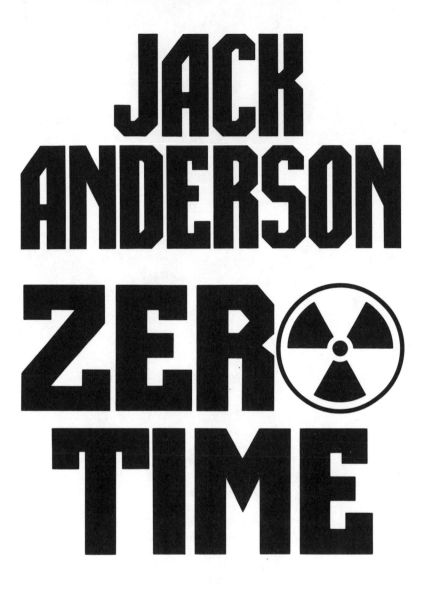

JACK ANDERSON

ZERO TIME

ZEBRA BOOKS
KENSINGTON PUBLISHING CORP.

ZEBRA BOOKS

are published by

Kensington Publishing Corp.
475 Park Avenue South
New York, NY 10016

First printing: September, 1990
Printed in the United States of America

*We must above all keep our hatred alive and fan it to paroxysm;
hate as a factor of struggle, intransigent hate of the enemy, hate
that can push a human being beyond his natural limits and make
him a cold, violent, selective, and effective killing-machine.*
—Ernesto ("Che") Guevara

The purpose of terror is to terrorize.
—Vladimir I. Lenin

Islam is justice.
—Ayatollah Ruhollah Khomeini

PROLOGUE

QOM, IRAN

AHMAD BIN RAZI HURRIED ACROSS THE TILED COURTYARD from the mosque tower, bearing his news like a head on a pike to the Grand Ayatollah Khomeini. Behind him stalked another mullah, bearded and fierce eyed, whom Razi was escorting to the Imam's presence. He was Ali Akbar Mohtashemi, the former Iranian ambassador to Syria, now minister of the interior. Within the circle of Khomeini's closest advisers, he had earned another title less known to the outside world: the Prince of Terror.

Their progress was interrupted by the call to prayer. The muezzin's chant floated over the city five times a day, and while Ahmad always anticipated the calls at sunrise and sunset, sometimes during a chaotic day it was easy to forget the precise times of the other three prayer periods. The exact moments changed each day, according to the time the sun rose and set.

When he heard the muezzin's cry, Ahmad had reached the covered gallery outside the ayatollah's study. He prostrated himself on the ground at once, facing Mecca, aware of the man behind him dropping to a similar posture. Because the ayatollah's study door was open, Ahmad caught a quick glimpse of the fierce old man inside, his bearded face pressed against the delicate colors of his prayer rug.

But Ahmad's attention turned to the glory of Allah while his fingers fumbled over his amber prayer beads. He had not carried his prayer rug with him, and the tiled floor was gritty against his knees.

"Praise belongs to Allah, the Lord of the worlds. . . ."

When the interval ended, Ahmad bin Razi slowly straightened up, feeling refreshed. He hovered outside the doorway to the study; it was a stark room, the furnishings austere. Inside, the ancient one had risen from his prostrate position and now sat cross-legged on large pillows. He stared straight ahead, his hands folded together, still lost in contemplation. Ahmad was forty-two years old, himself a distinguished mullah, a man of faith who had studied the scriptures. But he was in awe of the Grand Ayatollah. Like many other followers, Ahmad was convinced that Khomeini was truly the Twelfth Imam, who had vanished from the earth suddenly in the year A.D. 939 with the promise that he would one day return to earth to lead all Islam.

The ayatollah was a frail figure, wasted by the disease attacking his vital organs, but his manner conveyed authority. He resembled an Old Testament prophet, in a hard way, with a long white beard and angry black eyes. In contemplation, the ayatollah's face darkened into a menacing portrait, his classic scowl deepening, the eyes burning with a smoldering fury.

Ruhollah Khomeini bore the double burden, albeit confidently, of leading Islam to a glorious destiny and of shaping up its miserable disciples for the journey. Allah had given him poor, frivolous clay to mold. He molded them in his own image, teaching a puritanical Islam and inculcating fierce hatreds.

Aeons of solitary brooding had left him with a hoard of abrasive convictions, which had guided him through various stages of his long life: a religious dissenter; a political agitator; a back-alley conspirator; an organizer of cabals; a spinner of intrigues; an urban mob master and revolutionary leader; a manipulator of religion. All in the pursuit of the regeneration of his native land.

But Khomeini's vision extended beyond the borders of Iran; he thought in terms of remaking the world. He saw himself as the Sword of Islam, an avenger of terrible wrongs, the embodiment of the wrath of Allah. But he executed Allah's will less by strength than by prestidigitation—by slogans, intrigues, demagoguery to hold the faithful, terrorism to intimidate his foes.

His pervasive propaganda throughout Islam and his campaigns of subversion against regimes that opposed him had achieved considerable success. He had become a forbidding figure whose long shadow reached across the far-flung, disjointed, unruly Muslim world.

His bellicose hunger for kindling political tinderboxes had almost ignited the Persian Gulf. It had led to the devastating war with Iraq, confrontations with the Great Satan, and chaos within Iran. He had played out his relentless script, piling up day-by-day calamities, until he had brought Iran to the edge of ruin.

In the summer of 1988, Khomeini was still rallying his troops, vowing to fight on as long as they could still draw breath, disdaining talk of peace, when his string ran out. His soldiers began deserting en masse; Iran's economy was in shambles; the people were weary of war; he was compelled to sip the "poisoned chalice" of peace and to accept a cease-fire. Now the spirit of his people was undergoing the disillusions and recriminations that follow defeat.

But the ferocious old fanatic still had not given up his holy crusade. In February of the year 1989 he had shaken the Islamic world and sent shivers of fear throughout the West by condemning Salman Rushdie, the blasphemous author of *The Satanic Verses,* to death and authorizing a price on Rushdie's head of $5 million.

Meanwhile, he had directed his fanatical Revolutionary Guards to recruit an underground army of terrorists. In his name, they had gathered disciples from squalid Shiite enclaves along the curve of the crescent that spans two continents. They had sought out the deprived, the dispossessed, the disillusioned.

The scruffy, raw recruits had been indoctrinated and trained at terrorist camps in Iran and Lebanon. They had arrived as faceless nobodies; they had left as somebodies—transformed into Soldiers of God, driven at once by idealism and hatred: an invisible force who awaited the ayatollah's command. To stoke the fires in the bellies of these radical fighters, he needed only to send them on dangerous new adventures, to press hit-and-run attacks against his mortal enemies, to strike terror into his enemies' black hearts.

But the mullahs who surrounded him offered conflicting counsel. Many had found their will sapped by the long ordeal of the Iraqi war and the isolation of Iran from the international community. They had become pragmatists, led by the beardless Speaker of the House Hashemi Rafsanjani, who counseled exploring an accommodation with the world. They were bitterly opposed by the radicals, the hard-line religious fundamentalists, who were still determined to carry out Khomeini's legacy of hate and terrorism, led by the implacable Ali Akbar Mohtashemi.

The rivalry of these wily men was more than a clash of wills or personalities. With the Imam in failing health, the leaders of the two factions were fighting for nothing less than the future of Iran—its place in the community of nations, or its permanent exile.

It was Mohtashemi whose harsh whisperings in the Imam's ear most pleased the old tyrant. To achieve the final victory, Mohtashemi had urged, the ayatollah must leap into the unknown, do the unexpected, and trust the mysterious workings of fate.

There was one enemy above all others that the ayatollah had sworn would feel his terrible vengeance. Until now the Great Satan, symbol of all that Khomeini found detestable in the non-Islamic world, had remained untouched within its own borders. But Mohtashemi encouraged a plan that would plunge the sword of vengeance into the very heart of Satan.

Khomeini listened. His animus toward America produced a bitter bile within him that had probably helped prolong his life. He presumed that George Bush would prove no more effectual in dealing with terrorism than Jimmy Carter and Ronald Reagan had been. But for an eighty-eight-year-old holy man who would soon settle accounts with Allah, the risk was inconsequential.

There was one other factor. The plan had been brought to Mohtashemi by a special person—someone close to Khomeini's heart; someone who, unknown to the outside world, secretly carried the seed of hatred the Imam had planted and nourished; someone truly worthy to carry out his final design; someone who would strike a blow so devastating, so punitive, so shocking that history would not soon forget Ruhollah Khomeini. . . .

At last Khomeini rose painfully to his feet and beckoned. Ahmad stood before the cheerless old man, whose face bore the ravages of age, illness, and festering hatreds. Still, a fire blazed deep within him, and Ahmad warmed his spirit before that fire.

"You have news for me, Razi?"

"*Allaho Akbar!* God is great! Your loyal servant of Allah, Ali Akbar Mohtashemi, has arrived this hour from Tehran. He brings news from America, also from Kirovabad." The latter was a strategic rail center in the Soviet republic of Azerbaijan, across the Elburz Mountains from Iran's northwest border, whose ethnic strife made it a tempting target for what Mohtashemi called the Soviet option.

"Where is he?" Khomeini demanded. He spotted Mohtashemi in

the doorway and gestured impatiently. *"Tashrif beyarid tu,* Ali Akbar. Come inside."

"Salam Alekom," the mullah greeted him deferentially.

"Alekom-os-Salam," the Imam answered him. "Upon you be peace. Now what is the news you bring?"

Ahmad bin Razi withdrew discreetly, leaving the two men alone. Mohtashemi hesitated a moment. He bore both good and bad news. The news from Kirovabad was unpleasant; he decided he would dispose of that first.

"Well . . . what is it?" The ayatollah's voice quavered with age, but it was the vibration of polished steel.

"A loyal son of Islam, the one called Abu Hasir, has disappeared. He was the one who worked for the railroad the Soviets use to transport uranium to Baku, the one we hoped would carry out the first stage of our Russian plan. There has been no word from him for three days."

"What has happened to him? What do you think?"

"We must assume that Hasir has been taken prisoner by the godless Russians. He will be interrogated and tortured."

"Will he speak? What is your opinion?"

Would Abu Hasir betray his master? Mohtashemi spoke from the heart, not from his head. "He will die first."

The ayatollah's harsh expression changed perceptibly; he appeared pleased.

"The mission? Is it in jeopardy?"

Mohtashemi shook his head. "His capture was anticipated. A second son of Islam works in the railroad yard at Baku. He remains in place."

The ayatollah lapsed into a silence violated only by the audible wheeze of his breathing. To Ali Akbar Mohtashemi, the sound was ominous—a signal of the Imam's fading mortality.

At last Khomeini resumed the dialogue. "The Great Satan? You spoke of a message from America. Is there news of our preparations to assault the Great Satan?"

"Those whom the Imam has chosen to carry out his vengeance"— here Mohtashemi's voice trembled with fervor—"have crossed the Canadian border in small groups. From there, they have been taken to the chosen place."

He waited for the ayatollah's reaction and was rewarded with a flicker of a smile. The quiver in the younger mullah's voice now became a ring of exultation. "Everything is in readiness! It awaits only the Imam's word!"

For a moment Khomeini sat motionless. Then he reached for a sheet of paper and scratched some instructions in French. He sealed the paper in an envelope with a shaking hand, addressed it laboriously, and handed it to Mohtashemi. The mullah stared at the address: Post Office Box 837, Gibson, Montana, U.S.A.

He looked up at the ayatollah, meeting those burning eyes. "Let it begin!" the old man whispered.

Khomeini glared after Ali Akbar Mohtashemi until he had disappeared. The loyal Ahmad bin Razi hovered in the doorway, but Khomeini dismissed him. The ayatollah shifted his gaze to the window, his thoughts dissolving into the flaming sun beyond. The sky looked as though it were burning.

Gibson, Montana

TOM CAMERON LAY MOTIONLESS ON A SHELF OF ROCK, CONcealed by a projecting lip directly overhead, as darkness melted up the canyon walls toward him. Not since he was a boy had he kept a lonely vigil, heart pounding, at this spot. Then he had watched for savages, half-naked, daubed with slashes of paint, about to ride down the canyon on their war ponies. . . .

But that was a lifetime ago. The Indians had been imaginary; the real ones had been banished to their reservations even before Tom Cameron's time. Now he was crowding eighty, and the sun-dark figures he watched, squinting to sharpen his eyesight as daylight faded, were not Indians.

He wasn't sure who they were or what they were doing.

All Tom could say for certain was that a lot of strange things were going on in this corner of Montana. Trucks rumbling along the back roads at night, heading for nowhere. And crews of men trudging in and out of the mine shaft. Then there were those other mysterious men digging that irrigation ditch on the old Halston place, hard-working men, whatever else they might be, who never came to town. Not even on payday.

It wasn't natural.

He was tempted to crawl closer for a better look. It was dark enough now. He ought to be able to get right on top of them unseen, a man who had wormed his way into a hundred hostile Indian camps, invisible as a ghost, all those years ago.

But when he started to roll out from his protective outcropping of rock, Tom Cameron heard a sound that made him freeze and the hairs stir on the back of his neck. Lying flat on his stomach, holding his breath, he could feel his heart thumping against the hard rock.

A crunching footstep. A trickle of gravel running down the side of the mountain.

The old man lay still for several minutes. Just as he started to relax, there was another slide of gravel, then more steps, careless now, a man working his way along a steep, twisting footpath.

Tom tasted a little of his supper welling up into his throat, and he was angry with himself for his weak nerve. But he lay absolutely motionless, a shadow blending into a deeper shadow, as the unseen man made his way past the ledge and down the slope toward the cluster of tin shacks near the mouth of the mine.

A sentry, Tom guessed. The thought tingled in his mind like a small jolt of electricity.

When the footsteps had faded down the slope, safely distanced from the sheltered slab on which Tom lay, he lifted his head and peered down after the man. That was when he saw the rifle the sentry had slung over his shoulder, worn not like a hunter's but like a soldier's.

The curiosity now overwhelmed Tom. Something peculiar was going on here. Something was wrong, very wrong. And he had to know what it was.

Too many strange things had been happening lately, and he had a nagging suspicion they were connected in some mysterious way. The Halston place being taken at auction. Armed guerrillas stalking the mountains. Digging resumed at this worthless old gold mine. And now, Tom thought bitterly, his own spread up for grabs—the

land that had been his and his father's before him and his grandfather's before that, for more than a hundred years.

What the hell was happening?

Could it be the government? Secret military experiments of some
kind? Maybe it was connected with that storage facility the Department of Energy had taken over immediately adjoining the Cameron
and Halston ranchlands. The government had built fences and
posted guards. You couldn't trust the government any more, and
wasn't that a hell of a note, when a citizen couldn't trust those who
were elected to office, who were supposed to serve the people? Too
damn many government officials had the idea they were the masters,
and the people were supposed to serve *them*.

He had taken them on before, all of them—the looters and exploit-
ers of the land, the oil barons, the bureaucrats. He had become regarded as a gadfly, a Don Quixote in boots and Stetson, tilting at
abandoned windmills. This time, by God, he was going to get the
goods before he raised a ruckus.

He waited until he felt safe from discovery. Then the old codger
slid off his ledge and made his way through the hills, surefooted as
a cat in the darkness, to the wooded bottom where he had left his
Chevy pickup. He stood silently beside the truck, all his senses alert,
his ears straining for any discordant sound—a lean, leathery man
nearly six feet tall, thinning white hair under the stained cowboy hat,
wearing faded jeans and denim shirt and scarred boots. But the hush
of darkness was disrupted by only familiar, reassuring sounds—a
light-footed rabbit scurrying in the underbrush, the splash of a trout
breaking the surface of the nearby creek, the hoot of an owl, the night
breeze ruffling the feathers of the cottonwoods.

The old Chevy pickup fired up, and he wheeled it away. He ran
without lights for a time, the moon gliding from behind some clouds
and painting the dirt road for him, until he came to the asphalt of
the Montana state highway heading north. Then he flicked on his
headlights and pushed his foot down heavier on the accelerator and
sped through the darkness down the long straight road like a locomo-
tive on a track. Once he thought he heard the sound of another automobile. Slowing, he watched his rearview mirror, but there were no
headlights behind him. Nerves! he scolded himself.

He left the window down, his elbow hanging out, and let the night
air wash over him. It was a May night, crystal clear, star spangled,

with a touch of crisp cold after dark, the way it was in spring in the Big Sky country even when the days turned warm. Driving along the highway, alone with the rushing wind and the hulking hills and the vast emptiness all around, Tom Cameron felt the old familiar touch and taste and smell of this land, working its magic, stealing over him, becoming part of him. This country, so ruggedly beautiful, so stark and peaceful, got into a man's bones.

Lonely, too, sometimes.

He scowled, angry with himself for letting a thought slip out that he always kept suppressed, like old memories kept in a box.

Tom wound down out of the hills onto the flat plain. He could see the shine of the river off to his right, the tall black shapes of the cottonwoods defining the river bottom, the trees like huge ink blots, the river like polished silver in the moonlight. The river snaked back and forth, and the road ran straight as a plumb line, but the river and the road stayed together like two ill-matched dancers. After a while the land, which might have appeared formless to a stranger, one vast expanse of emptiness, took on familiar details and features. Tom knew, without needing a fence or a sign, the moment when he reached his own land.

Not yours anymore.

The thought hit him like a blow below the belt. And the anger rose like the mercury in a thermometer—the anger and the bitterness against those who were stealing land from the people whose blood and sweat were in the soil, soaked into it. And against those who would conduct their deadly experiments where they said no one could be harmed. Only the coyotes and the wolves, only the deer, only the cattle who strayed too close to something odorless and deadly, only birds that flew overhead.

God in heaven, what were the damned fools up to now? What could they be doing in that abandoned gold mine? One thing he knew: They sure as hell weren't mining gold.

Swerving the pickup off the highway, Tom Cameron bounced along some barely visible tracks down a short slope to a copse of trees beside the river. You could always locate the rivers on the plains of Montana. That's where the trees were. In between were only rocks and rattlesnakes, short grass and prickly pear. Tom rolled to a stop and got out of the truck and stood on the riverbank, trying to fight off the anguish that threatened to engulf him.

Beyond the river there was movement. A slow, shuffling drift of dark shapes. He watched the shaggy herd, those great clumsy beasts with their huge hairy heads purple in the night, grazing slowly across his grassland, nibbling on the short grass, thriving on it.

On his land.

A century and a half ago, millions of them roamed the West in enormous herds. They were part of the land, part of a frontier that resisted the onrush of time and change, that still survived here at this place he had called his own. The Indians respected the buffalo. They killed only what they needed for meat and hides, only what they could use.

Then the white hunters came, slaughtering the magnificent shaggy beasts, taking the hides for buffalo robes and leaving the meat to rot on the prairie, abandoning carcasses by the hundreds at first and then by the thousands. After them came the sportsmen, and the killing escalated. In fifty years, an animal which had overrun the plains had been almost wiped out. Where there had been millions, only a few thousand survived.

Tom Cameron's small buffalo herd, numbering about fifty head, was an anachronism. He admitted it—at least to himself. Oh, he sold a few for the meat, but buffalo steak had never caught on with people who thought a steak was something you shouldn't have to chew. Tom kept the buffalo on his land, cherished them, because he couldn't stand the idea that they might soon be extinct. "You're just a stubborn old man—you won't ever change! You have to have it all your own way!"

Luke's voice echoed in his memory. And his son was right, of course. Tom had to concede that he was stubborn, and old, and hard on people. He lived too much in the past, maybe because it seemed to him like a better place, at least a more honest place.

Any man who kept fifty head of buffalo on his land in this day and age was as out of place as a saint at a political convention.

His land. The land they were taking away from him!

Tom Cameron stepped down the low bank and crossed the silver stream at a ford where it ran shallow, and the water wouldn't wash over his boots. Some big flat rocks just below the surface provided stepping-stones as familiar to him as a staircase. Near the far bank, under the thick shadows of the cottonwoods, he peered ahead at a shaggy old bull who had heard him coming. "It's just me, you hairy old hump-headed son of a bitch!" Tom growled aloud.

And because he was talking aloud and not paying attention, and rummaging around in his head among old grievances and sorrows, he didn't hear the splash in the stream behind him. He didn't hear anything at all, but at the last moment he felt something, a rush of air. He started to turn his head; for a fleeting second, he was aware of a mass behind him soaking up the light. But the big rock was already smashing down on his skull, which cracked like an eggshell.

At the last moment, when he lay crumpled against the riverbank and saw the rock lifted high above him a second time, black against the sky, it was not his life that flashed before him but a searing regret, and he spoke through his pain to his son. I've made such a goddamn mess of things. I've driven you away, never saying the things that needed saying between us after your mom was taken. I've lost the land that should have been yours. Now I've let something loose on this land, something terrible, and I don't know what it is. . . . I sense it's evil, son, it's cold, it's . . .

Cold. Cold as the water in the stream spilling fresh from the mountains, flashing over rocks, washing stains away.

Cold as death.

PART ONE
HOMECOMING

PAMELA POVIC—SHE HAD NEVER QUITE FORGIVEN HER PARents for the alliteration—hustled down the aisle toward number 7B in first class, who was impatiently pushing the call button. He grinned at her, holding out his empty glass. With each drink, his grin became sloppier.

"Hey, little lady," number 7B said. "I'll have another . . . one of them pee-wee bottles of Jack Daniels."

She managed a perfunctory, "Yes, sir."

"Yes, *sir!*" he echoed, mockingly. His hand casually brushed her calf, fingers nipping. "Let's not be too formal, honey. This is a long flight."

"I'll be right back with your Jack Daniels." Keeping it business-like, still smiling but furious, she stalked off, thinking, "I am *not* your little lady! I am *not* your honey!"

Her job as a Pan Am flight attendant was a far cry from the glamorous vision that had lured her into the skies, she thought wryly.

Pam served number 7B his Jack Daniels, artfully avoiding his groping hand, then turned to help a little girl in 3A who was nervous about air turbulence. "It's just a few bumps in the road . . . ," she said, smiling at the girl. ". . . Air bumps. You can't see them, you just feel them. Would you like another 7-Up? No? How would you like to help me in the pantry? It's right behind the cockpit."

The little girl brightened, scooted from her seat, and followed the flight attendant up the aisle. Out of the corner of her eye, Pam Povic saw number 2B glance at her as she passed by. Now *that,* she thought, was why she had taken this job. Back when she fantasized

about *him* taking a seat on her flight, and then their eyes meeting . . .
Back when she was still a romantic.

Six feet two, she guessed; legs too lanky even for first class; healthy
tan; no stomach at all; broad shoulders; scars on his brown hands
and a tiny one next to his mouth on the left side; sandy, tousled hair
that needed trimming, strong planes in his face, a generous mouth . . .

All right, she thought, that's enough.

But even the name fit the portrait: Lucas Cameron.

There was, in fact, only one small imperfection in her portrait of
number 2B, only one little ingredient missing from the nearly forgotten fantasy. He didn't know her from the fixtures. For all the attention he had paid to her, she might as well switch assignments with
Dick in coach.

The problem was, Pamela Povic thought, as she ushered the little
girl into the pantry and started showing her the fascinating things
that flight attendants did, number 2B had something very heavy on
his mind. Yes, he ignored her, but he also didn't notice anyone.
When their eyes had momentarily met, the expression in them had
brought a tingle to her spine—a shiver of apprehension that, she was
now prepared to admit, had increased her interest.

What she had seen in those clear brown eyes was suppressed anger.

It *was* anger. A smoldering form of self-flagellation. He was furious at being in first class, courtesy of InCon, the company he worked
for. Nothing but the best for InCon people. He was furious at the
delays getting out of Punta del Ansa. Two days upriver in a slow
boat until he was met by the InCon Cessna and flown to Rio for the
connection with Pan Am's flight to Houston. He was furious at the
desultory Latino approach to any crisis. The telegram from the
Houston office had taken a week to reach him, hand-delivered at the
end of another slow journey on the riverboat.

His anger was irrational, but it wasn't every day that you learned
your father had died. Learned it out of the blue in a truncated message, without the softening of article or adjective. Lucas Cameron
had the telegram memorized.

REGRET TO INFORM YOUR FATHER KILLED IN ACCI-
DENT STOP RETURN HOME OFFICE IMMEDIATELY
STOP CONDOLENCES STOP CANSECO

Each word was like a hot coal feeding the flames of Luke's quiet rage. An anger directed not at InCon or the people of Punto del Ansa or Pan Am or Canseco. Directed at the one person responsible for Tom Cameron dying alone.

Luke himself.

Four hours later Luke was closeted with his boss, Canseco, in one of the company's white Mercedes stretch limos, in which Canseco had been driven to Houston International to meet him. After Luke cleared customs and emerged from the terminal, the white-haired chauffeur—Hurley was his name—had driven them slowly around the airport complex until Canseco directed him to one of the parking garages. The motor was still running, the air-conditioning purring softly. Outside, the temperature was slow-broil. The acres of airport pavement and the walls of glass, defining the nearby high-rise hotels, reflected both heat and light.

"I've got you booked by way of Denver," Canseco said. "It's the first connection I could get. The flight leaves in an hour, so there isn't time for you to come downtown. I brought everything that was on your desk."

Everything included a letter from a lawyer in Gibson, Montana; an auction notice issued by the Gibson Bank; and a third envelope that Luke had slid into his jacket pocket, unread. It was addressed in Tom Cameron's shaky script to Luke in care of InCon's home office in Houston. It had been postmarked two weeks ago—less than a week before Tom Cameron died.

"You want a drink?" Canseco asked. "We can use the Sky Club—"

"No." Luke Cameron had worked for Canseco since signing on with InCon. They were a team. Canseco was one of those rare bosses who gave as much loyalty as he demanded. He was a powerful man, with a wariness of eye and an intimation of the physical: bull necked, gray jowled, and crew cut. He had developed a paunch that was probably still hard enough to hurt your hands on. His short, square hands were tipped with immaculate fingernails. Luke wondered when Canseco had started having manicures.

"How's it going down there in Punto?"

"It's hot."

Canseco grinned knowingly. "Yeah." He paused for a moment.

His eyes were gray, shrewd, steely. "What do you think, can Williams handle it while you're gone? I'm not putting the screws to you to rush back there, don't get me wrong, what I mean is, do I need to send anyone else?"

"Williams can handle it. It's only a bridge."

"Yeah." Canseco grinned again. "It's only a bridge." Which, to a bridge builder, is like a Super Bowl coach saying, "It's only a game!"

"Williams is okay," Luke repeated.

"Maybe it's time we give him the ball, see whether he can carry it." The remark was irrelevant; it was not what Canseco wanted to say.

He gazed silently out of the black glass car window at the sheets of pavement, the acres of glistening cars, a jet soaring steeply into a white-hot sky. Finally, he said, "Take all the time you need up there in Montana, Luke."

Canseco understood why he had been reluctant to speak. He was apprehensive about Luke Cameron's going home. Because he suspected that going home had always been at the back of Luke's mind, stirring around in his head. Canseco feared that, once Luke planted his boots firmly back in his own territory, there was a chance he might choose to stay.

"The bank took over your dad's property before he died, that right?"

"That's what the lawyer says."

"I thought maybe the federal land bank stepped in."

"Not this time. The bank held a first mortgage and an equity loan to boot."

"Timing was kind of convenient." Canseco cursed himself. Now why the hell had he said that?

Lucas Cameron glanced at him. "The drought hit Dad hard, two years in a row. He wasn't the only one. Half of Montana is in trouble, I hear."

"Hey, not to mention Iowa and Texas. You should've heard the bleating here in Texas."

"Dad knew he was losing the place; it was no surprise. Maybe if I'd been there . . ."

"Don't start that shit. If you could've stayed, you would have. Isn't that the story? You didn't get along. Isn't that what you told me? I mean . . . you'd have died for your old man, but you couldn't live under the same roof together."

"Yeah . . ." Luke was startled at Canseco's bluntness. "Yeah."

"Then nobody's to blame. It's like nobody's to blame for being short or tall."

"Yeah."

Canseco grinned at him. "Okay, so I'm a horse's ass. Sometimes . . . what comes out of my mouth is horseshit."

Luke managed a weak smile, then lapsed into silence, engrossed in his own thoughts. Then he said, reflectively, "I guess you couldn't expect the Gibson Bank to be sympathetic. The local ranchers . . . they owe the bank money they don't have and, therefore, can't pay. I heard the bank almost went under a year ago. It was taken over by some foreign holding company."

"Too many bad loans, I suppose."

"Yeah, I suppose."

Luke Cameron thought, with silent despair, that his father belonged in that category: Someone who couldn't pay his debts. A deadbeat. What that must have done to his father's stubborn pride. Tom Cameron had tried to go through life without owing anyone a dime—or an apology. Modern ranching had made his code of life an anachronism. The equipment had become more high-tech, the operating costs more expensive, the markets more speculative, until you simply had to borrow just to keep up. Or you ended up selling out to one of the big combines that could afford large investments against long-term payoffs, one of the megaranches with the financial stamina to ride out bad years or bad luck. Tom had borrowed like everyone else, gambled like everyone else against the risks of a killer winter or a scorching summer. Staking his future, as cattle ranchers had done for a hundred years on the High Plains, on a rise in the price of beef.

He had lost his gamble, his range, his home, even its contents. And, finally, his life.

Justin Cranmer—the name was unfamiliar to Luke—was the Gibson lawyer handling what was left of Tom Cameron's estate. His letter had expressed sympathy while sounding a bit embarrassed—as embarrassed as a lawyer could sound—over having to inform Tom's only surviving relative that his father's entire estate had been insufficient to pay the debts outstanding to the bank. A land sale had taken

place before Tom's death; there had been no offers. The holding company that now owned Gibson Bank had then taken over the property.
"It has happened to several others in the area," Cranmer wrote, as
if that were some kind of consolation. "Your father was not alone
in facing hard times."

An auction of furnishings, equipment, and livestock would be held
on the premises under the bank's auspices. "We have a substantial
offer on the beef herd," Cranmer had concluded, "but there appears
to be little interest in the buffalo. However, I still have one possibility,
a rancher from Washington State about whom I am making addi-
tional inquiries."

The man beside him in the back seat of the long limo coughed.
"We better get going. I'll walk you to your plane," offered Canseco.

"You don't have to do that."

"Hell, it's no trouble!"

"Thanks for coming down, Tony."

Luke Cameron climbed out of the air-conditioned limousine into
the broiler outside, nodded at both Canseco and Hurley, then strode
off toward the terminal, lugging his one soft-sided suitcase. Canseco
watched his tall figure until the glass doors hissed shut behind him.

"Good luck," he said.

The Delta Airlines DC-10 dropped over the mountains and swung
in a wide, semicircular approach to the Helena Airport. The DC-10
came in low from the east, and Luke Cameron, in a window seat,
was able to peer north into the river canyon toward the Gates of the
Mountains—so named by the explorer Meriwether Lewis because
the steep, gloomy bluffs that walled both sides of the river had
seemed to draw apart before his approaching canoes, opening a
passage . . .

Luke had a glimpse of Helena off to his left, surrounded by green-
clad mountains. Then the ground rushed up toward him and the
plane's nose lifted, followed by a bump and rumble and the sudden
scream of the jet engines as deceleration kicked in.

Striding across the tarmac toward the terminal building, Luke experienced the first emotional tug that told him he was home. He
sucked in a long breath of sage- and pine-scented air. It was dusk;
the sun had already slipped behind the massive peaks to the west;
but there was a clarity in the air, a sense of size and space so alien

to the claustrophobic atmosphere of the South American jungle in which he had been working.

Inside, at the Hertz desk, Luke paused. Canseco had reserved a rental car for him. It occurred to Luke that his father's Chevy pickup would be at the house. Or was that also to be included in the auction? There had been nothing in the lawyer's letter or the auction notice about the truck. Luke seemed to remember that his own name was on the registration along with his father's. If anything happened to one of them, the other would automatically get the pickup.

He shook his head, remembering a thousand rides in that dinged and dusty truck. He wouldn't need a rental car if he stayed. But of course he had no intention of staying longer than was necessary to settle his father's affairs.

Hertz had provided a map of Montana in the glove compartment of the Ford Taurus. Luke had no need of it. He pointed the car in the direction of Gibson, Montana, and drove without thought, like an old horse given its head at the end of the day, turning for home.

He had nearly forgotten the pull of this land of his childhood, with its limitless blue skies. Coming over a rise, he gazed suddenly across the rolling prairie toward another range of mountains that appeared close enough to reach out and touch, though Luke knew they were fifty miles away. Thunderheads were building up over the mountains behind him. Luke had almost forgotten the tingle of excitement at the prospect of outrunning a storm to Gibson. How many times had he run this race, speeding through the gathering darkness while a storm rolled and crashed across the plains? You could always see the storm approaching from a long way off: you could watch the jagging streaks of lightning and hear the distant cannon fire and know it was coming your way like God's own wrath, and you'd better be ready for it, ready for hail the size of marbles, ready for winds that threatened to blow you skittering across the prairie like a downsized tumbleweed . . .

There was little traffic on the highway to intrude on Luke's thoughts. Occasionally a car's headlights would appear, visible a mile off, bobbing toward him until the vehicle took shape out of the murk of evening and whooshed past him. Everything was as Luke remembered it. The black clouds now filled up half the sky like spilled ink. Would this be the storm to break the drought? Farmers would be praying tonight. The short grasses leaned before the wind, and the cottonwoods thrashed in the river bottoms. He felt the wind rock the Taurus with a sudden gust that stirred an inward surge of emotion. How could he have ever left this land?

When Luke was a boy, his father had sometimes taken him to sites along the Lewis and Clark trail. "Those men and that little woman camped right here beside the river. Picked some of the berries from bushes just like those, maybe shot a deer for supper." At Great Falls, Tom Cameron had pointed toward an island covered with thick brush and a few trees. "They called that White Bear Island, because there were grizzlies living on it. They weren't really white, Luke, they were silvertips—you've seen 'em—but they were sure enough grizzlies. A hunting party crossed over to the island to rout a large bear that ruled the island. 'Our troops stormed the place, gave no quarter, and its commander fell,' one of the sergeants wrote. Pat Gass was his name."

Except for the fallen shaggy monarch, White Bear Island hadn't changed. The same was true of many places along the river where those intrepid explorers had rowed and poled and hauled their boats. You could read their journals, as Luke's father had done—especially Meriwether Lewis's when he became eloquent—and find yourself gazing at a scene through early nineteenth century eyes, knowing that nothing had changed.

Yet everything *did* change, including this rugged place. Farmers and ranchers, who had withstood the ravages of nature, had been uprooted by the onslaught of economics. There was a little oil exploration going on, some experimenting with coal and shale. Most of that was on hold until OPEC gathered enough strength to impose another squeeze.

Tom Cameron would never allow the oil men to drill on his land. "I don't fall for those TV commercials, with the birds singing among the pretty flowers, showing how they put the land back the way it was before they came with their bulldozers and oil rigs. They use fancy commercials to sell you what ain't true."

God he was stubborn! And most of the time, Luke thought grudgingly, he was right.

So Tom Cameron did it his way, as always. And this time it brought him more trouble than he could handle, trouble that he had faced alone. . . .

The letter was still in Luke's jacket pocket, the jacket now draped across the passenger seat of the car. He had read it on the DC-10 high over Montana. But he had quickly put it away, hoping to stifle the voice from the grave. For the words of his father had shaken him like something physical.

Luke could hear his father talking as he read the words, could hear every intonation, could see the old man sitting at the kitchen table and slamming his fist down, as he did whenever he got worked up, with enough force to make the china and silverware jump. Luke remembered once when the top of the sugar bowl hopped clear off the bowl and broke when it struck the table. He remembered how this old mule of a man went suddenly quiet, chastened, while Ma, without a word, picked up the broken pieces and walked away.

Tom Cameron had never asked anyone for help in his life. But less than a week before he died, he had called out to his son. And Luke hadn't been there.

Luke pulled the letter from his pocket again after he had calmed down. The writing was a jagged scrawl, nearly illegible in places. Like a great many isolated ranchers and cowhands, Tom had always read prodigiously, everything from dog-eared volumes of Shakespeare and Conrad to Hemingway's short stories, but Tom rarely wrote. And his handwriting had been awkward even before he got arthritis.

Like the telegram, the letter was burned like a brand into Luke Cameron's memory. . . .

"Luke—

"I don't like writing to you like this, but there's something you have to know. I always figured you'd come home some day, simply because it's home. And I took it for granted the place would be here waiting for you, passed on to you the way it was to my pa and then to me when our times came. Maybe it doesn't mean as much to you as it always did to me, but it would be here, and it would be yours.

"Well, things don't always work out the way you expect, as I reckon we both are old enough to know. What I have to tell you is, the bank's taken the place over. I couldn't pay them what was due. I got in debt to the vultures, which I promised your ma I'd never do, and now they're picking the bones clean.

"I won't give you a song and dance about why or how it happened. I guess you know there's been hard times hereabouts these past few years. It hasn't been a big thing like the Depression in the 30's, because that was happening everywhere. Our depression has been more private. The Halston place went belly up last winter after old Burt died, and I don't know why I should have been so sure it would be different with me and the Bar-C.

"Anyway, that's spilt milk, and nothing will put it back in the bottle. There's nothing you or I or anyone else can do about it. But seeing as how this is your loss more than mine, given my age, I thought you ought to know.

"That isn't the only reason for this writing, though I have a feeling it may all be linked together.

"There's something going on here I don't rightly understand. It's not just losing the Bar-C or the failure of the Halston spread or what happened to old Sorenson who lost the bank last year and then got himself killed. It's a whole pigpile of things. It's nothing I can spell out or prove in court. Maybe it's something that's happening to the whole country and I'm just imagining things, the way I imagine hearing trucks running on the back roads at night where trucks have no business to be. Maybe it's the bad feeling I have about this nuclear storage site over west of Halston's spread, behind a high wire fence here in Montana—where *it* has no right to be.

"All I can tell you, son, is there's something happening here I can't handle alone. And it troubles me. You're the only one I know of who could maybe solve the mystery, the only one I can trust.

"If you can come, fine. If you can't, I'll understand that, too. You've got your own life to live, I know that. Took me a while to find it out, I reckon. Come if you can.

Dad"

Cutting it off bluntly like that. No "Love, Dad." He could never bring himself to say it.

But the love, if silent, was strong. Luke knew that. He had a sudden image of Tom Cameron leaning over him that night in the darkness, his voice oddly gentle. "Come along, son. Your ma's goin' to the hospital."

She managed to smile faintly when Luke appeared, still struggling into his jeans, his shirt unbuttoned, hair spiky and eyes dull with sleep. But she wasn't able to hold the smile; it drifted off like the fleeting recognition in her eyes. They got into the pickup, the three of them, jammed together on the bench with Ma in the middle, Luke driving. He glanced once at his father, expecting the stoic, hard-bitten expression he knew so well. But in the glow from the dashboard, he saw wet tears glistening on his dad's face.

Other images. Tom Cameron always seemed to be waking him up for something. Mornings when it was still dark. They would go out before the rooster made up his mind, the air so cold it made your face stiffen. They'd climb in the pickup and drive down to some part of the river where the fishing was good, and they'd cast while standing in the water in their hip boots, fly fishing—"Fairer for the fish," Tom would say. Another early morning, Luke remembered his father rousing him to go off to college, saying nothing, his mother having to speak for both of them, saying how they would miss him and be sure to write and if you need anything, just let us know. And don't get hurt. Because he had a football scholarship, or he probably wouldn't have been able to go. And there was the morning his father woke Luke to say he'd been called up by the army, the Vietnam nightmare. Mom tearful that time, hiding her fear, unable to find the words.

That was the trouble after she was gone, Luke thought. There was nobody to translate for them. No one to articulate the deep feelings that the old curmudgeon never had a tongue for.

Except for scattered sprinkles, the storm fizzled out. The blowing wind carried more dust than water. The dust clouds obscured the road, forcing Luke to a roadside stop, where he slept in the car. He woke at daylight, the sky still gray but the storm heading east with its churning dark load. Catching breakfast at a truck stop on the highway, he reached Gibson just as the town was stirring to life.

Luke Cameron drove slowly along Clark Street through the center of town. Gibson appeared tired and dusty and unchanged. Luke recognized all of the older buildings—the hotel and the bank, the movie house, the Rexall drug, two gas stations still in competition on opposite corners of Clark and Main.

There were a few changes. A combination bar and keno parlor was new. So was the McDonald's, serving assembly-line hamburgers in competition with the old A&W Root Beer Drive-In. The frontage road leading into town had a couple of new motels, and there was a 4-B's family restaurant and motel close to the center of town, part of a popular Montana chain.

The town basked in the morning sun, which glistened off the store windows. It was unseasonably warm for May, and Gibson seemed gripped by lethargy. A few stores were opening, but there was little activity. A woman shopper angle-parked her station wagon in front of a market. A few cowboys and an Indian wearing a tall black Stetson ambled along the sidewalk.

Luke nosed the rental car into the curb, switched off the key, and sat in the car for a few minutes, listening to the ticking of the hot engine as it cooled. Wished himself a thousand miles away, and knew that he was home.

As he started into the bank, he had to step aside for a slim, dark-haired young woman just emerging. She had a look that was too sophisticated and elegant to belong in this setting. She wore the requisite jeans and a checkered blue cotton blouse, but the way her trim hips were molded into the jeans was Park Avenue or Rodeo Drive, not Clark Street. She flicked a glance at Luke Cameron in passing, but that was all. Mahogany eyes, he thought.

Inside, the bank was cool. The air-conditioning was a soft hum like background music. The interior had been extensively remodeled since Luke was here last. For a small-town bank that must still be burdened with many bad loans, it had a surprisingly modern, successful look.

Anne Carr presided over a desk off to his right. The small sign on her desk read Anne McAlister, and below that, Assistant Manager. She had spotted him the moment he walked in, and as she rose and maneuvered around her desk, her eyes sparkled with genuine delight. The expression shaded into regret when she remembered why Luke was there.

"Luke Cameron! How wonderful to see you!"

"You look marvelous, Anne."

"Are you kidding? Three kids and thirty pounds later."

"They look good on you." She was attractively businesslike in a beige linen jacket over a pale yellow blouse; the rich chestnut hair he remembered was now an artful nest of curls, her makeup skillfully enhancing high cheekbones and a generous mouth. But there was also a tired grayness around her eyes.

"I was sorry to hear about your dad. Everyone was. It was a shock. I mean, Tom was so tough . . . so solid . . . so rugged. You had the feeling he'd always be there, like one of those old black cottonwoods by the river on your place." She stopped abruptly, either because she felt she had said too much or was embarrassed by the reminder that "the Cameron place" was no longer theirs.

"Thanks, Anne." He glanced at the name plate on her desk. "Assistant manager, huh? What was it the high school yearbook predicted? . . . I remember . . . 'Annie Carr will travel far, and on her door will be a star.' You didn't have to go far to get *your* star."

His remark brought a touch of color to her cheeks, a clear pleasure at his remembering. Montana women still blushed, Luke thought. "Brad . . . ," she started to say. "Brad and me . . . we both belong here in Montana."

"How is Brad?"

"Oh, he's . . . fine." She rushed past the momentary hesitation. "So are the kids—two boys and a girl, since you haven't asked," she added quickly. "Come . . . sit down."

"I wanted to talk to your new bank president, Mr. Gilman. He sent me a copy of the auction notice. I heard about old Sorenson. I never thought he'd retire."

A flicker of apprehension appeared in Anne McAlister's eyes. "He had no choice . . . really. He was lucky someone wanted to take over the bank. And then to have that terrible thing happen, none of us has got over it yet." The consternation remained in her eyes. "I'll see if Mr. Gilman is available. But you've got to promise to come over for dinner. Promise?"

"It's a deal."

He wondered whether there was something wrong with the marriage, or just with Brad McAlister.

"It was a most unfortunate situation, Mr. Cameron." The president of Gibson Bank appeared to be a man who bore others' misfortunes with fortitude. "But you understand we had no choice but to foreclose."

"There's always a choice," Luke said. "Ranchers like my father built this territory."

Theodore Gilman smiled. "It's obvious you're not a banker."

Gilman didn't fit Luke's perception of a banker either. He resembled those overstuffed, fast-talking pitchmen you sometimes see on television hawking automobiles—no money down, easy payments, don't worry about your bad credit, we're ready to deal.

"We were, of course, shocked by your father's accident."

"His friends were," Luke said dryly. He thought Gilman wore too much cologne, perhaps because he sweated excessively.

"It had nothing to do with our seizure of the property, but the unfortunate timing was distressing to all of us."

Luke suppressed a rising surge of anger. "There's an old Chevrolet pickup. It's coregistered in my name."

"Yes, yes. I was going to mention that, Mr. Cameron. It's at the house, and is not on the list of items for the auction." Gilman patted his thinning brown hair while he appeared to wait for some expression of gratitude. When it was not forthcoming, he frowned slightly and continued. "Our parent company, which now owns the property, also has no objection to your staying at the house until after the auction. I'm sure there must be some personal things . . . small mementos . . . that you would like to preserve. We will have no objection, Mr. Cameron, within reason. We are trying to be fair."

"Good of you."

Gilman pulled a handkerchief from his hip pocket and delicately patted his forehead. "Contrary to popular impression, banks are not heartless."

"How many other properties in Gibson County do you expect to take over?"

Gilman flushed. "That is an unreasonable question, Mr. Cameron."

"Sorry," Luke said, "my timing was unfortunate."

He stalked out of the banker's office before his anger exploded, striding past Anne McAlister's desk without seeing her.

After Luke Cameron stopped steaming, he walked down the street to Justin Cranmer's office. It was on the second floor of the old, red brick building next to the turn-of-the-century Gibson Hotel. The only thing new in the office building was the air-conditioning unit mounted in one of the tall windows behind the lawyer's desk, the fan at the low setting but emitting a steady vibrating noise.

"Drives me crazy," Cranmer said. "But the damn thing keeps me cool, so I put up with the background dissonance."

He was a small man in his fifties, balding and overweight, who seemed happy to see someone who might need a lawyer. He was a native Montanan, he said, reciting his credentials without waiting to be asked. "Born over in Billings, even though I may lack the rough edges. My old man moved the family to L.A. in the thirties, when I was a kid, and I grew up there in La-La Land. Went to school there, too. How I ended up in Gibson is as much a mystery to me as it might seem to you."

"How did you?"

Cranmer's blue eyes flashed in their pouches. "I love to fish!" he said. "Came up here once for some trout fishing over by Three Forks. I was hooked more certainly than the fish." The lawyer grinned. "Kept coming back every chance I got, there's no fishing like it on earth. Then my wife died. . . ." The grin faded, the eyes clouded over, and Cranmer swung around his leather swivel chair to gaze out the tall window on Clark Street below. "My son—he was our only child—went to Vietnam and never came back. Then Jo got sick and . . . never came back . . . and . . . hell, there was nothing to keep me in L.A."

He swung the chair around again and managed a small, poignant smile. "You know I had to go back to school at fifty? Had to pass the Montana bar. Squeaked through. So here I am. Never more than an hour or two away from the fightingest fish that ever chased a fly. You a fisherman, Mr. Cameron?"

"Dad and I used to try our luck. Never seem to have the time anymore."

"Yes, that's what ails mankind. Too busy to live."

Luke relaxed in the chair across from Cranmer's battered oak desk, settling back. He had found a man who liked to talk, and there were things he wanted to know.

"What can you tell me about my father's accident? Everyone is sympathetic, but nobody has been specific."

Cranmer sobered instantly. "The sheriff has an accident report on it; I think you'll want to read that. But I can tell you the gist of it." The lawyer paused. He was used to confronting people with uncomfortable facts, but that never made it easier. "Tom was down by the creek, the one that crosses the southwest corner of your property. I'm sure you know it. It was in the evening, no one knows exactly what time. . . . The coroner put it around eight o'clock, but it could have been an hour or two either way, earlier or later. Tom wasn't found, you see, until the next day."

Luke Cameron winced. A protest was forming inside him like a shout yet to be heard. But except for a tightening of the jaw, he showed no reaction.

"Maybe he was out there checking on his buffalo. They meant a lot to him, you know. Sentimentally, not economically."

"I know." Luke had argued with his father about the buffalo herd, which Luke thought was an expensive indulgence. But for Tom Cameron, those buffalo were the incarnation of his lost frontier.

"He slipped crossing that creek to get to the herd. Maybe it was too dark. Maybe he had a stroke. No way to tell." Cranmer avoided Luke's eyes, allowing privacy for his grief. "Tom struck his head on a rock when he fell. He struggled to his feet somehow, and staggered out of the riverbed into that meadow, and . . ."

"Go on."

"He must have spooked the buffalo, reeling from his head injury, stumbling in the dark. But we don't really know. . . . He stampeded the herd. I'm sorry to have to be the one to tell you this, Mr. Cameron. Tom was . . . trampled."

Trampled by the buffalo he loved. Luke felt sick. He wanted to get up and empty his insides, to vomit up all the accumulated grief and guilt. But he just sat there, motionless. For a long time, there was no sound in the office except for the vibrating air conditioner and a creak in Justin Cranmer's chair whenever he stirred.

"Thanks . . . ," Luke said at last. "Thanks for telling me. I needed to know. The coroner's verdict was accidental death?"

"Yes. It was a . . . a stupid accident, Luke. Stupid and ironic, given the way your father felt about those bison."

"He wouldn't have blamed those buffalo," said Luke. "Just himself . . . for being careless."

And old, Luke thought. And tired. And scared. And alone.

He asked Cranmer about the bank foreclosure on the ranch. The lawyer confirmed the general outline of events. Against his instincts, Tom Cameron had borrowed heavily over the past three years to cover losses. Most of the cattlemen and farmers in the state had been hard hit, first with falling beef prices, then with consecutive summers of withering drought.

"The drought's affected everything and everyone," Cranmer said.

"The wheat farmers have had no crop for two summers. You know those big potholes you used to see across the plains? Thousands of them are dry pans now. The plains used to appear arid, dried out, but there was always water. Not any more. Those potholes used to be duck breeding grounds. Now half of them are gone. The marshes are drying up, too, if they're not bein' drained by farmers who need the water. It's the same all across the High Plains states—the Dakotas and Wyoming and Montana. That big Yellowstone fire . . . that did god-awful damage, too, to the wildlife as well as the forests.

"The fish . . . they suffocate," Cranmer said sadly. "By the millions. The rivers are shrinking. There's not enough oxygen when the water gets low; temperatures go up in shallow water. Best fishing rivers in the world . . ." His voice trailed off.

"That's why Gibson looks as if it's been sucked dry, I suppose," Luke said.

"Yes, that's about the size of it. You'll hear pretty much the same story in other towns, but especially the small towns like this—farm and ranch towns that don't get much of the tourist trade. They're all suffering." He was silent a moment. "I stopped to greet an old-timer on Clark Street the other day. He summed it up. We exchanged some comments about the hard times in Gibson. The old-timer spat some tobacco juice between his feet and drawled, 'Birds fly upside down over Gibson. Ain't worth shittin' on.' "

Luke smiled in spite of himself. Montanans had a dry sense of humor; they could poke fun at adversity. "Dad never told me how bad it was. We . . . we weren't in close touch."

Cranmer shrugged, his eyes sympathetic. "Yes, he told me." When he saw the surprise in Luke's face, the lawyer added: "We went fishing together a few times. I think Tom wanted to find out if he could trust me, and getting me out in a mountain stream with a rod and a fly was his way of finding out. He didn't think much of lawyers." Cranmer smiled reminiscently. "He liked to quote Shakespeare on the subject."

"First kill all the lawyers."

"That's the one."

"So you knew he was in financial trouble?"

"Trouble? No. I knew he was in debt to the bank. I knew he was upset when Sorenson retired after the bank takeover. But Tom never talked about his own troubles."

"Sounds like him."

The air conditioner's vibrating drone shifted to a higher pitch. Both Luke Cameron and Cranmer focused for a moment on the new sound. Outside, Clark Street looked weary and bleak under the rising sun, nearly deserted. Like a dying town, Luke thought. Why would a foreign investment outfit want to buy up property in a dying town?

He discussed the upcoming auction with the lawyer. Cranmer said he'd found a buyer for the buffalo herd—a good offer, he thought, from a Washington rancher. Unfortunately the proceeds, like those from the auction, would go to the bank.

"I met Gilman, the new bank president, a little while ago," Luke said.

The lawyer's gaze was noncommittal, waiting.

"If I had some Florida condos to sell, or some desert land, I'd hire him. He's a smooth-talking son of a bitch, and he sweats too much for a banker."

Cranmer smiled at the description. For a moment he seemed to weigh how much he wanted to say. Then he made up his mind. "My guess is he's a front man; the holding company gives him his orders. Oh, I suppose he's got some banking credentials, but if they were anything more than second rate, he wouldn't settle for the Gibson Bank, would he? The French company wanted an American figurehead, I suppose, which makes good sense for a foreign-held bank in this part of the country. You're right, Luke . . . Gilman should be selling limited partnerships or pushing shaky stocks."

"Anyone from the parent company on the scene?"

"No . . . no need . . . not with today's electronic banking and communications. Oh, there's the Frenchwoman and her workers, but she's not active at the bank."

"Frenchwoman?"

"A real dazzler. Her name's Picard. What I understand, her daddy's a big honcho with the French conglomerate."

Luke Cameron thought he had seen the Frenchwoman; that must have been her emerging from the bank. Not the kind of woman you'd forget in a hurry. Not Rodeo Drive, he thought, but the Champs Elysée . . .

"What happened to Sorenson, anyway? I was surprised to hear he sold out. He was no fisherman who couldn't wait to retire. I thought they'd have to carry him out."

"The bad loans got the bank in a hole too deep to climb out of. It was either find a buyer or wait for the FDIC to take over."

"How did Sorenson get himself killed?"

Cranmer nodded. "Shot by a robber. Some vagrant, they believe, broke into his place—it's kind of isolated there on the north edge of town, that big white Victorian house—"

"I remember it."

"Sorenson must have surprised him. Nobody heard the shot. His housekeeper found him when she came in next morning."

There was another lapse into silence in the high-ceilinged office. Both men stared out the windows. The few drops of rain in the night had spotted the windows without washing them.

Another violent death, Luke thought.

"How much do you know about this holding company that took over the ranch? Isn't it strange, a French company investing so much in western Montana?"

"Hell, no, not any more." Cranmer touched the tips of his fingers together, tenting them, bouncing the tips off each other as he talked. He had obviously considered the question, Luke thought. "You think the drought and the hard times here would scare off foreign investors, right? That's just what makes it a good investment. It's like down around Houston, where land prices took a big drop when domestic oil was so hard hit. The wise money moved in and snapped up those bargains. There was no way Houston land could go but up."

"Gibson, too?"

"Maybe not as high; maybe not as soon; but yes, in the long term. U.S. real estate is the best buy in the world. Foreigners are rushing in to buy it up with devalued dollars. The only surprising thing might be that the French moved in here before the Arabs or Germans or Japanese."

"What are they going to do with the property?" Luke asked. "Sit on it and wait for the value to go up?"

"They don't strike me as a sit-on-your-hands outfit. They seem to be enterprising. For instance, they bought up the old Wind Canyon Mine south of here. From what I hear, there's a lot of activity up there. Old-timers around Gibson are shaking their heads and saying I told you so. They're the ones who always believed there must be another big vein of gold in that mountain. The French have brought in modern equipment and mining techniques to make a dormant mine pay off again. Then there's this Frenchwoman I told you about; turns out she's a botanist. That's why she's here. What I understand, she's working on some big irrigation project on the Halston place—the company took that over, same as they did yours. This Picard woman has some fancy new ideas on land use." The lawyer smiled. "A lot of Montanans are sitting back and looking wise and waiting for one of our remember-when winters, or maybe a real howler of a wind that will move part of Montana over to the Dakotas."

"But you haven't heard their plans for . . . Dad's place."

"No. Only that . . . you'll probably be seeing the Frenchwoman there."

"Oh? Why is that?"

"Well . . ." Cranmer looked apologetic. He glared at his noisy air conditioner. "From what I hear, after the auction, she's planning to move into your place."

It was late afternoon when Luke drove up to the house along the long gravel road that led from the highway, past a line of cedar trees Luke's grandfather had planted. The sight of the house, silent and empty, brought an ache to his chest. He parked in the yard and walked past the dusty Chevy pickup and let himself into the house through the back door. His father had never gotten around to changing the rusty screen door.

Walking through the rooms, touching the familiar furniture, hearing the hollow echo of his footsteps, Luke found himself not alone but surrounded by voices, images, memories. They followed him from room to room—upstairs to his own old room, back down again to the kitchen—scenes of a thousand arguments, reunions, celebrations.

Luke drove back into town and checked into a room at the 4-B's Motel. Maybe tomorrow, he told himself. Maybe tomorrow I'll be ready to face the fact that he's gone, they're both gone, and it'll never be the same again.

Brad McAlister glanced at his watch. 3:25 A.M. He felt a small tingle of excitement, almost sexual. It was exactly five minutes before Henderson's lunch period.

Like most of the security officers on graveyard duty at the Energy

Department's Strategic Materials Storage Site twelve miles south of Gibson, Henderson liked to eat his brown-bag lunch during his duty hours, leaving his lunchtime free for a visit to the facility's weight room. It featured up-to-the-minute, state-of-the-art equipment, installed because a former site manager had decided that it would be a good way to encourage physical fitness among his employees—also because he recognized that one of the troublesome morale problems at the site was boredom. Quite simply, the employees didn't *do* anything. "We're goddamn babysitters," the manager had growled. "Those things out there are our babies. Nuclear babies. We don't even have to change their diapers. All we got to do is make sure they stay in their cribs."

Brad McAlister shared the former site manager's opinion. He viewed his night security duties with ill-concealed contempt, as make-work activity without meaning.

That was about to change with dramatic suddenness; now he approached his dull routines with new exhilaration.

Brad thought about Kali, the man who was responsible for the change. He would be meeting Kali in the morning after he got off his shift. Kali was not expecting Brad's news; Brad had decided on his own that tonight was opportune for the test.

He was pleased with himself and looked forward to this morning's meeting.

Kali thought that clandestine meetings at night, in some bar or keno palace, were simply an invitation to discovery—though that was how he had first met Brad. "People wonder what you're doing there . . . why you're not gambling or boozing it up." Kali didn't drink. "Or if you're a man there alone . . . even a couple guys . . . why you're not trying to pick up a couple broads."

Brad McAlister was amused at Kali's breezy slang, stilted and forced and often outdated. But Brad had to admit that Kali's advice made sense.

In a small town like Gibson, folks took quiet notice when you frequented a public place at night—especially if you were as well known as Brad was, a local hero, high school football star, first string in college at Western Montana, maybe not All-American, as everyone had predicted, but first-string tailback for three years.

Whenever Brad met Kali now, it was at some busy lunch counter or café or truck stop, maybe early in the morning, like they were just popping for coffee and a doughnut. Nobody noticed you then, Kali said—or if they did, they didn't think anything of it. Kali would wear old jeans and a jacket with the collar turned up, a working man's clothes, topped off with a cowboy hat, so he blended into the scene. In other circumstances, Kali might look foreign, with his dark skin and black hair and liquid brown eyes. But hunched over coffee at a counter or in a booth, wearing that weathered hat and soiled outfit, he seemed to belong. To a casual customer or waitress, he might have passed for an Indian if it weren't for the beard.

The one thing that Kali insisted on, though, was that Brad had to shuck his uniform before they met. Which was no problem. Brad hated the uniform.

The tickle of excitement came again. There was Henderson lumbering out of the alarm systems control center, heading for the weight room on schedule—3:40 to 4:10 every morning. He waved at Brad. "Hey, you workin' out tonight?" Brad shook his head, pantomiming a strained hamstring in his left leg. Henderson shrugged and walked on.

Brad McAlister waited until Henderson disappeared into the exercise room before he resumed his patrol, which took him along a wide aisle in the southeast quadrant of the facility. No rush, he cautioned himself. Give Henderson time to work up a good sweat. Make sure Rayburn over in the southwest quadrant was where he was supposed to be, and Danielson, the shift supervisor, was sleeping in his office as normal.

Two months earlier, Brad McAlister had requested the graveyard shift at Kali's suggestion. The request was soon granted because, in spite of a five percent pay differential, this was the least popular shift.

It was a quiet time, eerily quiet. Between midnight and eight o'clock there were few employees on duty other than the security detail, and almost no activity.

Brad's steps in his thick-soled black shoes—standard uniform issue—echoed hollowly along the empty aisle. He had often wondered why they didn't issue silent crepe soles. Why should a security guard announce his approach with a heavy clop, clop? He passed the security office, where mousy little Freddy Wilson, the night clerk, was shuffling paperwork at his desk. The door to Danielson's office was closed. The bank of television monitor screens on the far end wall showed several views of the facility, inside and out, with a security officer always assigned to watch them.

Henderson would be adding more metal now, stepping up the weight, in his fantasies going for the gold.

Brad glanced again at his watch and slowed his measured pace. He had planned to reach the alarm center at exactly 3:36. Two more minutes.

He could feel the tension building, the exhilaration. It didn't matter that tonight was only a dry run. The risk was still real. And the promise . . .

In the beginning, Brad McAlister had looked upon his job as a security officer at the nuclear site as a stopgap. "It'll pay the mortgage," he had told friends cheerfully, "until the business gets going again." He was a real estate broker, as good as there was in the area, with his own office for eight years. Had done all right, too, until about two years ago. Then times started to get hard in most of Montana, even in the mountain resort areas where Brad had invested heavily. Things got lean and tight. That was nothing new; you were supposed to suck up and gut it out until the next upswing. Except there was no upswing.

Suddenly Brad McAlister found everything disintegrating around him, as if he were a man surrounded by moving sands, not knowing whether, if he moved, he would be swallowed up by the sands. The Gibson Bank, taken over by outsiders when the bank itself got into trouble, began to call in its delinquent loans. The K-I Resort Development, in which he was one of the general partners—which would have been a real money-maker in good times and should have made Brad's fortune—went into Chapter 11, with ugly lawsuits pending from the limited partners. The deal on the shopping center also turned sour, the major investor pulling out, saying he didn't like the feel of things and was going to stay on the sidelines for a while. Then there was the Black Monday, the stock market dive, the last sand hill dissolving beneath Brad's feet.

He had lost the business. His mortgage was six months in arrears. There were no available jobs in his field—hell, there were no jobs, period. Half of the state was in trouble, farms and ranches failing, businesses struggling just to keep open, bank foreclosures and property auctions so commonplace they caused less excitement than a chicken barbecue at the Methodist church.

Brad McAlister had grabbed the job offer at the nuclear site—a payback for a favor he had done for the materials supplier who had won the cement contract when the facility was built—fully expecting it would be only temporary.

But there had been no sign of change, no evidence of improvement. Brad had wanted to leave Gibson, to strike out for somewhere fresh—California, maybe. "Houses sell for a small fortune out there," he had argued to Anne. "People line up to buy 'em. Some places they have to take tickets! All you'd have to do is sell one house a month at those prices and, Jesus, you'd be knee deep in CD's before you'd know it."

"Brad, don't swear."

"Oh, for Chrissakes, I'm not swearing. Anyway, that's no answer."

"Times will get better here; we just have to wait. You'll get your business back, right here where we belong, where you know everybody and everybody knows you."

"That's just the trouble. Everyone knows I'm a failure."

"You're not a failure! You've just had a temporary setback, that's all. No one blames you. It's the times. It's the recession. It has hit many people in this part of the country. Lord knows, it's no disgrace. When the economy picks up . . ."

"Oh, sure! When the economy picks up, Gibson's going to boom. People will flock to Gibson to spend their money. . . . Don't hold your breath."

"It's a good town, Brad. You grew up here. You always said you loved it here, that it was the best place on earth to bring up our kids."

"So they can grow up to be security guards . . . like their old man?"

"What's wrong with that? It's a respectable job. They wouldn't hire just anyone, you said so yourself. With what you make, and what I earn at the bank . . ."

"I wondered when you were going to throw that at me."

"I'm not throwing it at you! I just meant, until things get better generally, we could be a lot worse off. And things *will* pick up."

"As I said, don't hold your breath."

"Oh, Brad . . ."

There'd been a lot of Oh Brads lately.

Well, all that was going to change. He had come to hate his job; hate the sight of the nuclear facility each night when he drove through the tall, guarded gates; hate the quiet of these high-ceilinged buildings with their thick cement walls; hate the widely separated racks where the metallic uranium was stored in shielded containers; hate even the yellow lines painted on the floor as a reminder of the distances that had to be maintained between the shielded containers. Because, as Brad understood it, even a small quantity of weapons-grade uranium, harmless enough in isolation, would instantly become subcritical if it came too close to a similar mass, supercritical if the masses were large enough. But now, as Brad reached the alarm systems control center—Henderson's private domain—he felt not hate but pounding excitement.

Even his attitude toward his job had changed.

It had changed after he had met Kali.

At exactly 3:36 A.M., Brad McAlister peered into the narrow, crowded alarm center. It smelled of Henderson's sweat. Because the lunch period lasted only forty-five minutes, Henderson never allowed himself time to shower after his workout.

Behind Brad, the corridor was empty. No footsteps approached along the horizontal aisle where his patrol was scheduled to intersect with Jim Rayburn's in eight minutes.

Brad grinned as he saw the light go out that identified the camera used to survey the alarm control center. He stepped inside. Flaw in the system. And he was the one who had spotted it. Kali had been impressed.

The Strategic Materials Storage Site had two videotape recording systems, each wired to eight closed-circuit television cameras for security surveillance. That meant the cameras recorded in an automatic sequence, rotating from one to the next at thirty-second intervals. The rows of red and yellow lights on Henderson's control panel showed which two cameras, one in each system, were active at any given moment—red on, yellow off. No way this could have been spotted as a security weakness. It wasn't—unless you had someone on the inside who knew what the little red and yellow lights meant, knew the timing cycle, knew the locations of the switches that turned the various alarms on or off—*and* could put himself in a position to *see* those little lights and *reach* those little switches.

Someone like Brad McAlister.

He moved swiftly, each action preplanned. With the control center camera cut out of the cycle for exactly three and a half minutes, he was free from detection. He deactivated the ultrasonic intrusion alarms that, by means of a transceiver that sent out and received ultrasonic waves, detected any movement in the immediate vicinity of the stored cylinders of uranium. Any break in the wave pattern triggered the alarm. Quickly, deftly, he cut off the electromechanical alarms protecting the shipping and receiving bay in the southeast corner of the building and the fire door in the southeast outside wall. He hesitated, for a moment uncertain, fighting panic, before he identified the switches for the underground seismic pressure sensors buried outside the building between the wall and the perimeter fence. And, finally, he hit the switch that turned off the vibration detectors—the contact microphones attached to the perimeter wire fence to detect any attempted penetration by cutting or climbing the fence.

There was also an above-ground, invisible, infrared photoelectric beam system that normally protected the clear zone inside the perimeter between the fence and any structures. Because of recent false-alarm incidents, this system was down for repairs.

All of this took about thirty seconds before Brad McAlister was out of the control center and back in the main aisle. He walked quickly now, trying to make up the seconds he had lost. Then he slowed his pace before reaching the alarm room.

At 3:45, heart hammering, he met Jim Rayburn where their patrols intersected, dead on time.

Rayburn grinned at him. "Still awake, Brad?"

"I'm sleepwalking, can't you tell? If any terrorists break in, try not to wake me up, okay?"

"You never know, old buddy. Headquarters might pull one of their mock attacks any day now. We haven't had one in a while."

The bored guard spoke wistfully, reminding Brad of the turmoil and excitement back in March when an outside assault team had staged an attempted intrusion into the site. They had almost succeeded. Luckily one of the attackers had jumped the gun, cutting a fence about thirty seconds ahead of the other members of the assault force. That alarm had awakened the site's security response; the half-minute warning had been just enough to enable them to repel the attack.

At the time, there had been congratulations all around. Security Director Greg Danielson—asleep in his office when the assault team struck—had even received a letter of commendation from the secretary of energy in Washington for the alertness of his security unit.

What Brad McAlister had observed, however, was not the success of the security response but its vulnerability . . .

Brad walked on, listening to the fading clomp of Rayburn's steps. Brad's patrol route brought him to the service bay at 3:56 A.M. He walked past it to a door set in the southeast wall. Glancing down another long, brightly lit, empty aisle, seeing everything safe, no one in sight, he quietly gripped the bar handle of the safety fire door and pushed it open.

Cool night air rushed in from the darkness, the scents of sage and damp earth. The smell of wet soil came from the freshly dug irrigation channels on the Halston place, just beyond the east perimeter fence.

The smells, the darkness, the rush of wind startled him, like a breath of reality intruding upon his fantasy world.

But what he waited for, every muscle taut, was the scream of sirens, the pandemonium of shouts and pounding feet, the glare of spotlights focusing on a security zone when the door was opened.

Nothing.

There was no backup system that he had been ignorant of.

Brad McAlister stepped outside briefly, long enough to verify that he had successfully deactivated the seismic pressure sensors buried in the ground. He smiled at the recollection of a proposal by Danielson to bury mines in the clear zone. Washington had overruled the idea.

Reentering the building, Brad eased the door shut and glanced once more at his watch. 4:01. Cutting it close.

He completed the next stage of his patrol, where he had to use a key to punch in his time of passage—a process repeated at regular intervals along his route. With five minutes left before Henderson was due out of the weight room and back at the alarm systems control center, Brad McAlister hurried down another long, wide aisle, following the detested yellow lines. At an intersection, he crossed over to the main aisle and walked briskly—afraid to call attention to himself by the sight or sound of running footsteps—to the alarm center.

He reached the center at 4:08. He peered down the aisle, listening, especially for the bang of a door opening. Heard nothing, saw no one. Stepped inside and hastily began to flip open the switches he had closed a few minutes earlier, taking them one by one, counting them, making sure he hadn't missed one. He felt the wash of relief when the last switch was open; he stepped out through the door and glanced back, and . . .

His heart seemed to stop beating.

The red light on the video camera that covered the interior of the alarm center was on.

How long had it been on? Had the light been on when he was inside? *Think!*

He was out in the aisle, breathing again, walking away. He reached the side corridor seconds before he heard Henderson's heavy steps coming toward him from the direction of the weight room. *Too close,* he thought, *you cut it too close.*

He had wasted several seconds staring at that red light. Had he been outside the room before it came on? Yes, he had stepped back, surveying the panel to make sure he had activated all of the alarms. And the surveillance camera inside the room hadn't been on then. He would have seen the red light when he looked at the panel; he was sure of it.

Almost sure.

What would the camera have recorded if it was on? A security officer checking the control panel. Nothing incriminating in that.

Except that it wasn't Brad McAlister's job. He had no business being in the alarm center when Henderson was away.

Brad hardly remembered the rest of his shift. Long before it was over, at eight that morning, he had decided that he wouldn't tell Kali about the red light coming on. Only about the rest of it. Only that everything had worked precisely as planned.

The next time would not be a dry run. The next time would be the real thing.

Baku, the Caucasus

SERGEI MILOV SAT AT A TABLE AT THE ZHEMCHUZHINA, AN
open air café on the shore promenade just off the Boulevard of
Oilworkers in the coastal city of Baku. He sipped tea while staring
out to sea. A steady wind blew in from the Caspian. The temperature
was mild, but there had been a wind warning earlier that morning,
forecasting the possibility of a real howler called the Nord of Baku,
a wind of hurricane force that sometimes struck the city. Let it come,
Milov brooded with true Russian melancholy.

He thought of Natalia. Rarely did he think of her now. When he
did, it was only in moments of despair.

Captain Sergei Andreyevich Milov was a KGB counterintelligence agent assigned to the Cominform's IV Division, which was
responsible for Middle East terrorism, as part of the Second Department of the Second Directorate. He was a ruggedly handsome man
of 29, black haired, with strong, well-chiseled features and brooding
gray eyes that women found attractive. He had an arresting face,
which reflected a detached intellectuality at odds with a wariness of
eye. He was not tall. Just five feet nine. But because of his wiry, muscular build, he seemed to be larger and more powerful than he was.

All in all, the impression Milov projected was that of a young man
of character and intelligence, self-assured and ambitious. Yet there
was a tenseness in him, a sense of beleaguerment. Those with the
temerity to do so might wonder what he was doing stationed at a
remote outpost like Baku in the Caucasus. True, it was the capital
of the Azerbaijan Republic, a center of communications, and it was
in a region of strong nationalist demonstrations and an area frequently rent by ethnic violence. But this city on the Caspian Sea was
far removed from the centers of power. It wasn't Moscow.

Sergei Milov's good looks, so far as he was concerned, were his
curse. They had caught the eye of Anna Natalia Sidorin. They were
the reason for his banishment to Azerbaijan, where he would attract
the attention of his superiors in the Soviet Committee for State Security only if something went wrong. And, given the nationalistic fervor among Azerbaijanis, and their frequently violent conflicts with

the neighboring Armenians, there was a good chance that something would go wrong.

He had first encountered Natalia ("He calls me Anna. You will call me Natalia," she had said imperiously) at a performance of *Giselle* at the Bolshoi. She was standing with a young army officer during the first intermission, her mouth open in laughter so genuine and uninhibited that Milov could not help staring. As she became aware of his interest ("I felt those eyes of yours, Milov"), this beautiful woman glanced toward him. Her laughter faded into a thoughtful smile.

Milov wondered enviously who the lieutenant was. He seemed to dote on her.

During the next intermission, and again after the performance, Milov searched for her. She did not reappear. Her image, however, stayed with him. A woman in her twenties, he guessed. Blond hair cut fashionably short like a boy's, exquisite features, and a slender, diminutive body as graceful as a model's. Her fashionable, bare-shouldered gown, Milov thought, must have come from Paris or Rome.

The next time he saw her, she was riding in a black Zhiguli through Dzerzhinsky Square. Milov was returning to his office from lunch. For a moment, he had the astonishing impression that the black car was pulling away from the entrance to KGB headquarters at number 2. Not possible, he thought, staring after the Zhiguli as it sped away. For an instant, the same woman's face was framed in the window, her eyes wide in the cameo face, staring directly at him, her lips curved in a smile. Don't be a fool, he told himself. How could she possibly remember you?

Milov's superior in his section of counterintelligence, Colonel Vitaly Novikoff, approached him.

"Have you seen a ghost, Sergei Andreyevich?" Novikoff remarked.

"A beautiful one. That woman in the Zhiguli. Do you know who she is?"

"Anna Natalia Sidorin? You mean you don't know?"

"No . . . I've only seen her once before."

"Look but don't touch," Novikoff said with a chuckle. "My friend, that is General Sidorin's wife! There are those who say she is the most beautiful woman in Moscow—she was an actress before he married her—and the most dangerous!"

Milov was not stupid. He had proceeded to forget her. General Dimitri Yaslovich Sidorin was not only a Hero of the Soviet Union and a member of the Central Committee, he was also the head of the KGB's Second Directorate and close to Mikhail Gorbachev.

The next month, Sergei Milov did not see Anna Natalia Sidorin. He avoided the ballet and the opera. He concentrated on his work. After all, the world is full of Natalias, he thought.

But in his world, there was only one Natalia. She haunted his dreams.

The letter came one evening in November. It was not really a letter but a brief note, not really an invitation but a summons. A car would pick him up the next evening at his apartment at seven. It was signed simply "N."

Milov hardly slept at all that night. It was insane, he told himself. Idiocy. They had not even been introduced; only their eyes had met. Now this most beautiful, most desirable, most dangerous woman had sent for him.

General Sidorin was attending a Warsaw Pact meeting in Prague.

The Zhiguli was waiting at curbside at exactly seven in the evening. There was a light snow falling; Milov was grateful for the darkness and the snowfall. A young KGB sergeant drove the car, stone faced. Milov could only guess that he was absolutely loyal to Natalia. ("Grisha?" she murmured afterward, amused. "He would die for his Natalia." *His* Natalia, too? Milov wondered, acutely jealous.)

The car glided through the darkness to a dacha in the woods about a half hour from the perimeter of Moscow. The cottage was on a lake surrounded by fir trees. Milov was relieved to see only one other dacha nearby, half-hidden in the woods.

Anna Natalia Sidorin was waiting for him. There was a fire blazing in the stone fireplace, a bottle of Posolskaya on ice. Grisha, the chauffeur, disappeared without a word. Natalia lay on a blue sofa next to the fireplace, the vodka on the table before her in a bucket beside a platter of crackers and cheese. Milov could not take his eyes off her.

"Are you so shy, Captain Milov?"

"I shouldn't have come. General Sidorin—"

"Of course you shouldn't, but you did, so you might as well relax."

There was an amused twinkle in her eyes, a playful tone to her voice. He suspected she was laughing at him. Her eyes were the blue of the lake, cool and deep. "Do you like goat cheese? It's from Georgia. You are Georgian, are you not?"

"Yes. And I'm fond of our *sulguni.*"

"Are you going to stand there all evening, Sergei Andreyevich?" She patted the soft leather cushion beside her. When Milov sat in it, he felt afloat in billowing softness.

She spread some white cheese carefully on one of the ring-shaped crackers and held it teasingly toward him. When he tried to accept it from her, she murmured, "No, no, like this. . . ." She lifted the cracker to his lips and fed it to him delicately, as if he were a child. The tips of her fingers followed the cracker, nibbling at his lips.

With a gay little laugh, she leaned back in a corner of the sofa. Her white robe parted slightly to reveal the curve of a small, firm breast. When he reached for her, her hand restrained him. "Some vodka, my impetuous captain. Will you pour for us?"

His heart was hammering, his fingers clumsy as he poured the ice-cold Posolskaya into two glasses, spilling vodka onto the table. He started to wipe up the spill with a paper napkin.

She gently stopped him. "First a toast. Then you can clean. You can even vacuum if you like."

The deep blue eyes regarded him over the rim of her glass. They drank to the Bolshoi where they had first exchanged glances across a crowded lobby; to poor Giselle; to the sadness of true love. Natalia drank like a man, tossing the vodka to the back of her throat. He heard the glass click against her teeth. When she lowered it, he embraced her roughly, smothering her laughter with his hungry mouth.

They made love on the sofa, and again on the thick bear rug in front of the fireplace. It was still dark when she woke him, whispering, "You must go, my beautiful captain."

The uncommunicative Grisha chauffeured him back into the city. Two nights later, he came for Milov again, behind the wheel, silent as ever. Then, after two days had passed, Natalia came to Milov at his apartment. She drifted lightly through the two rooms—one of the valued privileges of his KGB rank—touching each piece of furniture, picking up the photograph of Milov's father in his World War II uniform, studying a cheap Utrillo print on the wall. Milov was struck as never before by the barrenness of his rooms. Except for his American jazz record collection, there was nothing of himself visible, as if the circumspection essential to his calling had defined his personal life.

She spun around, her eyes bright as if she were elated with what she saw. "Mischa returns tomorrow," she blurted. "We are wasting time."

She stayed until the cold gray of dawn lay against the shaded window. Then she rose from his bed, naked in the pale light, appearing smaller and thinner. He could see her ribs beneath the soft, smooth skin. She came to him fully dressed and kissed him softly, almost demurely, on the lips.

That was Saturday morning.

On Monday, without explanation, Captain Sergei Andreyevich Milov was transferred to the remote KGB field office in Baku. Although he retained his rank, Milov was quite certain that his career with the Committee for State Security had reached a dead end.

Not that there was nothing for him to do in Baku. Azerbaijan at the time was in the grip of one of its periodic pogroms, during which the numerically superior Azerbaijanis, who were mostly Shiite Muslims, slaughtered the minority Christian Armenians. The violence was concentrated in Sumgait, one of many mixed-population cities in Azerbaijan; the area was administered from Baku, and Milov was kept busy rounding up extremists and trying to prevent the spread of the violence.

But news of events in Baku then were little known, either in the world at large or in Russia itself; the era of openness had not yet begun. Milov's actions, however well carried out, would never be noticed. Baku was not Moscow. Because of his transgression, Milov believed, his banishment there effectively quashed any hopes he might have had for a promising future.

That bleak view prevailed until, eighteen months after he had left Moscow, the telex came from Moscow Centre.

It arrived on Sunday. Milov had been playing tennis when he was called to his office. He was wearing white cotton slacks and a knit shirt, appearing more like a tourist than a counterintelligence officer as he stood beside his desk reading the decoded telex. He was hot, sweat dripping down his back. Yet he felt a chill.

Top Secret
To Captain S. A. Milov
Investigate attempted theft of strategic weapon on the Baku-
Tbilisi railway line. Suspect in military custody at Kirovabad.
Proceed there immediately, take charge of prisoner and interro-
gate. Report as soon as possible.

Novikoff

Colonel Vitaly Yurevich Novikoff had been Milov's mentor as well
as his superior in the Second Department. He also reported directly
to General Sidorin. Milov had not heard from him in eighteen
months.

At Kirovabad Captain Milov had taken custody of the prisoner.
With the help of his assistant, Sergeant Yakov Zagorsky, and the
overeager cooperation of the local militia, Milov had interrogated
the thief for five consecutive days. His name—or the name he gave—
was Abu Hasir. That was the only information he volunteered.

Milov, who was persistent, knowledgeable, and highly trained in
the arts of persuasion, had persisted, knowingly and persuasively.
By the third day, when Abu Hasir babbled wildly in a mixture of
Farsi and French, Milov had determined that the young man was
not a member of the Azerbaijani Popular Front, an organization ad-
vocating Azerbaijani independence from the Soviet Union, or involved in one of the anti-Armenian extremist groups. He was, in fact,
Iranian but he had spent some time in France. This meant that he
was not a simple peasant chosen by his Iranian masters from Tehran's rubbish heap. Abu Hasir also talked about the cause of Azerbaijanian nationalism, but Milov suspected that this was part of a
rehearsed cover story.

Abu Hasir was in his early twenties, tall, swarthy, with curly black
hair and the mandatory full beard of some Shiite fundamentalists.
He betrayed a familiarity with an array of terrorist weapons. An
American-made Browning 9mm automatic was found on him when
he was captured; an orange plastic explosive of Czechoslovakian origin was concealed in a small bag in his room along with coils of wire,
a detonator and a timer. He was not, in other words, Milov observed
to Sergeant Zagorsky, your ordinary student of the humanities. The
sergeant's face was questioning.

"He's had terrorist training," Milov explained.

"Oh . . . Yes, Captain Milov."

"It's also clear that either he knows nothing of the attempt to steal a nuclear weapon, or he has a fanatic's will to resist."

Abu Hasir had already lost the skin from the bottoms of his feet, all but four toenails, most of his front teeth, and the first joint of one index finger. He could see out of only one eye, and that with difficulty.

"He seeks martyrdom, Yakov. At a certain level of fanaticism, pain becomes joy. But the medical supplies from Baku have arrived. Now we'll see if his will is as resistant to the subtle persuasion of drugs as it is to pain."

On the fifth day Abu Hasir, during the course of interrogation under sodium pentathol, slipped into a coma. The doctor in attendance checked the prisoner's eyes with a tiny, bright light and shook his head.

"Is it a toxic reaction to the drug?" Milov asked impatiently.

"I can't be sure without more tests."

Milov bent over the limp form of the silent terrorist, who was strapped to a narrow table, his arms and legs immobile. He slapped the bearded face and shouted, "Who ordered you to steal the weapon? Hasir, listen to me. Resistance is pointless. Who collaborated with you? What is his name?"

The prisoner was unresponsive.

"Can he hear me?"

"I do not believe it is possible." The doctor, who was attached to the local militia, was visibly nervous in the presence of the KGB.

Milov stared at the Iranian who had managed to frustrate him. "Go to heaven, you bastard," he muttered.

"What was that, Captain?" Yakov Zagorsky asked.

"Never mind. We'll let him sleep it off and try again in the morning."

On the morning of the sixth day of Milov's interrogation, Abu Hasir was dead. It was as if he had willed it, commanding his heart to stop.

Sergei Milov despaired. After eighteen months of exile, he had been given one last chance for redemption. He had failed.

An exchange of telex messages followed.

Top secret
To Colonel V. Y. Novikoff, Moscow Centre
Prisoner identified as Abu Hasir, Iranian origin, Shiite fundamentalist alignment, spent time in Paris. Terrorist training a strong possibility. Prisoner died during interrogation without revealing names of accomplices or source of support. Investigation continues. No priority weapons reported missing. Prisoner photograph and fingerprints are being dispatched to Moscow Centre this day via courier.

Milov

To Milov
Return to Moscow immediately.

Novikoff

Gibson, Montana

HONORING THE REQUEST IN HIS WILL, THE MORTUARY HAD buried Tom Cameron in a family plot beside his wife of thirty-five years, on a slight knoll in sight of the ranch house. The small private cemetery was defined by a low stone wall Tom had built himself, using rocks from his own land and fitting them together without mortar. There was no marker over the newly sodded grave. "We thought you might want to decide to choose the headstone," the funeral director had told Luke Cameron. "Tom didn't say anything about a stone or a marker."

There was a stone over Ellen Cameron's grave. IN LOVING MEMORY . . . followed by her name and the years bracketing her life. Tom Cameron had never been able to parade his feelings, however powerful they were. Luke was not surprised he had said nothing about a stone over his own burial plot.

There was an overturned basket of flowers at the foot of the grave, the flowers blown, dried up, and brown. Luke wondered who had thought to place them there.

The wind on the knoll was a steady force, a Montana wind. In the depression below, cars were beginning to bump along the gravel road from the highway toward the ranch buildings. Someone from the auctioneer's staff was directing the parking off to the left of the house. A large open area on the lawn in front of the house had been set aside for the auction, with rows of folding chairs lined up. Workers were carrying objects out of the house.

"You take anything you want that's personal," Bob Morrissey, the auctioneer, had told Luke. "That's what the Frenchwoman said I should tell you." Everyone in town seemed to call her the Frenchwoman.

"That's generous of her."

"Seems like a fine woman," Morrissey said with feeling. "I was sorry to hear about old Tom. Sudden like that . . . Most of the furniture won't bring much. . . ." Morrissey seemed relieved to divert his thoughts to business. " 'Cepting for that old rolltop and the tall clock. I'll hold out for a good price on them. There's buyers for the farm equipment, of course. Doesn't make any difference how bad things get, there's always buyers."

Luke watched the buyers gather, each new arrival stirring up dust along the gravel road. A dozen cars and trucks there now. Not all of them buyers, he thought. Some came just to look.

In the wind-stirred stillness at the top of the knoll, Luke Cameron heard voices raised in anger, his own and his father's. Tom sitting at the rolltop going over his books, turning in the wooden swivel chair to stare across the living room at his son. "You could be takin' an interest. It's as much your business as mine."

"No, it isn't."

"What do you mean, it isn't? You know damned well—"

"I'm just a hired hand who doesn't get paid."

"What the hell . . . You want some money? Why didn't you say so?"

"I don't want to get paid."

"Then what *do* you want?"

"Out," Luke said, not knowing the word was there until it was in the open, hanging between them. "I want out."

"I don't understand."

"How could you? You've never listened. This is your place, Pa. You run it the way you always have. There's no place on it for me. I can't just go along, saying 'yes, sir,' 'no, sir.' And that's what I'd have to do."

"You're sayin' you don't want to work on the ranch? You don't want to stay here?"

"I can't stay, Pa. We've been at each other's throats ever since Ma died."

"Leave her out of this."

"She *is* out of it. This is between us. Look, Pa, I have my own life to live. There isn't room here for us both. We'd butt heads every time there was a decision to be made. You helped me through college. Okay. I want to utilize what I learned."

"You can use what you learned right here on the Bar-C."

"You wouldn't let me. You'd do it your way."

"Horseshit!"

"No, you're too stubborn to listen, but it's time you heard the truth." Luke hesitated. He didn't want to hurt his father. Not even in anger. But he could no longer sacrifice his own future to gain his father's approval. It was best to speak up. "When Ma was here, she'd soft-soap the both of us, and we'd set aside our differences. We tried to get along because that's what she wanted. She—"

"I told you to leave her out of this."

"Goddamnit, listen to me for once!"

"Get out! Out!"

"So you won't have to listen?"

"Pack your things and get out. You want to live your own life. Then live it," Tom Cameron grouched. "You can stay the night, then get out. I don't want to see you in the morning."

"Pa . . ."

Tom Cameron closed the rolling top of the big oak desk with finality and stalked out of the room. Luke left in the morning.

A majority of the bidders were strangers to Luke. Young people, most of them, younger than Luke himself, hunting for bargains. Scattered among them were a few antique dealers, assessing the offerings with a professional eye. Luke recognized a few people, mostly older folks, Tom's friends. They came up to him and mumbled something about being sorry, and "Tom wouldn't have wanted to be alive to see this day." Old gnarled men in Stetsons and boots, straight-backed women with worn faces, standing silent in the yard.

Bob Morrissey was transformed into an automaton when he went into his rapid-fire auctioneer's spiel. "What am I bid for this fine oak table, who'll start it at a hundred dollars, do I hear a hundred dollars, they don't make 'em like this any more, solid oak, you'll need three people to carry it. Do I hear seventy-five dollars, seventy-five, sixty? Fifty dollars for a beautiful oak dining table—I have a bid, fifty dollars, fifty dollars, who'll give me sixty, sixty, yes, ma'am, back there on the left, sixty dollars now, do I have seventy . . ."

Commerce triumphs over sentiment, Luke thought wryly.

"It must be ver' difficult for you, yes?"

Luke turned to find a pair of large, dark eyes appraising him thoughtfully—perhaps sympathetically.

"It's not pleasant," he agreed.

"Is it true you are moving out today, Mr. Cameron? There is no rush. I understand, it is your home, yes?"

"It was."

"But you must still think of it so. It is so . . . peaceful here."

She had exotic features with clearly defined bone structure, and a long, straight nose. Her curly black hair was cut short, exposing the graceful line of her neck. When she looked up at him directly, her eyes—was it a trick of makeup?—seemed even larger, with exaggerated lashes. Though she was barely of average height, her trim figure made her appear taller at a distance than up close. She radiated an aura of sophisticated poise, of beautifully groomed elegance. The points of her lips curved upward slightly, delicately, as if on the verge of a habitual smile.

Luke Cameron was annoyed with himself for obviously staring.

"I am Micheline Picard." When she smiled warmly, Luke's heart gave a surprised lurch. "You must call me Micheline."

"Luke," he responded. *You own the house I grew up in, the land where my parents are buried. You can call me by my first name.*

She held out her hand in an impulsive gesture. Her hand seemed tiny in his, but her grip was unexpectedly strong. "I am glad you do not think of me as your enemy, Mr. Cameron . . . Luke."

"Why should I think that?"

She glanced around the yard, sweeping it with her long lashes.

"You have lost so much, and . . . I have gain so much."

"It's nothing personal, I'm sure."

"Mais non, of course not, but still . . ."

"Excuse me, there's something I must do."

Bob Morrissey was perspiring at his work. His voice was hypnotic. "Take a good close look at this beautiful desk, folks. A genuine antique rolltop desk, solid oak, nicked and scarred and as handsome as a first love. What am I bid for this piece of history? Look at those cubbyholes, you can put away a lifetime's worth of bills and forget them. Who'll bid two thousand dollars?"

"Twenty-five hundred," Luke Cameron said.

A hush came over the crowd. Everyone turned to stare at Luke. Even Morrissey was momentarily nonplussed. He coughed and nodded at Luke and hurried through the formality of asking for another bid. But it was clear no one was going to bid against Luke Cameron, knowing who he was and the harsh reality behind this auction. And even if someone might have wanted to up the bidding, Morrissey wouldn't provide an opening. He wound up the sale without pausing for breath. "Sold! To Mr. Cameron for twenty-five hundred dollars!"

The momentary excitement faded. As Morrissey returned to his wares, Luke wished he could also afford to buy the grandfather clock. It was an old Seth Thomas with a Westminster chime. He knew it would bring a good price, however, and he was near the bottom of his modest reserves. The rolltop would have to do.

As Luke turned his attention from the auctioneer back to the Frenchwoman, she nodded knowingly as if confirming his judgment. "It is a sentimental thing you do, buying the desk, yes? It is for your father."

"You could say that."

She smiled. "It is not such a bad thing, Luke, to be sentimental about someone you love."

Now Morrissey beckoned to her, and she drifted away. Luke made no attempt to observe or overhear the conversation. The auctioneer probably wanted to know how long to keep the auction going. He would soon run out of listed items. Some of the buyers were beginning to saunter toward their cars.

Luke had already packed up. Some boxes would be picked up later and stored. Others he would haul himself in the pickup. He would ask Justin Cranmer to keep the rolltop for him, maybe use it in his

office if he wished. Cranmer had already indicated a desire to buy
the Chevy pickup.

Luke didn't want to linger in the empty house any longer. Too
many shadows.

It was late afternoon. The yard was almost deserted. Most of the
oglers and buyers had disappeared in their battered pickups and se-
dans. Bob Morrissey was standing beside his van, talking with one
of his helpers, another day's work just about wrapped up. Luke
shouldered a trunk onto the bed of the Chevy truck, next to an old
leather suitcase and boxes packed with items he couldn't bring himself to part with—old photographs, musty books, childhood things
his mother had saved like his school yearbooks and a collection of
old baseball cards. ("Those cards are worth something, Luke," the
auctioneer had told him. "Be glad to take 'em on consignment for
you. They don't mean nothin' to the French.")

Micheline Picard emerged from the house by the back door and
descended the steps just as Luke slammed the tailgate closed. She
started toward Morrissey's van, then detoured over to Luke.

"It was nice to meet you, Luke. I hope we will be friends."

"I don't think there'll be much time for that."

"No? You are not staying in Gibson?"

"No, I won't be staying." She made him feel fumble-fingered and
clumsy, a country yokel. He ought to be angry with her, he thought.
After all, she was the one who was taking over his land, his home,
his birthright. But somehow the anger was diverted from her—toward himself for staying away, toward his father for driving him
away, toward the circumstances that made it possible for people who
had given their lives to a piece of land to be deprived of it by a piece
of paper. The Frenchwoman was hardly responsible for all that. Hell,
at least she planned to do something useful with the land. Luke said,
"I don't have anything to stay for now."

She seemed to hesitate. "I am very regret if I have been the cause
of your leaving."

Cute, he thought. "No need to regret. It's not your fault. From
what I hear, you have some construction plans for the properties
your company has acquired."

"Yes, it will be important what we do, I believe," she said seriously. "I would hope your father would not think this is such a terrible thing, what I try to do."

"No, I'm sure he wouldn't think it terrible."

Luke thought about what Tom Cameron might have said. *"She has a great ass, but she doesn't know a cotton-pickin' thing about Montana soil and Montana winds and Montana winters. She thinks she can turn it into a goddamn nursery!"* He would have paused a second or two, setting up the kicker. *"The trouble with this year's Montana topsoil is, next year it's in Wyoming."*

"He'd have told you to treat the land with respect, that's all," Luke said aloud. "I'm sure you'll do that."

"But of course," she said gravely.

Luke climbed into the pickup and drove away from the house, not looking back. The Frenchwoman watched him rumble down the long gravel road until the dust obscured him.

As dusk crept across the sky like a closing eyelid, Luke Cameron turned abruptly off the road to Gibson. He headed the Chevy pickup south along the Montana state highway that divided the Bar-C land and the Halston ranch. Off to his right, he could hear the sound of pumps—part of that new irrigation system he had heard about, he supposed. Earlier, he had observed activity far from the road, a few figures bent over in the fields, a pattern of trenches scarring the prairie—grazing land, in times past, for Halston's cattle. Now, in the fading light, the landscape was empty. No sign of activity except for the sound of the invisible pumps, pulsing in the distance.

Last night, Luke remembered, he thought he had heard the sound of a truck along this road long after midnight. It brought back to mind his father's letter.

In that moment, Luke realized where he was heading. He had told himself he was just going to take a last look around, maybe try to catch a glimpse of that herd of buffalo that would soon be moved all the way to eastern Washington. Now he knew he was about to do what he had put off ever since his arrival in Gibson.

He was going down to the creek where his father had died.

Luke left the pickup near the road and made his way down a gradual slope toward a clump of cottonwoods, their dark trunks silhouetted against the stream, whose surface glittered like a scattering of silver coins in the early moonlight.

That night had been overcast, the lawyer had said. Even darker down in the river bottom.

Luke stood on the bank, listening to the trickle of the water over its rock and gravel bed. No sign of the buffalo herd in the flat bottom-land, a rich grass meadow defined by some brown hills about a half mile distant. While he stood there, reluctant to retrace his father's steps—he simply didn't want to think about the ugly details—a question jumped at him, a question asked before and put aside: What was it that Tom was afraid of?

There's something happening here I can't handle alone. And it scares me. You're the only one I know who could maybe answer some of my questions, the only one I can trust.

What couldn't he handle? He certainly wouldn't be intimidated by a bank or frightened by a forfeiture.

Knowing Tom Cameron, who wouldn't have backed off from a confrontation if the devil himself had showed up in Gibson, there had to be a better reason for his plea. Then what was it? Why, after all this time, had he called out for help? A man who had never asked for anything in his life!

Luke stared down at the ford where his father had crossed the creek. Luke knew the crossing well. Upstream the river was confined into a narrower channel, where in normal times it ran three feet deep. It might run no more than half that depth now. But here at the bend the creek bottom widened, and the stream had always been shallow. Moreover, there were some large, flat stones scattered across the bed, slices of granite forming submerged stepping-stones, covered, Luke guessed, by no more than three inches of water. Tom Cameron and Luke had always used those stones to walk across the creek. Over the stones the current was a little more rapid than elsewhere, but not swift enough to knock a man down. Only when there was heavy rain in the mountains and a fast runoff could it be dangerous.

Montana was still in the grip of a drought. There had been no rain the day Tom died.

Luke Cameron glanced down at his scarred, comfortable boots, rescued from a closet in his old room, reflecting that it was easy to step back in time and place into old habits. This was not a country for low-cut Italian tassel loafers. This was boot country, and his old boots had absorbed more than their share of mud and snow and water.

He trudged across the shallow stream with no more than a casual glance down, knowing even after a lapse of years the exact location and contours of each stone step, using them as familiarly as one might use a stairway.

In half a century, his dad hadn't been away from the ranch for more than two weeks at a time. He had known these stones far better than Luke.

A man could grow old, of course, Luke told himself as he climbed up the low bank to the edge of the grass meadow. An old man could lose the spring in his step, the clarity of his vision. Stumble more. Tom needed glasses but would wear them only for reading.

He could also have had a stroke. Cranmer had suggested that possibility. Even a small stroke could cause an old man to become dazed or dizzy and take a misstep. No way to tell from the damage, the lawyer had added in an apologetic tone. Multiple cranial trauma, the coroner's report had concluded.

The scenario was plausible enough. Apparently the coroner was satisfied. Ed Thayer, the sheriff of Gibson, agreed it had been an accident. An old man, out walking on a dark night, had become careless while wading the creek, probably lost his footing and fell. Hit his head on a rock. Dazed by the blow, he had stumbled away from the stream onto the grassy table, dripping wet, reeling, perhaps groaning.

To the buffalo, Cranmer had speculated, Tom must have been a frightening apparition, lurching toward them out of the shadows by the creek. They stampeded.

"They're easily spooked, you know," he had said softly, diverting his gaze. "Especially at night. Anything out of the ordinary will spook them. Normally they would have recognized Tom, of course, but in the circumstances . . ."

The plausible story gave Luke Cameron problems.

Tom Cameron had walked across this shallow creek bed hundreds of times—no, thousands—ever since he was set loose on the ranch as a boy. In all kinds of weather. In rain. In snow. In fog and blizzard. He could have walked across the familiar ford blindfolded. Or drunk on those rare occasions that he tanked up.

Any man could slip, there was always a first time. And when you grew old and rusty . . .

Overhead, the cottonwoods stirred in the evening breeze like an expectant audience waiting for the drama to begin. Some clouds were rolling in like heavenly breakers, flooding the prairie and the nearby hills with darkness.

Still, the contrast between the riverbed and the open meadow was distinct, Luke saw, like stepping from a dark room into one that was dimly lit.

He hunched his shoulders uneasily. He had the feeling that he was missing something, something that his father had seen. Something that would explain what was tormenting him. Not the predictable bitterness, frustration, or anger that any man would feel over the impending loss of his cherished land. An alien emotion. Fear.

Why had Tom been afraid? What had he learned? Trucks running on the back roads at night, where trucks had no business to be, by themselves would not have unnerved him. Something at the Energy Department's nuclear storage site behind its high-security wire fence?

What was Tom doing here that night, down by the creek?

Preoccupied, Luke Cameron drove slowly, absently back along the highway. It was now full dark. From old habit, he turned automatically onto the gravel road toward the Bar-C. By the time he became aware of where he was going, he was already close to the house. He saw that it was dark.

He had not intended to come back. Besides, it belonged to the Frenchwoman now. He didn't know just when the Frenchwoman intended to move in. Not yet, he could see. At least not tonight.

Except for the impulsive moment when he bid on the rolltop desk, he had tried to stand apart at the auction, not watching what was sold or who bought it, pretending that it didn't matter. Now, as he parked in a shadowed slot between the dark, abandoned stable and the other outbuildings, he knew how much it had mattered.

He felt tired, dusty, jaded, in need of a shower. Hungry, too. He remembered there was a can of chili in one of the kitchen cupboards. Micheline Picard had told him he didn't have to clear out the cupboards unless he wanted to; she would take care of that.

The house was locked, but he still had his key. He stepped inside, trying to ignore the oppressive silence. He located the can of chili and heated it in a battered old pan that nobody had been willing to buy at the auction, not even for fifty cents. Luke had to fish it out of a plastic bag filled with disposables. He found a spoon in an otherwise empty drawer. Hard to empty an old house in a hurry, he thought.

The chili took the edge off his hunger. But he was left with a different kind of emptiness.

Slowly, he climbed the stairs. His waterlogged boots made a squishing sound with each step.

Micheline Picard saw the light in one of the upstairs rooms of the ranch house as she drove into the yard. Her first thought was that a light unintentionally had been left on.

She knew better than to rely on such an assumption. Her eyes quickly surveyed the compound. No other vehicle was in sight. She stole up the back porch steps and slipped into the house. It was unlocked. On cat feet, she walked through the kitchen and dining room, pausing apprehensively just inside the archway that led into the living room. It was empty except for its potbellied stove and the stack of wood next to it, ready for a winter that was still months away.

The downstairs was in darkness, the house quiet.

But not empty. Someone was upstairs.

She was a woman alone, a slight figure standing there in the dark living room. Yet she was neither frightened nor defenseless. She mounted the stairs slowly, her steps light, easing her weight onto the wood, making no sound at all until one of the old oak steps creaked. She stood very still, listening, one hand inside her purse.

Someone was indeed in the house, doing something very unusual for an intruder—taking a shower.

She eased her way quietly into the bedroom. There was no light in the room. She heard the shower shut off, a residual dripping, and the clack of the shower door opening. The bathroom was directly ahead of her, ablaze with light of a slightly reddish hue from a heat lamp in the ceiling fixture. In the shadows of the bedroom, she was a one-woman audience in a theater, staring expectantly as Luke Cameron stepped, naked and dripping, into the warm red glow of the spotlight.

Her breath caught.

She recognized Luke Cameron at once. She should have realized that anyone acting so much at home might very well *be* at home.

At the auction that day, she had been conscious of Cameron's presence all afternoon—he was not an easy man to ignore—but she had dismissed him as an appealingly sardonic, rough-hewn westerner. More interesting perhaps than the other men she had met in Gibson, but of no concern to her. Assuming he had moved out of the house and was departing town, she had dismissed his awkward presence from her mind.

Though brooding as he watched the sale, he had seemed to her acquiescent, not stubborn like his father. Tom Cameron had barged into the bank several times when she was there, truculent, suspicious, belligerent. Dangerous.

Luke Cameron had not seemed dangerous.

For a breathless moment, she stood transfixed in the shadows, staring at Cameron as he briskly toweled himself, unaware of her absorbed attention. A tall, muscular man, broad shouldered and lean hipped, he was deeply tanned from working shirtless out of doors, except for the white band around his loins and buttocks. To her startled gaze, he seemed to be all hard, burnished muscles, like the sculptured marble statue of an athlete, except that he was not cold, white marble but warm flesh, his skin reddening from the roughness of the towel and the radiance of the heat lamp.

Micheline Picard had known only a few men intimately. By Western standards, her upbringing had been strict, watched over first by the nuns in the convent and later by priests. She had never seen any man naked who looked remotely like Luke Cameron, standing there in the glowing light, oblivious, rubbing his body down with a thick white towel.

And she had never been so swiftly, strongly aroused.

Her breath came in short drafts. A shiver caused her to reel slightly. She withdrew her hand from her purse to grip the edge of the door, steadying herself.

The movement caught Luke Cameron's eye. For a moment he stood rigid. Then he snatched at the towel he had just draped over a bar.

Their eyes met. She felt flames in her cheeks, an awkwardness she had not experienced since she was a young teenager. "Mr. Cameron, I—I am so sorry! I didn't know anyone was . . . was . . . that is, I didn't know . . ."

She bolted from the room.

Stunned by her unexpected appearance in the empty house, Luke stared after her, listening to the tattoo of her footsteps retreating down the stairs.

By the time Luke had toweled himself dry, hastily run a comb through his wet hair, and scrambled into shorts, shirt, and jeans, his startled confusion had turned into wry embarrassment. When he had told the Frenchwoman he was leaving—he'd had every intention of catching the earliest possible flight from Helena to Houston—naturally she had believed the house ready to occupy. And she had every right to be there. The house belonged to her now. He was the interloper. He should have thought of the possibility she might move in that night.

When he descended the stairs, he was a little surprised to find her still there. She was seated at the maple table at one end of the big country kitchen, where Luke and his family had taken their meals unless there was company. Earlier, he had been surprised to find the familiar table and chairs in the accustomed places. She must have bought them through Morrissey, perhaps holding them out of the auction. For some reason, the discovery had pleased him.

Micheline Picard had even made some coffee. The aroma filled the kitchen.

Gratefully, Luke poured coffee into a mug and carried it over to the table where she was sitting. "Sorry I startled you—"

"I am so sorry—"

Having both started to talk at once, both broke off. Then slowly, their embarrassment dissolved into smiles. "I should have let you know . . . ," Luke said.

"*Mais non,* I did not expect anyone to be here, that is all. I was . . . very surprised. You must have thought I acted very . . . foolish."

His glance touched the woman's slender figure, memory supplying an image of the way she moved. "If it had been the other way around, I don't suppose I'd be able to talk yet."

She laughed. "I am sure you are not so easily flustered."

"That's because you don't know me. . . . By the way, what were you holding in your purse? A gun?"

Surprise flicked across the mahogany eyes, now cool and composed. "A foreign woman alone in Montana, Mr. Cameron . . ." She shrugged—a Gallic gesture, Luke thought. "I have heard a great deal about your American West. It is best to be prepared, yes?"

"I understand. But I don't think you have to worry. People in these parts respect a woman."

She smiled demurely.

Nice smile, Luke thought. Nice lips forming the smile. Maybe even old Tom Cameron wouldn't mind having her living in his house. "She can park her shoes under my bed any time," Tom might have joked—a man who hadn't touched a woman in the fifteen years he had been a widower, remaining faithful to the memory of the one woman he had loved. Tom would have liked this Frenchwoman trying to do something useful with the land, Luke thought.

"I understand you're a botanist?"

"Yes . . ."

"You studied in France?"

"Yes, at the Sorbonne. My degree is from the University of Paris. It is many different schools, you understand?"

"I think so. Like a university with many different colleges."

"*Oui,* but in different places, yes? Not all in one place." Her hands indicated branches of the university scattered across the city of Paris.. Her animated gestures, like her accent, were very French. She was olive skinned, her dark eyes lively and intelligent. If he had seen her, without hearing her speak or observing her mannerisms, he might have guessed she was Greek.

"It's a long way to come from Paris to Gibson to practice botany."

She gave another beguiling lift of her shoulders. "It is a small world we live in now, yes? You yourself, Mr. Cameron, you do not build bridges in Montana but in South America, is it not so?"

He was surprised that she knew so much about him. "You were going to call me Luke."

"But of course . . . Luke. I am interested in land usage. This land . . . so much of it is not used. So much of it is barren."

"It's a desert, essentially. We raise a terrific crop of prickly pear, far exceeding the demand."

She smiled tolerantly at his humor but brushed past it. Botany was serious business, Luke saw. "You also grow much wheat. And here on your own place, I have seen many fine grasses—bluejoint, blue grama, crested wheat, and one, it has a funny name, like for sewing—"

"Needle and thread?"

"Oui, that is it!"

Micheline Picard acknowledged the area's vulnerability to the capriciousness of wind and weather. Much of it was admittedly a desert. But with sufficient water, it could also be made to bloom. Proper irrigation, and the control of wind erosion, might transform unproductive land. Montana winters were long and harsh, its summers hot and brief, but there were now many new crops that could be grown in short seasons and at different times of the year. She herself was developing an irrigation project on land adjoining the Bar-C. "It was own by Mr. Halston, you know him? I would like to experiment with different crops. We have learn much, but agriculture is still a gamble, a . . ."

"Roll of the dice?"

"Just so! A roll of the dice." Her face was animated, enthusiastic. This was not the cool, sophisticated mannequin Luke had first observed emerging from the Gibson Bank.

"This holding company that bought the Halston spread and my place . . ." *My place,* Luke thought, interrupting himself. He hadn't said that to himself before. "It's French, right?"

"Yes, that is so."

"You work for them?"

"But of course. Now you see why I 'ave come such a long way from Paris. It was not for me alone to decide."

"It must be a big company. I mean . . . it's making some heavy investments in this part of the world."

"But that is good business, yes? To invest in America. Many companies, from many countries, invest in the United States."

"But why *you?* Why did *you* leave Paris and come to this obscure place? Why did *you* accept a job with *this* company to settle in Gibson?"

"But you do not know? It is my father . . . he work for them." She shrugged off her father's importance, then underlined it. "He is most important man with my company. I almost never see him, even when I am a schoolgirl. But he make it possible for me to study. He make it possible for me to come here. This work . . . it is ver' important for me, ver' good for me . . . you understand? It is something he does for me because he is my father. This is an opportunity for me; it is most exciting. You do not approve?"

"Taking advantage of Daddy's influence to get ahead?" Luke grinned at her. "Hell, that's the American way."

"Is it so?" She wasn't sure whether he was teasing her.

"What's to disapprove? You still have to produce on your own, once you get the opportunity. He may be able to open doors for you. After that, it's up to you. I don't suppose you'd be here, spending the conglomerate's profits, if you didn't have the credentials. Those multinational companies aren't noted for being sentimental."

"No . . . " She relaxed; it seemed safe to lower her defenses. "No, not even for Papa's girl."

Their conversation seemed to have run its course for the moment. The short silence that followed was disrupted by a whirring sound, then the mellow chime of a big clock striking the hour. Luke glanced toward the hallway, then inquiringly at the Frenchwoman.

"It's a magnificent old clock," she said softly. "I do not think old clocks like to move, so I buy it and keep it here. You do not mind?"

"No, of course not." He had listened to the steady ticking of that clock for most of his life, waited for the familiar chimes. Shaking off the attack of nostalgia, he asked, "Are you involved in opening up that old mine south of here? In Wind Canyon?"

She seemed disconcerted by the question. "The mine? I do not know. . . ."

"Your company has opened up an old gold mine, one that hasn't been worked in sixty years or more."

"Oh, yes, the gold mine . . ." This time her shrug was indifferent, dismissive. "I know nothing of such things. It is not my work."

"Funny thing for a French holding company to get involved in."

"Funny? . . . It is strange, you mean, yes? But who can know what these company do, or why? They think it might be valuable, yes? Mining is one thing they do, in many different places of the world. Who can say?"

She rose and took the coffee carafe from the coffeemaker to refill their mugs—thoughtfully emptying the tepid remains from Luke's mug before filling it. As she poured, her arm brushed against him. He was conscious of her scent, of the long, graceful line of her thigh, of the curve of her breast under her shirt. As if sensing his response, she moved away, returning to her chair opposite his.

This time the silence between them was longer and deeper, a simmering tension underneath. After a while she said, "I must go. This is still your house to stay in while you are in Gibson, if you wish."

"Not any more. I think I'm the one who should leave."

But he made no move. When their eyes met, Luke Cameron felt a tingle right down to his boots. *Hold on,* he said to himself.

Across the table from him, Micheline Picard had been having some difficulty concentrating. In the midst of talking—about her work, her father, her schooling—she would suddenly find herself contemplating the vivid image of Luke Cameron's naked body, bathed in a reddish glow, as his muscular arms lifted the white towel. It was as if the picture were burned into her brain, like an image on film, and all she had to do was push a button, as with a video recorder, to have the picture reproduced, remarkably detailed and decidedly unsettling.

"I'm already moved out," Luke Cameron was saying. "I think it might be better if I left."

He didn't want to spend the night alone, listening to the old clock in the hall, waiting for the chimes on the hour.

Luke scraped back his chair. The sound seemed loud in the empty house.

The Frenchwoman followed him to the door. Her car was parked outside. Not a Citroen or a Peugeot, Luke noted; a silver-gray Turbo Thunderbird. Part of that small world in which we all drive each other's cars.

He paused just outside the door on the small wooden porch, Micheline Picard behind him in the doorway, the screen door standing open. There was an immense silence around them, black clouds defining the lighter night sky with its points of light. A Big Sky kind of night, Luke thought, that made his private trauma a small event.

As he turned to say good night, the woman's scent filled his immediate universe. Suddenly he knew why she had stepped so close, letting the door swing shut behind her. He took her in his arms. Felt the small hard breasts against his chest, the slender, pliant firmness of her body, sleek as an otter's, melting against him. He tilted her head up and covered her mouth with his.

The door of the stables stood ajar. The smell of horses and manure lingered, though the stable's former inhabitants had been moved out. From the inky blackness within, a pair of black eyes, smoldering like coals, watched Luke Cameron climb into the Chevy pickup, shift into reverse, then nose it onto the gravel road. Kali watched and listened intently until the rumble of the truck's wheels died away.

The Frenchwoman loitered on the porch, gazing into the night that had just swallowed Luke Cameron.

Watching her through narrowed eyes, remembering the romantic scene he had just witnessed, Kali boiled with hatred.

Earlier that evening, while driving north along the highway, Kali had spotted that same pickup truck parked off the road near the stream, which meandered across the Cameron ranch from its source in the mountains to the south. At first, he had not recognized the truck. He had noticed only that a vehicle had pulled off the road.

Not parked just anywhere.

Parked where the old man had died.

Realizing he risked detection if he stopped, Kali had continued down the highway for another half mile until, just past a bridge, he found a narrow dirt track forking to the right. He pulled the jeep he was driving behind a thick tangle of brush and waited. After fifteen minutes, his patience was rewarded. He heard the growl of the pickup approaching the bridge. Then he watched it pass above him.

Kali gave the pickup truck time to proceed well down the road before he emerged from the brush patch and followed at a discreet distance.

The pickup drove directly to the Cameron place. Kali concealed his jeep in a grove of trees off the highway. In the thickening darkness, he hiked more than a mile across the prairie to the ranch buildings. He navigated through the underbrush by a light in one of the upstairs rooms. The rest of the house remained in darkness.

From the shadows of the stables, Kali had contemplated the actions of the pickup driver when the Frenchwoman drove up. He debated whether to follow her inside, but he held back, unsure. Who had driven the pickup? The old man's son, Cameron? Did the Frenchwoman know he was there?

Was he waiting for her?

While Kali pondered these questions, the woman burst into the kitchen, switching on a light. She appeared agitated, walking back and forth. But the pacing seemed to calm her. She began to busy herself in the kitchen.

So she *had* come here to meet the American!

When the man appeared in the kitchen doorway, tall enough to fill its frame, Kali recognized Lucas Cameron.

The table where they sat was directly in front of a large window facing the yard. Kali watched them sip coffee and converse. They seemed friendly, but not intimate. Still, their relationship, to Kali's conspiratorial mind, appeared close. What had happened between them? Kali was tormented with dark suspicions. Perhaps the two had met here by chance. But Kali didn't trust coincidence.

Cameron was an unwanted complication.

The American rose from the table and moved toward the door. The Frenchwoman followed him out to the porch, where Cameron gazed into the darkness as if communing with the night. In that moment, Kali felt he understood the man, for he himself felt Allah's presence in this immense darkness.

Then something happened that stunned Kali.

The American wrapped the Frenchwoman in his arms and kissed her. It was a long, passionate embrace. *She did not resist!*

Watching from the shadows like a voyeur, Kali felt heat surge in his loins. He was so betrayed by his body that he longed to whip and scourge himself. He could only stand in the gloom of the stables, quivering, until Luke Cameron abruptly swung on his heel, stalked down the porch steps in two strides, climbed into his pickup, and drove away.

Kali wanted to smash his fist against the wooden planks of the stable door.

When he had stopped trembling and could trust himself to look again at the back porch, it was empty. The woman had gone inside. The light in the kitchen went out.

Kali stood in the doorway of the stables for a long time, watching the house, seething with hate.

The next morning, Kali met Brad McAlister at a truck stop on the main highway that bypassed Gibson. Trucks were diverted around the business route that ran through the center of town. Several big rigs squatted on the oversized parking strip in front of the café. Inside, Kali settled into a green vinyl booth at the far end, his back to the room, eyes fixed on the highway.

Brad McAlister was late.

The American's earlier enthusiasm, fueled by frustration over his financial setbacks, was cooling. It was time to sink the hook deeper.

Kali had met Brad McAlister at the Gibson Bar & Keno Parlor a little over three months ago. The meeting had not been random. Kali knew exactly who McAlister was and had intimate knowledge of his financial history. Kali knew that the American was deeply in debt, that his real estate development business had failed, that he had lost still more money gambling to recoup his losses, that the Gibson Bank was threatening to call the mortgage on McAlister's house.

Brad McAlister was in deep financial trouble, and he was bitter about it. He was exactly what Kali was looking for—the right man in the right place with the right weakness. An earlier attempt to recruit a prospect working at a Colorado nuclear production facility had come under official scrutiny, forcing Kali to depart the area in haste. So with McAlister, Kali had been more careful.

It had been easy enough to cultivate McAlister's friendship. All it had taken was some banter about the basketball game showing on the television in the bar, a little flattery over the "discovery" that Brad had been a football star, generosity in paying for drinks. In western America, men tended to be open and to accept a stranger at face value. McAlister had been friendly from the start. Two hours and four beers later, he was telling Kali his troubles. "They say all you have to do is work hard, have what it takes, keep your nose clean and grab the brass ring when it comes by, right? That's what you've heard since you were a kid. This is the land of golden opportunity, right?"

"That's what they say."

"That's what they say, all right. That's the American dream. Well, let me tell you"—Brad leaned toward Kali, jabbing a finger at his chest—"that isn't the way it works. Not any more. You can't beat the system."

"I'll bet *you* can beat the system."

"Damn right. Listen, I'm as good a salesman as there is in Montana. I know real estate; I'm good at my job. Confidentially, I was making six figures. That's right, six figures. But then . . ." The clarity of Brad's vision slipped and his tongue thickened. "Then the insiders . . . you know, the guys who control the system, they pulled the wrong wires. They let the sharks loose on Wall Street; they let the big conglomerates and takeover artists swallow the little fish;

they let the foreigners come in and take big bites of America. The insiders . . . they didn't care what happened to us outsiders."

Kali tried not to show his disgust over McAlister's whining. "They got theirs, and you got shafted, right?"

"Right!" McAlister stared mournfully at the empty bottle of beer in front of him. "Look, Cal," he finally said. "I gotta run. Getting late, and the little lady will be worried . . ."

"Hey, you got time for one more, Brad. It's my round. One more, right? Go for the gusto."

"Well . . . yeah, one more maybe." Brad McAlister grinned. This dude was okay. Ought to scratch the beard, but what the hell. Be yourself, that's what everyone said now. Hell, at the site, they wouldn't even let you *grow* a beard.

Kali saw the scowl. "Did I say somethin', man?"

"Nah . . . I was just thinking . . . this job I have, they wouldn't let me grow a beard like yours. I've got to wear a uniform, polish my shoes, punch in, punch out, you'd think I was in the army!"

"Where d'you work?" Kali asked innocently.

"The Department of Energy has a nuclear storage site just outside of town. I'm a security guard . . . a security *officer.*" Brad felt a perverse need to improve the status he despised.

As the night wore on, Brad McAlister told his sympathetic new friend about his troubles—about the run of bad luck and bad timing that had bankrupted his business, about the shortage of job opportunities in the area, about his reluctant acceptance of a demeaning job at the nuclear facility. The man who called himself Cal listened and sympathized and shared Brad's outrage.

When McAlister at last took his leave, somewhat unsteadily, the two men had become fast friends. McAlister hoped he would run into this bearded dude again.

He did. Not until several drinking sessions later, however, was Brad told that Cal was the foreman of a crew working for the French company on the Halston place. At first, Cal said he just supervised the irrigation project. Then he spoke of other opportunities that he hoped would advance his career. After dropping a few careful hints to stimulate Brad's interest, Cal came right out with it: Some of the people he worked for would pay good money for information Brad might be able to provide. Harmless information, Cal said, but information that would give his company a competitive edge. The French company, having invested heavily in the Gibson area, was naturally interested in what the Energy Department's plans were, what was happening at the site, what might transpire in the future.

Brad McAlister balked at first. Kali immediately pulled back—hey, no problem, it was just a thought.

Kali waited. A week later, it was Brad McAlister who brought the subject up again. This happened on another Monday evening—Brad was working days then—at the bar and keno parlor. Brad had recklessly lost his whole paycheck. He would have to withdraw money from his dwindling checking account without Anne knowing—no small accomplishment, since she worked at the bank.

"What is it these people you work for are so interested in?" Brad wondered aloud. "Hell, there aren't any secrets at the DOE . . . at least not at this site. There's nothing going on."

"What do you do there?"

"Nothing. That's the point."

Kali disappointed Brad by showing no more interest. Instead, he became philosophical about the way the world was shrinking. Look at us, he said. Americans are driving Japanese cars, watching TV sets put together in Korea, wearing shirts made in Hong Kong. A Canadian had bought up some of this country's most prestigious department stores—even Bloomingdale's! A Dutch company owned Shell Oil. Britishers and Germans were taking over American publishing companies. The Japanese already owned half of Hawaii, and now they were buying up Southern California.

"My company is owned by the French, but by world standards, it's small potatoes. We own the bank here, and the Halston ranch, and I think we're gonna take over Tom Cameron's place, the Bar-C. But that's small potatoes."

"Didn't you open up that mine down south?"

"In Wind Canyon? Yeah . . . that, too." Kali shrugged. "They're just playing the game, you know? Like Monopoly. Buy some property, put a hotel on it. Dig up some gold."

The conversation was drifting away from the subject Brad McAlister wanted to raise. He practically had to compel Kali to return to the questions Kali had been priming Brad for weeks to ask: What information would his employers pay for? And how much would they pay?

"Hell, I don't know," said Kali, letting Brad down again. "They're involved in all kinds of development projects, you know, including nuclear power. People are scared of nuclear power in this country, but other countries—like France—are developing nuclear power on a big scale."

"I don't have any knowledge of that stuff."

"I'll ask," Kali promised offhandedly. "Maybe there isn't anything they want, Brad. It was just a thought that came to me while we were bullshitting. But I'll find out if maybe there isn't something you might be able to peddle."

"I was kind of hoping . . . I could get an advance," Brad said awkwardly.

"What's the problem?"

McAlister glanced over at the keno tables, busy even on a Monday night. "I dropped my whole week's pay. My wife'll kill me when she finds out."

Kali regarded him with contempt. American men let themselves be bullied by their women. "What? You need a few bucks on account? No problem, man."

Kali pulled a roll of money from his pocket. Brad McAlister stared at the thickness of the roll, impressed. For the first time, the thought flickered in his mind that his friend Cal, his good drinking buddy, might be something other than what he appeared. But damn it, Brad needed the money! And Cal was right, the world was becoming one big commercial enterprise ruled less and less by politics, more and more by economics.

Everyone had a finger in everyone else's pie. What difference did it make if Brad picked up a few bucks passing on information that didn't hurt anyone?

"What do you need, Brad? How much you lose?"

"I get four hundred a week," Brad said quickly, exaggerating the figure a little. Why not? And no need to remind Cal that his take-home pay was reduced more than twenty-five percent by all the withholding taxes.

"Four hundred?" Kali repeated. "You got it."

That was how it began.

Kali sipped his coffee, watching the highway impatiently. He liked his coffee strong and black, and this particular café made it that way. To help the truckers stay awake, Kali surmised. Most Americans seemed to prefer their coffee weak and watery. Turks made the best coffee, Kali thought. It was the only good thing he had to say about Turks.

Brad McAlister had made the mission easy for him. Over a period of two months, doling out small sums to the American for useless information, Kali had slowly steered him toward more important matters: spec sheets on the materials stored at the site (McAlister had found them surprisingly easy to pull and copy). Details on security protection. Quantities of materials stored and frequency of shipments. The fact that the latter were always accompanied by armed custodial teams, vital intelligence for Kali's mission.

Brad McAlister had convinced himself, with Kali's help, that what he was doing was neither unethical nor unpatriotic. It was what any smart operator would have done, given the chance to dig himself out of a bad hole that wasn't of his own making. With contemptuous ease, Kali played this weak, greedy American like a fish that did not know it had taken the hook.

Two weeks ago, Kali had finally told Brad McAlister that his principals now wanted nuclear materials. Appalled, Brad had started to protest. Kali had cut him off. "Hey, Brad, it's a little late to be developing a conscience. You're in deep, man."

"What do you mean?" The American looked bewildered, like a small boy suddenly confronting a frightening adult world.

"Come on, Brad . . . you've sold me things. Classified information, stuff like that, to a foreign power."

"Foreign power?" McAlister repeated weakly.

"What did you think? The French may be allies, but they're foreign, right? Hey, don't look so worried. Nobody's gonna know. Just don't give me that shocked, oh-I-could-never-do-that routine." With a grin, Kali slapped Brad on the shoulder. "Shit, man, all it means . . . you're not a virgin any more, right?"

Brad McAlister stared at the bearded man in numb despair. He wished Kali would stop trying so hard to sound like an American. "Who are you? Who do you work for? Israel?" he demanded hopefully. Like most Americans, he harbored a vague sympathy for Israelis and their beleaguered country. If Cal worked for them, it might not be so bad.

Kali smiled. "Maybe it's better you don't know. What you don't know can't hurt you, okay?" Then the smile faded, the black eyes became hard and cold, the tone turned vicious, whiplashing the confused American. "What are you crying about? You picked up a few bucks, nobody got hurt. All you have to do now is take the next step. You're already compromised, man, you don't want anybody to know. Besides . . . who's gonna be hurt? Not your country. You got more nuclear weapons than you can ever use. You store them like surplus wheat. And we're not talking weapons here, we're talking raw materials. Maybe the Israelis want to build a nuclear power plant, who knows? You could be doing them a favor."

Seeing the shock in the American's eyes, Kali relented, smiling once more. Brad McAlister was alarmed by what he had gotten himself into, frightened by the growing dimensions of it. But he suddenly had a feeling that he should be even more scared of Kali.

Three nights ago, McAlister had come through for him. He had figured out a way to deactivate the alarm systems in the southeast quadrant of the nuclear materials storage facility. When he reported his success at their morning meeting, he had been so excited that Kali nearly laughed at this amateur, suddenly caught up in the thrill of the game. But instead, Kali had been generous—with praise and money.

That was Wednesday morning. The following night, for the half hour between 3:40 and 4:10 A.M., Kali and his crew had dug a tunnel under the nuclear installation's security fence and across the fifty-foot stretch of open ground between the perimeter and the wall of the storage building. They had used a power corer that cut swiftly and fed the dirt back along the tunnel to Kali's men. The noise of the power equipment had been muffled by blankets placed over the end of the tunnel and camouflaged by the beating motors of the nearby irrigation pumps. The vibration of the digging had gone unnoticed because the seismic detectors had been deactivated.

Thursday night, the diggers had cut it close. They barely escaped from their tunnel, capping it, before the 4:10 deadline Brad had set for reactivating the alarms.

When Kali had emerged from the tunnel that night, he had found that McAlister had carried out another important part of their plan. He had dumped two thick-walled steel canisters, each approximately two feet long, over the fence. The empty containers had come from a storage room and were identical to those used to store the uranium metal. Kali smiled at the image of McAlister struggling to lift them over the fence.

During those two nights of digging, Kali and his crew had come within a foot of the warehouse wall. The end of their tunnel lay next to the concrete footings.

They could proceed no farther. Now they had to come to the surface. If Kali's calculations were correct, they would emerge from their tunnel within a few feet of the fire door in the southeast wall of the main storage building.

Kali saw the American's five-year-old Mercury Grand Marquis—purchased in better times, when McAlister wanted a big, comfortable car in which to chauffeur prospective clients—pull off the highway and nudge past one of the truck rigs into a parking place around the side of the café. Out of sight.

Kali smiled without humor.

Brad McAlister said, "We've got to hold off a while, Cal. I can't do this every night! Christ . . . last night, Henderson almost caught me, and you were late getting out. I think Henderson's getting suspicious. He regards the control center as his private little domain, and he watches over it like a mother hen."

"Take it easy; have some coffee."

"You're not listening to me, Cal!"

"Everybody else in the place is." The quiet venom in Kali's voice caused McAlister's mouth to hang open. "You want to make any public announcements, hire a hall. Otherwise shut up!"

"You . . . you can't talk to me like that."

"I just did." Kali leaned across the formica-topped table. "It gets a lot worse . . . or it gets better. Now—*you* listen." He kept his voice low, inaudible to anyone in the noisy café except the nervous man across the table from him. "We're almost there. One more night with the corer, and we'll pop out like gophers . . . next to that fire door. You've done a great job so far. Don't get cold feet now."

"We have to wait . . ."

"No, we have to go for it. The longer we wait, the greater the risk someone will see something they shouldn't."

"You can't mean you want to steal something now! We don't know if there's been any suspicions about those alarms. We can't be sure."

"You'd have heard. What did you think, McAlister, that we weren't really going to do it? That we were just playing games?" Kali smiled at the American's flustered, panic-stricken expression. "To-night we finish digging. You don't work weekends, right? That's okay, gives us the weekend to get ready. Then Monday we make the strike—"

"No! Not Monday!" McAlister was desperate. "Henderson is off Mondays. His sub, Gleason . . . he eats his lunch right there in the alarm control center. He watches his monitors all the time, even on his lunch hour, like he's watching TV."

Kali sat back, studying the American. "How come Henderson doesn't work Mondays?"

"I don't know; it's the way they have it set up. He works Saturdays instead."

"Saturday," Kali mused. "Maybe you should work Saturday—a quiet night. Be a good time for us."

"How can I do that? I don't set the schedules. It would just draw attention to me."

Kali studied the American's eyes for any flicker of deception. McAlister looked as if he wanted to cry. He wasn't lying about Henderson, Kali decided. He didn't have the smarts for it, nor the guts. The delay was unwelcome, but there was work still to be done at the mine in preparation. Anyway, it couldn't be helped.

But he wasn't about to let the American stew through the whole weekend. He had to give him something else to think about. He said, "Ten grand."

Brad McAlister stared at him. "What . . . ?"

"We do it Tuesday night," said Kali. "If you've given me the straight dope, if it comes off like we got it planned, you have ten thou-sand bucks to put in your pocket Wednesday morning." He paused to let it sink in, then added: "In cash."

Moscow

THE SINGLE CLASS TUPOLEV 134, A REAR ENGINE JET THAT carried seventy-two passengers, hit the runway with a jolt at Vnukovo Airport near Moscow, the terminal for internal Aeroflot flights. Smaller than Sheremetyevo, Moscow's international airport, it was also busier at this late hour. But the grim-faced passenger, KGB Captain Sergei Milov, was waved quickly through the gates to a waiting Chaika, with a KGB corporal behind the wheel.

He was whisked through darkened Moscow directly to Dzerzhinsky Square, named after the revolutionary leader whose statue stood at the center of the square facing the KGB's main headquarters. This was the heart of the dreaded organization that had evolved from the original Cheka, which Dzerzhinsky had directed. Both the circular "square" and the broad expanse of Marx Prospekt were deserted. Moscow's night air was cool to someone coming from the south. Milov shivered. Was it the change of climate? he wondered, or the dread over being summoned abruptly back to Moscow after the disaster in Kirovabad?

Colonel Vitaly Yurevich Novikoff was waiting for him, alone in his office. The light from the single brass lamp on his walnut desk was soaked up by the room's dark wood paneling, leaving the corners and ceiling in eerie shadows. Novikoff was reading a report and did not immediately look up. Milov stood fidgeting in the center of the room, like a schoolboy called before his headmaster.

It took Novikoff an anguishing two minutes to finish the report. He initialed it, placed the folder in his "Out" box, and looked up. "Sit down, Sergei Andreyevich," he said. "You're brown as a berry. Playing tennis must suit you."

Milov flushed beneath the deep tan. To cover his discomfiture, he sat in one of the black leather chairs to the left of Novikoff's desk, near the wall-mounted pictures of Vladimir Ilyich Lenin and Mikhail Gorbachev. He felt their eyes on him.

In his mid-fifties, Vitaly Novikoff still had a thick head of hair so black that it appeared dyed. The colonel was a short, stout man, built like a robot but small enough to fit comfortably into one of the tanks he had led into Hungary during the uprising against Socialist order. Novikoff had once described himself to Milov as a survivor. KGB chiefs had come and gone, rising or falling, for a quarter century. But Novikoff had managed to keep his head an inch above the purge line. "I am a useful man," he had said to Milov in a moment of candor. "You understand?"

Now his shrewd blue eyes examined the younger man silently, intently, for a long moment. Then he smiled. "You are a fool, Milov. But you're the only kind of fool I can tolerate, a romantic one. But only once, Comrade. There can be no more mistakes. Even the spirit of *perestroika* does not condone foolishness in the Cheka."

Milov's relief was so extreme that he was momentarily speechless. Novikoff grunted, a sound that might have meant anything but was actually a sign of approval. He didn't like subordinates who gushed or talked too much.

"You have made your penance. You see, I have not forgotten my early indoctrination by the priests—but you wouldn't know about that, would you, Sergei Andreyevich? The Party is your religion."

"Yes . . . yes, sir." Milov would have agreed to almost anything.

"Now tell me about this Iranian."

Milov summarized what he had learned about Abu Hasir from the interrogation and his own inquiries. Hasir was a railroad yard worker in Baku. "A laborer, not a technician. He could not have known when we were making a shipment of nuclear weapons or materials—"

"Which means he had help. He was part of a network."

"I believe so, Colonel. Because he was a Muslim fundamentalist, the first possibility is a small group of Islamic extremists."

"You do not suspect those bloody Azerbaijani nationalists? They might want a bomb to blow up some Armenians. Or something even more sinister, perhaps a foreign power?"

"I don't think so. His roots are Iranian. All of the Muslim fundamentalists now look to Iran. Qom has become their second Mecca," said Milov. He knew more about religion perhaps than the comrade colonel had thought.

"I agree. Khomeini's fingerprints are on this adventure."

"Hasir's attempt was doomed from the start," Milov continued his report. "He had no backup, no transportation. He took the train alone to Kirovabad where the attempt was made. He tried to divert the attention of the local militia at the Kirovabad rail yard by the crudest of methods, starting a fire and taking advantage of the excitement to cover his penetration of the railroad car. Hasir did not know that one of our protective military teams was inside the car. He was easily taken."

"What exactly was in that car? What did he hope to steal?"

"One of our smaller ADEs."

"ADEs?"

"An atomic demolitions explosive device. Our comrades in nuclear armaments tell me, technically speaking, it is not a nuclear weapon. These devices were to be used in some underwater demolition tests. The attraction for a terrorist is that the smaller ADEs are designed to be used by one or two men. They can be triggered by a simple, built-in timer and detonator. Not exactly an atomic bomb. But in the right situation, such an explosion could be a devastating propaganda weapon."

"An ideal terrorist weapon . . . if planted in a populated area."

"Yes, Comrade Colonel."

Novikoff was already familiar with the bare bones of the incident. But he was still trying to put flesh on the bones. For Milov's benefit, he contributed a new piece of flesh. "Your man Hasir . . . he has been identified as one who received revolutionary training in a camp in South Yemen."

"One of our camps? With Soviet instructors?"

"Soviet and Cuban and Korean. His training lasted six months . . . long enough, don't you think, to advance beyond the amateur level? Tell me, Milov, why would such a man make so transparently doomed—I think that was your word—an attempt to steal a nuclear device of limited value? Having no means of transportation or escape, knowing that he was almost certain to be captured and interrogated? To carry the question further, why would those *behind* him formulate such a foolish plan?"

"I . . . I don't know." Milov was beginning to feel uneasy.

"I can think of one possibility, Sergei Andreyevich." Novikoff's use of the patronimic could have been friendly—or mocking. "It would not be so stupid, in fact it would border on the clever, if the intention was to cause us to reveal the nature and level of our security protection. Perhaps the terrorists merely wanted to learn how vulnerable our nuclear materials or weapons are in transit . . . perhaps on that railroad line. That would also explain why Abu Hasir was able to resist nearly six days of interrogation."

"Why he endured? . . ."

"He told you nothing because he knew nothing. He had no visible backup, as you say. He was, perhaps, recruited for the mission without knowing its true purpose. These Khomeini fundamentalists are easily manipulated on behalf of their cause. In capturing him, you already knew everything he had to tell you."

"So you think his capture was part of the plan. He was a sacrifice."

"Of course, Milov! Perhaps a willing one, a martyr, who was promised direct passage to heaven. It was a test, a diversion. It forced us to respond and to expend our resources in the wrong direction."

"Whoever is behind him is planning another strike," Milov said.

"One with a better chance of success. We must prepare for it. Most likely it will be made against the same railroad line, which is heavily used by the military in the Caucasus. The next time, there will be more than one man, and the plan will be more sophisticated. We should anticipate, too, that the target might be greater—more dangerous than one of our ADEs. A tactical nuclear artillery weapon, perhaps, or a warhead. This is speculation, Sergei, but we must find out. That is your assignment. You will return to Azerbaijan and find out where Hasir has been, whom he knew, who might have recruited him."

Milov could not conceal his disappointment; he had allowed himself to hope for a transfer back to Moscow. "Yes, Comrade Colonel. I will leave at once."

"You will leave tomorrow. What is the matter with you? You look ill."

"I had hoped . . . ," Milov confessed, "that I might be returning to Moscow."

"Don't be an idiot!" Novikoff snapped impatiently. "This is your chance, Sergei Andreyevich. It is what I have waited for. General Sidorin is old and ill; he no longer cares so much whom his Natalia entertains at his dacha. You will follow this wretched Iranian's trail wherever it leads. To Azerbaijan, to Armenia, to Iran, to Paris, even to America if necessary. We must know who is behind him, Milov. The man who brings me this information will return to Moscow in triumph!"

Sergei Milov held his breath, knowing that he could not voice his gratitude; that was not permitted. "I may need men," he said. "Travel forms, authority to—"

"You shall have whatever you need. I repeat—we *must* know who is behind this terrorist—and where they will strike next time."

His emphatic directive delivered, Vitaly Novikoff leaned back in his leather chair. The lamp on his desk gave the cold blue eyes a deceptive twinkle. "And now, my impetuous young friend, do you remember where I keep my bottle of Kubanskaya?"

Milov's glance darted toward a dark corner of the room where, behind a plain, steel-gray filing cabinet, was the squat cubic shape of a small refrigerator. "Yes, Comrade Colonel."

"Well, then, what are you waiting for?"

Washington, D.C.

"ALL RIGHT, MEL, GIVE IT TO ME STRAIGHT. ARE YOU TRYing to tell me some of our nuclear weapons are missing?"

"No, Mr. President."

"Then what the hell are you saying?" George Bush demanded.

"I'm saying there've been some unusual attempts to penetrate our strategic weapons and storage sites."

"Doesn't that sort of thing go on all the time?"

"There have been isolated incidents. These are different."

Mel Durbin, a national security specialist, hated being ambiguous with the president, but he didn't want to appear as an alarmist. Still, he had come away from the latest committee meeting on nuclear security with an uneasy feeling, a vague concern that kept nagging him. And Durbin hadn't got where he was—a specialist assigned to the National Security Council with access to the president of the United States—by ignoring his gut feelings.

He hadn't reached the pinnacle by being shy around strangers, naive about politics, or indifferent to the mystique of power, either. But that didn't explain his present status, not only as a policymaker on the National Security Council but as a friend of the president.

Durbin had gained his eminence by pure, blind, dumb luck—the caprice of fate that had tossed him into the same freshman class with George Herbert Walker Bush at Yale.

Together they had endured freshman hazing and the other familiar rites of passage of young men. Durbin did not have Bush's silver spoon background, but in spite of this—or perhaps because of it—Bush made a point of including his young friend in his circle. It wasn't enough to get Durbin into Skull and Bones, but it made him a loyal, lifetime friend.

The tall, lean Bush was a patrician American aristocrat, and, though he liked to play down the fact, son of a distinguished U.S. senator, S. Prescott Bush. "I couldn't help where I was born," he would sometimes joke. "I wanted to be near my mother." He had enjoyed a childhood in Connecticut, summers boating in Maine, sports at Andover, before arriving at Yale. Mel Durbin had grown up in the rough-and-tumble of Detroit's lower east side, street smart, wary of eye, watching his neighborhood turn into a ghetto. While Bush went fishing off Kennebunkport during summer vacations, Durbin was learning how to dribble a basketball around taller, stronger players on Detroit's macadam basketball courts. Unlike Bush, who had been predestined for Yale from birth, Durbin was recruited on a basketball scholarship. He never knew his father, who absconded when Durbin was three years old. Bush was a quintessential WASP, Durbin a bare-knuckled black.

But in spite of their differences they had remained close. Through the years of making his fortune in Texas oil, the seemingly inevitable progression toward the seat of power in Washington, D.C., terms as ambassador to the United Nations, envoy to China, head of the CIA, Bush had carried Durbin along with him, a trusted aide and friend.

It was during his first term as Ronald Reagan's vice-president that Bush had used his White House connections to place his friend on the NSC staff. But Durbin had stood, firmly planted, on his own feet; he had quickly earned the respect of his superiors, including President Reagan himself.

During the election that had lifted George Bush from the vice-presidency into the Oval Office, Durbin had remained out of the limelight, wisely leaving the management of the campaign to political professionals, though he had contributed some effective street fighter suggestions for attacking Bush's opponent, Michael Dukakis. Following the election, he had remained on the NSC staff, but also on Bush's brain trust, a close personal confidant, someone Bush could rely on to give him honest answers however uncomfortable or unwelcome those responses might be.

The suggestion Durbin was making now was certainly an uncomfortable one, George Bush thought. But he valued Durbin's instincts. "You'd better give me the whole story, Mel," he said. "Just what the heck's got you all stirred up?"

"Intelligence reports, Mr. President . . . from the FBI, the Defense Intelligence Agency, the DOE, Naval Intelligence, the CIA . . . They've all recorded incidents over the past few months. Intrusion attempts, bribe offers, aborted physical penetrations. They've occurred in different areas of the country—all involving strategic materials."

"You mean nuclear?"

"Yes, sir."

The president let the information sink in for a moment. "Patterns?" he asked. "You see a pattern here, Mel?"

"I think so, Mr. President."

"Who do you think is playing games with us? Friendlies?"

Durbin knew the president was asking about the Israelis. Both men were familiar with the rumors—some had appeared in the national media—about small amounts of America's nuclear materials disappearing from inventory years ago when Israel was trying to develop an independent nuclear deterrent. No one had been greatly disturbed about the possible diversion of small quantities of these highly sensitive materials to Israel, given its volatile and vulnerable situation in the Middle East and its historic ties to the United States.

But Mel Durbin didn't think the Israelis were responsible.

He described an acrimonious NSC meeting that morning. Brian Clancy, the CIA specialist, had been the first to point out the possibility of a pattern of probes into nuclear facilities. He had not previously brought the subject before the NSC because the CIA's information was too tenuous.

The Pentagon's representative, Eldon Riggs, was piqued but not alarmed. Ted Chandler from the FBI's antiterrorist unit had picked up reports that terrorists might be involved. He complained petulantly that the other agencies could spook the FBI's sources and disrupt its operations if they pursued their own "tenuous" investigations. This threw the meeting into turmoil over jurisdiction and priorities.

"They all seemed more concerned about protecting their turf than protecting our nuclear stores . . . except the DOE's man, who's responsible for the SAS and SMS sites—"

"Whoa, Mel, talk English!"

"I'm talking about special ammunition storage and strategic material storage sites. . . . Where we store nuclear weapons and materials that aren't checked out to the armed services, sir. They've had a number of incidents."

"Go on."

"The reason we haven't gone on red alert, sir, is that the incidents seemingly have been random . . . unrelated. A fence breached at an SAS site in Pennsylvania last February. A break-in at a Navy storage yard that houses nuclear fuel. An attempt to recruit an employee at a DOE uranium factory in Colorado. Increased activity around one of our strategic weapons storage sites in West Germany. If there's a pattern, sir, it has no recognizable shape."

"What do you make of it?"

"I can only speculate, Mr. President. It could be an amateur group of terrorists who want to get their hands on a nuclear weapon—any kind, anywhere."

The president frowned. "We can't afford to ignore that possibility."

Thus encouraged, Durbin tried to clarify his thoughts. "I think someone is trying to steal a nuclear weapon, or the materials to make one. All these different probes in widely separate areas . . . I think we may be dealing with an organized group rather than individuals."

"Somebody like Qaddafi?"

"Or Khomeini. Someone with fanatically loyal followers."

The president made an instant decision. "Maybe the FBI and the CIA are right. Maybe there's nothing there but smoke. But I'm responsible for this country's nuclear arsenal, and I can't take the chance they might be wrong. I want our entire strategic nuclear inventory verified. Let's find out if we've got a problem, Mel, before we let this threat become visible. The last thing I want right now is a nuclear scare on the evening news."

"Yes, Mr. President."

Mel Durbin took a deep breath. Down in his gut, he knew that someone was threatening the nation's nuclear integrity.

☢ PART TWO
THE PROFESSOR

Los Angeles

D R. HASSAN KAMATEH WAS A SMALL, DAPPER MAN OF DARK complexion, with curly gray hair and a mustache to match. His face was ruled by his nose, a prominent prow that reminded colleagues at UCLA of the late Mohammad Reza Shah Pahlavi. Kamateh smiled diffidently but nervously at the comparison, but it was not altogether farfetched. He was the last of a distinguished family that had retained its social status under the shah of Iran. The family fortunes had deteriorated after the shah was driven off the Peacock Throne by the cantankerous Ayatollah Ruhollah Khomeini.

Kamateh had received an aristocrat's upbringing and a scholar's education. He had studied at American University in Beirut, at London University, and at Columbia. He had earned a doctorate in physics; his specialty was nuclear research.

On a campus with an informal California dress code, Kamateh always appeared manicured, soaped, pressed, pomaded, and attired in a suit of conservative cut and color. In his breast pocket, he wore an immaculate white handkerchief like an identification badge.

Though a reserved and solitary man, Kamateh was quite popular in the university community because of his neutrality in campus controversies, his abstinence from departmental politics, and his impeccable manners. He was content to channel his excess energy into research, closeted in his tiny, musty study.

On Sunday evening, the Iranian had been entertained by university friends at the Brentwood Hills home of the chairman of the physics department, not far from the Westwood campus. Kamateh had been reluctant to sanction a party in his honor, but he could not offend his departmental chairman. He had dutifully remained until midnight, sitting quietly in a corner, sipping tea (he neither smoked nor drank hard liquor) and responding politely if distractedly to the good-humored comments and well-wishes of the more festive party-goers.

When Kamateh departed shortly after the stroke of midnight, his host wondered aloud what was on the little Iranian's mind. Was he worried about going back to his wife in Iran? The little joke at Kamateh's expense drew appreciative liquored chortles.

The small bash had been arranged as a going-away party. Kamateh was leaving on Monday for a summer vacation with his family in Tehran. He would join his wife and two children, who had returned to Iran in late February for a visit that had been prolonged.

Kamateh had informed his apartment manager that he would be away for the summer; the implication was that he would return in time for the fall semester. He had canceled his subscription to the *Los Angeles Times* and had arranged to have his mail held in a rented post office box.

At 9:45 Monday morning, the familiar figure of the fastidious little Iranian professor, wearing a natty blue suit and carrying two gray Samsonite suitcases, boarded a Supershuttle airport bus at the front of his Westwood apartment. The bus stopped in front of the international terminal at LAX at 10:20 A.M. Kamateh had plenty of time to complete the preboarding routine for an Alitalia nonstop flight to Rome departing at 12:05 P.M.

After completing the ritual and clearing the security gate, the Iranian professor bought the late edition of the *Times* (the paper had not been delivered to his apartment that morning) and found a small table in the spartan cafeteria. While he waited, he drank coffee and read the sports section. He was a Dodger fan.

From another table, an unobtrusive, middle-aged man in a rumpled beige summerweight suit silently scrutinized Kamateh, his trained eye automatically registering such descriptive details as the big nose, the curly gray hair, the trim mustache. With a twinge of envy, the watcher saw the dapper, dark-skinned scientist board the plane shortly before noon. He waited until the doors were shut, the umbilical corridor withdrawn, and the Boeing 747 eased away from the terminal toward the runway. Only then did the observer light a cigarette and stroll over to a telephone bank. He selected a telephone that accepted credit cards and placed a terse long-distance call to a number with the 202 prefix of the District of Columbia.

"He left on schedule. Alitalia flight 10, nonstop to Rome."

"Good."

The watcher hung up. Rome would be beautiful in May, he thought, the envy resurfacing.

Gibson, Montana

"**H**AVE SOME COFFEE, LUKE," SAID ED THAYER. "IT'S BEEN simmering just about long enough to get some character."

"Thanks."

Luke Cameron poured thick black coffee from the pot kept warm in a corner of the sheriff's office. The coffeemaker was a Braun, a model whose sleek, modern design was at odds with the rest of the setting, which looked like a picture from the pages of *Country Living* magazine. Thayer had started his day at eight o'clock that morning with coffee, so it had been acquiring character for about two hours.

Ed Thayer had been Gibson County's sheriff for twelve years; before that he had been a deputy for six years. He was a quiet, dogged man whose amiable, easygoing manner was deceptive, as the town's few troublemakers—mostly drunks and joyriders—were quick to discover. He was steady, solid, not at all flamboyant. But he had been reelected sheriff by a widening margin every time he had run. The sturdy folks of Gibson County weren't about to change from a man they trusted to do his job.

Gibson was a neighborly town. Luke had known Thayer since he was a young deputy and Luke a rambunctious teenager; they had a loose, casual relationship.

"You want to know about your dad, I reckon."

"Yes."

Thayer gave him a copy of the accident report—more detailed and graphic in its particulars than Justin Cranmer's account had been, but with the same improbable, though seemingly credible, circumstances. The details, by their bizarre nature, made the conclusion all the more convincing.

"I did the investigation myself," the sheriff said. "At first, I didn't believe it was an accident. I didn't buy it. But the more I looked into it, Luke, the more I could see it was just one of those things. It happened. My guess is, Tom had a stroke. You'll note from the report that he'd seen Dr. Hastings about six months ago. He'd had some numbness in his left arm. The doc did some tests, but they were inconclusive. Now he thinks Tom may've had a small stroke—they're common enough for any man his age—that he got over. But the next time . . ."

Thayer left his conclusion unspoken. No one would ever know for sure, he said. But there were no unanswered questions about Tom's death, other than the cause of his fall, whether it was a stroke or he just slipped.

Luke listened intently as he sipped the sheriff's high-character coffee. In the pit of his stomach, he wasn't satisfied with the explanation of his father's death, but he had nothing specific on which to hang his dissatisfaction. Except . . .

"Tom wrote me a week or so before he died."

Ed Thayer showed his surprise.

"I got the letter in Houston on my way here."

"Oh hell, Luke, that's a damned shame! To have that letter waitin', like him talkin' to you from the grave . . . that must've hit you hard."

"The point is, Ed . . . he was scared of something. He wouldn't say what, but you knew Tom. When did you ever hear him admit that he was scared?"

"Never," the sheriff agreed, clearly puzzled.

"He didn't like what was going on around here."

Thayer shifted his considerable weight in his oak swivel chair. He glanced longingly at a drawer on the right side of his desk. "Lots of folks feel that way, Luke. These have been rough times. Folks don't like what's been happenin' to our economy. They don't like the way foreigners have been buyin' up so much of our land. Folks hereabouts tend to say, let 'em have Los Angeles, but this here's the heart of America. Tom felt the same way the rest of us do. And you got to remember, he'd just lost the Bar-C. That ranch was his whole life. It'd been in your family for three generations. Now it's hardly surprisin' Tom would start thinkin' that everything was going to hell.

If somethin' like that happened to me, hell, I'd start believin' the bank itself was in league with the devil!"

"Not the bank, the government," Luke said quietly.

"The gov'mint?"

"Dad thought there was something more going on at the nuclear facility than they're telling the public. Did he raise his usual rumpus about it? Go around asking questions? Or making noise at the city council meetings?"

"Well, now . . . sure he did. You know how Tom was when he got a notion in his head. Nothin' would shake it loose. He came in here once or twice . . . muttering about sinister goings-on behind that fence out at the DOE. There wasn't anythin' to it, Luke."

"Our government's been known to lie."

"That may be . . ." Ed Thayer squirmed uncomfortably. Then, with a decisive move, he opened the right-hand second drawer of his desk, dug out a blackened briar pipe, and began to stuff it with aromatic tobacco from a tin of Captain Black. "You mind, Luke?" He gestured with the pipe before he struck a match.

Luke Cameron shook his head. Pipes were a good way of stalling, he thought.

When the sheriff had his pipe painstakingly lit, which required two matches and considerable puffing, he said, "I can't get away with this when Thelma's in the office—that's my secretary. She's off today. One of her kids broke a collarbone."

"We were talking about the DOE."

"Near as I can gather, there's nothin' mysterious goin' on . . . nothin' at all. That doesn't mean I like the idea of all that uranium sittin' out there, so close to where folks live. But the experts all say the same thing, there's no radiation hazard or any other kind of hazard." He paused. "They don't have weapons there. I mean, nuclear bombs."

"The officials say what they're told to say."

"I didn't take their word at face value, Luke. I have my own sources. I asked some questions. I did a little readin'. I got kids here of my own, and a duty to the people of this town. From everythin' I could learn, they're tellin' the truth about the level of risk at a nuclear materials storage site."

Luke remained silent for a moment. The office was filling with aromatic tobacco smoke. Someone outside might look in, he mused, and think the place was on fire.

"You're saying Dad was wrong."

"I'm saying he could go off half-cocked. You know that for a fact, Luke. I tell you what, you want to know more about that DOE site, why don't you go on over to Butte and talk to the FBI agent there? Joe Springer's the one to see, the agent in charge. You can use my name. I think Tom may've gone over there. And there's someone else you can talk to, closer to home."

"Who's that?"

"Brad McAlister. One of your old school buddies. He's workin' at the DOE now, since his business folded. He's a security guard."

Anne McAlister appeared genuinely delighted when Luke stopped by the bank. "4-B's cooking is family style," he said cheerfully. "Did you say you can do better?"

"You bet I can! When can you come over?"

"How fast can you cook?"

She laughed. "Give me one day to plan, okay? How does tomorrow night for dinner sound?"

"Like fresh trout sizzling in the pan."

"I can't promise trout, but I'll find something edible." She hesitated, dismissed a thought, and said, "Brad works nights but he'll be there until midnight. That should leave plenty of time to visit. I know he's really looking forward to seeing you again. Can you get there about six?"

"Great."

Luke left feeling a little guilty about her enthusiasm. He *was* looking forward to the evening, now that he'd wangled an invitation, but there was no denying his real motive.

He wanted to pump Brad McAlister about the DOE's nuclear materials storage site.

Dark came slowly to the high country. The mountains faded into shadowy hulks of gray and blue and purple; the dusk flooded the deep canyons; the endless sky began to fill up with countless stars. You could read a newspaper by the stars, Luke Cameron swore, on a clear Montana night.

But he had been hoping for clouds.

Luke bought dinner that evening for Justin Cranmer, who had done him a favor; the lawyer had returned the rented Ford Taurus to the Hertz lot at Helena, where he had gone on business. Cranmer was interested in buying the battered Chevy pickup for himself, if Luke decided to sell.

Macon's Gibson Café served basic, hearty food, but his specialty was homemade pie. If there were a culinary heaven, it would feature Carl Macon's pies. Huckleberry pie when Carl could get fresh huckleberries from the Bitterroot Valley. Apple pie every night. Tart lemon meringue, the meringue about three inches high and sticky with egg whites. Peach in season, and when Carl felt like baking it, a coconut cream pie that some Montanans would drive a hundred miles for. This did not happen to be a coconut cream night, but Luke couldn't fancy anything tastier than the apple pie.

"It's as good a pie as you ever wrapped your tongue around," Cranmer admitted, "but you really should've tried the lemon. My lips may be permanently puckered up."

Carl's coffee was rich and savory, mingling delectably with the flavor of the pie. Good coffee and pie went together, Cranmer said, like beer and pretzels.

"You got to drive down to Dillon with me sometime," the lawyer said. "There's a woman there makes pies that are positively sinful."

"If I'm still here," Luke said, suddenly returning to reality from the relaxed, comfortable state induced by Carl Macon's steak and potatoes followed by pie and coffee.

"Your dad's letter is still eating at you," Cranmer said.

"The feeling won't go away that he was trying to tell me something."

Luke dropped Cranmer off at his office and drove back to the 4-B's Motel. He turned on the television, planning to wait until midnight before going out. He fell asleep.

When he awoke, the TV set was flickering with static; the station had gone off the air for the night. Luke's watch showed 1:42. He felt stiff of limb and foggy of mind. He was tempted to call off his project. Then, out of irritation with himself for dozing off, he splashed cold water over his face to wake himself up, pulled a jacket over his rumpled shirt, and slipped out of the room.

The town of Gibson had long been slumbering. Luke was alone driving along deserted Clark Street up the highway leading out of town. It wasn't the overcast night he had wished for, but there was a drifting cloud cover. Maybe if he timed it right, he could find a dark cloud to hide under. As for his late start, that might even work to his advantage. . . .

He drove south along the highway that bisected the Bar-C to the east from the Halston ranch to the west. Although the road marked the western border of his family's former acreage, the old ranch buildings were not visible from the highway, concealed by an intervening ridge. But the Halston ranch buildings, about a half mile away on the level plain, could be seen clearly from the road in daylight and were visible at this dark hour if only as black outlines, with an old windmill rising above them like a fragile steeple. The hired hands recruited by the new French owners were said to be divided between the main house and the bunkhouse. When the clouds broke for a moment, Luke thought he could make out several trucks next to the buildings. The place was dark. Not so much as a lamplight. Hardly surprising at two in the morning.

Luke rumbled on south in his pickup through the vast emptiness. Without warning, coming around a curve out of a dip in the road, he was confronted suddenly by the onrushing mass of a huge truck running with its headlights dimmed.

He felt a stab of alarm, a shock of adrenaline. The truck's bright beams flashed on, blinding him. He jerked the wheel to the right. The big rig thundered past him. The wind of its passage buffeted the smaller pickup. The Chevy's right front tire nudged the shoulder. He fought the wheel, trying to keep the pickup from slewing off the road into a drainage ditch.

Pulling out of the skid, he braked to a stop. But his heart kept racing. He looked back in anger and watched the truck disappear around the curve as if it had driven into a tunnel.

Luke stared after it. He suddenly realized that, in the moment before rounding the curve, the driver of the truck had once again dimmed his headlights.

In the darkness, it had effectively vanished.

One of Dad's mysterious trucks, Luke thought.

There were any number of good reasons for trucks to travel at night off the main interstate—and a few bad reasons for driving in the dark. Rustlers? Modern-day horse and cattle thieves used trucks. Smugglers? Possibly. For that matter, legitimate haulers might have reason to roll south along this road, trying to make up some lost time on a schedule that was always tight. But . . . not without headlights.

In his mind the question became linked with the highway that passed south of the DOE site. The intersection was only a mile or so ahead.

Luke drove to the junction and turned right, heading west. He continued for another five miles along the highway before he saw the high cyclone fence that defined and protected the edge of the government land. It wasn't a western fence, Luke thought, seeing it through his father's eyes. It wasn't designed to keep cattle from straying, or to keep out wild critters. This was a people fence, about eight feet high, with three strands of barbed wire strung along the top on elbows that jutted outward. Inside the fence and snug against its base was a thick coil of barbed concertina wire about three feet in diameter.

A fence to keep out trespassers.

On this back part of the property, the fence was set a good distance from the roadway. Perimeter lights, mounted on high standards, had been placed well inside the fence, with the lights glaring outward. They were intended to shine into the eyes of an approaching intruder while leaving the facility behind them in total darkness. About a quarter mile to the north, some railroad tracks appeared to enter the facility, presumably through gates that were too far away for Luke to see in the blackness.

Luke drove on, circling the property, which was bordered by highways on three sides. Only along its eastern flank did it border upon private lands—the Halston range.

The highway on the north side brought Luke past the main entrance to the installation. Along the way, he strained for a view of the site. There was little he could see. Just a collection of large, warehouselike structures presenting solid, windowless faces to the outside world. He took mental note: high wire fence. Security patrols. Floodlights where they could be set far enough from the public roads not to blind passing motorists. Fresnel strip lighting along the main highway, which ran closer to the perimeter fence than the side roads did. Guarded gates with a watchtower at the main entrance and the side entrance. An unobtrusive sign on a strip of lawn near the front gates identifying Department of Energy Strategic Materials Storage Site 14.

Visitor and employee parking lots were situated outside the perimeter fencing, near an administration and information center. Not even employees could drive in. They had to park outside and walk past the security gates.

Tight security, Luke judged. But, given the nature of the strategic materials stored here, security was essential. It could appear sinister to someone inclined to see it that way, a man already suspicious and bitter. But the precautions for protecting the site, no doubt, had been mandated by the Nuclear Regulatory Commission or some similar authority in Washington. It could not be faulted; more blame would be attached to careless security.

Luke Cameron returned the way he had come, making the circuit that took him south of the DOE site along the back road. As he cruised past the southern perimeter, he noted that the cloud cover had temporarily thickened, blotting out most of the stars. He thought of the railroad tracks that ran parallel to the highway.

About a quarter mile past the southeast corner of the site, Luke parked off the road. He hurried across the highway, climbed through a low cattle fence loosely strung with barbed wire, and struck out across the open grassland. He saw no sign of Micheline Picard's irrigation project. That was farther to the north, closer to the DOE's bulky storage buildings.

The night breeze whispered through the short grass, and grasshoppers whirred into the air wherever Luke stepped. Otherwise, the night was dark and still.

He reached the railroad tracks abruptly. There was no dip or shoulder alongside the rails, which ran straight across the level prairie, almost hidden by the short grass and low cacti. Luke followed the tracks westward a short distance before he was able to make out the high DOE fence and a pair of huge railroad gates set into it.

The blackness of the night had made a surreptitious approach seem safe enough. Luke wasn't sure exactly what he hoped to find. Something . . . anything . . . out of the ordinary. Something his father might have discovered. Luke knew his father; he had no doubt Tom Cameron had thoroughly scouted the DOE's perimeter. The problem was that the darkness, coupled with those floodlights in his eyes, made it impossible to see much of anything inside the DOE site.

He studied the railroad gates. They appeared to be heavily padlocked. Except for some rust on the sides, the tracks were shiny. This indicated they had seen regular and recent usage.

Luke shifted his shoulders uneasily. Something was teasing his senses. Nothing he could see. A sound . . . or a feeling.

Dropping to his knees, he leaned his ear to the ground. And heard—or felt—a rumbling heavy enough to shake the earth.

The sound stopped abruptly. Luke wondered what it was. He thought of the big truck that had passed him on the highway earlier in the evening. Had it been heading for the Halston ranch? What time was it now?—2:32 A.M., the faintly fluorescent numbers on his watch told him. Had he heard something as routine as a truck hauling irrigation pipe? Or was it something more sinister?

He stood still, listening, a couple of minutes. But the truck, if that's what it was, had stopped. Finally Luke turned with a shrug, back toward the railroad gates. He examined the heavy chain and padlock. Both secure. Gates snug, too tight for a man to squeeze through the break. He crouched down to see how much space there was where the tracks ran under the gates.

Without warning, a searchlight stabbed toward him.

Because he was already crouching low and because he dove away from the gates, instantly flattening on his belly, warned by peripheral vision a fraction of a second before the searchlight reached him, he lay unseen as the powerful beam swept across the open grassland and the empty tracks.

Before the arc of the probing searchlight returned, Luke scrambled to his right. His body rolled naturally into a shallow runoff in the plain, like a golf ball finding a divot in the fairway. The light passed over him again.

Had he triggered some kind of alarm, Luke wondered, sonic or seismic or whatever? Or had a passing patrol actually spotted him? Either way, it was time to get the hell out of there.

The searchlight winked off. Guessing that it might be followed up immediately by physical surveillance of the area, Luke was up and running the instant darkness returned to the plain. He raced straight back along the railroad tracks for a quarter mile and swung toward the road. Not far behind, he heard the sound of a vehicle approaching fast.

Dropping behind some low willow brush, Luke peered back toward the DOE site. He saw a security patrol Jeep jerk to a stop beside the railroad gates. Two armed guards jumped out of the Jeep.

The guards carefully inspected the gates and the fence for thirty yards in each direction. Luke stayed where he was. He had broken no law, as far as he knew, but it would be awkward if he should be caught sneaking around an off-limits government facility at 2:30 in the morning.

The security guards eventually climbed back into the Jeep and roared off. Luke watched the bobbing headlights as the vehicle followed the fence line to the north.

Then Luke trudged back to his pickup, relieved at his escape and a little chagrined over the game of hide-and-seek he had played with the site's security staff. He found the pickup where he had parked it. He climbed in; it started on the first turn of the key; and he drove back to town, wondering what he had learned.

Maybe Brad McAlister would be more revealing.

Unknown to Luke Cameron, his empty pickup parked off the highway had been observed by an earlier DOE security patrol. Darrell Johnson, the officer on a routine sweep, had found the vehicle apparently undamaged, its driver nowhere to be seen. He wrote up an incident report to turn in at the security office at the end of his shift. He noted the time, 2:21 A.M., the vehicle's location and condition, its make and color, its license number, and the absence of a driver.

The report seemed unimportant. So Johnson made no comment about it to his shift supervisor when he went off duty at eight in the morning.

The incident report was filed with a stack of routine paperwork, and Darrell Johnson soon forgot all about it.

Rome, Italy

A T 11:57 A.M. ON TUESDAY, NEARLY AN HOUR LATE, THE ALI-talia flight from Los Angeles taxied to the terminal from the runway at Rome's Leonardo da Vinci Airport, more often identified with its location at Fiumicino. A young American named Rich Osborne, who had arrived early to meet the flight, waited impatiently for the arriving passengers to retrieve their luggage and pass through customs.

Except for his keen interest in the Los Angeles passengers, Osborne might have been a tourist himself. He wore a pair of casual, light gray, pleated cotton slacks and a white cotton shirt. He looked tanned, fit, and relaxed—like a young man on a holiday.

The flow of passengers was met by enthusiastic crowds, mostly Italian, of demonstrative relatives and friends. The young man eased his way among them, smiling at the shrieks and cries and tears. The smile disguised a rising anxiety. In all this turmoil, it would be all too easy to miss someone. . . .

Osborne relaxed. A dapper, dark-skinned man with a gray mustache, about five feet six and slight of build, emerged from the tunnel. His fashionable blue suit was slightly wrinkled from traveling. He appeared to be about forty—the telex description had said forty-four. His gray hair was curly. The observant Osborne noted that the quiet little man took a furtive interest in the laughing, full-bosomed young Italian women in the reception parties.

Rich Osborne had not been eager to drive to Fiumicino that morning. He had made a tennis date with Amy Turner, the daughter of the American ambassador's assistant protocol director. Amy was a mature nineteen, in her first summer in Rome, an engaging figure in the short-skirted tennis outfit that displayed her golden legs. She was all he could handle on the court. Osborne had not advanced beyond tennis with her, but he was hopeful. Sunday night at the ambassador's dinner, he had caught her studying him with a speculative eye.

It was one o'clock before the physics professor from Los Angeles cleared the airport. His taxicab followed the Number 8 highway to-

ward the center of the Eternal City. Osborne followed in his white
Alfa Spider, the top down so he could bask in the sun. It was a warm
Mediterranean afternoon under a cloudless sky. As they approached
the city, the boulevards were jammed with fast, aggressively driven
little Fiats, Golfs, and other small cars. Osborne threaded his way
confidently through the chaotic traffic, giving no quarter to the Italian drivers who regarded a traffic circle as a challenge to manhood.
Osborne, nevertheless, drove with one hand on the wheel, the other
drumming to the beat of a Doors tape on his stereo. As a Fiat cut
across his hood, he gave the wheel an expert twist, cleared the other
car's fender by inches, and used his free hand to give the offending
driver an Italian finger.

Although it was the beginning of the long midday siesta, which
in Rome meant a languid three hours of minimal activity, there was
enough traffic and construction blockages to drag out the twenty-one
mile drive to forty minutes. At the end of it, to Osborne's mild surprise, the taxicab deposited its passenger in front of the elegant little
Hotel d'Inghilterra on Via Bocca di Leone, around the corner and
a couple short blocks from the foot of the Spanish Steps.

Osborne deposited his Alfa in a security-protected parking lot;
even if he could have found a spot, he wouldn't risk parking the Alfa
in the street. He tipped the attendant, asking to have his car located
near the exit, ready for a quick departure if necessary. Hurrying back
to the hotel, he strode into the tiny, gilt-and-marble lobby just in time
to observe Dr. Hassan Kamateh stepping into an elevator. Osborne
continued on through the lobby into the English-style bar, found a
seat that offered a view of the lobby, and ordered a Campari and
soda.

Our professor isn't skimping, he mused. The d'Inghilterra happened to be one of Osborne's favorite Roman hotels. Last year, he
had booked his parents here on their vacation visit, and he had admired the antique-furnished rooms and the quiet efficiency of the
service. It was also just steps away from the city's best shops as well
as the Piazza di Spagna at the foot of the Steps. This elegance and
convenience in the heart of Rome didn't come cheap. Osborne
guessed at least two hundred dollars per night for a single.

He glanced at his thin gold wristwatch. Any chance that Amy
might still be on the courts? After he was assigned unexpectedly to
meet the Alitalia flight from Los Angeles, he had called her unhap-

pily to cancel their date. Amy had accepted the news with such cheerful nonchalance that it perturbed Rich all the more.

He sighed helplessly. Amy Turner couldn't be told the real reason for breaking their date. She had no idea that he was attached to the U.S. embassy in a cover role. To the Italian society in which Osborne mingled and to the American colony in Rome, the slender, boyishly handsome young man with the shock of thick blond hair, the long, thin nose, and the engaging grin appeared to be just another of those appealing, lightweight young men of proper manners and background who found the Foreign Service an agreeable playground.

Osborne enjoyed his role, which provided adequate cover for his intelligence assignments. To date most of those had been no more demanding or dangerous than tailing the Iranian professor. Osborne had been recruited out of Georgetown while he was still trying to decide what to do with his life. He was still only a junior assistant to the agency's chief of station in Rome. If he didn't trip over his own feet, however, he could expect more exciting assignments.

But for the moment, he had to keep an eye on Hassan Kamateh as long as the Iranian remained in Rome.

Thinking of Amy Turner in her tennis briefs, Osborne fervently hoped that the Iranian did not plan on a long stay.

Gibson, Montana

"WHAT'S IT LIKE IN PUNTA DEL ANSA?"

"It's a jungle out there," Luke Cameron said with a smile.

"Do they have boa constrictors and pythons?" asked Brad McAlister, Jr.

"And piranha fish?" asked Rob, the younger brother. "Did you lose any of your crew in the river?"

"Nary a one."

"You're disappointing them," the boys' father said. Brad McAlister deftly turned a steak over on the barbecue grill. Flames flared up from the red-hot coals as fat dripped onto them. "In their favorite videos, someone is always being eaten alive."

"Or swallowed up in a bog!" Rob said enthusiastically.

"Gross," commented Patty, the third and youngest of the McAlister clan. She was ten—one and three years, respectively, behind her brothers. "Totally gross."

"She's scared of snakes," Rob confided to Luke.

"You sure you wouldn't want to adopt one or two of these kids, Luke?" Brad McAlister asked cheerfully. "We haven't been able to find any local takers. How'd you say you wanted your steak? Dripping red?"

"Yuk!" Patty said.

"Medium rare will do."

"She likes hers burned to a crisp," Rob said, with brotherly scorn for a kid sister.

"Cremated," agreed the father of the brood.

"Well, I don't like it *raw* like some people I know."

"Do people eat snakes raw in South America?" the older boy wanted to know.

"That's enough, Brad," the mother said as she emerged through the back door with a bowl of cole slaw.

"No, but the boas swallow the people raw," Luke said.

"Luke!" Anne McAlister cried.

"Totally gross," Patty said.

"I agree," said Anne, grinning in spite of herself.

"Okay, boys, bring the plates," Brad McAlister ordered. "Medium rares first."

"Sorry about the trout," Anne apologized to Luke. "I couldn't get any fresh."

"You never have to apologize to me for barbecued steaks."

"Anne's big on apologizing," Brad said. It was the first jarring note of the evening, the first hint that the idyllic family portrait Luke Cameron had been admiring might have a crack in the frame. Luke caught Anne's quick glance at Brad, the fleeting hurt in her eyes. He even sensed a moment of wary silence from the three youngsters, as if they were familiar with the verbal warning signal.

But then Brad was spearing thick sirloin steaks from the grill and distributing them on plates. The boys carried them to the outdoor picnic table in the big yard, where huge bowls piled with potato salad and slaw and corn on the cob were awaiting. But the pièce de résistance was a basket of fresh, homemade bread. "I got up at five this morning to bake it, I'll have you know," Anne admitted when Luke exclaimed over the crunchy crust and soft freshness of the bread.

"One of her specialties," Brad said loudly, as if trying to make up for his earlier putdown.

Brad McAlister was an overweight, overly talkative man with an outgoing geniality that probably held up, Luke thought, as long as things were going well for him. He was a big man of loud boasts and voracious appetites, once hard muscled, now soft around the middle.

Brad had been a sensational tailback in high school, where his size and strength had simply overpowered average opponents. He had expected to continue his gridiron heroics in college after being heavily recruited. Instead, he had found himself playing with athletes just as big and just as strong as he was—and frequently faster. Brad was simply a step too slow to dominate the game any longer at the college level. He was an adequate but unspectacular player, Luke remembered, a reality that Brad had never been able to accept. In Brad McAlister's view, he had been poorly coached and ineffectively used, his running skills wasted on a pass-oriented team.

When Luke had arrived at the comfortable, brick-and-clapboard house with its wide front porch, he had felt a sting of envy. The street was tree shaded and tranquil, the house warm and restful—the way small-town houses built in the 1930s were. The broad front lawn was dappled under old shade trees. The friendly, sit-down porch invited you to relax. The house had a look of solidity and permanence.

The McAlister children, the boys sturdy and sunburned, full of curiosity, and the younger Patty, shy of a stranger, had made Luke feel the emptiness of his own solitary and transient life. If there had been a false note at all, it was in the effusiveness of Brad McAlister's welcome, gripping Luke's hand and banging his shoulder and exclaiming, "God, Luke, it's been a long time! Great to see you, buddy!" They had never been close friends. They had merely gone to the same school, played the same games, known the same girls.

The outdoor barbecue meal, hearty and solid and delicious, revived Luke's earlier feelings. Afterward, dark closed in rapidly under an overcast sky, an enveloping darkness as if Gibson were a spaceship drifting alone in the void. There was distant lightning, too far off for any thunder to be heard. After awhile, a rolling rumble became audible, the warning of an approaching storm. The wind picked up, sending sparks flying from the dying coals in the barbecue kettle. Brad doused them with water and clamped the lid down over the grill, and Anne suggested everyone should go inside.

Sheltered in the big, comfortable living room, with its overstuffed furniture that was beginning to show frayed elbows, the McAlister kids off in another room watching television, the wind outside thrashing the trees and whipping up dust clouds, Luke Cameron sensed an underlying tension that had been hardly detectable out of doors. Brad McAlister seemed to become nervous and fidgety as the evening wore on. He glanced often at his watch, or rose to peer outside at the gathering storm. Anne's worry kept pace with his edginess. Marriage, Luke thought, must mean never having to worry alone.

As the first big drops of rain slapped the window, Brad muttered, "Shit!"

"Brad!"

"Look at it, goddamnit! I've got to go to work in a couple of hours."

"The state is drying up, and you're complaining about *rain?* About getting a little wet?"

"It's not me I'm worried about. . . ." Brad caught himself. "I just don't like to drive in it, that's all."

Anne managed a lame laugh. "It isn't as if you have to work outside, honey."

"Yeah . . . well . . . we can sure use the rain."

Luke seized the opportunity he had been waiting for all evening. "Anne was telling me you work over at the DOE."

Brad glared at his wife. "Yeah."

"In security?"

Luke thought Brad stiffened a little, but he answered mildly enough. "That's right. It's a high-security installation."

"High security? In the middle of Montana? . . . What are they doing there?"

"I'm not supposed to talk about it, Luke."

"I see. My dad had got into his head there was something sinister about that site."

"Sinister?"

"Something the government wouldn't want us to know about, I suppose. You know how Tom felt about cover-ups."

"There's nothing sinister going on there, believe me."

"Just nuclear weapons?"

"Not even that," Brad said. "Hey, it's supposed to be classified information."

"No problem. I just thought it would be common knowledge around town."

"Well, I suppose it is." Brad's edginess seemed to have eased, as if he were relieved rather than disturbed by the direction of Luke's comments. "I can tell you it's a strategic materials storage site. Hell, that's on the sign outside the gates. That's government jargon for nuclear materials. Not weapons, just the raw stuff."

Luke was disappointed. The presence of nuclear materials might very well have upset his father but not enough to account for the dramatic tone of his letter.

"And you can forget about sinister experiments in some secret laboratory," Brad went on. "There's nothing there, Luke. The military isn't even involved—just the Energy Department. I don't know what your father could have been thinking about, but there's nothing at our site that should have alarmed him. No mysterious experiments, no radiation leaks, nothing at all."

Brad sounded a little too emphatic, but Luke dismissed that as defensiveness about his job, which Brad obviously considered beneath him. Losing his business must have been a hard fall for Brad.

Hard on Anne, too, Luke thought. Which might explain the dark hollows around her eyes and the worried expression that threatened to become permanent.

Oddly, as the time came for Brad McAlister to leave for work, his edginess returned. The rain, which would be blessed all over Montana this night, let up after a half hour of heavy pounding. It was reduced to a steady drizzle when Brad ordered the kids to bed. They protested and pleaded with him.

Annoyed, Brad cut off the pleas. "You heard me, it's late. You've got school in the morning."

"Aw, Dad, Jimmy Miller gets to stay up for David Letterman," young Brad protested.

"I don't care if Jimmy Miller stays up all night; you don't. It's time for bed. Turn that TV set off."

"Daddy . . ."

"One more whining word, and there'll be no TV for a week! That's it . . . now get to bed!"

In the awkward silence that followed, as footsteps trudged heavily up the stairs, Luke sensed both embarrassment and resentment in the suddenly charged atmosphere—Anne McAlister embarrassed, Brad resenting the presence of an outsider. The gladhanding was over, Luke thought.

"I gotta go to work," Brad said abruptly. "Glad you could come over, Luke. Maybe we'll see you again before you go."

"I don't plan on being in town long. . . . I should head back to the motel"—he smiled, seeking to soften Brad's outburst—"before Brad sends *me* off to bed."

Brad McAlister glared at him, eyes suddenly cold. "Don't rush on my account. I'm sure you and Anne will have a lot to talk over . . . after I'm gone."

He stalked out. Anne McAlister and Luke Cameron listened in silence to the banging of the door and the grinding of Brad's starter, its sound muffled in the smothering dampness of the rain. The house was quiet then, and the tension slowly began to evaporate. Luke could hear the boys' voices upstairs.

Anne said, "Would you like some more coffee?"

"If I have any more, I'll stay awake all night." Luke admired her self-control, and the pride that made it possible. "Doesn't Brad wear a uniform at the site?"

"He won't wear it until he gets there." She paused. "Don't be too hard on him, Luke. Losing his business . . . it's like losing a job. They say it diminishes a man, makes him feel like a failure. It wasn't really his fault, you know. Maybe it was mine. He wanted to leave Gibson, make a fresh start somewhere else. I wouldn't let him."

"Don't dump on yourself, Anne. You're no failure, not with those fine kids, and loyalty to Brad."

She saw him to the door. There was a moment, standing together with the door open and the night weeping quietly beyond the porch overhang, when Luke felt a yearning in her, a vulnerability born of unhappiness.

They looked at each other for a long moment. Anne smiled. "It's been fun, Luke. The kids think you're terrific. It'll be weeks before they stop talking about you."

"I think they're terrific."

"Good night, Luke."

He walked out into the drizzle.

Why had Brad become so edgy toward the end of the evening, Luke wondered.

Did he hate his work that much?

Or was something else bothering him?

Or was Luke himself just grasping at straws?

Punching in almost simultaneously with Burt Henderson, Brad McAlister commented on the rain. "Rain's cooled things off. Good night for a workout."

Burt Henderson coughed, his face flushed. "I'm not workin' out tonight. No way."

"What? . . . Why?"

"I gotta cold."

Brad's leap of elation at Henderson's indisposition was short lived. He was eager to embrace any excuse to postpone the break-in. But then he thought of Kali's reaction, and his brief euphoria gave way to panic.

"A little cold's gonna stop you, Burt?"

"Colds drain the energy right out of me. I couldn't hack it to-night."

Brad's mind began to reel. Kali would never believe him. He would think it was an act of desperation, an attempt by Brad to wea-sel out of his commitment. Kali had given him a phone number to call—to use only in an emergency. Well, this was sure as hell an emergency. Should he try to reach Kali now? What if he wasn't there? If Henderson meant what he said, the whole mission had to be called off no matter *what* Kali thought.

Buy some time. Maybe you can still figure a way out of this.

It was the same inner voice that kept asking him how he had ever let himself become involved with Kali's schemes.

"You should sweat it out," Brad suggested as the two men entered the main building. "The cold, I mean."

"Yeah?"

"I mean it. It's good for a cold. Sweat out all the poison; cleanse the system." Henderson was big on laxatives.

"Yeah?"

"You don't have to go all-out. I mean, you could drop down a couple weights; still work up a good sweat."

"I don't feel like it."

"Hey, it's your body." Brad forced a smile, feeling sick himself. "But I'm telling you, sweating it out is the way to purify the system."

That was at midnight. Two hours later, Henderson was still waffling. Brad McAlister placed a frantic call from a pay phone in the employees' lounge. Two men were sitting at one of the tables, desultorily playing gin. Brad mentally began coping with the problem of communicating with Kali in an improvised code.

The phone kept ringing. Each ring tightened Brad's rising desperation another notch. *Where was Kali? He'd said he could be reached at any time. Why didn't he answer?*

Brad finally hung up. He was sweating so much the phone nearly slipped from his fingers.

In just ninety minutes, Henderson would be starting his lunch break. Ten minutes after that, on a split-second timetable, Kali and his men would break through the earth's surface a few feet from the fire door in the southeast wall of the main storage building.

Unless Henderson changed his mind, as soon as the first shovel dug into the earth, warning lights on the alarm control panel would signal an intrusion and pinpoint the location. The alarm system response would be activated instantly. . . .

Let it happen, the cautionary voice whispered. *What can Kali do? It's not your fault—you warned him this could happen. And anyway, how can he implicate you?*

But a cold, rational part of his brain answered that there was a great deal Kali could do. That he was not a reasonable man. That too many people had seen them together. That he had involved Brad in actions that could be called treason. That he could show copies of documents Brad had smuggled out of the DOE site for him.

And the rational voice added something else: *Ten thousand dollars, Brad. Enough to ease the financial pressure. And there'll be more. A second installment. You'll really be breathing easy again. And who gets hurt? Nobody.*

He was hurrying back along his patrol route, trying to make up the time lost while he detoured for the phone call, when a door opened ahead of him and Burt Henderson emerged from a restroom, still zipping up. "Hey, Brad! You know what? I think you're right. I'm gonna sweat my cold away."

Brad McAlister didn't know whether he was more relieved or dismayed.

The theft was on.

Kali was just emerging from the shed when he heard one of his men shouting. The phone in the Halston house was ringing.

None of the crew was allowed to answer the phone. For one thing, most of them spoke little English, and that was heavily accented. Kali didn't want to draw attention to them.

Who would be calling at this hour—two in the morning? Kali could think of only one person: McAlister.

And he could think of only one reason: McAlister was getting cold feet. He wanted to call it off.

Kali headed for the house on the run. As he burst through the door, the phone gave a last strident ring. Before he could reach it, the instrument fell silent.

Kali stared at it, waiting, breathing hard from his run. The silence stretched out. If it was McAlister, he would call again.

After five minutes, Kali concluded that the call had been a false alarm, perhaps a wrong number.

He glanced at his watch. An hour and a half. *Time to get this show on the road.*

He had attended school in America; he spoke the idioms like a native. Soon he would be adding something else to his lexicon.

How about the Big Bang?

In the beginning it all went exactly as Brad McAlister had programmed it.

Henderson lumbered out of the alarm control center at 3:32 A.M. Four minutes later, a yellow light on the monitor panel blinked off; the surveillance camera in the right-hand corner near the ceiling was cut out of the cycle. Brad stepped into the narrow room.

After rehearsing for three consecutive nights the previous week, he flipped the right switches with methodical efficiency. Brad had time enough to double-check the routine and was still out of the center in twenty-five seconds.

He forced himself to walk at a normal pace. At 3:45 A.M., he met

Jim Rayburn, exchanged banter, and continued on toward the shipping and receiving bay. By this time, he guessed, Ali Kali and his forty thieves should be popping out of the ground like circus clowns emerging from one of those little cars in the center ring.

When he reached the last aisle, his steps quickened. He broke into a trot. Excited now. Scared but excited, the adrenaline spurting into his bloodstream. Reaching the fire door, he glanced up the aisle behind him once more. No problem. Why should there be? This time of night, especially at midweek, everyone on the site was sleepwalking.

He leaned his weight against the door's panic bar and felt the rush of cooler night air as the door slowly opened. The rain had stopped.

For a moment, Brad stood in the doorway, experiencing momentary shock. He stared at the hole in the ground at his feet as if it were a gaping wound in the earth. Although he had anticipated it being there, the reality was still stunning. A dirt-coated head and shoulders appeared. Dark skin, oily black hair, a man Brad had never seen before. A small man—no, a kid, for God's sake! He looked like a teenager.

The youth reached down into the tunnel to help another emerge, this one eighteen or nineteen at most.

"Where's Cal?" Brad asked the first youth. "I have to go . . . make my rounds."

The kid stared at him blankly. Not a friendly stare, Brad registered. Stone-faced kid. Foreign, he concluded.

Who the hell are they? Where is Cal?

To his infinite relief, Kali climbed out of the hole. Brad welcomed him as an old friend—at least the guy spoke English! The bearded man pulled up a leather apron, then a weighted rope ladder, that were shoved to him from the tunnel.

Brad looked at him questioningly.

"To go over the fence, man," Kali said. "Cover up after us, right? Close the tunnel and make it look right. Then I go over the fence. No sweat. Simple, huh?"

Brad understood. The apron would take care of the barbed wires across the top of the fence and the weighted rope ladder could be thrown over the leather. "Hurry!" he urged. "I still have to finish my round and clock in along the way. I told you—"

"Take it easy. Just show us where the hot stuff is."

As Kali spoke, one of the men still in the tunnel shoved one of the steel cylinders up through the opening. The youth who tried to lift it showed the strain.

"What did you fill the container with?"

Kali grinned. "Lead buckshot."

"Does it weigh the same as the real metal? They're checked by weight. . . ."

"Hey, man, we went over all this. Stop sweatin' it. We got it right on the nose. With the buckshot, each cylinder weights 102.5 pounds. Okay?"

Brad nodded jerkily. "I gotta get going."

"Show us the way."

Until now, with the alarms shut down and the intrusion on Brad's watch, the risk had seemed remote. But as Brad led Kali and his followers through the fire door into the huge building, he suddenly became almost paralyzed with fear. God in heaven, what was he *doing?* If they were caught now, inside the building, if Brad were seen escorting nuclear thieves into a government facility, there would be no acceptable explanation, no way to evade the terrible consequences.

The band of dark-skinned young men gaped around them at the silent warehouse, the wide aisles, the march of storage units along the walls, the painted lines McAlister had described to Kali.

"Follow the yellow lines," he whispered hoarsely. As if whispering would help him now!

"Where's the stuff?"

Brad checked his watch, felt his heart skip a beat. "I have to clock in! I'm late. . . ."

"Just show me, man."

Brad McAlister led Kali and his men to a nearby bay, housing rows of widely separated cylinders exactly like the one Kali had lugged back through the tunnel. Only one cylinder would be switched tonight. Brad had emphatically described the dangers of trying to take two of them at once. If two masses of enriched uranium of sufficient size were brought too close together, either in the tunnel or during shipment, there would be a risk of the material going critical. Kali had reluctantly agreed that the necessary amount of U-235 would have to be taken on separate nights. The added risk of discovery from different intrusions simply had to be accepted.

As soon as Kali and his followers went to work, Brad hurried back along his regular patrol route. He was nearly five minutes late at the first clock. He could make up most of that before the next station, he thought. But there would be a record—proof that, on the night of a theft of U-235 from the site, Brad hadn't been where he was supposed to be on his route.

His real hope was that the theft would not be discovered for a long while. Then no one could pinpoint the night of the intrusion. There had been no recent shipments from this particular site. With a matching replacement cylinder set in place for each one that was stolen, even a normal inventory would not reveal anything amiss. Brad had observed the carelessness of those checks. No one ever expected anything to be missing; the inventories had become too routine. Unless something happened to arouse suspicion, there was a good chance that a bogus cylinder wouldn't be detected for months. But if there should be a serious investigation, Brad fretted, any break from his normal patrol pattern would be noticed and questioned.

Like everyone hired at the DOE site, Brad McAlister had undergone stringent vetting conducted by the Department of Energy and the FBI. His profile was all-American. He was an upstanding citizen. He had lived in Gibson all his life. He was well thought of. He had served two years in the Montana National Guard. He had never been convicted of a felony, never even participated in a student demonstration. Lately he had experienced a financial setback, but so had half of the people in Montana.

At the time of his hiring, gambling had not been a problem. He had admitted playing a little keno or poker—hell, everyone did. But he hadn't been betting—and losing—so heavily then. Now any thorough investigation would uncover large gambling losses. It wasn't a crime to lose money, but it would be a red flag no investigator could overlook.

At the far end of his patrol loop, where Brad was scheduled to punch in on the hour, he was still two minutes late. That meant, according to his own timetable, he had only eight minutes to get back to the alarm control center. The clock at the loop was located next to a fixed security station, manned on this night by a guard named Alex Velasco. It was boring duty, and Velasco liked to break the monotony.

"How about that rain tonight, Brad? We sure needed it."

"Yeah, it's about time the clouds unloaded."

"Still comin' down, you think?"

"It'd stopped when I—" Brad checked himself. "—when I last heard."

"I just planted some corn, you know. Hey, we get some real rain, maybe I'll have me a crop."

"We can all use it." Brad glanced conspicuously at his watch. "I'm late on my round, gotta get moving."

Velasco seemed not to hear him. "Sweet corn, you like sweet corn? I been lookin' forward to fresh sweet corn all winter. But they got these limits on how much water we can use. . . . Homeowners and small growers, I mean. They let the big growers waste it . . . but not us. But hey, the rain comes down equally on the poor and the rich. . . ."

"But who gets soaked?" Brad forced a laugh as he started walking. "See you, Alex. I'm late . . ."

Velasco called after him. "Hey, maybe we could have a barbecue, huh?"

"Great!" Brad looked at his watch again. My God, five after three!

He forced himself not to run, keeping his pace to a fast walk. He thought of those Olympic walkers he had watched on TV, looking stiff legged and silly the way they moved, arms pumping and legs kicking out in a jerky half-walk, half-run. As Brad cut across the main aisle past the security office, he began to relax. He would be okay if Henderson didn't cut his workout short because of his cold.

Brad came in sight of the alarm center. No sign of Henderson yet; he *was* going to be on time!

Then, far down the aisle, a figure scurried furtively across the line of his vision. Then another.

Kali's men! They weren't out of the building!

Brad McAlister stopped short. His breathing was constricted. His thoughts moved sluggishly, as if drugged with cold. What had gone wrong? Why weren't they out? He couldn't activate the alarms until every man was back in the tunnel. And what about Kali trying to climb the fence? He would never make it. *There wasn't enough time.*

Brad saw Kali waving at him. Grinning, damn him! He gave an all-clear signal before he turned and sprinted toward the fire door. Seconds later, listening acutely, Brad heard the heavy door close.

He started toward the alarm control center. He had to force himself to move. His legs felt as if he were walking in water. He knew he was panicking, losing control, feeling helpless.

He reached the alarm center. Stared into the narrow room. 3:12 A.M. on the wall clock—two minutes behind schedule! Henderson would arrive any second. And—oh, God—the surveillance camera inside the alarm control center was on!

The thirty seconds while he waited out the camera's cycle seemed an eternity. All the time Brad kept listening for the sound of Henderson's heavy footsteps. His thoughts tumbled over each other. Had Kali got the uranium out of the building? Would he be caught going over the fence? Twenty-one, twenty-two, twenty-three seconds . . . How would Brad explain to Henderson? What could he say? Twenty-eight seconds . . .

Now! The camera's warning light blinked off.

Brad's sluggishness dropped away as he darted into the control room and began to flip switches. He had moved onto another plane, ruled not by fear but exhilaration. His hands flew with the swift, sure touch and coordination of a former athlete. In less than twenty seconds, he had reactivated all of the alarms for the southeast quadrant of the building—and there were no telltale flashing lights, no bells and whistles. It had worked! Kali and his followers were out of the building, out of the facility! Safe!

Brad McAlister turned to leave the alarm control center, weak kneed with relief.

Burt Henderson filled the doorway. "Smile," he said. "You're on Candid Camera!"

Whatever expression of shock or terror appeared on Brad McAlister's face, it caused Henderson to laugh aloud. "Don't drop dead on me!"

"I . . . I just stopped by . . . I wondered how you were making out."

"Hey, you were right, you know? Sweating it out was just the ticket." Henderson slapped Brad so heartily on the back that for a moment Brad couldn't breathe. "You look like you been haulin' ass yourself. You're sweatin' like a pig."

Brad thought numbly that the description applied more accurately to Henderson. As usual the big man had not showered after his workout, and the smell of sweat was strong in the confines of the control room.

"You okay, McAlister?"

"Yeah, sure. Maybe . . . maybe I'm fighting your cold."

"Hey, take the cure. Pump some iron."

Brad McAlister stumbled past Henderson into the aisle, escaping the locker room smell and the stench of his own fear.

He walked the rest of his patrol blindly, the way you can sometimes drive for an hour and arrive at your destination without knowing quite how you got there, the mind having taken its own journey.

Not until two hours later, taking his ten-minute coffee break at six in the morning, did Brad remember the ten thousand dollars.

His hand shook as he lifted the styrofoam cup, and he spilled coffee onto his pants leg.

He didn't even feel the burning.

Joe Springer studied the man across his desk. Tall, lean, tanned, weathered, big shouldered, hard muscled, hands you wouldn't want raised against you in a barroom brawl. Looked like a westerner, in the John Wayne mode.

You could see the father in him, too—the same stubborn jaw. But the old man had come equipped with a louder mouth.

Springer remembered Tom Cameron clearly, though not favorably. He had come into the office with a chip on his shoulder, not seeking help or information but making unfounded accusations and expecting everyone to jump. It had been the wrong approach entirely with Joe Springer, a veteran FBI agent who had a stubborn streak of his own.

The G-man respected Ed Thayer, the sheriff in Gibson, and Springer liked to cooperate with local law enforcement. It made things easier all around, especially in a state as wide and empty as Montana. But friendly cooperation had its limits. Springer decided to cut Luke Cameron off at the pass.

In fact, there was a directive burning its imprint on his desk right now (which he was not about to mention to Cameron) from the J. Edgar Hoover Building in Washington over the signature of Ted Chandler, an associate director, asking field offices to investigate any possible penetration or sabotage of nuclear storage sites. Now here was the second Cameron within two months asking questions about the nuclear facility outside Gibson.

Joe Springer didn't need any local gadflies telling him his job; he had already acted on the Chandler directive. He had called Greg Danielson, the security chief at the Gibson site, and asked him about any recent incidents. Danielson had chuckled tolerantly. Not a whisper of trouble, he had said. The ring of certainty in his voice gave Springer a slight twinge of unease. If a man in Danielson's position got too confident, he might overlook something.

But the flicker of doubt in the back of Springer's mind did not make him appreciate someone stirring up wild rumors about nuclear mischief where none existed.

"So you remember my father coming to see you?" Luke Cameron asked.

"I remember him," said Springer. "Even if I didn't, we keep records."

"Would you mind checking your records? I'd like to know just what was on Dad's mind."

"Don't need to."

Cameron showed his surprise. "You remember him that well?"

"Your father had a way of making himself remembered," the FBI agent said dryly. He didn't mention that he had reviewed Tom Cameron's file after the directive had arrived from FBI headquarters.

Cameron smiled in acknowledgment. "He made a complaint?"

"Not exactly. I would call it more of . . . an accusation."

"Who was he accusing?"

"The U.S. Government. The Department of Energy. The Montana State Police. The FBI. You might call it a blanket accusation."

Cameron's face had stiffened as the agent talked. "He was a crackpot, is that what you're saying?"

"I didn't say that, Mr. Cameron. He was upset. He thought something was going on at the DOE site near Gibson. He thought the government was covering it up."

"It wouldn't be the first cover-up. The government has lied to us before."

"Us?"

"The people . . ." Luke Cameron said, ". . . who own the country."

"Ah . . . well, you see, I'm one of the people. That's why you find me here in Butte, Mr. Cameron. You know what Butte was considered to be in Mr. Hoover's time? It was exile. Siberia. A dead end. It was where maverick agents were sent when they didn't play the game by Hoover's rules . . . when they ruffled the wrong feathers. J. Edgar Hoover's gone, but Butte's still here. And it hasn't changed. I was in the New York field office for fourteen years, Cameron. That's where the action is. A bank getting hit. Contraband goods smuggled across the state lines, spies setting up drops in Central Park, Wall Street stings—you name it, that's where it was happening. I was doing what I joined the Bureau to do. Never a dull day . . ." Springer's voice trailed off. He stared thoughtfully out the office window. "If I'd learned how to keep my mouth shut," he mused, "I'd still be there."

Luke Cameron studied the G-man with new eyes. But he let Springer go on talking.

"I'm a long way from Manhattan now, Cameron. I'm here in Butte. I'm like the Maytag repairman. This is not exactly a hotbed of crime. . . . So I think I understood your father. No, I didn't let what he was saying go in one ear and out the other. There's a little of him in me. A man who won't bridle his tongue. A maverick. A boat rocker."

"That was Dad, all right."

"Trouble was, he didn't have any evidence to back up his charges. He just got it into his head that there was something sinister about the nuclear storage site in Gibson. Some mysterious experiments. Or radioactive leakage. He had in his mind all kinds of wild possibilities." The agent tilted forward in his chair to look Luke Cameron straight in the eyes. "It's not happening. Wasn't then. Isn't now. I told your father as much. No experiments. No radioactive fallout, no cancer-causing chemicals, nothing to justify his dark suspicions. Hell, the nuclear materials at that site aren't even weapons, Cameron."

"You know that? You investigated my father's charges?"

Springer scowled at him. *Jesus Christ, how much plainer could he make it?* "We investigate when there is reasonable suspicion of a violation of federal law, Mr. Cameron. There was no such suspicion. Then or now."

But to himself, Springer wondered. *What had got Washington stirred up? There must have been some reason behind that directive from headquarters.*

For a minute Luke Cameron sat silently, contemplating his next move. He had anticipated what Springer would say even before driving over to Butte that morning in response to Ed Thayer's suggestion. Luke recognized that he was just going through the motions, just trying to do right by his deceased father.

Dead end, Luke thought. For Joe Springer, who had dead-ended in Butte.

For Luke as well.

On the drive to Butte, descending a long grade, Luke Cameron had found his foot hitting the floor when he stepped on the brake pedal. By alternately coasting and crawling, he had eased the battered pickup into Butte and had dropped it off for repairs. Then he had set off on foot for the FBI field office. When he returned for his truck, he found it high on a lift, front and rear wheels removed.

The mechanic's name was Clyde. He had a prominent Adam's apple, which wobbled when he talked. "Lucky you could coast into town," Clyde announced when Luke approached.

"Bad brakes?"

"No brakes at all. When's the last time you had them checked?"

"I just acquired it. Been driving it only a few days," Luke said. "What exactly is wrong with the brakes?"

"You need new linings. Maybe I can turn those rear drums, maybe not. And the master cylinder's leaking."

"Which means?"

"You need to replace it."

Luke shrugged irritably. Clyde showed him the worn linings and evidence of leaking. He couldn't drive through mountainous country without brakes. "How long will it take you?"

"A good brake job?" The mechanic peered up at him. "You don't sound like no easterner."

"Why?"

"They're always in a hurry."

"You're right, I reckon," Luke said in his best Montana drawl. "I come from over Gibson way. Montana born . . . Chevy parts shouldn't be hard to find."

"Maybe not," Clyde said more agreeably. "But I wouldn't count on goin' anywheres today, son."

"Be ready tomorrow morning, you think?"

"I reckon so."

It meant a night in Butte, not one of Luke Cameron's favorite towns. He carried in his memory an image of the mile-wide, open copper mine that had slowly been devouring the city, bite by bite, until the Anaconda Company stopped expanding the hole in the direction of the city's center. His father had shown Luke the gaping hole on a boyhood trip to Butte. "That's man for you," Tom Cameron had said. "The only animal that will foul his own nest."

No longer a wide-open boom town, Butte was a bustling metropolis, nevertheless, compared to Gibson. Luke reconciled himself to an overnight stay, a couple beers, a steak, a motel with cable television.

He wondered how Joe Springer spent his nights.

Rome, Italy

FOR TWO DAYS, RICH OSBORNE CONTINUED HIS DILIGENT SURveillance of the man called Hassan Kamateh. The subject did nothing that would suggest he was other than a visiting tourist enjoying the sights and sounds of Rome. He seemed determined to miss none of the city's delights before resuming his journey to Iran.

At midnight on Tuesday and Wednesday, Osborne was relieved by Douglas Hodges, a seedy mercenary with a shadowy past who was used occasionally by the chief of station for routine, free-lance assignments. Hodges smelled of body sweat and alcohol breath. His shirt—he wore the same one both nights—was soiled and wet with sweat. He wheezed when he had to undertake any physical activity, even walking. Osborne had an appalling vision of Hodges trying to follow Kamateh up the Spanish Steps, all 138 of them.

Rich Osborne could not understand why the chief used a free-lancer of Hodges's uncertain character. It had something to do with a Cold War escapade back in the early sixties, when both men had been stationed in Berlin. Loyalty was admirable, Osborne thought, but Hodges was a caricature of an undercover man. He was an embarrassment to the Agency.

On the first day, Hassan Kamateh emerged from his hotel at five in the afternoon—refreshed, presumably by a nap and a shower. Osborne, in contrast, was feeling sticky and tired from his vigil. Kamateh strolled along Via Condotti, Rome's posh shopping strip, just around the corner from his hotel. He lingered before the window displays at Ferragamo's and Gucci's and the other fashionable shops. Then he retraced his steps to the Piazza de Spagna, where he stopped to watch with silent amusement as an elderly man held up a small boy to drink from the Barcacci Fountain, designed by Bernini in the late sixteenth century. It was reputed to have the sweetest water in all of Rome.

Rich Osborne tailed the diminutive professor up the Spanish Steps, which were crowded on this sultry spring evening. The Spanish Steps were actually built by the French in the eighteenth century. They acquired their name from the Spanish embassy, then located at the bottom of the steps which led up the hill to the French church of Trinita dei Monti at the top. After absorbing the atmosphere of the old church, Kamateh strolled on into the Borghese Gardens and to the Pincio, where he paused to drink in the sweeping panorama of the entire city, dominated by the dome of St. Peter's off to the left.

As Rome bathed in the golden glow of sunset, the Iranian visitor, followed by the dogged Osborne, walked down the hill past a number of the fountains to the busy Piazza del Popolo. Unhurried, Kamateh stopped at Rosati, one of the popular, open-air cafés. He lingered over a drink while the colorful scene swirled around him—the cruising Maseratis, the young men in their silk shirts and balloon-leg pants, the elegant young women on display in their airy spring dresses. The Iranian had a ringside table for the evening *passeggiata;* Osborne stood at the bar, where the drinks were cheaper. The professor, he noted, seemed to have no concern about expenses.

They dined at separate tables that night at Nino's, a Tuscan restaurant on Via Borgognona not far from the Iranian's hotel. Though hungry after missing lunch, Osborne contented himself with the Francovich soup and some pasta. Kamateh dug into the house specialty, *bistecca alla florentina.* Thick T-bone steaks might be questioned on Osborne's expense chit.

The two men ambled back to the d'Inghilterra at midnight, a half block apart. Out of the corner of his eye, Osborne spotted Doug Hodges at a nearby café. Showing no awareness of the other agent's presence, Osborne watched Kamateh disappear into his hotel, then peeled off and retrieved his Alfa from a parking garage, swearing at the hostage fee he had to pay.

Wednesday was the same; only the sights were different. Again, Dr. Hassan Kamateh was the model conventional tourist. He began his day with an expensive breakfast at Babington's, a tearoom on the Piazza de Spagna. Later, he paid a ritual visit to St. Peter's Square; inside the Basilica of St. Peter's, he gazed rapturously at Michelangelo's *Pieta,* but ignored the cathedral's ornate and gilded interior.

Rich Osborne took over from Hodges at noon, just in time to accompany his subject to the gardens of Cucurucu overlooking the Tiber for lunch. Hassan Kamateh, who had a hearty appetite for a small man, ordered lamb and rabbit grilled over the open fire. Osborne settled for a salad.

In the spirit of the siesta, Kamateh scattered some seeds for the pigeons and dozed in the shade of one of the old umbrella pines in the Borghese Gardens, while his food digested. He returned to his hotel to freshen up—Osborne was feeling hot and sticky again—and emerged about six in the evening. Then he toured the shops on the wide, tree-lined Via Veneto, bought a pair of handmade Italian shoes at Ribot and stopped in Harry's Bar at the top of the road for a drink. Osborne was tempted to duck into the nearby American Embassy; he was becoming bored with Hassan Kamateh. But he thought better of it.

He bitched about the dull assignments to Doug Hodges before turning over the surveillance to him. This time they huddled briefly at Hodges's café table to compare notes. For Kamateh was scheduled to leave for Iran after the next shift. "I don't know why anyone's interested in this guy. My surveillance report reads like a tourist guide," grumped Osborne.

"What'd he do today?"

Osborne wondered if the chief knew that Hodges drank before going on the job. "The usual things." He gave a brief rundown, concluding, "Tonight we had dinner at Mastrostefano."

"What'd he order?"

"Seafood," Osborne answered, surprised by the question. "With curried rice."

Hodges licked his lips hungrily. "He must be on an expense account."

"Yeah," Osborne muttered. "How much do professors make, anyway?"

Hodges responded with a twisted smile. "What happened after dinner?"

Osborne shrugged. The overweight, perspiring free-lancer was beginning to annoy him even more than the little Iranian did. "He wandered around the piazza, admired the Church of St. Agnes, ordered some *tartufo* at Tre Scalini . . . picked up a woman."

"Ahhh," Hodges sighed appreciatively. "Where'd he pick up the woman?"

"At one of the bars there."

"On Navona?"

"Yeah."

"She come after him?"

"She was at one of the tables. Can't be sure who made the first move."

Hodges smiled again—an irritating twisted smile, Rich Osborne thought.

"He bought her a drink, they talked awhile. She came back to the hotel with him." Osborne glanced across the street toward the hotel. "She's still there . . . nothing worth putting in a report. Like I said, it's been a waste of time."

"He's put himself on display," Hodges said.

"Display?"

"He's made himself conspicuous . . . easy to follow."

Osborne swallowed a derisive retort. Leave it to the old Cold Warrior to manufacture intrigue where none existed.

"Well, you're welcome to him for the rest of the night. He's still booked on that flight to Tehran tomorrow?"

"That's what the ticket says."

"I'll be here at eleven, then, instead of noon."

"Fair enough," said Douglas Hodges. "Get some rest."

Osborne was tired after the long drudgery and he passed out when his head made contact with the pillow at about one o'clock in the morning. He awoke before dawn, feeling chilled in the darkness of his room. He couldn't help wondering whether he had missed something these past two days that an over-the-hill, whiskey-soaked free-lancer had detected easily.

On Thursday, the Iranian physics professor boarded a 12:30 P.M. Gulf Air flight for Tehran. Rich Osborne made himself part of the anonymous human flow at Fiumicino long enough to see him off, then returned to the embassy to write a detailed surveillance report in triplicate. He stayed at his desk into the evening, when the duty officer brought him a coded telex from Tehran.

Osborne typed the meaningless message into his word processor, activated the code, and read the translation printed out in green on his terminal screen.

The man listed as Hassan Kamateh, identity confirmed by description and flight manifest, had arrived at the Iranian capital on the Gulf Air flight from Rome. The CIA agent in place, who was of Iranian nationality, had made no attempt to follow Kamateh from the airport. The Agency lacked the manpower and the means for any more than the most urgent assignments in Iran. Kamateh had come to Tehran to join his wife and children, who had extended their Iranian vacation, and to visit his aging parents, who still lived in the city. Clearly, his visit was not a matter of great urgency.

Kamateh left the Tehran airport in a taxi and disappeared into the city.

Rich Osborne completed his report, thought again of Douglas Hodges, but dismissed a fleeting moment of unease.

He wondered whether it was too late in the evening to call Amy Turner.

Los Angeles

As dusk overtook Rome and Osborne waited for the telex from Tehran, it was still Thursday morning in Los Angeles. A man remarkably similar in size, complexion, hair color, and general description to the Iranian professor boarded a USAir shuttle to San Francisco. He arrived in time to make a leisurely connection with a Northwest Airlines departure for Helena, Montana.

No one paid attention to the quiet little man in the nonsmoking section, with the exception of a flight attendant. When she offered liquid refreshments, he was the only passenger who politely asked for tea.

Butte, Montana

T HE CHEVY PICKUP WAS READY, BRAKES INTACT, AT TEN o'clock Thursday morning. The sky was vast and blue and empty, except for a blazing sun that caused the air to shimmer above the highway. In the distance the High Plains stretched out, clear to the eye, for a hundred miles.

The mechanic in Butte had given the motor a minor tune-up without being asked—"It sounded a mite rough," he told Luke—and the pickup hummed over the highway with renewed vigor. Though the truck still transmitted each jolt in the road straight to the base of Luke's spine, it assaulted the highway with an authority that created a sense of security. Luke was developing an affection for the old truck, which had acquired a personality of its own. He decided it deserved a name more befitting a pickup of such character. Henceforth, he would call it "Old Brown," which somehow seemed to convey its brown, mud-splattered individuality.

Between his communion with his vehicle and the lure of open spaces, Luke Cameron was in no hurry to end the drive. At a junction with a road that connected to the northbound interstate, he impulsively headed Old Brown off the freeway along a narrow road that meandered southwest through mountainous heaps of rock alternating with verdant river valleys.

A small-town, roadside café offered a palatable hamburger, savory coffee, and the traditional homemade pie. Luke chose the apple—a Montana specialty.

His belly satisfied, Luke drove on—on into the afternoon like a miniature figure in a tiny toy truck under that brilliant, vaulting sky. Without focusing his mind on it, he understood in his heart that he was saying farewell to the place of his birth, perhaps never to return. An orphan now, he drifted across the broken landscape without direction or purpose.

In time, he approached the Wind Canyon Range, one of the knuckles on a great fist of the Rocky Mountains.

At an intersection with another north-south Montana state highway, Luke stopped short, wondering what subliminal sense of direction had brought him to this junction.

A north turn would take him back to Gibson in about two hours. The road, in fact, led past the Bar-C ranch. Journey's end, or beginning, depending on how you looked at it.

To the south was Wind Canyon—formed by a mountain stream that, over millennia, had cut its way between solid granite cliffs. Somewhere in those rugged hills, Luke suddenly remembered, was the Wind Canyon Mine.

The area was familiar to him. As a boy, he had hiked over these hills and fished for trout in Wind River. He had even explored some of the abandoned mine shafts that pockmarked the faces of the bluffs. Most of the mines dated back to the nineteenth century and, as Luke's father had never tired of telling him, posed the constant danger of cave-ins and trapped gases. The warnings had merely added to the thrill of wandering through the dusty, cobwebbed old shafts.

Every Montana boy knew the story of the four defeated prospectors who decided to abandon their search for a fortune in these mountains and were headed back toward their home in the South. Their journey brought them through a picturesque valley west of the Missouri appropriately called Prickly Pear Valley. Hell, they told themselves when they came upon a cut in the rugged terrain, let's give it one more try, long as we're here.

The gold they found in Last Chance Gulch was one of the richest bonanzas ever struck in the West, and the town that grew up around that mining camp was said to have more millionaires per capita among its citizens than any city in America. They named it Helena.

Oddly, it was copper, not gold or silver, that eventually came to rule Montana. But the story of Last Chance Gulch had kept prospectors and mining companies digging in the neighboring mountains for decades.

Wind Canyon, Luke recalled, had been one of the smaller strikes, abandoned early in this century.

Until now.

He thought he could find his way to the Wind Canyon Mine, but the warren of dirt roads and fire trails defeated him. After nearly an hour of backtracking that led nowhere, he nosed Old Brown up a narrow, corkscrewing road that climbed one of the steep hills. The canyon opened as he climbed. It offered a vista of rugged beauty, but it wasn't Wind Canyon. There was no stream at the bottom of the deep cleft in the hills.

Near the top, the twisting road leveled out onto a narrow strip of meadow. Looking across a deep gully, Luke saw the mouth of a mine shaft framed in weathered timbers. Above it rose a steep bluff that nudged the sky. The road was bad, rutted from runoffs and littered with fallen rocks. He growled ahead slowly, carefully around the head of the gully. The road ended in a loop—a small turnaround. But the twin ruts of an older trail led on another fifty yards to the abandoned mine he had spotted.

The rugged canyon was stark, silent, empty. There was life down there in the canyon, Luke knew, but it was watching and waiting, wary of his intrusion. As he hiked slowly up the grade toward the mine shaft, Luke tried to figure exactly where he was and how he had lost his way. The mine ahead wasn't the one he had been searching for.

He inspected the opening of the shaft. Even the bright afternoon sunlight on this western face of the mountain did not penetrate far into the gloom of the mine.

Luke had an emergency flashlight in the pickup. He would need it if he wanted to penetrate this old hole.

"You'll get yourself killed pokin' around in them shafts." Tom Cameron's warning echoed, a quarter century old.

As if mindful of that voice from the past, Luke turned away from the mine and followed an old animal trail that climbed to the top of the bluff, where he hoped to be high enough to get a fix on his location. The trail was steep. Though he was in good condition, he was laboring before he reached the crest.

He was a few feet short of it when the silence of the mountain was broken by an alien sound: the growl of a motor, also laboring.

Instinct caused Luke Cameron to approach the top of the bluff cautiously. It was bare rock, rounded on the west slope but sheared off to a steep drop on its eastern face.

Luke crawled up the rounded slope and peered over the rim.

About a quarter mile below him, some tin shacks were clustered on a narrow shelf near the opening of a mine. A car and a couple trucks were parked near the shacks. Some men were hauling wooden crates from one of the trucks into the mine. About a mile down the mountain from Luke's vantage point, another truck was grinding up a switchback road toward the mine.

Luke had found the Wind Canyon Mine.

Curiously, he watched the activity below, but he saw no evidence of mining. These people were moving something into the shaft, not bringing gold out. He guessed that the crates might contain mining equipment.

Then Luke saw something else of interest. About a hundred yards below his perch, sitting with his knees drawn up and a rifle at his side, a sentry commanded a view of the hills and anyone approaching Wind Canyon Mine from any direction except the sheer cliff that Luke had mounted from the rear.

The sentry, whose face was hidden by his wide-brimmed hat, lit a cigarette and casually flipped away the used match. *Wet the hot end, you son-of-a-bitch,* Luke thought with reflex anger. A fire in the dry brush of the canyon would torch this whole mountain.

As the sentry pushed to his feet, stretched, and turned his head, Luke ducked back out of sight.

A number of questions hurtled at him like darts of light, each one exploding in his brain.

Why armed guards? To protect the gold scrapings that might still be scratched out of the veins of this mountain? What equipment was being unloaded from those trucks? And were those the same trucks Tom Cameron had heard on the back roads at night? Like the one that had nearly run Luke down?

Had his father come here, as Luke had, to investigate what was going on at the Wind Canyon Mine?

What had Tom seen?

The questions reverberated in his head as Luke scrambled back down the western slope of the mountain. At the abandoned mine opening, he stopped. A fresh possibility nudged him. He studied the scratches and marks of birds and animals in the dust. No human footsteps here.

He guessed that his descent from the rim had brought him close to the level of the Wind Canyon Mine on the other side of the mountain.

On impulse, Luke hurried down to the pickup. He returned a few minutes later with the emergency flashlight. It had two bulbs—one for a red flasher, the other a powerful white beam.

He aimed the beam into the shaft, lighting up a gossamer of interlaced cobwebs. Brushing past the webs, Luke entered the mine.

He had explored many such shafts as a youth. What he had suddenly remembered was that mining companies in the old days would sometimes work both sides of a mountain, cutting into it from more than one direction. If Luke's hunch was correct, this abandoned shaft might have been sunk by the same people who worked the Wind Canyon Mine on the east face. The secondary bore would have been intended to cut through to the main shaft, in the hope of accessing new ore.

As Luke penetrated deeper into the mountain, the air became stale and musty. At one point, he had to crawl over the debris of a partial cave-in. His light poked into the blackness of the tunnel, playing over fallen rocks and dried-out wooden beams and braces. Here and there an abandoned shovel or pick lay on the floor, unrusted in the dry air.

The shaft angled downward, at times steeply, and, it seemed, endlessly. Luke was about ready to turn back when his light darted down a side shaft cut at right angles to the main bore. The light stopped against a wooden barrier.

There had been a cave-in here many years ago. The shaft supports had been buttressed, and planks had been nailed across the opening.

Luke glanced around uneasily, feeling the massive weight of the mountain pressing down.

He approached the wooden barrier cautiously, shutting off his flashlight and standing in total darkness. The blockage was not a solid wall. The planks had been nailed into place hastily, leaving wide gaps between them. Luke was sure he could tear the boards away with his bare hands. They had been erected merely as a warning.

A cool draft blew through the cracks and caressed his face.

The temptation to break through the barrier was overwhelming. He fought it off, remembering the sentry and his automatic rifle.

He was convinced this shaft cut through to the original dig. But how bad had the cave-in been? And if he should get through, what would he face? He didn't know how many men were inside the mine or how far they were from this spot. Some of them, like the sentry he had seen, might also be armed. It was not a situation to blunder into, brandishing a flashlight.

Luke Cameron left the shaft the way he had come. Emerging into the brightness of late afternoon, he was almost blinded by the light. He rubbed his eyes and breathed deeply, inhaling a lungful of fresh air, feeling the crushing mass of the mountain lifted from him.

He bounced along the back roads toward Gibson deep in thought, carrying a burden of unanswered questions that seemed as heavy as the mountain.

His father's letter had taken a new hold on him.

In the kitchen of the Cameron ranch house, Micheline Picard stared at the words she had written in her precise, convent-school handwriting. "Our American venture is on the brink of success. There is great enthusiasm here for your products, and the initial sales have been completed as we had hoped. We anticipate an early fulfillment of our goals. . . . "

The men who would read her report were paranoid about the possible interception or censorship of any message from America. They held this country in awe and in contempt at the same time. Where America was concerned, they were startlingly naive—unrealistic, unworldly, unable to . . .

She broke off the thought.

Impulsively, she crushed the sheet of paper into a ball and brushed it aside. It would be wiser, she thought, to report an actual success rather than an anticipated success. Meanwhile, the outlook was favorable. The only unpredictable element was Luke Cameron—and he would soon be gone.

She rose from the kitchen table and paced restlessly through the quiet downstairs rooms. It was a warm evening, and she undid the top buttons of her blouse. Kali would be shocked, she reflected; no

Iranian woman would display any part of her breasts, even in her own home.

An image of the damp, cold stone walls of the convent intruded—so far in her past, yet so near in her memory. The feelings of a small girl, alone, abandoned, returned with a rush. Shivering in the early morning. Herded to chapel with the other girls for morning mass. The nuns hushing the giggling babble. Then the clear, high voices rising in unison in the chill air.

The rush of memories caused an involuntary quiver. *How could her father have left her there?*

The tall clock in the hallway chimed. She remembered Luke Cameron's face as he listened to the clock, the softening expression in his eyes.

Again, Micheline shivered, not with cold.

The house was permeated by the American's presence. Upstairs, in the room where he had stayed, the scent of him lingered. In the bath, she saw the image of his lean hard body as he stepped from the shower onto the mat. On the stairs, she heard the clump of his boots. In the kitchen, she watched his strong, scarred hands engulf a coffee mug. Even in the empty rooms, she sensed his powerful physical presence, heard his voice, felt his eyes upon her.

She hated the weakness that such feelings betrayed. She had stifled them ruthlessly in the past, sublimated them to her dedication to the real purpose in her life—a burning desire to make herself worthy in the eyes of her father, that commanding, intimidating, terrifying figure for whom she would willingly give her life.

The specter of Cameron would fade, she told herself, now that he had departed for his distant jungle. She was relieved, she tried to convince herself, that she was rid of his disconcerting presence. Better to . . .

She stood motionless in the kitchen doorway. Stared out the window intently as headlights slashed across the yard. Felt her heart begin to pound. She wanted to turn, to flee up the stairs. She knew instinctively who it was.

A car door clunked shut. Footsteps thumped up the back porch steps. She hadn't moved since hearing the sound of the engine and watching the headlights dance into view. Her eyes were fixed on the back door. It was locked, but a key turned noisily in the lock.

Luke Cameron stepped into the kitchen.

The isolation of the ranch house had pleased her. She had no need of company, no desire for visitors. But suddenly that isolation had become a danger; it had left her vulnerable.

"Mr. Cameron! I . . . I thought you had left. . . ."

"Luke," he reminded her gently.

"But I . . . I don't understand. Why . . . why are you here?" The question faltered. A tremor in her voice betrayed her.

"I saw the light," he said, as if that were a complete explanation. "I was heading back to town. . . . Been over to Butte. . . . On business . . ."

None of it mattered. Both knew he had come to the house because she was there, because of what had happened between them, if only for a moment. She was part of what held him in Gibson. How? Why? He was not yet sure.

She hadn't realized how much she had been aroused by her thoughts of Cameron until he was standing there in the kitchen, just a few feet away, looking down at her. She felt the electricity flowing like a live current between them. Her mind warned her against what was happening, but she could no longer trust her body.

Once, when she was sixteen, one of her black-robed teachers, a man she had looked up to, a man of God, had entered her room unexpectedly, invading her privacy late at night, much as Luke Cameron had arrived tonight. She had been surprised but not frightened. A girl, trusting. He had bent over her to see what she had been reading at her desk. Smiling in approval, he had patted her arm, and let his hand rest on her shoulder. She had smelled his breath, the rotten odor of bad teeth.

Then he was pawing her. His long, harsh beard scraped against her chin as his lips sought hers. His breathing was quick and ragged. His callused hand groped under her robe and closed cruelly over a small, firm breast. She was instantly overcome with disgust and fear. She felt violated and betrayed.

She squirmed free and flung herself across the small room. The tall, narrow window behind her was open. She was a slim girl, the window was wide enough. It overlooked a cobbled street three stories below. Her eyes were wild, desperate. "Don't come near me! If you touch me again . . ."

She edged closer to the open window.

Her warning cry penetrated the haze of the man's passion. To continue meant death for her and disaster for him.

He had assigned her to another tutor after that. Though neither of them had ever spoken again of the incident, her hatred of him smoldered silently, understood between them, requiring no words.

When Luke Cameron's hands took her shoulders, she felt not revulsion but a thawing of resistance, an abandonment of reason. *It is too dangerous, I must be careful.*

But her lips responded to his, parting, as soft and eager now as they had once been stiff and reluctant. Her body was like hot wax.

Luke awoke to the reveille of a distant rooster. Slowly reality began to seep back into the house with the gray light of early morning. The doubts that had given way to the dreams of the previous nightfall now rushed back.

He felt the warmth of Micheline Picard's sleek body beside his own, curled in sleep. Her back was toward him, her hair a small dark nest against the pillow. Soft and delicate on the outside, a core of steel within. There had been a part of her he had never penetrated, a secret inner person as yet unexplored.

He slipped quietly from under the blanket's warmth, shivering reflexively at the touch of cooler air. The warmth of a Montana summer evening didn't prepare you for the dawn's chill, when ice might form on an oar dipped into a mountain stream.

Dressing hastily, he started for the stairs, moving noiselessly, carrying his boots in one hand.

In the bedroom doorway, he paused to look back. The Frenchwoman had not stirred; the slender figure under the covers was still turned away from him. Yet he sensed that she was awake.

Like himself, he thought, she chose the refuge of silence. What had happened between them last night had happened. But Luke's troubling questions remained unanswered.

He wondered what questions tormented her as she lay still in the bed.

He crept downstairs, pulled his boots on in the dimness of the kitchen, and let himself out into the yard.

For a moment, he stood on the porch steps, feeling absurdly like a fugitive. But the silence had been a mutual pact, he thought, like the reckless passion that preceded it.

He fired up Old Brown and nosed her down the long gravel road to the highway, wondering if it was for the last time.

Kali was in the kitchen, waiting for her, when Micheline Picard descended the stairs.

She wrapped her thin robe about her, unconsciously tightening the cord belt in a protective gesture. She could see the barely controlled outrage in Kali's flared nostrils, the red slash of his mouth behind his beard, the blazing eyes.

"You've been spying on me," she said coldly, speaking in Farsi, a language in which she was also fluent.

"You have betrayed our cause—the cause of Allah!"

"I have done nothing of the kind. Do not talk like a fool!"

"If I talk like a fool, you act like a whore!"

She struck swiftly, without warning, her fingernails leaving thin trails of blood where they raked his cheek. Never had Kali been struck by a woman—never! His hand leaped to the knife carried in a sheath attached to his belt. But the woman, who had come downstairs wearing only a robe loosely tied, quite obviously naked beneath it, dipped a hand into the large pocket of the robe as Kali bared the steel of his blade.

The gun, suddenly appearing in her hand, stopped him. It was a small automatic pistol—the one she normally carried in her purse—but the black hole at the end of the muzzle looked large and ugly.

Kali trembled in his rage, but in the woman's eyes he saw a fire as hot as his own. Behind the hot eyes was a pitiless coldness that Kali recognized and understood.

The knife receded into its sheath.

"You have no right!" hissed Kali.

"I have every right. I command here. It is you who will obey. You have received your orders. It shouldn't be necessary to repeat them."

"The man Cameron is our enemy . . . a dangerous enemy. He threatens our sacred mission. And you bed with him!"

"What I do is not for you to question . . . not for you to understand," she answered icily. "I will decide if Cameron is a threat. I will decide how to deal with him. Your spying eyes have led you to the edge of danger. You will obey, not question. You will attend to your mission, not to mine."

"And you will answer to the Imam," Kali whispered hoarsely.

"Yes . . . but not to you. Is that not yet clear?"

Kali did not reply, his silence sullen.

"If you call me a whore again, or question my devotion to our cause, it is you, Kali, who will face the wrath of the Grand Ayatollah. The mission will continue without you."

"You would not . . . !"

"I would do it as easily as I would swat a fly. You do not matter . . . I do not matter. Only Islam matters."

The words struck Kali in the gut like bullets from her handgun. He struggled to control his rage and humiliation. To be made subservient to a woman—to suffer such humiliation before her—was almost unbearable. It was equally hard for him to understand.

Because of his schooling in America and his devotion to the ayatollah, Kali had been assigned to seek out a potential traitor who worked at the Rocky Flats Plant near Golden, Colorado, which processed plutonium for nuclear weapons. A promising effort had failed when the intended recruit reported Kali's overtures to superiors. The anguished Kali learned about his betrayal just in time to effect a hasty disappearance from Golden.

He had been directed next to Gibson, Montana. Upon his arrival, he had been shocked to find a woman in command—even more astonished to discover that the mission had originated with this woman in Paris. She was the one who had conceived and planned this bold thrust of the knife into the heart of the Great Satan. This mere woman, this petite female, was in complete command of an operation that would build the ultimate weapon from ingredients stolen from nuclear installations in the United States and the Soviet Union. She was in charge of an effort that had already penetrated strategic weapons storage sites in Colorado, New Mexico, Pennsylvania, and Soviet Armenia.

The Frenchwoman, Kali learned, had received her indoctrination in France, where the great Khomeini had spent many years in exile and had developed a large following. Unaccountably, the woman had become a revolutionary leader in France, where the Party of Allah was strong. Her plan came to the attention of Khomeini himself, who not only approved it but entrusted the implementation to her—to Kali's utter astonishment. She had recruited devoted, English-speaking Islamic followers to search for weaknesses in America's nuclear arsenal, and she had enlisted Russian-speaking counterparts for a similar mission in the Soviet Union.

Kali found everything about this infuriating, disconcerting female to be an affront—even her beauty, which fired unwanted desire in him. To a radical Shiite fundamentalist such as Kali, a woman's role was decreed by God. Khomeini himself had said it! A decent woman covered herself from head to toe when she was in public. The chador assured that her hair and face would not be seen. She wore subdued colors; she eschewed makeup and other Western decadences such as plucking eyebrows and shaving legs—legs that should never be displayed in public. An Islamic woman wore perfume only at the request of her husband, for his pleasure alone.

The Frenchwoman had been trained in the faith. Yet she defied all of this. She had sold her soul to the devil. She had displayed, even flaunted, her body before the eyes of all. Her Western clothes, in forbidden hues of bright red and blue and yellow; her uncovered face; her eyes made large with makeup; the scent that hovered about her and inflamed a man's blood—all of this violated everything that Kali believed and felt about women. They were the actions of one who belonged not in the City of Faith but in *Dar al-Harb,* the place of the infidels, the City of War.

And yet everything she did, Kali had been firmly informed, was necessary.

She had been chosen by the Imam himself for this mission.

The woman had brought no recruits to Gibson from France. The field workers and trench diggers on the Halston place, like the guards in the mine, were part of Khomeini's Revolutionary Guard. Their faces were unknown to any intelligence agency; there was no record of their fingerprints in the computerized terrorist files of Interpol. They had been gathered up in Iran, trained in the hot desert camps, slipped without difficulty into Canada, and filtered across remote outposts of the western Canadian-American border into Montana. Like Kali, they were volunteers for a mission that promised great honor—perhaps even the ultimate glory of martyrdom.

Kali was not one of them; his revolutionary development had been quite different. He was older, better educated, better trained. He had been selected for this mission by his teacher in Tehran. His full name was Rahmat-Allah Kali. He had grown up in relative affluence in Tehran and in New York City. His father was a businessman who, like most of his class, had cooperated with the shah's democratic reforms in the 1960s and 1970s. It was a time of controversial change in the country, producing a volatile clash between older cultural values and the shah's twentieth-century ideas.

Business had taken the family to New York during Kali's adolescence. As a stranger in Long Island's public schools, he had sometimes been teased and humiliated. He had welcomed the family's return to Tehran.

During the seventies, Kali had been radicalized at the University of Tehran by the ferment of resistance to authority—especially to the shah's Savak, the hated secret police. He had become converted to the Islamic revolution after reading the fiery pamphlet called *"Kashfal-Asrar,"* written by Ruhollah Khomeini when he was a rising rebellious mullah in Qom many years earlier. Khomeini's "Key to the Secrets" was a call for a return to fundamental Islamic tradition and a violent rejection of all Westernisms advocated by the shah.

During the turbulent decade leading up to the revolution, the Imam's words—spread in smuggled writings from his exile at Al-Hajaf in Iraq and later from France, proclaimed in taped messages delivered to a Soviet courier and broadcast over a clandestine radio station near the Soviet-Iranian border, repeated by sympathetic mullahs in their Friday sermons—fueled the resistance to the Pahlavi government and the shah's reforms.

Kali's parents had sent him back to America for further studies, hoping to extricate him from Tehran's radical atmosphere. He was studying at the University of California in Berkeley when Khomeini launched his Islamic Revolution in 1979.

Abandoning his studies, Kali rushed home to Iran, eager to enlist in the *jihad,* the holy war against the enemies of Islam. He joined the Party of Allah, which had been revived by Khomeini and which soon embraced all disparate Islamic fundamentalist and terrorist groups under a single leader. Their slogan became "Only one Party, the Party of Allah; only one leader, Ruhollah!"

Khomeini's crowd-enrapturing orations struck a deep chord in the Iranian psyche. His appeal was hypnotic; it incited a worshipful hysteria that ran amok and dislocated Tehran.

Kali joined fervently in the bedlam. He fought in the streets with youthful revolutionaries—armed at first with knives, clubs, acid, and firebombs, then with guns. He rejoiced in the overthrow and exile of the hated American puppet, Pahlavi. He shouted in triumph at the humiliations of the mighty Satan, culminating in the detention of the American hostages in their own embassy.

In the turmoil that followed the revolution, Kali was singled out for special training. The first terrorist school for the *Goruh Zarbat*—Khomeini's strike force of urban terrorist guerrillas—opened in a former nurses' training school in the suburbs of Tehran, nestled among the shade trees of Manzariah Park, home of three of the shah's summer palaces and, during Pahlavi's reign, the site of international Boy Scout jamborees. Instead of teaching how to relieve suffering and save lives, the new Niavaran training camp offered a different curriculum. A faculty of skilled Cuban and North Korean killers and saboteurs taught the grim arts of assassination, sabotage, and hijacking. The pernicious instruction was supplemented with intense ideological indoctrination. Kali had been a good student.

For the first graduating class, Khomeini himself had given an audience. Like the other graduates, Kali had received an armband, the *ta'awidh,* which he always wore under his shirt, and a small square of cloth that had been cut from one of the Imam's turbans. They were his most precious possessions.

For the holy man whose patch of cloth Kali carried, he would give his all—even his life. A suicide course had been part of his training at the Niavaran terrorist school.

Not long after graduation, Kali had utilized his new skills on the firing line against Iraq. He had returned from the battlefront with an injured leg, ripped by shrapnel. While his leg mended, he had been assigned as an instructor at a Revolutionary Guard training camp at Saleh-Abad, north of Qom.

Then had come his big assignment; he had been chosen to strike a massive blow at the Great Satan. Because of his familiarity with American customs and idiom, he had been sent to America on a secret, sacred mission. It would bring glory to him, if not in this life, then in the next.

Not until he had come to Gibson after his failure in Colorado had he discovered that his mysterious superior was a woman. This was not a joke; Ruhollah Khomeini was not a frivolous man. The orders had come from the Imam himself; his authority was absolute. In Kali's mind, Khomeini embodied Allah's will on earth.

"Kulunna Khomeini," he murmured, as if the words came of their own force, without his will. "We are all Khomeini."

The Frenchwoman fixed him with a long, silent stare. Then she nodded. "So be it."

Quick as a cat, she slipped her weapon back into the pocket of her robe. Calmly, she filled the coffeepot with water. The pot gurgled noisily as it completed its automatic brewing cycle. Micheline Picard waited in silence, relaxed, then poured herself a mug and carried it over to the table. She did not pour for Kali, who wanted coffee but hesitated to serve himself.

"Coffee?" she asked. "You may help yourself. It has not been poisoned by my touch."

Slowly, uncertainly, Kali sidled over to the coffeepot. The woman smiled thinly. "Understand me, Kali. I will say this once only. I know you would gladly die in the service of Allah. I would do even more. I would bed a man, without love."

"This man—"

"Knows nothing . . . I will deal with him." Her eyes turned cold and menacing. "You will stay away from him, is that understood?"

"But he is suspicious. He tries to investigate his father's death. . . ."

"He would have nothing to investigate if you had not killed the old man," she blazed. "The killing was unnecessary. It could have attracted attention. It could have aroused suspicion. Now I must divert the son from stirring up trouble for us. . . . The professor? . . . He has left Los Angeles, is it not so?"

"He is in Helena. He arrived last night. I will take him to the mine later today."

"You have served well, Kali. . . . The other American, McAlister, is your responsibility. Leave Luke Cameron to me."

Kali remained silent, which would indicate acquiescence. The Islamic tradition of *taqiya* justified his silence although it meant deceiving the woman. The code sanctioned even deliberate falsehood if the deceit was committed for a higher purpose.

Let the woman think what she would.

Kali had his own agenda.

Baku, the Caucasus

"**P**RAISE IS TO ALLAH," THE YOUNG MAN SAID.
Sergei Milov, disdainfully sniffing the smells that filled the small, stuffy room, had not come for a religious discussion. "Tell me about Abu Hasir."

A shrug of thin shoulders. "What is to say? I know nothing."

The young man's name was Mohammad Yavlevi. The dingy room was his kitchen, bedroom, and living space. It was an anonymous building in a complex on the north side of Baku. It was favored by oil field workers and their families, but Yavlevi worked on the railroad—in the same Baku railroad yard as Abu Hasir. The two had been seen together at a local mosque.

Like the late Hasir, Mohammad Yavlevi was a Shiite fundamentalist. Unlike Hasir, he was not an Iranian but a native Azerbaijani. Studying the young man, Milov thought he detected something else different about Yavlevi, something missing from his eyes: the fanaticism of the true martyr.

"You were friends. You were coreligionists. You talked about striking a blow for Islam against the Motherland." Milov did not make it a question.

"That is not so. We never spoke of such things."

"You work in the dispatch office at the railroad yard, is it not true?"

"Yes."

"You have access to shipping information."

"It is my job."

"Including military shipments."

"No," Yavlevi replied quickly. "Those are different. They do not go through our procedures."

Milov smiled. "But you know of them," he said in a confidential tone. "There are ways, aren't there? A car diverted from its route, a delay in linkups, a change in normal time schedules, priority shipments . . . You would notice these things."

Yavlevi hesitated. Yakov Zagorsky shifted his weight, a shoe scraping on the gritty floor, and the young man's eyes darted apprehensively toward Milov's companion.

"You know of them, and you informed Abu Hasir."

"It is not so!"

"What other shipments did you report?"

"I know nothing of such things."

Milov appraised the young Shiite silently, then circled him in his chair. Yavlevi's eyes followed him. "Did you meet Hasir in Paris?" The question was conversational. "Or were you already friends?"

"I . . . I have never been to Paris."

Milov smiled. "That is a foolish lie, Yavlevi. I have been patient with your lies. They are only to be expected. But that is a stupid lie. There are passport stamps, customs records that can easily be checked. We know that you were in Paris at the same time Hasir was there. Do you now wish to tell me the truth?"

"I know nothing. . . ."

Milov kicked the chair from under him. The young Azerbaijani spilled onto his back. His head struck the leg of a wooden table. He lay on his back like an overturned beetle, legs in the air, unable to right himself.

Milov kicked him cruelly in the groin. Yavlevi's howl of pain was inaudible, shut off by the blow that had provoked it, though his mouth remained open in agony. His eyes bulged and there was blood on his lips. He had bitten his tongue.

"Tell me about Paris," Milov said. "I can wait."

An hour later Milov delivered Mohammad Yavlevi to Baku's militia major, who placed him under formal arrest. The specific charge would be determined; it would, of course, involve illegal acts against the state.

It was night. The fresh air off the Caspian Sea was welcome after the rancid confines of Yavlevi's grubby room. The breeze was stiff, as usual. Most large buildings in Baku were constructed, like Mohammad Yavlevi's apartment building, with the small end toward the sea. They were never built broadside to the winds.

Despite the spirited breeze, the temperature was mild. Milov reflected that there were more people out strolling at night than would be seen in Moscow. Kirov Park was crowded with speechmakers and demonstrators, ignored by the militia, a tribute to the remarkable changes in the Soviet Union under Gorbachev's *perestroika*.

Milov walked leisurely beside Sergeant Zagorsky, who prudently kept silent. At last Milov said, "There are many sins committed in the name of religion."

"Yes, Comrade Captain."

"What have we learned here, Yakov?"

"I am not certain. . . . "

"The Shiite fundamentalists mounted an attempt to steal a nuclear demolition device or devices from a rail car in transit. Mohammad Yavlevi is an assistant dispatcher in the Baku railroad office. He had access to information about such shipments, and he was an associate of Abu Hasir. So . . ."

"He informed Hasir of the shipment."

"Yes, and this information was communicated to Hasir only . . . to assure that Yavlevi did not know anyone else in the cell."

"You do not think he held back names?"

"He told us all he knew," said Milov dryly.

"Then we have come to a dead end."

"Not exactly a dead end, Yakov. What else did he tell us?"

"There was nothing . . ."

"Paris," said Milov.

"Paris? Yes, he said he had been recruited in Paris where he also met Hasir."

"Recruited in Paris . . . but by whom?"

"I am not sure . . ."

"He spoke of a woman, Yakov. A daughter of Allah whose Islamic fire burned hotter than any man's."

"A woman who used only a code name."

"Ah, yes! But a woman who set him on fire."

Yakov Zagorsky shrugged. "How much can we learn about Mohammad Yavlevi's crimes by investigating his love affairs?"

"Yavlevi did not speak of her captivating beauty," Milov reminded him. "No, it was not her seductive appeal that impressed Comrade Yavlevi. He spoke only of her passion for the service of Allah."

Their stroll in the night had brought them along Communist Street to Nizami Square, with its statue of the Persian poet, the most celebrated in Azerbaijanian literary history. Shortly beyond it was bustling Kirov Prospekt. Suddenly Milov realized he was famished. "Let us eat," he said to his sergeant. "The Shirvan is just ahead. Have you tried their *yarikh dalmasy?*"

"No, Comrade Captain." Zagorsky did not say what he was thinking: That his pay was insufficient for him to dine in fine restaurants.

"Then it's time you did. It's Grecian-style, you know, the meat and pilaf wrapped in grape leaves. And the red wine is excellent."

"Yes, Captain." Zagorsky hoped that Captain Milov planned to pick up the check.

"Afterwards," Milov said, spotting the Shirvan Restaurant across the way and quickening his pace, "our real work begins."

Yakov Zagorsky, who had hoped his long working day was over, hesitated to ask. "What are we looking for next?"

"I am curious, Comrade . . . how many Shiite fundamentalists, now available to us in Azerbaijan, have spent time in Paris during the past year? Or the past two years?"

"Not many, I would think."

"And how many, do you suppose, were recruited for their glorious cause by a fiery woman?"

"A woman?" Vitaly Yurevich Novikoff repeated with an ironic smile. "With you, Sergei Andreyevich, it is always a woman."

When Milov and Zagorsky finished their leisurely dinner and returned to his KGB offices on Oilworkers Boulevard, the captain was astonished to find Novikoff sitting behind his desk, feet propped up, eyes closed as if he were dozing. When they entered the office, Novikoff's eyes popped open. For someone who had been napping, he seemed wide awake.

"If I had known you were coming, Colonel," Milov said, "I would have met you. . . ."

"No, no." Novikoff waved off the protestations. "The trip was quite sudden. You had no warning."

The trip had been too sudden, apparently, for Novikoff to change clothes. In his woolen suit, he was overdressed for this southern climate.

Milov sent Zagorsky to fetch a bottle of vodka and some glasses. Colonel Novikoff beamed. When they were alone, he said, "You have had a useful evening, Captain?"

"Yes, Colonel. Yavlevi was very helpful."

"And you think the Paris connection . . . this woman . . . could be significant?"

"Yes."

"Hmmm. So do I, Sergei Andreyevich. So do I." He glanced around Milov's spartan office with its beige painted walls and government furniture of steel and plastic. But the view to the south, of mountains rising abruptly from the sea, was spectacular even at night.

After delivering the vodka and glasses, Yakov Zagorsky went off to initiate the tedious process of collecting passport records. Alone, Milov and the colonel settled down to vodka and tactics. Milov reviewed his interrogation of Mohammad Yavlevi in detail. At the end he said, "It seems clear that the Iranians were behind the aborted theft."

"Is not Yavlevi an Azerbaijanian?"

"He is a Shiite extremist. He is dedicated to Ayatollah Khomeini and his Islamic Revolution."

"And this woman in Paris? Is she Iranian?"

"French . . . Iranian . . . Arabic . . . we cannot be sure. But what woman would inspire young men like Hasir and Yavlevi?"

"She must be an extraordinary woman," Novikoff agreed. He remained silent, reflecting. He liked Milov's logic—and his vodka. He held out his glass for a refill. The colonel's capacity was remarkable, as Milov knew from experience.

"You knew, of course, that the Iranian National Front was based in Paris in the 1970s. It was there that Khomeini's revolution was nurtured. But do you know what France was called during that period?"

"No, Colonel Novikoff."

"The Land of Asylum. It was a mecca, if I may use the word metaphorically in this context, for political exiles of every description—the Baader-Meinhoff Gang, Italy's Red Brigades, the Japanese Red Army, the Palestinian European Directorate—the group headed by Ilyich Ramirez Sanchez; Carlos, he calls himself—the Turkish People's Liberation Army—all the revolutionary movements.

"The ayatollah was there for two periods—when he was first exiled from Iran in 1964, and later when he was banished from Iraq. For a time, the Iranians shared a villa in a Paris suburb with Carlos. And we supported Khomeini during that period. He was useful to us." Novikoff frowned. "And we were enormously useful to Khomeini."

"We bankrolled his revolution?"

"Yes," said Novikoff with a wry smile. "And I was his banker."

The KGB colonel became expansive as he recalled his role in bringing down the pro-American government in Iran. He spoke of the tumultuous times when Iran, with its vast oil reserves, was a most valuable pawn in the world chess game. An exotic old bird, named Mohammed Mossadegh, had risen to power. He showed the advantage of being ugly, Novikoff suggested with a chuckle. For Mossadegh was ugly—frail, hairless, wrinkled, banana-nosed. He bore this unfair burden up through Iran's chaotic politics, weeping in public, perpetually on the verge of feigned or actual collapse, until he got a hold on Iranian emotions and drove the shah off the Peacock Throne. This had to bespeak the inner superiority that unkind fate can nurture—the compensating enlargement of brains, tenacity, and guile that Mossadegh employed to triumph over his physiognomy. The colonel laughed out loud at his own analysis.

But Mossadegh's wits were no match for the CIA's power, Novikoff recalled ruefully. The CIA reacted swiftly. Mossadegh was overthrown by a street uprising with the not-so-covert aid of CIA agents, and the shah was safely reinstalled.

The chess match, though, was not over, and the KGB played it with more subtlety and skill, Novikoff boasted. He had then been assigned to the IV Division, which was responsible for the Arab network. The Iranians, of course, were not Arab but Indo-European. But geography was given precedence over genealogy, and Iran was counted, for the KGB's purpose, as Arab.

The colonel recounted nostalgically how he had recruited an Iranian, named Musavi Khoiniha, who had studied at the Patrice Lumumba University in Moscow. Khoiniha became a trusted "agent of influence," who joined Khomeini's movement and gained the personal confidence of the ayatollah. For the years 1965 to 1975, Khoiniha had shuttled between Baghdad and Leipzig. Novikoff would meet Khoiniha in East Germany two or three times a month to exchange suitcases. Khoiniha brought back to the ayatollah a suitcase packed with cash to finance his revolution. Novikoff carried tapes of the ayatollah's sermons to the Soviet-Iranian border, where they were beamed across the border to Iran. These were inflammatory sermons that not only stirred his followers but gave them secret, coded instructions, Novikoff chortled.

In 1975, the shah brought pressure on Iraq to oust Khomeini, who transferred the operation to Paris. Since this was a more agreeable place, Novikoff often carried his own suitcase to Paris.

"I went once a month, Milov."

"And you delivered the funds yourself?"

"Not caviar to tempt the Parisian ladies, Milov. Money. Rubles for the revolution. Money for the Iranian mullahs."

Money that brought Khomeini to power. Khomeini launched the final stage of his revolution from his Paris base. Now after ten years of bloodletting, Milov thought, Khomeini turned against those who had helped him.

"You met Khomeini?"

"Many times. A charismatic man. But I sensed that he hated us. He hated us, but he needed us."

"I believe he was behind this nuclear theft in Baku."

"It's possible, Sergei Andreyevich. Now we must make sure. A large Iranian revolutionary presence still exists in Paris. You say both Hasir and Yavlevi were recruited there. You say both were influenced by this woman. An Iranian Joan of Arc, eh, Milov?"

"Joan of Arc . . . ?"

"Ah, again you betray a deficiency in religious history, my friend. She was a French martyr who rallied the people to follow her, and was burned at the stake for her pains." The colonel suddenly brought his palm down hard against the top of Milov's desk. "We must find this Iranian woman. If Khomeini is behind her, and thus behind this attempted theft, we must know it. And there is only one good way to find out."

"Yes, Comrade Colonel?"

"You will go to Paris, Milov." Novikoff tossed off his vodka and studied the glass as if he could find meaning in the droplets remaining, as a soothsayer reads tea leaves. "Every young man should go to Paris once, Sergei Andreyevich. I envy you. But please, my friend . . . This hot-blooded Parisian lady is not to be courted. She is the enemy."

Helena, Montana

AFTER SPENDING A SLEEPLESS NIGHT IN A MOTEL OFF THE highway in Helena, the true Dr. Hassan Kamateh was picked up by an Iranian driving a jeep. The driver called himself Kali.

The two men traveled south and then east. Soon they left the city behind and entered a mountainous, unpopulated wilderness that reminded Kamateh of Iran, of the rugged beauty of the Elburz Mountains north of Tehran. They drove in hostile silence. Eventually Kamateh broke it to ask politely, "How far are we going?"

"You'll know when you get there."

Kamateh had not expected courtesy or even civility. He was, after all, being blackmailed by religious zealots.

He had been approached in March by an Iranian, a scowling, black-jowled man, who spoke with earnest ferocity about the Khomeini revolution. He accused Kamateh of betraying his Iranian heritage and making a pact with the devil. There was need for nuclear scientists in Iran; he should be serving Allah, not the Great Satan, the man said.

This dark and gloomy stranger had appeared at Kamateh's door one night, asking to come in. When Kamateh hesitated, the man said, "I have word of your family."

Even in that instant, Kamateh had felt a tremor of fear. He had allowed the man to enter his apartment. Inside, the man glanced around with contempt for the luxury he beheld. "Your family will not return from Iran," he said, without preamble.

"What . . . what are you saying?"

"They will not be permitted to leave. What happens to them depends upon your cooperation."

"They have done no wrong. I have done no wrong. You have no right!"

"We have every right. We are the Party of Allah, and we are at war."

"At war? What does this have to do with me?"

"You are either with us or against us. If you are against us, this means you would let Islam die."

"No, no, no . . . I am not involved."

"You are now," the stranger said fiercely.

He summarized Hassan Kamateh's situation in stark terms. His wife and children had not been harmed, but their future safety depended on Kamateh's willingness to serve Allah. If he did as he was directed, his family would be returned to him. If he did not, he would not see them again. Simple as that.

At first the alternative seemed unthinkable, more horrifying to a nuclear scientist than the terrorizing of his wife and children. These fanatics intended to steal the materials necessary to build a nuclear bomb. Hassan Kamateh was essential to their plans.

He was to assemble the bomb.

Over the next few weeks, the plight of his family—verified by pleading notes from his wife and his daughter—escalated in his tormented mind. Their predicament came to seem more terrible, the alternative less so. What was asked of him, after all, was a problem in physics. Others could solve the problem if he would not. He was not asked to *invent* the damn bomb, just to *assemble* it.

The bizarre nature of the proposal removed it so far from reality that it seemed less alarming. He persuaded himself that the terrorists would never be able to collect all of the necessary ingredients. Meanwhile, he could stall them, or merely pretend to acquiesce.

That was two months ago. Reluctantly, Kamateh had supplied list after list of the materials he would need—lists that his blackmailers verified from other sources. Whenever he tried to omit something, the fanatic Iranian would challenge him . . . and renew the threats.

Now he was being driven to this remote location in the mountains of Montana, to a place where the ingredients for a bomb had been brought. The horror he had mentally rejected had caught up with him. It was happening. The nightmare was real. He thought of the phony Hassan Kamateh, the look-alike who had assumed his identity and carried his passport. Foreign nationals working in the nuclear field were kept under discreet surveillance when they traveled outside the country. His captors had not wanted the real Kamateh's disappearance to arouse unwanted attention. The double should be landing in Tehran about now, ostensibly for a summer vacation with his family.

In an area of craggy brown hills, treeless except at their heights, the jeep began to climb a twisting mountain road. The rutted surface was studded with rocks. The vehicle bounced and rocked, jostling its passengers. Kamateh grabbed on to a panic bar.

Not far from the top of the mountain, the road wound around a deep gorge and suddenly leveled out. A cluster of tin mining shacks appeared on a long, narrow shelf. Nearby was the timber-framed opening of a mine.

Several young men appeared out of nowhere to stare curiously at the arriving stranger. Most of them wore the white shirts and pants of Iranian peasants. But some were dressed in Western jeans and shirts.

Several carried guns.

They were all, Kamateh guessed, Iranians.

Not one of them appeared to be twenty years old. Children of Allah. Ayatollah Khomeini's Allah. Uneducated children enlisted in a fanatical cause.

Most of them grinned as they clustered around him. Kali shouldered his way through them and led Kamateh into the mine. The shaft was illuminated by lights strung along the top. After a short descent and a right-angle turn, they entered a large, high-ceilinged cave.

Hassan Kamateh stared in growing astonishment.

What he saw, so incongruous in the bowels of this mountain, bathed in the harsh brightness of rows of overhead fluorescent lights, was the rough laboratory he had sketched for his Iranian contact in Los Angeles. Along one wall were the separate workrooms he had prescribed, heavily reinforced in concrete. There were the work tables, high-fidelity monitoring equipment, a heavy-duty lathe and drill, CCTV scanners, a computer, remote-handling equipment still in boxes, mazes of electrical wiring, and, set off at the far end of the cave, a large ceramic funace.

Kali began to grin for the first time. "Okay, professor? It's everything you asked for. Anything else you want, just let me know. Okay?"

Kamateh's visual surveillance took in the ring of teenage terrorists who surrounded him again, their faces lit with pride and excitement. He could see how much his arrival meant to them. To them as much as to him, their mission must have seemed unreal. Until now . . .

His heart lurched painfully.

He spotted two gleaming steel cylinders set against a far wall about fifteen feet apart. "You . . . you've actually stolen uranium?"

"Yes, yes, two times now. It is what you asked for."

Kamateh approached one of the cylinders, which had a beautifully machined screw top. As he began to unscrew the lid, he heard a collective gasp behind him. Even Kali appeared uneasy.

Kamateh calmly continued to unscrew the top of the cylinder. Setting it aside, he peered at the lump of metal inside. U-235. Earlier it would have been silver in color, like aluminum foil. It had oxidized, acquiring a distinctive brown coloration. "You can look," he said for the benefit of Kali and the others. "The metal is harmless in this state. Just keep the two cylinders separated. Never bring them any closer to each other than they are now. Yes, and don't pick at the metal or scratch it. The oxidized coating is toxic . . . very toxic."

The professor's authoritative tone silenced Kali. For the moment, Hassan Kamateh was in command. Not wanting to show fear before the others, Kali moved closer and peered into the cylinder. The others hung back, afraid of the unknown.

Except for one youth. He was taller than average, slim and lanky, with a long, thin face and dark eyes alight with eagerness.

"This is Yusef, professor. He is to assist you. He is an expert metalworker, is it not so, Yusef?"

"Yes, yes, praise Allah!"

"He makes jewelry," Kali added.

Yusef was a little older than the others in the group—all of twenty-one, Hassan Kamateh guessed with dismay. An expert metalworker? Experienced in making trinkets!

This completed the metamorphosis that had begun in the jeep; Kamateh came to grips with reality. He realized the full horror of what he had been coerced into agreeing to do. He could no longer wish it away.

Here, inside this mountain, guarded by youthful fanatics who were prepared to protect him with their lives, he was to construct for their beloved Imam the ultimate weapon.

A nuclear bomb.

As a youth, Luke Cameron had crisscrossed the Halston range by horse and truck a hundred times. The Halston and Cameron outfits had commonly joined up for the spring roundup and the branding of calves and yearlings. He might not have explored every nook and gully as he had done at the Bar-C, but he was thoroughly familiar with the Halston spread, even in darkness. He could guide Old Brown off the road under the cover of darkness, without worry of bogging down in a creek bed or plunging into a hidden gully.

He switched off his lights as he left the highway. Slowly, cautiously, he drove across the level plain, following the irregular course of a dry wash. It twisted back and forth, so it took two miles of driving to cover a half mile of distance. That brought him to a copse of willow and cottonwood trees, a shadowy oasis that he remembered on an open prairie. He stopped, cut the motor, ran the window down, and leaned an ear to the night.

Grass stirred in the night breeze. Crickets chorused. In one of the tall cottonwoods, an owl hooted. The sounds of a Montana night.

Luke judged that he was less than a mile from the Halston ranch headquarters—yet far enough, he thought, that the low-gear growl of the pickup should have been inaudible as he rumbled across the prairie.

He couldn't suppress a nagging curiosity about the activity on the Halston property. He was drawn here, in particular, by the incident at the DOE site—the appearance of heavy equipment moving in the small hours of the night.

He heard nothing now.

Luke left the pickup and began to walk, following the bed of the dry creek as it wormed in a generally southeasterly direction across the prairie. After a short distance, he came to the first of the shallow irrigation trenches he had been expecting to find. In a matter of minutes, he was able to trace a checkerboard pattern of ditches that reached as far as he could peer in the darkness. To the west, the channels appeared to extend all the way to the border of the DOE property.

But there was something peculiar about the irrigation trenches; they were dry.

No water.

Luke Cameron quickly rationalized this incongruity, reminding himself that he was unfamiliar with the ways in which such systems might be tested or used. But the engineer in him remained curious about Micheline Picard's experiments on the Halston land.

He hiked away from the dry wash to the crest of a low rise. Beyond, on a long downward slope that ended near the old ranch buildings, some watering had been done recently. For the grass was long and lush. It swayed and rolled as if alive. It reminded Luke of sports fans doing the Wave in a huge stadium. This stadium, however, was lit only by the stars, and the players were invisible . . . ghostly, silent. There was only the wave itself, accompanied by its own rustling voice that rose and fell like a soft moan.

Luke could see lights in the windows of the ranch buildings—signs of habitation about a half mile away. Sounds carried a long distance in the stillness of the plain, and he clearly heard the thump of a car door closing. Then a pair of headlights tunneled through the darkness. He could hear the engine first gargle, then purr. The vehicle backed, then started forward, the headlights swinging in an arc toward Luke Cameron's position. He ducked involuntarily and stepped backward. But the long reach of the headlights was an illusion. The path of light diffused into the dark void before it could illuminate him.

He watched the headlights as they moved off. Not east, toward the highway, but west. Toward the DOE site.

Curious about what in the world was going on at this hour, Luke set off in the direction the headlights pointed, angling toward the dirt road, but keeping carefully wide of it. There was little cover here—the grass was too short, the brush too sparse, the moon too bright, and the clouds too few. Luke began to feel uncomfortably exposed in the open plain. Exposed and vulnerable.

He unexpectedly intersected the dirt road, no more than a pair of worn ruts, which had taken an unseen curve around a dip in the terrain. Luke could see the headlights bobbing off to his right, still moving away.

Then the headlights went out.

As Luke stared after the vehicle, he heard the sound of another car's motor approaching from the direction of the ranch buildings.

A lot of traffic for the middle of nowhere.

He trotted away from the dirt tracks and flattened on his belly as a new pair of headlights slashed through the darkness toward him. Not long afterward, a truck rumbled past him. Luke was close enough to see that it was an open-bed truck with slatted wooden sides. It carried a number of men, some standing up and holding onto the sides, others hunched down.

A work crew, Luke thought.

What kind of late-night work were they up to? He wondered if he could safely get close enough to find out.

From here to the western flank of the Halston range, the prairie was open and level, without much grass. There would be no place to hide on such a clear, starlit night. If Luke tried to get close to those trucks, he would be too easy to spot.

He had almost been caught by security guards at the DOE the other night. He had no intention of risking exposure again. He was trespassing on private land, with no real justification for being there beyond a vague uneasiness about his father's accidental death.

He decided to wait for another night—a dark night, with good cloud cover.

His walk back to his truck was uneventful. He followed the dry wash, which led him back to the copse of brush and trees where Old Brown was hidden. He noted that he was unable to see it himself until he was close, even though he knew it was there.

He drove slowly back to the highway, holding down his speed more to minimize the engine noise than to negotiate the rough terrain. The night was bright enough that he could pick his way across the open prairie without lights.

The highway was deserted. He pulled onto the road and pushed down the gas pedal. After a short distance, he flipped on his headlights.

How much had he learned from all his poking, prying, and stumbling around? Armed guards and unexplained activity at the Wind Canyon Mine. But nothing concrete. Empty irrigation ditches on the Halston property. Blanket denials of any mysterious activity at the nuclear storage site.

Tonight's surveillance on the Halston place had been an impulsive, poorly planned, halfhearted attempt to give shape and substance to his suspicions. Once again he was left unsatisfied.

He wondered if it was time to pack up and leave.

The town of Gibson had been named after one of the original "nine Kentuckians" who had signed up as volunteers for the Lewis and Clark expedition in 1803. It was situated in a broad valley bisected by one of the lesser tributaries of the Missouri River. The highway approached the town across the high plains, then slumped down a rather steep grade from the bluffs to the valley floor. As Luke Cameron started down the grade, he could see the river off to his right, a wide but shallow stream whose banks were lined with brush and the overhang of tall cottonwoods. The lights of Gibson twinkled in the distance. To his left, the wall of the bluff shouldered close to the two-lane road, a sheer mass of solid rock. To his right, the drop-off was steep.

As his speed increased, Luke Cameron tapped the brake pedal.

Old Brown failed to respond; it continued to gain speed.

Damn! Clyde the mechanic must have forgotten to put in brake fluid after the repairs were completed!

But even as this thought crossed his mind, Luke knew better. The brakes had worked fine on the mountain drive around Wind Canyon. He had continued to run up mileage, without intimation of trouble. A sudden rupture in the line? Something he had struck while driving across the prairie? No, he would have felt the impact. He was sure of it.

He stared down the grade, saw a curve approaching, and leaned on the wheel.

The tires squealed in protest. The pickup heeled over as it hung through the turn and straightened out—gaining speed, racing faster and faster.

Free fall now, Luke thought coolly. There were a couple hard, tight curves ahead before he bottomed out.

The wind howled through the gaps in the windows, which couldn't be shut tightly. He jammed the shift into third gear to cut some of his momentum, downshifted again as he screamed through the first of the two remaining curves.

The plummeting charge of the pickup slowed perceptibly.

Luke peered ahead through a film of sweat. He was still doing fifty miles an hour. Too fast. Much too fast. No way could he stop his headlong fall through the last curve. Too sharp a turn. Luke calculated his chances as if gauging the stress factor in a bridge. No, he wouldn't make it.

He swerved to the left side of the road and scraped against the wall of rock.

The action was deliberate. He held the pickup against the rock face, metal screeching and sparks flying, hoping the friction would slow his plunge.

Not enough. Try again. Maybe . . .

Another car loomed ahead on the road, climbing toward him in the inner lane, barring that side of the road for Luke's desperate maneuver.

He rocked over to his own side of the road.

There was a sharp explosion beneath Luke's feet. The clutch seemed to have broken loose. He had a sudden impression of metal teeth flying. Old Brown hurtled forward like a wild beast released from a harness. It highballed out of control toward the last curve.

The approaching car in the inside lane swept past him. A white face, frozen behind the windshield, mouth open.

Luke saw the sharp turn beginning its sweep. The asphalt ribbon curved sharply and disappeared around the wall of rock on Luke's left. To his right, the drop from the shoulder had narrowed to about fifteen feet, diminishing fast.

In the blur of the onrushing terrain, Luke tried to focus his mind on the landscape at the bottom of the grade. He visualized in quick flashes the contours of the river bottom east of the highway, the brush and trees, the gullies and runoffs. There was no time to catalog every detail. No time to analyze his options. There was only a fleeting whirl of images and blind calculations.

He made his choice.

At the beginning of the curve, before centrifugal force caught the pickup in its tight grip, he spun the wheel to the right. The truck shot off the highway into the air.

Although the drop from the shoulder was now only a few feet, it had the impact of a body slam that rattled Luke's bones and teeth. The wheel was wrenched from his grip. Old Brown bounced and rocked. Yet miraculously, the runaway truck righted itself and plunged through grass and brush toward the river.

Luke remembered only one dangerous gully ahead, a fissure cut into the level bottom about three feet deep. He grabbed the wheel again and tried to steer away from the gully. Cottonwoods loomed dead in his path, willows on his left. The car's careening progress began to slow. The brush and deep grass of the river bottom dragged at the wheels and undercarriage.

The Chevy struck a large rock and lurched crazily. Luke's head banged against the roof of the cab and one knee cracked off the dash.

As the truck neared the river, it rattled over a washboard of dry furrows, bounced through a shallow dip, missed the looming trees, and thrashed blindly through head-high willows. The ground was soft now, sandy, slowing the mad dash.

He dropped off the shallow bank into the river.

The grass and brush and sand had done their work, diminishing his speed and minimizing the impact with the water. The drag of the river did the rest.

He came to a stop in midstream. The water sloshed around the pickup's wheels, not much more than hub deep, barely covering the bumpers.

Luke felt the pain and bruising then, the battering his head and body had taken. None of it mattered.

He had survived. That's what mattered.

Because now there was something he had to do.

No accident, he knew as the rage surged inside him. No crack in the brake line or mechanic's carelessness. A staged accident, the lining cut or fluid drained while Luke was exploring Halston's property. How long had he left the Chevy unattended? A half hour at least. Maybe an hour.

Long enough.

No accident, by God! Because he had been asking too many questions, poking into the operations of that French holding company. *Asking the same questions his father had asked!*

And he suddenly thought of Sorenson, forced out at the bank, only to become the victim of another mysterious and violent death. Had he also asked too many questions? Or had he been in a position to know too much? It was possible.

But Luke knew that someone had *definitely* tried to kill him.

And that answered the aching question that had brought him home. His father had not stumbled in the creek and struck his head on a rock. He hadn't suffered a stroke, and he hadn't been trampled to death by his beloved buffalo herd.

Someone had murdered Tom Cameron.

Tehran, Iran

Ahmad bin Razi stepped quietly into the darkened room. The curtains were drawn, for the bright sunlight hurt the Imam's eyes. Several whispering men, part of the legion of forty doctors who were in attendance, broke off their conversation as Razi entered. They had been conferring with specialists about the video cameras that had been installed to monitor the Imam's movements around the clock.

Ruhollah Khomeini lay still as a corpse on his hospital bed. His body was frail, his skin drawn tightly over the bones of his face. His breathing, though not visible, was audible. The sickness that was eating away at his body showed in the gray pallor of his skin and the deep, dark hollows into which his eyes had sunk. Because of sudden complications—severe vomiting and stomach pain—he had been brought to the clinic in north Tehran, where his doctors consulted anxiously, fearful of a wrong decision.

Ahmad did not wish to wake him, but . . .

"What is it, Razi?" The voice was unexpectedly strong. The ayatollah could still rouse himself when he wished.

"There is word from America. Allah be praised!"

The eyes glared from their sockets. "Tell me!"

Ahmad glanced at the doctors. The Satan option was still secret. He bent close to murmur so that only the Imam could hear him. "The nuclear material has been taken from the Great Satan. It is even now in the hands of the Children of Allah. And the professor— he who will build the weapon—has arrived at the place of hiding." Ahmad's voice trembled with emotion.

Khomeini collapsed back on his bed. For many minutes, he was silent, his eyes closed. At last Ahmad thought he had fallen asleep. Ahmad turned to go, his steps noiseless on the polished tile floor.

Khomeini's voice stopped him. Not forceful and commanding, but a whisper. "I must speak with Mohtashemi."

Ahmad's eyes quickly searched the outer room. Ali Akbar Mohtashemi was among the cluster of mullahs in attendance. Ahmad noted, with silent satisfaction, that Rafsanjani the politician was not present. He hurried toward the interior minister, who stepped forward to meet him. "He wishes to speak with you," Ahmad said.

Mohtashemi glided into the sickroom and crossed over to the ayatollah's bed. The minister was conscious of the eyes of the video cameras recording his movements, as the sensitive microphones would also record his words. But he disdained both. He had the fanatic's absolute certainty of the rightness of his actions.

Mohtashemi had to lean close as the old man's dry lips moved. "My daughter . . . I must speak to her."

"Zahra Mustafavi?" Mohtashemi asked, surprised, referring to the forty-eight-year-old daughter of Khomeini's Iranian wife. "You wish me to bring her to you?"

Khomeini's hand checked him irritably. "My French daughter . . . she who is called Micheline."

Mohtashemi tried to hide his confusion. "Yes, Imam . . . I will fetch paper and pen. . . ."

"I do not wish to write a letter!" Khomeini said harshly. The effort cost him. He sank back, a racking cough shaking his whole body. Several of his doctors moved toward the bed, but the old man waved them off. His sunken eyes found Mohtashemi. "I want to speak to her directly."

"Yes, yes . . . I understand. . . ." But Mohtashemi remained confused. Always the Imam's messages relating to the nuclear mission had been communicated through Mohtashemi himself, who bore responsibility for commanding terrorist operations. What the Imam now requested was a startling departure.

He wished to speak directly to the terrorists in the field. To their leader. To the Frenchwoman.

"It is time she heard my voice," the old man said.

"We have established shortwave radio communication with our soldiers at the site where Allah's work is underway. But they cannot respond without revealing their location to the American authorities, who monitor all our communications. The Frenchwoman can receive your message, which can be delivered in code."

"I will speak without code. Let the Americans hear what I have to say," said the Imam, wheezing. "I will deliver a message of terror for all enemies of Islam. My words will pour like poison into their ears."

"Yes, my Imam," Mohtashemi whispered, inwardly exulting. He was moved by the passion he heard in his leader's voice. "I will arrange a time."

"My health . . . we cannot wait."

Mohtashemi had an inspiration. "We can record your message immediately on tape here in your room. It can then be transmitted when the right moment arrives." A tape could be edited, he thought, should the Imam have an attack of pain or coughing while he spoke. His voice could also be amplified to sound stronger.

Khomeini nodded, satisfied. "Whatever good there is exists thanks to the sword and in the shadow of the sword," the old man said, quoting what he had once written. "She has put a sword in my hand. Where others have failed, she has succeeded. Arrange it, Ali Akbar! I will speak to my daughter!"

PART THREE
THIEVES' NEST

Gibson, Montana

K HOMEINI'S ARMY OF REVOLUTIONARY GUARDS HAD BEEN recruited largely from the slums of Tehran. Most were young, thin, hollow eyed. The Children of Hell. But he had transformed them into the Children of God.

Some were volunteers recruited shortly after the outbreak of the revolution. Khomeini's stern visage, staring from posters and handbills, had urged mothers and fathers to "offer one of your children to the Imam" for the war against the enemies of Islam. In two weeks, the movement gained over a million volunteers, ragtag soldiers barely in their teens.

Where they had nothing, the ayatollah gave them purpose. And passion. He gave them love. And hate.

Most of all he gave them hate.

Hatred became a bile that consumed them, simmering at first deep within them, then welling up until it overwhelmed them. They drew daily nourishment from Khomeini's own bitter bile. His acrid words poured over them, engulfing them, submerging them.

His voice rang in their ears, amplified by blaring radios and tinny loudspeakers. He glared down at them from a thousand walls, tall roadside signs, and overhead banners. Scolding them. Admonishing them. Teaching them to hate.

Khomeini distrusted the older generation. They had been tainted by the Great Satan, corrupted by his ways. But the children were Khomeini's to teach, to train, to mold. He had turned them into living weapons to be hurled against the enemies of Islam. He gave them guns when their arms were almost too weak to hold them, their hands too small to grip the stocks.

In the ugly war against Iraq, the children were wasted like bullets. When the mine fields had to be cleared, the children were sent forth. They ran blindly, chanting their slogans, until the antipersonnel mines exploded beneath them and slivers of steel sliced away hands and arms and feet. Obliterated faces. Tore thin bodies to ribbons. They went willingly, for they ran not toward death but to the ultimate joy that Allah had reserved for them. They clutched the Koran in one hand, a rifle in the other. Around each neck dangled a plastic key to heaven.

Some of those sacrificial children, torn by shrapnel, found the strength to hold their mangled bodies intact as they stumbled over the mines. They wrapped their blankets tightly around themselves so that shattered bones and shredded flesh would not be lost. So their torn bodies could more easily be put back together.

They advanced screaming Khomeini's name.

They worshiped him.

The favored of Khomeini's children—the strong and the gifted, the quickest of eye and the sharpest of mind—were singled out for special training.

They were sent to the terrorist camps at Saleh-Abad near Qom, Parandak west of Tehran, Behjeshtieh far to the northwest (where women were among the trainees). Or to the Gorgan Plain and Tariq al-Qods and Vakil-Abad near Mashhad in the east.

These were schools of death where the trainees were taught to kill and to die. They learned to use the instruments of death—the handgun, the rifle, the machine gun. They were taught the handicraft of death—how to make a firebomb, a dynamite bomb, a plastic bomb. They studied the handiwork of death—how to kill by hand, by foot, with the lid of a tin can. And they learned other arcane skills—sabotage, hijacking, hostage taking.

A small band of honored graduates, twenty in all, had been chosen as a spearhead for the secret mission aimed at the heart of America. They would bring death and terror to the Great Satan, the most powerful of the enemies of Islam.

Most of them had slipped across the Canadian border near Glacier National Park in the north of Montana. A truck had picked them up at a secret rendezvous and driven them across the treeless plain on the eastern flank of the Rockies, down through the Blackfoot Indian Reservation, and south across Montana to their destination.

They had passed through Gibson after dark, without stopping. They had neither seen the town nor been seen by it.

Most were small in stature, lean and wiry. Their faces were alike—thin and dark and passionate. They were hard to tell apart, their names a jumble—Ali, Baran, Ebrahim, Hadi, Jaafar, Mostafa, Reza, Selim, Taghi. Some bore the name Muhammad in one of its forms, as if annointed at birth to be soldiers of God.

A few stayed at the Halston ranch as workers. Most were quartered at the Wind Canyon Mine.

They had made it an outpost of Islam. Arrows painted on the walls of the tin shacks, even inside the mine, pointed in the direction of Mecca. In the mornings and evenings, the call of a muezzin drifted out over the rugged sandstone bluffs and pine-covered peaks, down a steep-walled canyon and over treeless meadows . . . the Islamic call to prayer. In this remote spot in Montana, the quavering cry seemed eerily out of place.

As the call died away this evening at sunset, the young penitents prostrated themselves on the stony ground.

In unison they repeated their nightly prayer. *"Khomeini mi razmad! Amrika mi larzad!"*

Khomeini fights! America trembles!

Not long after the evening prayers, a car was spotted approaching the mine—a sleek, silver car whose appearance caused the guards on the bluffs to come to admiring attention. Dust drifted in its wake as it wound up the canyon. The sentries called out to each other, relaying the message swiftly up the mountain in advance of the silver Thunderbird. A runner raced into the mine.

With a small swirl of dust, Micheline Picard braked the car to a stop beside the cluster of tin shacks on the shelf outside Wind Canyon Mine. Kali was already emerging from the entrance. He stared with disapproval at the woman's boldness as she stepped from the car with a flash of silken legs. Grudgingly, he had accepted the necessity that she must mimic Western customs and clothes while in Gibson. But not here, among the scandalized Children of Allah, who gaped at her.

To Kali she was an unwelcome sight. To the others gathered on the mountain, she was a mystery, seldom seen and never before up close. She was a remote figure who was part of their mission but apart from it. That was necessary, they had been told, because of her visible role in the camp of the enemy.

They were not entirely certain of her status. It was Kali who gave them their orders.

But the woman, it had been whispered, spoke for the Grand Ayatollah.

That meant her word was law.

Kali greeted her politely enough. *"Salam alekom.* I did not expect you so soon . . ."

She cut him off. "I will speak with you in private." She addressed him in French, a language none of the young *fedayeen* understood.

"The professor is at work inside the mine. I am sure you wish to meet him."

"I will talk with you—now!"

No woman since his mother—and then only when he was a small child—had ever spoken to him in such a tone. The blood rushed to Kali's face and neck. His fingers brushed against the knife handle protruding from the sheath at his waist.

The woman saw the gesture. She smiled, with a slight, sardonic quirk, as if daring him to act. The smile challenged him.

Seething with rage, Kali followed the Frenchwoman into one of the tin-roofed mining shacks, now used solely for storage. He closed the door behind him. Cracks in the walls and around the lone cardboard-covered window admitted enough light for him to see the icy calm of the woman's face.

I could kill her now, Kali thought.

Yet it might not be so easy. He knew she had completed intensive terrorist training at Behjeshtieh on the island of Kharg, one of the Revolutionary Guard training camps for women. Still, he was confident of his own lethal skills. The knife would be quick and silent. No one among the followers at the mine would dare to challenge his action.

A minute had passed since he had entered the shack with Micheline Picard. The heat was stifling, trapped in the tiny structure from the day. Kali felt sweat trickling down his neck, causing his shirt to stick to his back.

"You will not attempt it," the woman told him coldly, speaking now in Farsi. "Because you are not sure if you would succeed . . . and because it would be a sin against Islam."

"*You* are a sin against Islam!" At last Kali's fury found its voice. "With your naked, painted face and your Western whore's clothes."

"The clothes are necessary to accomplish my mission," she said tersely. "I have no intention of discussing this further with you."

"The clothes, perhaps. But not the whore's colors," he muttered. Even the bright pinks of her patterned blouse were an offense to decency.

"You speak as a child. Worse, you have acted as a child."

"You lie!"

"Don't speak to me of lies! I warned you not to take independent action against the American, Cameron. You arranged a stupid accident. Yet your tongue was silent."

Though Kali was shaken over the exposure of his private, little plot, he recovered quickly. "It is permitted to be silent for the good of the cause. It is permitted even to lie if that is necessary! Cameron was a threat to us."

"Because of your stupidity, he is now a much greater threat. He has now been alerted. Had he been killed, his death would have alerted the authorities. Are you so foolish as to believe no one would have suspected a second accident so soon after the father was killed? You have jeopardized our mission by trying to kill him. Then you couldn't even do that. Tehran will hear of your incompetence!"

Kali's dark eyes blazed with defiance, but the woman's hot words put him on the defensive. "No one suspected us of the banker Sorenson's death," he spat back.

"He was one person, not two of the same family. And his death was necessary. He knew too much of our activities, and he had begun to question them. Cameron knew *nothing!* He had no reason even to stay in Gibson. He was prepared to leave. He had nothing to justify his doubts about his father's death. Now he *knows!*"

"He still knows nothing. His brakes did not work. What does that tell him?"

"Fool! His brakes had just been repaired! He knows they were tampered with! He knows that an accident was arranged. And this will be proof to him that his father's accident was also arranged."

"You can't know this. You are guessing," Kali retorted.

Her demeanor abruptly changed again from hot fury to icy calm.

"The sheriff, this man Thayer who is his friend, has impounded his truck that was towed from the river where it was found. Do you not yet understand?" Micheline Picard leaned close to Kali, perceiving his hatred, clearly aware of the knife so close to his hand but defying him to reach for it. And—when he failed to act—she edged closer, increasing her vulnerability and his humiliation.

And in that tense moment, he was stirred in spite of himself by her beauty, her fire—and now her cold courage.

"An investigation has begun where there was none. New questions are being asked."

"They will bring no answers."

"No?"

For a long minute she was silent, watching him through cold, calculating eyes. The moment when Kali might have struck her was past. But she had not yet dealt her final blow.

"He has left the country," she said.

Kali stared at her, momentarily puzzled, not grasping the significance of her announcement.

"No one had seen Cameron after his car was found abandoned. I contacted our people and discreet inquiries were made." She paused again, for the first time revealing a crack in her rigid self-control. "He is in Paris."

"Paris!"

"Yes, you idiot—Paris! He is investigating the French company that now owns his land. Because of *you,* he is investigating *us,* Kali. He is investigating *me!*"

When Kali descended into the mine in the company of a striking, elegantly dressed woman, a startled Hassan Kamateh gaped at them.

Aside from the young and eager Yusef, who was proving to be an enthusiastic if ill-trained assistant, Kamateh had kept aloof from the ignorant young revolutionaries with whom he shared Wind Canyon Mine. They were omnipresent, but they were nonentities. They weren't even there to guard him, he realized; his captors were not worried that he might attempt to escape. The Revolutionary Guards—Khomeini's violent children—were there to keep out the curious or troublesome. In a sense, to protect Kamateh.

Kali was another matter, a man to be reckoned with. He had been a student in America, with a peculiarly Iranian mind-set that made a bright young man susceptible to the harsh, fundamentalist rhetoric and extremist views of the Ayatollah Khomeini's Islamic revolution. Kali was a highly trained terrorist and a remorseless fanatic; this made him truly frightening.

That others like him held Kamateh's family hostage in Iran—his wife, his two children, his aging parents—was even more terrifying to the scientist.

Kamateh was a decent man, with a tolerable measure of human compassion. Yet he wondered whether he would have had the courage to defy these people if he had had only his own fate to consider. . . .

Hassan Kamateh thought of himself as an ordinary man, even though in his work he dealt with quite extraordinary matters. He recognized that he was not exactly a dynamic person. His attitudes tended to be as conservative as the blue and gray suits that hung in his wardrobe. Yes, his personality was so bland, so unremarkable, that he was quite certain half of his students, if they had encountered the man impersonating him outside the classroom, would easily have mistaken the imposter for Kamateh.

His thoughts were rambling now. He must pull himself together.

Who in the world was this woman? She was an unexpected factor, an unknown quantity. Beautiful. Chic. Immaculate. Supremely composed. What was such a woman doing with Kali?

Kamateh noticed the way the youthful band of terrorists stared covertly. They had probably never been so close to a woman of such style and sophistication. She must seem to them like a princess. Kamateh was less overwhelmed. He had met many such women, in Tehran, in New York, in Los Angeles, where he had learned that beauty may be only makeup deep. Though not indifferent to her glamour, he was not in awe of her. He assumed that she was of some uncertain use to the shadowy people behind Kali. Kamateh's safest course, he decided, was to respond to Kali's cues.

Her first question after Kali completed the introductions seemed to confirm the scientist's estimate. She pointed to the lump of metal that rested like a crown jewel on a table in a small, isolated room that Kamateh had arranged. Removed from its cylindrical container, the shapeless lump of uranium seemed an ugly, dormant thing, in no way frightening or dangerous. "That is the weapon, Professor?"

"That's the uranium," he answered with just a hint of condescension in his voice. This woman was nothing to him. Let Kali humor her. "It is not by itself a weapon. It could be used to make a weapon."

"And what progress are you making in that direction, Dr. Kamateh?"

Kamateh glanced at Kali. Although he did not share the extreme views of Islamic fundamentalists, who sought to turn back the clock, Kamateh nevertheless shared their cultural heritage. He thought of himself as enlightened of course, long exposed to Western ideas. Still, he was impatient with this woman's presence.

"Well?"

"I'm sure Kali can answer your questions, Mademoiselle Picard," he said formally. "We're conducting an experiment. It is not so simple a thing to construct a nuclear weapon in"—his glance took in the immediate surroundings, the crude laboratory in a cave inside a mountain—"in such circumstances, and with the facilities at my disposal."

"I asked you a question!" the Frenchwoman snapped.

Something in her tone brought Kamateh to full attention for the first time. He looked into the cold, dark eyes. An involuntary shiver goose-bumped up his spine. *Who was she?*

A glance at Kali's bitter expression confirmed his sudden intuition. "I . . . I'm sorry . . . I didn't realize . . . ," he stammered.

"You do now, Doctor. Answer my question. Can you build such a bomb here in this mountain?"

"Yes . . . yes, it can be done. It won't be easy . . . but . . . we now have a sufficient quantity of U-235. I have confirmed it is highly enriched . . . seventy, perhaps even seventy-five percent."

"That is pure enough?"

"Yes."

"Show me what you are doing."

With an apprehensive new respect, Hassan Kamateh showed the woman through his crude laboratory. He pointed out the ceramic oven, in a separate shaft that was vented out the side of the mountain. It was capable, he said, of being heated to temperatures up to 1,500 degrees Fahrenheit, and would be used to melt the uranium down when it was molded. "We use what is called the 'lost wax' process," he explained. "Even the American Indians were familiar with this technique. A mold is made into which the metal is poured. When it has cooled and hardened, the wax is peeled away."

"The metal is to be formed into a ball?"

"Yes, with a hole penetrating to its core. Then we must make a kind of bullet to fire into this center . . . ah, it is like the male and female part." She smiled faintly in acknowledgment, her eyes cool. "But the bullet must be fired at great velocity, or there will be no explosion. All of this must be precisely defined, but it is essentially simple. That is why I chose an atomic bomb rather than a hydrogen bomb, which is many times more powerful."

He led her through the partitioned rooms, pointing out his measuring instruments, the computer used for his calculations, the power source feeding down from the top of the mountain—connected to the Montana power company's lines more than a mile away—and the auxiliary generator.

"Tell me, Doctor," she said at one point, "if a hydrogen bomb is so much more powerful, why exactly did you choose not to build one?"

"It is much more difficult, much more exacting. The hydrogen bomb requires an implosion, rather than an explosion. It is essentially a uranium bomb enclosed in a tritium envelope, with two triggers that must be perfectly timed. Not only is the sophistication of the device a difficult challenge under the most controlled circumstances—impossible in our circumstances—but the use of tritium made it out of the question. Tritium is in very short supply, closely guarded and virtually impossible to obtain. I had really no alternative."

Micheline Picard, back in the main room of the cave, stared once more at the innocent mass of brown metal isolated in its own compartment. "How will the weapon be triggered?"

"For safety, a radio signal can be used to trigger an electrical impulse into a high-explosive charge. This will fire our neutron bullet into the critical mass of the uranium. If our calculations are correct, a chain reaction will be produced . . . which will be contained by the bomb's steel cylinder."

She was silent. How many would die? she wondered. It would depend, of course, on where the bomb was placed when it was triggered.

"How large will it be?"

"Kali has told me it must be small enough, and light enough, to be transported in a truck."

"Is that possible?"

"Yes."

There was another long silence. Hassan Kamateh saw one of the teenage guards, an assault rifle cradled in one arm, sidle along the back wall of the cave to gain a better view of the Frenchwoman. If she was aware of the lascivious attention she attracted, she gave no sign.

"What you tell me is satisfactory, Professor," she said at last. "I will notify Tehran. I am sure the news will be well received."

The intimidated Kamateh said nothing.

"Let us understand each other," she said, as if reading his uncertainty. "Your wife and daughter are well. They are being cared for and are under no constraints . . . except that they cannot leave Iran."

"My son . . . ," he said hoarsely.

"Yes . . . your son Mahmoud . . ."

"Is he . . . all right?"

"He has been corrupted by the secularism that he learned in America. That was your doing, Dr. Kamateh."

"He was raised in obedience to the laws of Allah."

"He learned disobedience, not obedience."

"My God! . . . What has happened to him?"

Micheline Picard stared at him, making him wait, allowing the fear to tighten around his heart. "He is alive. He is being educated in the truths of Islam. There may yet be hope for him . . . if all goes well with us here in the land of Satan. . . . Do you understand me, Professor?"

Hassan Kamateh understood; the threat was stark enough. It was also clear who commanded this horrible mission in which he had become a coerced accomplice. He saw before him a passionate, intelligent, dedicated fanatic—lovely to behold but more dangerous than Kali. A woman who knew all about him, who understood why he had been brought to this cave in the mountain.

Who might even, he suddenly thought, have planned the mission.

"You too may yet be redeemed, Professor."

"Yes?"

"You have an opportunity to serve the cause of Islam instead of serving the U.S. dollar. And the opportunity to ensure that your family will one day be returned to you."

The professor nodded humbly, his every gesture conveying his capitulation.

He had never had a choice, not really, he thought as he watched the woman walk out of the mine, each smooth swivel of her hips watched hungrily by a dozen pairs of eyes. From the moment he reached the mine and saw the cylinders containing the enriched uranium waiting for him, he had known what he had to do. The horror of it had turned his life into a nightmare.

Washington, D.C.

CONCEALED FROM PUBLIC VIEW IN THE WEST WING OF THE White House is the National Security Council conference room. Directly adjoining it is the White House communications center, which has direct links to every nerve center of the government—the Pentagon across the Potomac, the CIA's Langley headquarters, the FBI director's office in the nearby J. Edgar Hoover Building, the National Security Agency, Norad's Command Center in Colorado Springs, the Strategic Air Command in Omaha—and the Energy Department's Nuclear Emergency Operations Center. Among the men who took their places at the long, oval conference table that morning there was growing apprehension that they would be discussing a report more ominous than the dozens of nuclear threats the FBI had recorded and investigated over the past two decades. Most of those had been hoaxes, but this one was something very different.

This perception had altered the makeup of the NSC meeting. The State Department was represented by Secretary Jim Baker himself. He was accompanied by the deputy secretary for terrorism, Robert Shirek, a blunt-spoken former corporation lawyer who was already acquiring a reputation for his lack of deference before congressional committees. The deputy director of the CIA had been replaced at the table by the director himself, William H. Webster, the durable former judge and former FBI chief. Ted Chandler, an associate FBI director, was present because of his expertise on terrorism. So was

Eric Sanderson, who had first brought the potential problem of nuclear theft to the attention of Mel Durbin, the president's national security specialist, and who was coordinating the Energy Department's investigation.

This meeting reminded Mel Durbin of a game at the end of spring training, when most of the heavy hitters were inserted into the lineup. The real season was just around the bend. . . .

Eldon Riggs, deputy assistant secretary of defense in charge of special operations, sat next to the assistant secretary, James McKechnie, former CEO of a major aerospace firm. The lean, boyishly handsome McKechnie came across as an Ivy League hatchet man who, in an earlier generation, would probably have been recruited by Wild Bill Donovan for the original OSS. Next to him, representing the Joint Chiefs, was Army Chief of Staff Alfred Vuono.

Studying them down the length of the long table, Durbin felt a tickle of excitement. He'd stuck his neck out on this alert. Now he was getting action. . . .

George Bush had been sipping his coffee and conversing amiably with Jim Baker, getting a private report on the secretary's recent visit to the Middle East. The president glanced at his watch, set down his cup, and coughed for attention. The table conversation faded into silence.

"Maybe we should get started," he said. "You all know what's at the top of the agenda."

William Webster stepped smoothly into the opening. "I may have picked up something. One of our people in Rome recently did a routine surveillance of an Iranian nuclear scientist on summer leave from UCLA."

"We've got an Iranian nuclear physicist at UCLA?" Bush asked incredulously.

"He's an American citizen now, and he has impeccable credentials."

"What was he doing in Rome?"

"He was on his way to Tehran to join his family, who had been vacationing there."

"I don't see a problem," the president said.

"Our agent assigned to check on Dr. Kamateh—that's his name, Hassan Kamateh—didn't see anything out of line either. But one of our other people, a veteran with a good nose, smelled something.

Kamateh put himself very conspicuously on display. He spent too much money, ate like Orson Welles, behaved like a tourist on the town. He was too typical . . . too easy to follow. Our man submitted a backup report suggesting that we take a closer look at Dr. Kamateh and his trip to Iran."

"And?" Bush was becoming impatient. William Webster had a methodical, orderly mind and a tendency to take his time getting to the point, preferring to get there step by step.

"I requested the FBI to conduct an investigation." He nodded toward Ted Chandler. Since Webster's appointment by Ronald Reagan to succeed William Casey as CIA director, cooperation between the Bureau and the Agency had improved remarkably.

Chandler began a terse briefing: "Kamateh's family flew to Tehran in February, intending to stay there only about two weeks. Their return flight was booked before they left. The kids were expected back in school, and their mother had signed up for a weaving class at the local community college. In other words, there was an abrupt and unexplained change of plans. They've been in Iran now for three months, with no apparent explanation. Some of their friends thought it unusual."

Everyone around the table was staring at Webster. The sudden hush made Mel Durbin feel self-conscious when he stirred in his chair and it squeaked.

"Our report from the Los Angeles field office also notes that Dr. Kamateh was acting nervous and distracted recently . . . ," Ted Chandler added. "As if something was on his mind."

"What are you suggesting?" asked the president.

"There's more." Chandler glanced at William Webster, who nodded, signaling the FBI man to complete his briefing. "We've had reports on the activities of a West Coast chapter of the Islamic Student Society, which is funded by an Iranian front called the Foundation of the Oppressed. One of its members is under FBI surveillance. He was seen on several occasions meeting Dr. Kamateh at the scientist's home and on the university campus."

"You think all this adds up to a problem?"

"Yes, sir, we do."

"Do you still have this man in Los Angeles under surveillance?"

Ted Chandler looked uncomfortable. He cleared his throat before he spoke. "He's disappeared, Mr. President. Right now we're looking for him."

Bush frowned. "I'm still not sure what this has to do with the possible theft of . . ." His voice trailed off.

Everyone's eyes were on the president. Everyone waited respectfully for him to complete his thought. After a moment of silence, William Webster spoke up: "Our man in Rome believes that the man he watched in Rome might not have been Dr. Kamateh. If that's right—and it's beginning to look that way—we can build a scenario."

"Do it," George Bush snapped. "Spell it out."

"Our analysts suggest this is what happened: Dr. Kamateh's family flew to Tehran in February, intending to stay only two weeks. They were prevented from leaving. The probable purpose was to put pressure on Kamateh. At a predetermined time, a look-alike took Kamateh's place, flew to Rome, made certain he was observed, and then continued on to Iran, where he disappeared. Anyone watching him was supposed to assume that Dr. Kamateh had joined his family for the summer in Tehran."

"What happened to the real professor?"

"He disappeared, too."

"Where? Why?"

"If they're going to steal nuclear material for a weapon, they need someone who can assemble it . . . say a nuclear scientist with the ability to build a bomb. Either they must have someone in their organization with the necessary qualifications . . . or they must find someone."

"Good God!"

A murmur of alarm rippled around the conference table. It stopped at the chair occupied by General Vuono. "So far this is nothing but speculation," he growled. "Let's not get worked up into a lather until we know something's been stolen."

"We do." Eric Sanderson, who had kept still through the briefing, spoke somberly. "We've had reports from all of our sites. You have to understand that materials are sometimes in transit . . . that inventories are not always completely up to date . . . that there can be paper discrepancies . . ."

"Good God!" Bush exclaimed again. "We're not talking about a shortage of toilet bowl lids or computer paper, we're talking about strategic weapons materials."

Sanderson flushed. Everyone around the table had more ego than normal or he wouldn't have been occupying a chair at that table. But every ego was necessarily subordinate to the president's.

"At any given moment," Sanderson explained, "there may be discrepancies between computerized file figures and on-the-spot physical counts, for a variety of reasons that don't involve anything sinister."

"I certainly hope you can reconcile your computers," said the president. "Go on."

"In one of our facilities, Strategic Materials Storage Site Number Fourteen in Montana, two cylinders containing weapons-grade U-235 have been tampered with. We might not have detected it if you hadn't requested a special inventory, with an eye out for theft or sabotage. Normally the inventory would have involved a physical count of the cylinders stored at the site. They're checked both by sight and by weight. But this time, gamma ray detectors were also used and readings taken."

He paused. There wasn't a sound in the room. The president of the United States seemed drawn and older, as if he already knew what was coming. If nuclear material had been stolen and turned up in a bootleg bomb, no one would ask what he might have done to prevent the theft. History would record only that it had happened on his watch.

Sanderson took a deep breath and continued: "Two of the cylinders at SMS Number Fourteen showed minor variations in weight. In itself this might not have appeared significant. But each cylinder also showed a sharp drop in gamma radiation."

"The uranium is gone?"

"Yes, Mr. President."

"What was put in the cylinders to bring them up to weight?"

"Lead buckshot."

General Vuono swore, then glanced from under thick eyebrows at the president, who was himself so dismayed that he hadn't even noticed the breach. George Bush, perhaps mindful of the Nixon tapes, had made it clear there were limits on permitted language both in the Oval Office and at the conference rooms in the West Wing.

"We don't know exactly when the switch was made," the unhappy man from the Energy Department said. "The facility has an excellent security record—"

"Not any more," Bush retorted. "Where is this site?"

"Outside Gibson, Montana. That's a small town somewhat south of Helena."

"Yes, I know." One thing about running for president, Bush thought, you became knowledgeable about the geography of the United States.

Bush recalled the crack of a grizzled pilot who had flown him across Montana. "This isn't really the end of the world," the old codger had drawled, "but you can see it from here!"

Eric Sanderson was staring at the president with a startled expression. George Bush realized he was smiling at his recollection— hardly an appropriate response to the news he had just heard.

He hastily swallowed the smile. "What action have you taken?" he asked sternly.

"We've invoked our Nuclear Emergency Crisis Plan. A NEST team is en route to Gibson. . . . That's the Nuclear Emergency Search Team."

"I'm familiar with your alphabet," said Bush.

"The FBI's nuclear crisis management team has also been activated," Ted Chandler spoke up. "Because of the possible Iranian connection, we have ordered a Bureauwide alert. Every suspected terrorist in the Islamic Student Society is under surveillance. We're also checking out every Iranian national who has entered the country during the past six months. And we have thirty agents searching for Hassan Kamateh."

"It was right to alert the Bureau, but I don't want to alert the media," the president said. "Let's keep a lid on this." His gaze challenged the group one by one. Everyone murmured or nodded agreement. "I want to keep this quiet until we know what we're facing." He turned to Chandler: "So far there's been no overt threat against the United States, no demands of any kind?"

"That's correct, Mr. President."

"The uranium might even be out of the country by now," Mel Durbin suggested, speaking for the first time.

Bush glanced at him, nodding thoughtfully. "So we don't really know what we're up against. We can't risk a media circus, or a stampede to get out of Montana."

The president turned to the Energy Department's representative. "Does your NEST team make periodic inspections?"

"It's an emergency team, Mr. President—a crisis team. It also tests security; it runs mock attacks on nuclear installations. But we also have inspectors and investigators, of course."

"Who can operate under wraps?"

Sanderson nodded. "Yes, Mr. President."

"All right . . . get your investigative team in there, but make it look routine. Until we hear otherwise, we'll treat this as an investigative problem, not a terrorist threat. We need to know who stole that uranium, how much they took, how they did it, where they've taken it. And we have to find out without any embarrassing questions from the media."

"Excuse me, Mr. President," said James McKechnie. "We're talking about weapons material here. The Defense Intelligence Agency should be directly involved in any investigation."

"You will be. But I don't want any turf squabbles over this."

"No, sir, Mr. President . . . but this is clearly a military matter."

"We'll do this my way," Bush said coldly.

Once again, he looked along the table, meeting every pair of eyes. This was George Bush at his best, calm under pressure, wise in the ways of Washington. He was by nature a cautious man. His policies were sometimes like jello; they were slow to set and tended to wobble. But when the heat was turned up, he kept his cool.

"Let me repeat . . . ," the president spoke slowly, each word like a drop of water from a dripping icicle. "Not a word of this must leak out. Whoever violates this order—I don't care who—will dearly regret it. I promise."

There was a hasty chorus of assent, a dozen voices exclaiming "Yes, Mr. President!"

The president began his final instructions. First, he addressed Sanderson. "Stay in touch with me around the clock. I want to know what your NEST team learns the minute they learn it."

Bush turned next to Chandler. "I want the FBI to use every available resource, to check with every possible informant. I want your antiterrorist SWAT team on full alert."

To McKechnie and Riggs, the president said, "I want the army's First Special Operations Forces Detachment, the Delta Force at Fort

Bragg, moved into position out West just in case. Make it look like maneuvers, a drill."

Finally, he included everyone at the table. "Whatever these terrorists are up to, whoever they are, whatever their demands, this time they're operating on American soil. We have to show them—and the world—that was a mistake!"

Paris, France

IT WAS LUKE CAMERON'S FIRST DAY IN PARIS, HIS FIRST VISIT to France, his first view of the Champs Elysée. He slid into a chair at an outdoor table at Fouquet's, a café so old a Parisian tradition that, like the Louvre and the Eiffel Tower, it had been declared a national monument, to be protected in perpetuity. Around him swirled the activity of what had been called the world's most beautiful street. It was not what he had expected.

The famous avenue was beautiful enough, with its broad sidewalks and tree-lined curbs. Wide as a football field, it retained the splendor of its anchors at opposite ends—the place de La Concorde at one end, marked by a tall obelisk, and the magnificent Arc de Triomphe at the other. But in between was a string of auto dealerships, sweatshirt emporiums, one-hour photo shops, record stores, video-game arcades, and fast-food restaurants—including McDonald's and Burger King.

Luke felt a sense of unreality about the scene, as he did about his own presence in the midst of it. He was waiting to meet a European representative of InCon.

Luke had telephoned Anthony Canseco at InCon's home office in Houston while he was waiting for his plane connection in Denver. Briefly he had explained what had transpired in Gibson and where he was now going.

"Why Paris?" Canseco asked bluntly.

"That's where this French company, IBZ International, has its headquarters. They're the ones who seem to be buying up half of Gibson."

"That's not news, Luke. Foreign companies are investing heavily in America. Hell, that's what I'd do if I were in their shoes."

"This is different," Luke insisted. "Everything keeps coming back to them . . . and to this Frenchwoman. I'm convinced that, somehow, IBZ is connected with what's been happening to people in Gibson who got too curious."

"Including your dad."

"Yes."

Canseco grunted. "You've got no proof, Luke. It's all circumstantial." He didn't say what he was thinking, that Luke Cameron might be reacting emotionally, not logically.

"I'm not looking for something that'll stand up in court. I'm looking for something that will satisfy *me.*" There was a short pause. "I have to know why my father was killed."

"Okay," Canseco said decisively. "If it's somethin' you gotta do, it's somethin' you gotta do. That's one of my wise sayings."

"You're a wise man."

"Then you should listen to me. You don't want to do it stupid, Luke. You're going to France; you don't know the language, the people, the terrain; you need somebody."

"You have someone in mind?"

"Our man in Paris, who else? We at InCon are a family, Luke. Wait a sec, I've got his address and phone in the Rolodex . . . somebody should invent a better system . . . okay, here it is. You got somethin' to write with?"

"Fire away."

"His name's Frank Delaney. He's not a Frog, but he's the next best thing. Lived in Paris the last fifteen years, supervises a dozen French nationals. He knows his way around, speaks French, has friends in key places. You go in there on your own, Luke, fresh off the plane, unable to speak the lingo . . . I've got to tell you, the French aren't going to fall over themselves being friendly."

"You've been spoiled by your visits to New York. You can't expect the French to be as friendly and charming as New Yorkers."

Canseco chuckled. "Point is," he said, "Frank can help."

"It isn't his problem."

"Talk to him."

"Okay. I really appreciate this, Tony. This is something I've got to do."

"I know. The whole thing smells and you've got to find out where the stink is coming from." Canseco paused. Ghost voices whispered on the line. "Watch yourself, son. Don't want you having another accident."

It wasn't like Canseco to be melodramatic. Luke Cameron realized he wasn't. He was dead serious.

"I'll watch my back," he said.

Now, here in Paris, there was a burst of shouting on the sidewalk near his table. A pair of blue-jacketed gendarmes were herding some ragged children away from a couple of bewildered tourists, one of whom was anxiously looking for his missing wallet. Horns blared as several of the children broke away and dodged through the traffic, darting across the wide avenue. The security police glanced at each other and shrugged. They made no attempt to pursue the little band of pickpockets. One gendarme turned toward the tourist, an angry American, and listened to his protest with studied indifference.

"Welcome to Paris," a voice said. The accent was so markedly French that Luke looked questioningly. "Frank Delaney. I'm your date."

They shook hands and Delaney took a chair facing Luke, with his back to the busy street. Delaney was a small, round-shouldered man in his forties with thick chestnut hair, alert brown eyes behind gold-rimmed glasses, a thin-lipped mouth that clamped shut over a jutting chin. He reminded Luke of photos of James Joyce, an Irish expatriate in Paris of another era. Like most Parisians Luke had seen, Delaney was also dressed like a fashion model.

"Sorry I couldn't meet your plane," Delaney apologized. He glanced around at the crowded sidewalk tables. "God, I never come here any more. But it seemed like an easy place for you to find. They charge you an arm and a leg."

"I wouldn't know. The waiter hasn't brought a bill."

"He won't want to discourage you. He'll wait until you're ready to leave. Anyway, this is on me . . . I mean, InCon. Canseco's orders."

The two men appraised each other in silence for a moment. "Your hotel okay?" Delaney asked.

"Not bad."

"I didn't know if you wanted seventeenth-century picturesque or twentieth-century comfortable. The Sofitel is new by French standards. Napoleon didn't sleep there, but it's well run."

"The hotel's great," Luke Cameron said indifferently.

"It should be quiet. Many of the small, older hotels are right on the street. You have to keep the windows open if there's no air-conditioning, and you get picturesque Paris street noises. Worse than a baby bawling in the next room."

As if to punctuate the comment, high-pitched taxi horns started a dialogue nearby. "So I hear," Luke said wryly.

"You want to go inside and talk?"

Fouquet's bar was wood paneled and subdued—more elegant than its other furnishings would have suggested. Perhaps it was only the patina of age, Luke thought. The two men found a table in the corner, and Delaney ordered two crèmes. He studied the tall, rugged westerner for a moment. "Canseco didn't say much, except that I should be helpful. Why don't you fill me in?"

Luke Cameron explained his interest in a French holding company he knew only by its initials, IBZ. The company had taken over a large number of properties in the Gibson, Montana area—including the local bank and Luke's father's ranch. Luke omitted the circumstances of his father's death and his own close encounter.

"I'm sure there's more to this than you're telling me," Delaney guessed shrewdly. "But I don't need to know all the whys and wherefores. Canseco's word is good enough. Let me ask you just one thing, Luke. You're suggesting there's something about IBZ that's not kosher. . . ."

"That's what I want to find out. I'd like to know more about the company. Who are the principals? Where are their offices? What are their aims? In particular, what are they doing in Gibson?"

"Mmmm. That may not be easy. Some of these international holding companies are secretive. They don't want to be scrutinized too closely by outsiders."

"I'm interested in a man named Henri Picard. He's one of the directors of IBZ. His daughter works for the company . . . she's in Gibson now. She's some kind of plant specialist. Has a degree in botany from the University of Paris. That couldn't have been too long ago, because she can't be more than twenty-five."

"I'll raise my antenna." Delaney shrugged, sipped his crème, glanced around the room at the well-dressed men and women scattered among the tables. "Let me see what answers I can pick up."

"What's your timing?"

"Give me twenty-four hours. Go do some sightseeing, Luke. You've never been in Paris before?"

Luke shook his head.

"Then you owe yourself, *mon ami.* Paris in the springtime is the most beautiful city in the world."

"I didn't come here for sightseeing."

"You've got a day; it'll take me at least that long. Go up the Eiffel Tower, visit Napoleon's tomb, the Flea Market, the Louvre—"

"All in a day?"

"Then do the Louvre, and walk across the Pont Neuf to the Ile de la Cite and Notre Dame. And eat. You're in Paris for Chrissakes!"

Luke Cameron had dinner at Le Petit Nicois, not far from his hotel on the Left Bank—a place enthusiastically recommended by Frank Delaney. Luke let the waiter select the dishes for him—it was easier than trying to translate the long menu—and wolfed down a fresh English sole, a truffle salad, and a superb dessert, with a name he couldn't pronounce. He suspected from the waiter's raised eyebrow that he should have lingered longer over the meal.

If his eating habits seemed barbaric to the French, he finished dinner in time for a leisurely stroll along the cobbled banks of the Seine. On the ornate Pont Alexandre III with its statuary and elaborate Florentine lamps, he paused to gaze down at the river as a boat passed beneath him, carrying diners who were still sipping wine and supping at tables with white cloths and candles. The evening breeze carried the light ripple of a woman's laughter. Luke was instantly reminded of Micheline Picard; she belonged in this beautiful, elegant city, he thought.

She definitely didn't belong in Gibson, Montana.

A gendarme, swathed in a drooping old-fashioned cape that must have been uncomfortably warm on this humid evening, paused near Luke.

"Bon soir, m'sieur."

"Bon soir," Luke answered in his high school French.

"Ah, vous ête Americaine! You are unwell, *m'sieur?"*

"No, I feel fine, thanks. Just enjoying the view."

"Ah, oui!" The policeman moved on, satisfied. Luke wondered if many people tried to commit suicide by jumping into the dark, placid waters of the Seine. The bridges weren't tall enough for serious jumpers, he thought.

A short distance away the Eiffel Tower rose, spidery, graceful, into the night sky, seeming taller than it actually was. Luke's sense of unreality, standing there on the ancient bridge and staring up at the tower, with the massive, spotlit Arc de Triomphe visible off to his right on what Parisians called the North Bank, and the gothic Notre Dame Cathedral behind him on its own island in the river, left him feeling cut off from his purpose, adrift in a strange land.

First day feeling, he decided. Paris was not a city to be experienced in this way, peripherally; its beauty and magic were something to be savored, not a distraction.

He wondered what Frank Delaney would learn.

Luke started back toward his hotel, impatient for the day to end.

Gibson, Montana

MAY, ANNE MCALISTER THOUGHT, WAS USUALLY HER FAvorite month, but Montana was suffering through an unseasonal hot spell. Or was it really the weather that caused her to feel so tired and listless these days? Maybe she was simply getting older.

When she stepped from the shimmering heat of Clark Street into the bank building, she welcomed the sudden rush of cool air. The French owners—no one ever used the name of the holding company, IBZ—had done one thing for which she renewed her thanks each hot summer day: they had installed central air-conditioning. She wasn't sure how she had functioned before.

"Good morning . . . good morning." Even when she was dragging, fighting off depression, she tried not to let it show. Aside from not wanting to burden others with her personal problems, or to put private unhappiness on display, she knew that employers had little patience with an employee's reasons for being surly, moody, or difficult to get along with.

Put on a happy face.

For the next hour she was too busy to think about herself. She sorted out the documents that passed over her desk, and routed those she couldn't handle herself to the loan committee, the accounting department, the personnel manager, the auditors who were currently preparing their annual report.

As she shuffled her papers, a letter turned up addressed to Mr. Gilman, the bank's president, bearing a French stamp and postmark. She stared at the envelope, reminded of her earlier reflections about IBZ. She didn't even know what the letters stood for. She understood only that the name was an umbrella to cover a highly diversified conglomerate headquartered in a suburb of Paris.

Oddly enough, she had never seen the names of any of the subsidiaries or affiliate companies—most were European, she guessed, and the names would have meant nothing to her anyway.

Shortly after 9:30 A.M. Mr. Gilman himself strode to the front of the bank to unlock the double doors. Micheline Picard swept in.

Swept was the appropriate word, Anne thought. The Frenchwoman—no one in town referred to her in any other way—entered the bank with a regal flourish. Mr. Gilman stopped just short of bowing to her. She walked briskly through the bank, not waiting for Gilman to catch up to her after he relocked the doors. She looked stunning in a white linen jacket over pale blue slacks. She caught every eye in the bank, those of men and women alike.

Anne wondered if her own negative reaction was jealousy, or envy. Or was it part of the resentment she felt toward foreign companies coming into Montana and buying up troubled properties at bargain prices, displacing people whose whole lives had belonged to this land, changing the nature and face of the land. . . .

As if sensing hostility, Micheline Picard slowed as she approached Anne's desk, pausing long enough to offer a nod and a smile that revealed perfect white teeth but failed to light the cold dark eyes. "Bonjour, Madame McAlister," she said, in what everyone in Gibson called her delightful French accent. "It is such a lovely day, yes?"

"Yes, it really is."

Gilman caught up to the Frenchwoman at the low barrier that

screened employees from customers. He held it for Micheline Picard to pass through and ushered her quickly into his office.

Sometimes, he acts as if he's frightened of her, Anne thought, wondering at such a perception. Or was it that, like everyone else in Gibson, especially the male population over the age of ten, he was merely smitten?

Like Luke Cameron, she thought.

And the thought of Luke's name triggered some mixed feelings she had been trying to sort out.

She had tried to call Luke at the 4-B's Motel when she heard about his accident, but he had checked out. No one knew where he was.

Luke's pickup truck had been found in the middle of the river south of town on Sunday morning. There were rumors, small-town gossip being what it was, that Luke had got drunk Saturday night and had driven off the road in the dark. Lucky he didn't kill himself, some people said. Someone claimed to have seen him driving erratically down the long grade—toward the sweep at the bottom that teenagers called Chicken Curve.

But to Anne McAlister, this rumor somehow didn't fit Luke Cameron.

Sheriff Thayer had arranged for the truck to be towed into Gibson. But after a couple of days, he had released it to Justin Cranmer, the lawyer, who seemed to have become friendly with Luke. The rumor was that he had bought the pickup from Luke.

None of this explained why Luke had left town so abruptly. But there was no doubt he was gone.

Back to South America, Anne thought. Where was it? Punta del Ansa, something like that. Washing his hands of Gibson, probably. Shutting off the past.

Knowing that Luke was gone brought an odd feeling of relief: she wouldn't have to deal with an unexpected stirring she had felt that night when Luke was leaving her house, a feeling she had put down to her low state of morale at the time and her unhappiness with the way Brad had acted. But the relief was accompanied by a wistful regret. . . .

When the bank's doors opened for business at ten o'clock, Anne once more became too occupied to think about her own problems. Micheline Picard left shortly thereafter, stepping elegantly and coolly into the heat of Clark Street. Mr. Gilman called Anne into his office to give her some letters he had signed, ready for mailing. When she returned to her desk, she became absorbed again with a new account application.

She almost missed Brad, who was waiting in the line before Ruth Waldmeier's window. Brad must have entered the bank while she was in Mr. Gilman's office.

Her desk phone buzzed urgently. After she finished the call, Brad had left the teller's window and was crossing the carpeted floor toward her desk. Anne looked up at him, trying to shake a heavy feeling.

"How goes it, Mrs. M.?" Brad seemed to be in an uncommonly cheerful mood, considering that he couldn't have slept at all since the end of the shift. He hadn't reached home when she left the house at nine. "You're a sight for sore eyes, or haven't I told you that lately?"

"No, you haven't."

He leaned over the desk toward her, a broad, infectious grin spreading over his face. God, how she used to melt when he turned on that grin! In a low, conspiratorial voice he said, "We've got to stop meeting like this . . . people will talk."

"You're in a cheerful mood this morning."

"Why shouldn't I be? It's payday, remember?" The grin teased her, a secretive quality in it. He held up the savings passbook, which surprised her. Usually both of their paychecks went straight into their joint checking account to pay bills due. There wasn't enough left over to add to their meager savings. "Want a peek?"

"Brad . . . what's got into you?" She saw Mr. Gilman peering around his door. "You'd better go home and get some sleep."

He flipped the passbook onto her desk. It landed on an auto loan application she had typed up. Anne stared at it, for some unaccountable reason afraid to pick it up.

"Go ahead." Brad's tone was insistent. "Have a look."

Anne picked up the passbook, hesitated, then opened it to the last entry.

Her heart seemed to stop. It was like a freeze-frame in a movie. Even the normal, muted sounds of activity in the bank—murmuring voices, the slap of the outer door opening and closing, typewriters clacking in the background—were momentarily stilled.

"What . . . my God, Brad, what is this?"

He shrugged with elaborate nonchalance. "Hey, I told you my luck couldn't stay as bad as it's been. I know, you don't like my gambling . . . and you're right, I've taken some chances I shouldn't have with the mortgage money. But old Lady Luck smiled on me last night."

"But . . . ten thousand dollars! You couldn't have won that much! Not in one night. It . . . it would be all over town!"

The smile began to fade. A sullen expression replaced the good humor—that unhappy little boy look she had once found so endearing and now so exasperating.

"You calling me a liar?"

"Brad . . . please! Tell me where you got this." She was becoming self-conscious, sensing that not only Mr. Gilman but other bank employees were staring curiously at her and Brad.

At first, he seemed determined to stick to his story—using anger to cut off communication, a sequence that was becoming all too familiar. Then he thought better of it. "I didn't want to tell you yet. I didn't want you getting your hopes too high. You remember some of those investments I made in the ski resort project? We figured they were all down the drain, right? Well, the bad news is the resort project is dead. But the good news is that the land is still worth something. A new lawyer has come into the picture. Our limited-partner interests that I'd written off are now worth something. I agreed to sell mine, and this is the first settlement payment. There should be at least one more payment, maybe even as big as this one. Now what do you say?"

"Oh, Brad, that's . . . wonderful!" The news should have left Anne elated. Somehow it didn't.

"Hey, how about a little more enthusiasm? You can see what this means—there's enough to catch up on the mortgage"—Brad caught Gilman's eye and smirked—"and get this bank off our backs."

"That's not fair, Brad. They've been good about our falling behind."

Brad gave Gilman a cheerful wave and turned back to her. "With another chunk like this, honey, who knows? Maybe we can trade in that old clunker of a car and fix the roof."

"Let's not get ahead of ourselves." She tried to respond brightly. "It really is marvelous; I had no idea. I just need a little time to absorb it. You should have told me."

"Well, it wasn't a sure thing. I figured I'd made enough pie-in-the-sky announcements. Hey, I'd better let you get back to work. Big Brother is giving us the evil eye."

"You'd better get some sleep; you must be dead tired." But he wasn't, she saw clearly; Brad was on a high, pumped up in a way she hadn't seen in years.

"I'm fine; stop worrying. Maybe you can stop worrying about a lot of things. Maybe you'll even start believing in me again."

She watched him stride out of the bank, his step bounding. Instead of the relief and joy his surprise revelation should have brought, she felt only the return of the morning's depression.

How can I believe in you, she asked silently, as her husband disappeared into Clark Street, *when you've just lied to me?*

Al Trautman frowned at the strict orders he had received. How in the world could he conduct a thorough investigation in a small town and an isolated government facility without tipping off the thieves, terrorists, nuclear protesters—whoever they might be—that an investigation was underway? There was a chance the bad guys would make another attempt—so far two thefts had been verified—but not if they knew their earlier strikes had been detected.

More by good luck, Trautman thought, than good management.

Trautman was staying at the 4-B's Motel, Gibson's best. It was located right in town, was new enough that the plumbing still worked, and had cable TV and an attached restaurant. In strange towns, Trautman didn't like exploring for a place to eat.

Al Trautman was a special investigator for the Energy Department, part of a Nuclear Emergency Search Team, known inside the federal bureaucracy simply as NEST. He wasn't one of those scientists who wandered around in white laboratory jackets with gamma ray detectors and neutron sniffers. Those members of NEST had also descended on Gibson, primed to practice their magic. By contrast, Al Trautman, in his own blunt view, was just a seat-of-the-pants cop. The White Jackets could say whether or not some strategic material had been taken or tampered with. With a little luck, they might even be able to track it. If they could focus on a specific location, they could detect the presence of a nuclear mass even from the air. What the White Jackets weren't trained to do was track down the people who might have taken the stuff illegally and arrest them—by force if necessary. That's what Trautman did.

He was not an impressive man in appearance, a fact that often worked to his advantage. He was fifty-two and looked older. The hair was gray and thinning. He was vain enough that he had taken to a different way of combing it, letting it grow longer on the sides and folding it over the top, contemptuous of himself for doing so. The paunch was not only threatening; it had settled in for the duration. His left hip ached when the weather was cold or wet. His features were nondescript, the nose mashed in from past encounters with bare knuckles, the jowls sagging, the brown eyes deceptively bland.

Under the extra weight, however, was a conditioned, hard-muscled body. Behind the bland eyes was a constant wariness. Beneath the relaxed mouth was a stubborn chin. Trautman had served in Air Force Intelligence until early retirement, then had gone to work as an investigator for Treasury. The Energy Department, in quest of experienced investigators, had drafted him and had assigned him to NEST.

Since his arrival in Gibson, Trautman had deliberately stayed away from SMS Number 14. That was the last place he wanted to be seen. For Trautman was convinced that someone on the inside was implicated in the theft of uranium. He had reviewed the security with a professional eye. In his judgment, it was adequate to trip up any thieves on the outside—unless they had help from the inside. The White Jackets could investigate the site in the guise of inspectors; such visits were part of the normal routine for all nuclear storage sites. And one young investigator on Trautman's team, Rob Gillespie, was already inside as a new hire. Gillespie was a baby face, whom no one would ever suspect of being a federal undercover man.

Trautman saved for himself the outside investigation. So far, he had only one lead.

Copies of the incident reports at the site for the past three months had been delivered to Trautman's room at the motel last night. He'd spent the evening poring over them, the tedium broken by a couple of beers and snatches of the evening news, winding up with a few minutes of Johnny Carson. Except that Johnny was on vacation and Jay Leno was subbing for him. Leno's lines were funny, but he couldn't match Carson's bemused expressions.

At 11:36 P.M., in the middle of Leno's opening monologue, one of the incident reports leaped out at Trautman. A security officer on the graveyard shift at the nuclear site, one Darrell Johnson, had spotted a pickup truck parked off the highway that ran along the south border of the site. The truck was not on government land, but its presence near the perimeter had been enough to generate a routine report. The bare facts had caught Trautman's attention not because a truck was parked at the site's edge, with no driver in sight, but because of the hour: 2:21 A.M.

He scanned the incident report quickly. The security officer had followed through, checking the location an hour later, at 3:30 A.M., and noting the pickup was gone.

Sometimes you get lucky, Trautman thought.

He debated talking directly to the security officer. But Johnson probably had little to add to what was already in his report; the license number of the vehicle, a full-size Chevy pickup, not one of those downsized imports. Talking to Johnson, though, would add another person to the number of people who knew about a NEST investigation—a person who worked inside the DOE facility. Not worth the risk, Trautman decided.

He picked up the phone, which offered direct dialing. The number he tapped out was the home phone number of Joe Springer, the FBI agent in charge in Butte, Montana. The phone rang seven times before it was picked up. There was a grunt, then the clatter of a sound as if a telephone was being dropped. Finally a voice, fuzzy with sleep, spoke: "Yeah? Hello?"

"Springer?"

"Yeah?"

"Al Trautman. I left a message earlier."

"Oh, yeah, yeah, the NEST guy."

"Right. You know about our investigation at the nuclear materials storage site in Gibson. You were the one who passed along the report from the security manager about missing uranium."

"I got a memo from Washington about you, Trautman." The sleep was banished from Springer's voice. "What's the urgency?"

"I need help." He gave Springer the make and license number of the pickup and the reason for his interest. "I need an I.D. on the registered owner."

"Tonight?"

"Yesterday."

"Where are you?" Springer asked. He scribbled down the name of the motel and Trautman's room number. "I'll call you back."

Jay Leno was talking to a guest, a young actress Trautman didn't recognize. She was wearing a black leather miniskirt that was so short it exposed her hips when she crossed her legs. She kept crossing and uncrossing her legs, as if she were nervous or self-conscious. A leering Leno kept leaning over for a better view.

In less than ten minutes, the FBI agent called back with the information Trautman wanted. There was an undercurrent in Springer's voice that caught Trautman's attention. "The truck is coregistered to Thomas Cameron and Lucas Cameron, father and son. The father is deceased but his name hasn't been taken off the registration yet."

"You know them?"

"Yeah . . . Thing is, both of them came by my office the last couple of months—not together but separately. The old man was in maybe a month before he died."

"Natural death?"

"An accident. He was trampled. It may sound crazy but it's true. He was trampled by a herd of buffalo."

"Sure."

"I'm telling you, it's true. He slipped and hit his head on a rock. This must have spooked a buffalo herd which trampled him."

Al Trautman contemplated this for a moment. He decided not to ask Springer how come a herd of buffalo was running loose in Montana. "What did he come to see you about?"

"Among other things, the DOE site just outside Gibson." Joe Springer paused to let Trautman absorb this information. "He thought there might be something going on at the site that the government was hiding. Radiation leaks or mysterious experiments . . . or whatever. He wasn't a crackpot, really, just a suspicious old guy. But he didn't have anything to back up his suspicions . . . just smoke."

The girl in the short leather skirt was leaving the stage, giving the crowd a little-girl wave to thunderous applause. Trautman said, "You said the son also came to see you. Lucas?"

"Yeah, Luke."

"What did he want?"

"Funny thing, he asked pretty much the same questions his father did. Except that he was also upset about his old man's fatal accident."

"I don't remember seeing a report about their complaints."

"Well . . . there was no reason to alert your people." Joe Springer sounded defensive. "There was nothing substantial . . . just complaints, coincidences, suspicion, speculation . . . nothing substantial."

"I've cracked many cases that started with suspicion." Trautman's tone was not unfriendly. He didn't want to alienate the local FBI. He might need more cooperation. "Thanks for the information. I'll be in touch."

"There's one other thing."

"What's that?" Trautman was suddenly attentive; he had detected something in Springer's voice.

"A vehicle accident report was filed with the state motor vehicle department. Seems that pickup truck had to be towed out of the river just south of Gibson Sunday morning. Brake failure the report says."

"Anyone hurt?"

"The driver was lucky. It was Luke Cameron."

There was a long moment of shared silence. Springer felt the same instincts he did, Al Trautman thought. They were both old-timers, whose minds were moving in the same direction: two complaints about mysterious doings at the nuclear site . . . separate complaints from a father and later his son . . . both of them involved shortly afterward in strange accidents, one fatal. And all of this happened just before the discovery that uranium was missing from the same site.

"I'll let you know what turns up."

"You do that."

Each man thought there were too many coincidences.

No one in Gibson, Montana, seemed to know where Luke Cameron had gone—not even Ed Thayer, the sheriff of Gibson County. Thayer had sent a tow truck to haul Cameron's pickup out of Gibson Creek and tow it into town. He had impounded the car while a mechanic checked it over. The mechanic had found the brake fluid reservoir empty.

"Break in the line?" Al Trautman was questioning the sheriff. "Or a cut?"

Thayer shook his head. "Uh-uh. Just empty."

"Somebody forgot to fill it?"

The sheriff smiled. "Luke drove that Chevy over to Butte last week. He developed a brake problem and took it to a garage for repairs. I called the mechanic, name of Clyde Turnbull. No good mechanic likes to admit he made a stupid mistake, like forgetting to add fluid after finishing a brake relining. But this guy's story rings true. He remembers adding fluid himself, and he checked for leaks. He also gave the car a test drive before Cameron got his truck back. Brakes worked fine."

The two men studied each other. Thayer's office was as sparse and plain as a country store. But Trautman felt at ease in it, as he did with the sheriff. Cops the world over, in Al Trautman's experience, are on the same wavelength. They tend to identify with one another. Like aliens in a strange country.

"Where's the truck now?"

"I released it to Justin Cranmer . . . a friend of Luke's. He's buying the pickup. . . . I had no reason to hold the vehicle. There's no evidence of wrongdoing. I had to treat it as a minor accident . . . truck's got a few scratches and rock dings . . . that's all. Luke walked away from it."

"Where's Cameron now? I'd like to talk to him."

"I understand he's left town. He was staying at the 4-B's . . . where you are." Thayer shifted vocal gears. "Mind telling me why you're looking for him?"

Al Trautman took his time. Some small-town cops had big mouths. He decided Ed Thayer could be trusted. But he paused for effect before he spoke. "His pickup was logged last week . . . parked off the highway south of the DOE facility after midnight."

"Doesn't surprise me," the sheriff said. "Both Luke and his dad had questions about that place, suspicions, bad vibes. My guess is, Luke was checking out his suspicions . . . doing a little quiet snooping."

"Know him well?"

"Since he was a kid. Know him well enough to trust him. There's an old saying in this country: *a man to cross the river with*. That's Luke Cameron."

"Dependable," Trautman summarized.

"Yup."

"Patriotic?"

Thayer nodded, the curiosity deepening behind the steady brown eyes. "Did his time in Vietnam when he was called up."

"His father . . . patriotic, too?"

"Hell, yes . . . what's up, Trautman?"

"We've got some nuclear material missing. That's for your ears only."

"Understood." Thayer's eyebrows, usually steady as his gaze, rose perceptibly.

"Two containers of weapons-grade U-235 have been stolen. Not just mislaid. Not lost in inventory. Stolen. The missing containers were replaced by identical ones containing buckshot."

The air in the sleepy office was suddenly charged. They were two lawmen confronted with a major crime on their turf—Trautman's federal turf, Thayer's local turf. This was an affront to both of them. They belonged to a breed of lawmen who took such encroachments personally.

"I need to talk to Cameron," said the man from NEST. "You may be right about him. He's probably not a criminal. But he may know something."

"Talk to Cranmer. He drove Luke to Helena. My guess is, Cranmer drove him to the airport."

"Where, in Helena?"

The first thought that flashed into Al Trautman's mind was, *If he's not guilty of anything, why is he running?*

At dusk, Al Trautman headed his rented Toyota for Helena. The evening was cooler than he had expected after a day in the seventies. The breeze gushing in the car's open windows was soft and scented. And the sunset over the mountains, he had to admit, was spectacular—a palette of pinks and oranges and reds over the green forests and the purple peaks.

Approaching Helena, the main highway, Interstate 15, was wide and divided. It cut surgically through steep, pine-covered hills. All nature was hushed, disrupted only by the occasional swish of a passing car or rumble of a semi trailer. The drive allowed him to sort out the interviews he had conducted during the day, the answers he had obtained, and the questions that had been raised.

The least productive meeting, although it had been revealing to a lawman accustomed to dealing with lawyers, had been with Justin Cranmer.

Lawyers, not unlike cops, had their peculiar ways, and Cranmer had been predictably guarded in his responses. Yes, he had purchased the Chevrolet pickup from his friend Luke Cameron, and yes, it was now in his possession. The brakes worked just fine. Yes, he'd driven Luke over to Helena. To the airport? Yes to that, also. Did he know where Cameron was going? No, Cranmer couldn't say. Luke had kept his own counsel. And what was this all about, anyway?

Trautman had been equally circumspect. He just wanted to talk to Luke Cameron. No, Cameron was not the target of his investigation. It was possible that Cameron himself had been the target of a criminal act—that the brake failure that sent his pickup hurtling off the road might not have been an accident.

Cranmer, Trautman thought, did not seem surprised.

"Of course, I can locate Cameron and trace his movements, Mr. Cranmer," Trautman said finally. "I thought you might save me the trouble."

"Then I suggest you do what you say you can do."

"It might be helpful if I knew what was in Cameron's mind—why he decided to leave so suddenly."

"He returned to Gibson because of his father's death. It's possible he had simply accomplished all he could here."

"Uh huh. Yeah, that's possible. Not likely though."

Al Trautman had learned one thing from his interviews in Gibson; Luke Cameron seemed to have some good friends.

And at least one enemy.

Trautman met his boss, Lee Hamilton, at a Best Western motel just off I-15 at the edge of Helena. Hamilton was using the motel as headquarters for the NEST investigative team. Obviously, they couldn't set up shop in Gibson without attracting attention. Two undercover men—Trautman in the town and his assistant, young Gillespie, at the SMS site—was as conspicuous as Hamilton wanted the investigation to be.

Lee Hamilton, as Trautman saw him, was an administrator, not a cop. A bureaucrat who knew his way around the federal maze. Yet he was no paper shuffler who found his *raison d'etre* in the regulation books. His eye was on the bottom line, not on the fine print. He was more interested in results than in protocol—as long as your methods didn't backfire and cause embarrassment. You simply got the job done, or he found someone else. Trautman didn't like the man—but even if Hamilton had sensed this, he would have disregarded it. By his lights, liking or disliking had nothing to do with their assignment.

The team commander, in deference to the late hour, had settled into a soft chair and switched on the TV set when Trautman knocked discreetly on his door. But even in a relaxed mood, Hamilton was in command, leaning forward in his chair. A NEST agent opened the door a crack, eyeballed Trautman, and stepped back to let him in.

From his chair, Lee Hamilton nodded. His only concession to relaxation had been to remove his jacket, unbutton his collar and loosen his tie. Trautman didn't understand how anyone could sit and watch TV with his tie on.

"We checked on your suspect," Hamilton said.

Trautman dropped into one of the chairs facing a circular lamp table near the front window. The drapes were drawn across the window. He wanted to light a cigarette, but Hamilton didn't tolerate smoking in his room or car.

"He's not my suspect."

"He caught a flight to Denver Saturday."

Trautman waited.

"He's gone," Hamilton said. "Flew the coop. Left the country."

Trautman's surprise stimulated his senses and cast off the fatigue that had overtaken him. He analyzed the new information for a moment and announced, "He's not our man."

"That's your conclusion? You think it's a coincidence that, all of a sudden, he bolts out of Gibson and flies off to Paris."

"Probably not."

"Probably not?"

"I've checked him out. He's not the type who would cross his country."

"Not the type? No doubt that's your gut feeling. I need more than your gut to convince me."

"There's more. It's beginning to look like Cameron's been a target himself. Someone tried to kill him . . . and someone may have killed his father." Briefly, Trautman sketched the series of events surrounding the elder Cameron's death and his son's return to Gibson, culminating in Luke Cameron's downhill plunge in his pickup truck after the brake fluid had been mysteriously drained. "No . . . Cameron's no fanatic engaged in nuclear terrorism. He's not the type. The circumstances don't fit. It just doesn't add up," Trautman concluded.

"Maybe he had a falling out with his accomplices. There's more than one man involved in this. . . ." Hamilton jabbed a finger at Trautman. "Luke Cameron's your man, all right. He may not be one of the bad guys, but he's involved. Find out how he's involved."

"How'm I supposed to do that? I'm in Montana and he's in Paris."

"That can be overcome." Hamilton reached out to a nearby dresser and picked up an envelope. He flipped it onto the bed within Trautman's reach. "Your ticket to Paris. Find the son of a bitch."

Paris, France

"THAT'S THE PLACE," FRANK DELANEY SAID. It was a lackluster office building, located in the Eighth Arrondissement in a district called La Defense, reached by driving west from the Arc de Triomphe and crossing the Seine. The area had become a center of business and finance for the city. With its modern, high-rise office buildings of steel and glass, it was part of Paris, Luke Cameron reflected, that could have been a Houston transplant.

Delaney had picked Luke up at his hotel. The InCon man maneuvered his black Peugeot deftly through the morning traffic snarls, circling the Arc de Triomphe and heading west on the avenue de la Grande Armes past the Palais des Congres. After crossing the river at Pont de Neully, he darted into a forest of high-rise structures and parked in an underground garage identified by a large letter P. On foot, he led Luke to a small café off the avenue Gambetta, where he ordered coffee and rolls.

With an eye on the building across the street, Delaney dunked his croissant. "To a Frenchman, this is sacrilege," he confessed, with a grin.

"How much did you learn about IBZ?"

"You're all business, aren't you?" Delaney's gaze returned to the glass face of the office building. "IBZ is a mystery company. It's registered, it has a board of directors, it has an office address. But nobody . . . I mean nobody . . . knows anything about the outfit. Except for one thing . . ."

"What's that?" Luke pressed.

"It's not French." Delaney tore off a bit of soaked croissant. "My informants tell me IBZ is a foreign-held company with a French facade. That's not unusual with international investment and development companies. The principals like to stay behind the scenes and maintain their privacy."

Luke stared at him, thinking of Micheline Picard, wondering how much of her was genuine and how much subterfuge. "What about Henri Picard?"

Delaney shook his head. "There's no such animal."

"That's impossible."

"It's a common name, but there's nobody connected with IBZ called Picard. If he's as important as you suggested, he should be one of the listed officers or directors. He ought to have *some* visible profile. He does not . . . not with IBZ or any other international company. I checked out all the standard business directories, the French register of corporations, I asked questions of people who ought to know," he said with deliberate vagueness. "Your Monsieur Picard is even more of a mystery than IBZ."

"I'd like to have a look at their offices."

"You want a translator along?"

"Maybe it would be better if I went alone . . . and played the part of the bumbling American."

"I'll bet you lunch you don't get past the receptionist."

Luke went straight to the IBZ offices, which were located on the ninth floor. The receptionist was pretty as a dream, petite, chic, perfumed, and coiffeured. She also spoke tolerable English.

"I wish to see Monsieur Henri Picard," Luke said.

"Mais, non, monsieur, c'est impossible. There is . . . no Monsieur Picard. You have mistake."

"I'm quite sure of the name." He spelled it in case the receptionist didn't understand his pronunciation clearly. "I have an appointment."

"I am sorry, monsieur." She offered him a lovely smile to ease his disappointment and cover her own sorrow.

"Could I talk to someone else? Do you have someone who speaks English?"

"*Anglais? Non, monsieur.*"

"Anyone at all."

"I am very sorry. May I suggest . . . you should write and ask for an appointment. I am sure it will be arranged."

"Maybe I have the wrong office," he suggested, frowning.

Behind the tastefully extravagant receptionist's office, which was dominated by her desk in the center, decorated by several original oil paintings, and framed by expanses of opaque glass partitioning, there was a hush of important silence.

Luke Cameron had a strong feeling there was nothing else.

They had lunch at the Sebillon-Paris-Bar on avenue Charles de Gaulle in Neuilly—Delaney's choice because Luke had insisted on picking up the check. The restaurant was a popular, bustling place. Although the *boeuf a la ficelle* was delicate and delicious, Luke Cameron toyed pensively with his food.

Over coffee, Delaney studied Luke with mild skepticism. "What's next, *mon ami?*"

"I'm not sure."

"Why do I get this feeling you know exactly what your next move will be. The boss will have my ass in a sling if I let you get into trouble in Paris."

Though Luke welcomed Delaney's assistance, he was reluctant to confide too much. Delaney might say the wrong thing to the wrong person. "I just can't understand it. . . ." Luke said tentatively. "There doesn't seem to be any Henri Picard."

"No one by that name at IBZ?"

"But there *is* a Micheline Picard. At least she *calls* herself Micheline Picard."

Delaney's gaze behind the thin, gold-rimmed glasses was shrewdly perceptive. "She's the real reason you're in Paris."

"She may be the key to the mystery."

"Then let's try the key. I'll check her university credentials. What else do you know about her? Anything about her personal life? Where she was born? Where she grew up?"

"Not much. She said she was brought up in a convent somewhere near Paris."

"It shouldn't be hard to verify her academic credentials . . . if she studied under the Picard name. It may be more trouble locating an unnamed convent. Did she mention anything specific? Any details about the village? How old the convent was?"

"Ancient, I think. It was near a river, or on one, and . . . not far from one of the great forests. Vincennes?"

"Bingo! Would the river be the Marne?"

"Could be . . ."

"Let me do some more digging and get back to you."

"Do you mind if I rush you a little?"

"Give me another day. You visit the Louvre yet? No? I didn't think so. Relax, Luke. Be a tourist."

The two Americans in the Peugeot, absorbed in their own concerns, did not notice the small gray Renault that had followed the Peugeot from La Defense to the Sebillon-Paris-Bar. Nor was either man aware of being followed later on the return drive into the center of Paris.

When Delaney dropped Luke off near the Sofitel, the driver of the Renault lingered, ignoring the angry shouts of a passing taxi driver who had to swerve around him.

Not until Luke entered the hotel lobby did the Renault move on. Then it pulled over to the curb outside a small café.

The driver sauntered inside, asked to use the phone, and dialed a Paris number. The proprietor of the café paid no attention to the brief conversation, other than to note that it was not in French.

Sergei Milov had a love affair with Paris.

The City of Light sparkled for the Russian by day and dazzled him at night. The sun seemed brighter, the springtime balmier—and the heart certainly beat faster—in Paris.

He paid homage to a few of its old churches, concentrating on Notre Dame and Sacre Coeur—as a nod to his friend and mentor, Colonel Vitaly Novikoff, who was certain to ask about them. The cathedrals inspired wonder in him not only for their soaring beauty but as testament to the astonishing depth of religious faith among their medieval builders. Besides these architectural marvels, Milov loved the bridges over the Seine, the river itself, the museums and gardens, the evidence on all sides of the French people's reverence for their past, which appealed to his Russian soul.

He marveled at the little shops and great department stores with their delightfully decadent bounty of jewels and fashions and artistic treasures. Moscow and Leningrad had great churches and museums of art; also ancient bridges and opulent castles that had once housed kings and queens, emperors and empresses. But nowhere in Russia would you find such extravagance and abundance on display—available to anyone.

He basked in the joys of Paris: his freedom of movement; the noisy confusion of traffic; the warmth of the shopkeepers and restaurant proprietors; the daily feast at every table.

But most of all, Milov loved the women of Paris. Wherever he went they caught his enchanted gaze—trim, chic, sophisticated women, dressed in the latest fashions, so confident and sure of themselves, apparently so free of drudgery and dowdiness that they could devote their lives to making themselves vivacious and beautiful.

Of all the Russian women he had known, only Anna Natalia Sidorin was like them.

Sergei Milov had to force himself to concentrate on the mission that had brought him to Paris. That, too, centered upon a woman of intrigue.

The KGB's extensive intelligence network in Paris was at his disposal, and the anonymous agents had done much of their work before he arrived. From their reports, Milov learned that the Party of Allah was strong in France. It was France that had granted Ayatollah Ruhollah Khomeini sanctuary when he was banished from Iraq, where he had been carrying out his revolutionary activities against the shah of Iran from exile. Khomeini had set up headquarters in a villa in Neuphle-de-Chateau, a suburb of Paris. He had used his prominence to exploit the Parisian media and to make himself the spokesman for revolutionary Islam recognized throughout Europe. Until he came to France, he had been a dominant religious leader in Iran recognized throughout the Middle East; in Paris he moved onto the world's stage.

Assigned to assist Milov was a KGB agent attached to the Fifth Department of the First Chief Directorate. The latter had ultimate responsibility for all foreign operations, while the Fifth Department covered most of Western Europe. The agent, Major Alexei Pichenko, outranked Milov. He had also spent enough time in the Western world to have acquired an air of superiority about his London-tailored suits, his command of French, his French mistress. Milov's first impression was that Pichenko was an arrogant bastard. Nevertheless, the major proved to be cooperative; he had been impressed by the level of authority directing him to assist Milov.

On Milov's third day in Paris, Major Pichenko drove him to the Marne Valley. They stopped for lunch in a small restaurant in Villiers-sur-Marne, a picturesque and peaceful town that seemed inviting even though a soft rain was falling, misting the wooded slopes east of the town and shrouding the banks of the meandering river.

At a nearby table, two dark-skinned, bearded men were dining. They spoke quietly and ignored others in the restaurant, although Milov was certain that he and Pichenko had been quietly observed.

"This village is the headquarters for the Iranian Islamic revolutionaries," Pichenko explained. "I will show you their villa after lunch, although there is little to see."

"There's an active Islamic fundamentalist group here?"

"Here and throughout France."

"As you know, I'm interested in one person in particular, a woman who was here a year ago. I don't know how long she had been here; I don't know whether she's still in Paris. If she is, she might be part of the group located here—if this is the control center for Iranian revolutionaries." Villiers-sur-Marne seemed a long way from revolution, Milov thought. But so Paris must have seemed to the French nobility two hundred years ago, on the morning of what came to be called the Terror. . . .

"We are making inquiries as Moscow Central requested," Major Pichenko said. "There was such a woman . . . oddly, she appears to have been French rather than Iranian. She was said to be recruiting the most ardent Iranian supporters of Islam for a special mission. Her activities were investigated by the Direction Generale de la Securite Exterieure—the DGSE—and the French international intelligence agency—the DST. Apparently they did not find anything substantial."

"She supported Khomeini's revolution?"

"Passionately, it seems."

"I wonder why. A Frenchwoman, I mean. Do you have a name for her?"

"Not yet. It is not certain that she is French. Some of the Iranians refer to her as a true Daughter of Allah. But they tend to speak of such matters with exaggerated fervor." Pichenko nodded at Milov's plate. "You find the duck tasty, *n'est-ce pas?*"

"Yes." But Milov was not to be distracted. The mysterious Daughter of Allah was more interesting than French cuisine. "I need to know if she is still in France . . . and if not, where she has gone."

"We should have news from our informants soon."

The rain dissipated before they finished dining. When they emerged from the restaurant, the sunshine was filtering through the clouds. "Is there anything else you wish to see, Captain Milov?" Pichenko wondered aloud.

"Tell me . . . how far is it to Orleans?"

"Maybe . . . a hundred fifty kilometers. You wish to go there?"

"That's where another revolutionary Frenchwoman won a great victory . . . more than five hundred years ago."

"Joan of Arc?" Pichenko responded curiously.

"That is the one," Milov said with a smile.

Vitaly Novikoff, he thought, would be very pleased.

Gibson, Montana

ROB GILLESPIE COULDN'T QUITE EXPLAIN HOW HE HAD BE-come an investigator for the Nuclear Emergency Search Team. It certainly wasn't a planned career. What he knew about nuclear energy could have been stuffed inside the rolled-up law school diploma that he had earned from Georgetown University. He had quickly concluded that he could expect a mediocre future in law. Having placed in the bottom third of his class, he had been passed over by all the prestigious law firms scouting the campus for future junior partners.

At that vulnerable moment, he had been approached by an FBI recruiter. Oddly, the recruiter was prospecting not for the Federal Bureau of Investigation but for the Department of Energy. With some skepticism, not really expecting anything to come of it, Gillespie had filled out an application. To his surprise, he had been hired.

Not that he had any complaints. The work stimulated his inner sense of intrigue and spirit of adventure. He also liked working for Al Trautman, who was a demanding but patient teacher. For an unspectacular lawyer, the job also offered stability and advancement. Given Trautman's age and incompatibility with their boss, Lee Hamilton, Rob figured Trautman wouldn't stay at DOE much longer. Which meant Rob Gillespie had a possible future with NEST.

At age twenty-seven, Rob Gillespie looked more like twenty-two. He had soft, wavy blond hair, guileless blue eyes, and a deceptively boyish appearance that had proved to be an advantage in his work. No one ever took him for a wily investigator, with a keen eye for detail.

As his cover at SMS Number 14, Gillespie posed as an accountant with the General Accounting Office who had been assigned to help complete a routine audit. But back in his motel room in Gibson, he had spent endless hours feeding video tapes through a rented VCR.

The tapes had been recorded by the surveillance cameras at SMS Number 14. The scenes picked up by the rotating, time-lapse cameras were brief, fragmented, repetitive—and so routinely boring that Gillespie had twice fallen asleep while viewing them. At first, he had rewound the tapes and watched the segments he had missed. Then he stopped bothering.

He almost missed the crucial scene in the facility's alarm control center. His glazed eyes caught a break in the routine, but it barely registered on his numbed brain. He stopped the tape, ran it back and replayed it. His heart started to pound. Not just from the discovery of something unusual on the tape; even more from the sudden frightening thought that he might easily have overlooked it—or slept through it.

Gillespie played the scene for a third time, this time in slow motion. It showed a tall, muscular security guard turning away from the control panel inside the tiny room. It was not clear from the tape whether he had actually touched the controls; the camera cycled on a moment too late. His back was to the camera, so Gillespie couldn't see his face. But when Burt Henderson—whom Gillespie recognized as the man in charge of the alarm control center on the graveyard shift—suddenly loomed in the doorway, the other man's body language was unmistakable. He froze. The rigidity of his body telegraphed shock—or fear.

This told the NEST agent viewing the tape that something was wrong.

Quickly, Rob Gillespie checked the date and time. He already knew the incident had occurred between midnight and eight A.M. The log showed the time as 03:12:30.

The site's cameras provided video coverage, not audio. Watching intently the silent exchange between Henderson and the other man, Gillespie yearned for sound to tell him what they were saying. The unidentified guard quickly departed and the segment ended.

Gillespie considered the importance of what he had seen. There was nothing certain, nothing incriminating, just something unexplained; the guard's presence in the alarm control center at three in the morning when he didn't work there, and his nervous reaction when Henderson caught him inside the room.

It was no more than a flicker of light through the fog. But it was the only clue Gillespie had found in endless hours of scanning tapes.

Rob Gillespie wished Trautman were available; he could have turned his findings over to the rumpled senior agent, knowing Trautman would latch onto the discovery like a bulldog and know exactly what to do. But Trautman had gone off on another pursuit without any explanation to his assistant.

Because of the lateness of the hour, Rob Gillespie hesitated while he argued with himself, then telephoned Lee Hamilton at his motel in Helena. The boss of the NEST investigation didn't hesitate; he routed the assistant manager of the DOE site out of bed—he was one of the few who knew of the investigation—and explained tersely what was needed.

An hour later, the assistant manager himself, a harried bureaucrat named Sindell, knocked softly on Gillespie's door.

"You Gillespie?"

"That's right."

"These are the logs you requested . . . and the personnel files. I'll have to have them back before morning." After handing over a cardboard box filled with papers and files, he stood in the doorway, irresolute. "Is that . . . is there anything else?"

"No, that's all, thanks."

When Gillespie volunteered nothing else, Sindell left. The NEST agent watched him duck into a white Dodge sedan and drive away. Then Gillespie shut the door and dumped the files and reams of computer paper onto the bed.

It took him thirty minutes to find what he wanted. The computerized logs recorded all activity of the alarm systems at SMS Number 14; on the night in question, they showed that alarms in the southeast quadrant of the facility had been deactivated for a period of twenty-four minutes, ending at 03:12:28.

The security guard who had intruded into the control center had been recorded on tape the instant after he had reactivated the alarms. There was no doubt about it.

Helena, Montana

A T THREE O'CLOCK THAT MORNING, ROB GILLESPIE HAD LOST control of his leaded eyelids. He had slumped back on the motel bed, dead asleep, fully clothed, in a tangle of computer paper. As a consequence he was late for the special meeting that morning, held in Lee Hamilton's room at the Best Western motel in Helena. When Gillespie arrived after a high-speed drive, haggard, red-eyed, hungry, but triumphant, the meeting was already in progress. Lee Hamilton rewarded him with a frosty stare and signaled him to sit down. When Gillespie tried to speak, Hamilton silenced him with a curt gesture.

The White Jackets were delivering their report, upstaging Gillespie's announcement.

The White Jackets were the scientists who comprised the heart of the NEST investigation. Using their gamma ray and ionization detectors, they had discovered where radioactive material had been taken from the site, by way of an emergency fire door set in a wall in the southeast quadrant. At that exit, they had discovered a tunnel from the storage building to the other side of the perimeter fence.

The detectors had tracked the stolen uranium through the tunnel to the point where it merged with a newly dug irrigation ditch on the adjoining Halston ranch property. There, the trail vanished amid the tire tracks of at least two different trucks.

"There's no way of determining where the material was taken once it was loaded onto the trucks," a White Jacket said.

"Could it still be on the property?"

"It's possible. . . . We used a pretext to visit the ranch headquarters in one of our vans. Our equipment picked up no trace of uranium there."

"Could the same people who dug the irrigation channels also have dug that tunnel?"

The White Jacket, who was a physicist, not a detective, shrugged his shoulders. "Anyone could have taken advantage of the presence of the irrigation ditches. All I can tell you is, it's almost certain that the stolen uranium was removed from the area. It must have been done at night . . . in secrecy. Once it was loaded onto the trucks and hauled away, we have no way of tracking it."

This somber pronouncement dampened the eager excitement that had pervaded the crowded motel room. There was a long, frustrated silence. Then Lee Hamilton turned to another man, whom Rob Gillespie did not know, and said, "The next step . . . check out the people on the Halston property. They may be innocent . . . but those ditches were too convenient."

"We'll take care of it," Ted Chandler said.

Hamilton turned to Gillespie. "Good of you to come," he said with heavy irony, causing the young investigator to blush. "These gentlemen are from the FBI—Ted Chandler and Joe Springer. What have you got for us? It had better be good."

"It is."

Gillespie told them of the incident recorded by the surveillance camera covering the alarm control center. The alarm condition logs, he reported, confirmed almost identical periods of downtime for the alarms in the southeast quadrant of Building D, not only for the night when the guard was filmed but for several nights the previous week and one subsequent night. "Those logs mean that the alarms were shut down, presumably not only for the two times uranium was stolen, but also for the nights the tunnel was dug under the fence and over to the building. Otherwise the vibration from the digging would have been detected."

The room buzzed with excited comments. The team already knew that two cylinders containing U-235 had been stolen. Now they knew exactly when and how the thefts had taken place.

"Have you identified the security guard who was in the alarm control center that night?"

"Yes, sir. His name is Bradford McAlister. He works the graveyard shift. His patrol route covers that fire door."

"Why was the control center empty?"

"The duty officer—his name is Henderson—was on his lunch period. He usually spends the time working out for about a half hour in the weight room."

"Presumably, McAlister knew that?"

"Everyone did."

"For Christ's sake, you mean to say the alarms are unmonitored while he's having lunch or working out?"

"No, sir. There's a security guard at all times in the main security office who watches the monitor screens. Those screens cover the entire facility, including the alarm control center. Henderson's job is not surveillance, but to make sure the equipment is functioning. The cameras rotate . . . they provide only time-lapse coverage. There are sixteen of them, two groups of eight, working on four-minute cycles. That means any specific area is on camera for only thirty seconds every four minutes." He paused. "It's considered effective coverage. The only way you could beat it would be if you knew the exact times and the rotation sequence. . . . Obviously, McAlister did."

"Then why did he let himself be caught on camera?" one of the FBI men growled, the one identified as a field agent named Joe Springer from the office in Butte.

Gillespie looked at him apprehensively. Tough son of a bitch, he thought, suddenly wishing Al Trautman was present. "My guess is that he had it timed closely, and he just ran a little late. He probably expected to be out of the room before the camera cycled on . . . and before Henderson got back."

"Why didn't the man monitoring the screens see him?"

"Maybe he did. . . . It might not have meant anything to him. I mean, all the tape shows is a security officer in the room for a few seconds. Then he's seen talking to Henderson. . . . No reason to suspect anything wrong."

Springer grunted. He glanced at his superior, who had arrived the previous afternoon from Washington, with a team of agents. Springer knew he had been included only because this was his territory. "We don't have proof of anything," he grumped.

"We have enough to act on," Chandler said.

"You want McAlister picked up?"

"No . . . not yet. We knew there had to be an inside man. Almost certainly, he's our man. But we still don't know who has the stolen nuclear material or where they've taken it. The inside man isn't likely to be the ringleader. He probably doesn't even know where the stuff is. He's just someone who's been bought. But if McAlister is involved, maybe he'll lead us to some of the others. We'll put him under surveillance." Chandler turned to Joe Springer. "I'd like to find out if he's made any large bank deposits lately. Like I said, people like him usually have one primary motive."

Hamilton and the FBI man from Washington withdrew to a corner of the room to confer quietly while the others helped themselves to coffee and doughnuts. Rob Gillespie gratefully wolfed down a Danish with his coffee, accepting congratulations from the others for his discovery.

Lee Hamilton called the meeting back to order and gave out assignments. An FBI team would set up discreet, twenty-four-hour surveillance of Brad McAlister. Rob Gillespie would continue to work undercover at the DOE site, but he would now take the graveyard shift. The NEST White Jackets would continue to search for the missing nuclear weapons material, on the presumption that it might be stashed in the vicinity of Gibson.

"What about the missing suspect, Luke Cameron?" asked Rob Gillespie. "The one Trautman was investigating."

"He's in Paris," Hamilton said. "So is Trautman."

While Gillespie gaped in surprise, Joe Springer said, "I think we should debrief this Henderson character."

The suggestion was greeted by silence. Then Hamilton said, "That would mean exposing our investigation."

"Not necessarily. Henderson doesn't have to know why we're questioning him. Make him think it's simply a breach of procedure . . . leaving McAlister alone in his control room. Make Henderson think *he's* in trouble, not McAlister."

"What can he tell us?"

"We don't know that, do we? Not until we question him."

After some discussion, it was agreed that Springer should approach Henderson, without giving away the reason. Henderson should be warned to keep silent; a slight scare might keep him quiet. They hoped he wouldn't risk jeopardizing his job by loose talk.

Ted Chandler took over. He would submit a preliminary report to the White House, he said. An FBI antiterrorist SWAT team had been placed on full alert. And the Army's First Special Operations (SOF) Detachment-Delta had left Fort Bragg en route to an air force special operations site just outside Great Falls, Montana. It would be joined by Army Task Force 160, which provided helicopter and attack support for the Delta Force. The president—acting in consultation with the National Security Council, the Joint Chiefs, the assistant secretary of defense for special operations, and the FBI director—would decide the next move. Just as soon as the uranium—and those who had taken it—were found.

"Everyone is waiting . . . waiting for us to find the missing uranium. . . ." Lee Hamilton told his NEST people grimly, ". . . before someone uses it to build a nuclear bomb!"

Paris, France

FRANK DELANEY ARRIVED AT NINE IN THE MORNING AND INsisted they go to Aux Deux Magots on the boulevard St. Germain for coffee and rolls. They sat at an outdoor table, watching the passing panorama—throngs of Parisians hurrying to work, tourists emerging from their hotels for the day's outing, vendors spreading out their wares.

"This used to be a French intellectuals' hangout," Delaney said. "Sartre, Camus, all of them, would come here to sit and talk. It's not quite that popular today with the intelligentsia, but it's one of the best people-watching places in Paris."

As if to illustrate the comment, a gaggle of students passed their table, young girls chattering animatedly. "Your Micheline Picard would have been one of those," Delaney said. "She studied at the university, and her degree is real. The woman seems to be genuine . . . so far. That surprise you?"

"She's real, all right."

"Try one of the croissants, Luke. As good as you'll find in Paris. They bake 'em fresh on the premises."

"So she is who she says she is. . . . What else did you find out?"

"This may surprise you. I've had a friend of mine, a French journalist with good business and financial connections, quietly digging into IBZ. He verified that it's a front for foreign interests."

"We knew that much."

"We didn't guess who was hiding behind the facade. The word is they're Iranians. Not exiles . . . Khomeini's boys."

An image of a young, dark-skinned, bearded sentinel on a mountain, armed with an AK-47 assault rifle, leaped into Luke's mind. An Iranian? Even when he first saw the sentry on the rocky hillside above the Wind Canyon Mine, Luke had been reminded of the common television images of young Palestinian or Lebanese terrorists, skinny little teenagers with adult eyes and adult weapons.

"Iranian involvement in IBZ might explain the secrecy behind the company's purchases of U.S. properties," Delaney suggested. "An Iranian company would have aroused suspicion and encountered resistance."

"It doesn't explain Micheline Picard. She's French, Western in her ways, a woman. . . . Not a person Khomeini would put in charge of an American project . . . or any project. And she was sent to America by a father who doesn't seem to exist."

Luke found he had devoured the flaky, buttery croissant without thinking. At Delaney's signal, the waiter appeared at their table with more coffee. Some English tourists settled at a nearby table. One of them, a teenage girl with enormous blue eyes, watched Luke Cameron covertly. Luke wondered if he was so obviously out of place and thus so easily identifiable in a French crowd. Delaney, by contrast, appeared more French than a Frenchman. Even on this warm morning he wore a linen suit, silk shirt and tie, polished loafers. Luke felt underdressed and conspicuous in his tan cotton pants and denim shirt.

"Okay, let's *cherchez la femme*. What I did was, I got a rundown on old convents east of Paris, within reasonable distance of Vincennes and the Marne. I had no idea France had so many convents. We're going to have to visit a lot of convents, Luke . . . unless we get lucky. Unfortunately, Micheline Picard's university records don't list a convent. She had good private schooling before the university, but I ran into a blank there as well. . . . Kind of unusual."

"How so?"

"No mention of birthplace. Usually there is."

"How would that help?"

"That might have led us to the right convent. Now all we can do is take my list and hunt them down, one by one."

"Have you got the time?"

Delaney grinned. "You think I want to tell Canseco I was too busy to help? It's a good day for a drive in the country."

St. Genevieve-sur-Marne, France

SISTER EUGENIE WAS EIGHTY-SIX YEARS OF AGE. THOUGH HER mind was still active and lucid, it tended to wander. Of all the nuns at St. Genevieve, she was the only surviving sister who had been in the convent during World War II. Yet half a century ago, she had already become a fixture. For she had first come to the convent as a young woman, a novice in the order, in 1930. Oddly, though recent events seemed hard to keep track of, sometimes eluding her memory, those of long ago frequently stood out like Mont-St.-Michel rising above the surrounding sea.

What was it the young man wanted to know? *Ah, oui . . . Micheline.* He wanted to know about a little girl.

"Mother superior tells me there are no records of what happened to her," the young man said in English, which Sister Eugenie understood perfectly well. American, he was. Good strong bones. The openness one often saw in American faces, like the young soldiers in the war. And he was so tall, he towered over her. "But she said you might remember."

"Oh, yes, I have a very good memory. I remember many things. I was here, you know, during the war. We had many children then, even—." She paused, her watery eyes uncertain, as if even now there were secrets that must not be spoken. But that was so long ago, what could be the harm? "Even Jewish children. We hid them, you see, from the Boche. It was the charitable thing to do. Such frightened little things. And pretty, with their huge sorrowing eyes."

"This would have been much later," the American said patiently. "In the early 1960s she would have come here. Mother superior says that convent records were destroyed in a fire some years ago, so there's no record of what happened to the girl. Do you remember her? A little dark-haired girl, very pretty?"

"Oh, there are so many, so many with dark hair. How can one remember just one? Such innocent creatures they are," she added. "God must love them most of all."

"Micheline Picard? Twenty, maybe twenty-five years ago? Would you remember who brought her to the convent? Or when she left?"

"It's been such a long time ago." Sister Eugenie was feeling tired. The effort to remember was tiring her.

"Is Micheline a common name?"

"Oh yes, quite common. I have known many of the girls with such a name. . . ."

A memory suddenly surfaced, rising out of the mists. Micheline . . .

Sister Eugenie's heart began to race. She felt faint, dizzy, and frightened. It was as if, rounding a corner in bright sunlight, she had caught a glimpse of something dark and evil.

"Are you all right, Sister?"

"*Oui . . . non, je suis . . .* I must rest."

"I'm sorry to upset you. It's very important."

"I think it would be best if you let her rest, Monsieur Cameron." Another voice, concerned, firm with authority. Ah, the mother superior, of course! Sister Eugenie felt the weight lift slightly from her breast. Her heart still pounded.

"Just a few more questions—"

"I am sorry, monsieur. You can see that Sister Eugenie is not feeling well. Perhaps another time."

The American stared down at the elderly nun, at the wrinkled face framed by a stiff, old-fashioned white cowl—the kind you didn't see any more in his country. The nuns in America all dressed in street clothes, Sister Eugenie thought, as if they weren't nuns at all. It was hard for her to imagine what it would be like after so many years to feel the sun on your face and legs, the wind ruffling your hair, to know what it would be like to walk freely without the long, enveloping skirts of her habit. . . .

"Sister Eugenie?" The tall American's voice was gentle. "Would it be possible for us to talk again?"

His eyes were kind. She remembered the kindness of the American soldiers who had come to the village after the Germans left. They had been so sympathetic and generous, bringing butter and chocolate and tins of fruit. So full of life they were! The girls had been so taken with them.

"*Oui,*" she said. "I would like that."

"Perhaps you'll be able to remember more about the little girl, Micheline Picard."

"I will try. Yes, yes, I'm sure there was such a girl, a pretty thing. So many, you know."

She was feeling better now, her heart no longer thumping, as the necessity to respond was removed.

But the memory she had shied from so strongly still hovered in the shadows of her mind.

"Tomorrow," the American said. "Is it all right if I come to see you in the morning?"

The mother superior was watching her, with that stern expression of hers. She might forbid it, Sister Eugenie thought. But it seemed important, somehow, that she do what this young American asked.

"Yes, I would like that," the old nun said. "I am sure I will remember more in the morning."

Sergei Milov, from the passenger seat of a Citroen, watched the tall American emerge from the convent and stride down a steep, stone-paved path to the road. A black Peugeot, which had been parked below, pulled up in front of the tall man, who folded himself inside. After a brief conversation, the two men in the Peugeot drove off. The driver, a small, immaculate man, looked French.

"What do you wish to do now?" Major Alexei Pichenko asked.

"Follow them," said Milov. "Without alarming them."

The driver of the Peugeot seemed to know exactly where he was going—not a tourist, Milov decided. A U.S. agent stationed in France? CIA? What had aroused his interest in Villiers-sur-Marne and St. Genevieve? And who was the tall man? At lunch earlier in the day, Milov, sitting at a nearby table, had heard them talking in English. It was the dapper, smaller man who had to address the waiter in French. The tall one—a cowboy, Milov speculated; he was fond of American western movies—was, like Milov himself, newly arrived in Paris. Like Milov, he spoke little or no French.

And like Milov, he displayed an interest in Iranian revolutionaries. Milov had noticed a Peugeot had parked for a time near the headquarters of the Party of Allah in Villiers. By training, he had developed an eye for detail.

Milov suppressed a surge of excitement. Not only were the Iranians involved in this mission, but the Americans as well! The investigation that had begun for Milov in Baku and extended to Moscow and Paris, now reached across the ocean to the United States. The convergence of their separate inquiries was too extraordinary to attribute to mere chance.

The KGB's station in Paris, on instructions from Moscow Central, had made inquiries about a woman—French or Iranian—who might have been involved in the Iranian revolutionary movement in France within the past year. The Americans, it seemed, were making similar inquiries. The two searches had converged upon the convent at St. Genevieve-sur-Marne.

On the drive back into Paris along the A-4, Sergei Milov ruminated upon the questions that spun in ever widening circles, with the mysterious Frenchwoman at the center. The Citroen tagged along behind the Peugeot at some distance, and there was enough traffic for their pursuit to go unobserved even by an attentive driver.

Then suddenly, Pichenko said, "We have a problem, comrade."

"They've detected us?" Milov had grudgingly approved of Pichenko's techniques of automobile surveillance. He didn't see how the Americans could have spotted them.

"No . . . *we* are being followed."

Milov resisted the impulse to turn around. Instead he said quietly, "You are quite certain?"

The car behind them, a gray Renault, had been in Villiers earlier in the day, Major Pichenko explained. It had appeared again shortly after the Americans left St. Genevieve to return to Paris. The driver of the Renault was proficient but unschooled in professional surveillance. He had followed too closely and, on one occasion when the other two cars changed routes, the Renault had clung to them much too doggedly. "There are two men in the car. I saw one of them clearly in Villiers."

"Where, exactly?"

"Coming from the garage behind the Iranian Islamic Party's headquarters."

Milov considered the implications. "Let them follow. They must already know enough to identify us. We shall give them something else to think about. If we have puzzles, why shouldn't they?"

Puzzles, indeed.

Why was the cowboy asking about the woman the KGB had identified as one Micheline Picard? Was it possible—here Sergei Milov made one of those leaps not yet justified by the evidence—that the Americans were interested in the woman for the same reason Milov was?

Was there a nuclear connection?

Traffic thickened as they approached the center of the city and were forced to drive along surface streets. Pichenko, carefully keeping several cars behind, stayed on the tail of the black Peugeot, whose driver showed an admirable familiarity with side streets and traffic buildups. He escaped the crowded boulevards on the Right Bank and crossed the Seine. The Russian major, after several searching glances into his rearview mirror, murmured, "I think we've lost them."

"Maybe they know where we're going," Milov said.

"*Pardon?*"

"*Pardon?* What's that, Major Pichenko? You have been in France too long, I think. You're beginning to dress and act and talk like a Frenchman."

"Is that so bad? I am a Russian, Captain, down to the bone marrow, but there is much here to like. Have you enjoyed the company of your first French woman yet, Milov?"

"I haven't had time."

Pichenko laughed. "With you, Sergei Andreyevich, surely it wouldn't need to take so long, eh? You cannot spare a minute or two from your busy day?"

Sergei Milov smiled. It was the first time Pichenko had addressed him in the familiar Russian way. "Maybe you're right, it would not take much time."

Pichenko focused for several minutes on the tangle of traffic along the narrow streets that threaded past the university district before he spoke again. "What was it you said? That those men behind us already knew our destination?"

"It was the Americans they were following, not us. And my guess is they know where at least one of the Americans is staying. Ah, you see? They are stopping now."

Pichenko pulled over as the black Peugeot stopped near the entrance of the Sofitel-Bourbon hotel. The tall cowboy climbed out of the car and exchanged a few words with the driver, who apparently had a different destination.

"I'll get out here," said Milov. "See where the driver goes and what you can learn about him."

"How will you . . . ?"

"I will catch a taxi to the embassy."

The sidewalks were thronged, as usual. The faces of Paris were in their varied hues and structures a testament to the lure the city has for people of all climes. Mingling with them, Milov was able to approach inconspicuously within a few steps of the hotel. At the entrance, where the tall American had gone into the lobby, Milov paused to light a cigarette. His cupped hands half covered his face as he glanced inside. Then he entered the hotel and went straight to the bar.

Though Milov did not obviously glance around the lobby, he noted the American talking to the concierge, then turning toward the elevator.

Milov also observed the rumpled, heavyset man in the beige suit and large, scuffed shoes who was settled in a wicker chair in a corner of the lobby. The man slowly lowered his paper and stared after the tall American.

Sitting at the bar with a glass of Stolichnaya, Sergei Milov decided that anyone who merited so much interest from so many sources definitely deserved his close and personal attention.

The cowboy is in Paris for the same reason you are.

He was looking for the woman. A beautiful young Frenchwoman with an interest in nuclear weapons.

Al Trautman didn't notice Milov enter the hotel and deploy to the bar off one side of the lobby. But he spotted Luke Cameron striding in from the street; the description fit the tall, ruggedly handsome American.

The investigator made no attempt to intercept Cameron. That could wait.

As soon as the elevator doors closed behind Cameron, Trautman went to the concierge and asked how he could make an international phone call. He was directed to a pay phone, with a fistful of French coins which the concierge was happy to supply.

The French, Al Trautman thought as he waited for his call to be placed to Helena, Montana, sure knew how to run a hotel.

Tehran, Iran

A LI AKBAR MOHTASHEMI'S DEVOTION TO THE IMAM AND THE Islamic Revolution was so complete, so absolute in its fervor, that it would rarely occur to him to withhold information from Ayatollah Khomeini. But now he approached the old man's room with trepidation.

This should have been a time for rejoicing. The Imam, though weakened by his long battle against the voracious cancer cells in his body, not only had survived eight hours of surgery but had seemed to improve visibly. The dark frowns of his doctors had begun to lighten.

Earlier in the day, Mohtashemi had spoken briefly to Khomeini, who had appeared to be winning his stubborn battle against the ravages of disease and the frailties of old age. Mohtashemi had been moved to offer prayers of gratitude to Allah for the Imam's recovery.

Now, the news Mohtashemi brought was positive—except for one jarring element that made him hesitate outside Khomeini's room. He drew in a long breath and released it slowly, invoking calmness upon his spirit. Then he entered the room. A phalanx of doctors turned in unison as he appeared, but they knew better now than to defy the Imam's edict that Mohtashemi should have access to his bedside.

The old man lay upon his bed, his long face drawn, causing the deep-set eyes to appear even larger in their dark pouches. The flowing beard was completely white, setting off the fierce dark eyebrows that still held their color.

His head turned on the pillow as Mohtashemi entered the room. His eyes were bright, perhaps from his persistent fever, but also with sharp awareness. During Mohtashemi's earlier bedside visit, medication had dulled the old man's senses and stilled the turmoil of his thoughts.

"*Salam alekom,*" Mohtashemi said, bowing. "*Che tor hastid?*"

"*Emruz halam khob shod,*" Khomeini whispered.

"*Al-hambo-lellah!* Praise to God!"

"You have news for me, Ali Akbar?"

"Yes, Imam, from America."

"Tell me."

The ayatollah listened impassively to Mohtashemi's detailed report of the theft of uranium-235 from the storage facility in Montana. The metal had been tested and found to be of excellent weapons grade. Work on a bomb was proceeding in the secrecy of an abandoned mine, which had proved well suited to the purpose.

"When this bomb is completed, will it serve our purpose?"

Mohtashemi hesitated. "It will not be a large bomb . . . more symbolic than an instrument of true destruction. To build such a weapon in the camp of the enemy, to demonstrate that the arm of Islam can reach into every corner, that is its true purpose."

"It is well spoken." For a few moments the Imam was silent. Then he asked, "How many will die?"

"That will depend upon where we choose to explode the weapon. Perhaps twenty-five thousand people . . . perhaps thirty thousand . . . would perish in a small city in the American West, though the direction of the winds could increase that number. But in a large city . . . in one of those evil ghettos in the land of Satan . . . there would be more deaths . . . many more."

After another silence, during which Khomeini turned his gaze toward the shuttered window behind his bed, the old man said, "It is enough."

One of Khomeini's familiar sayings flickered across Mohtashemi's mind, a slogan that was frequently seen scribbled on walls in Qom and Tehran and such distant Islamic strongholds as Beirut: "The purest joy in Islam is to kill and be killed for Allah."

Mohtashemi made no move to leave.

"The coming carnage in America . . . this troubles you, Ali Akbar?" asked Khomeini, his eyebrows wrinkling perceptibly.

"Allah is my witness, it is not so!"

"Then you must tell me what is in your heart that makes it so heavy."

Mohtashemi sighed. Even on his deathbed—please God, let the angel of death pass him by—the Imam was able to peer into a man's soul. "There is a potential problem . . . ," Mohtashemi began.

"It will not become less by your silence."

"The woman entrusted with the Imam's mission in the land of Satan has become . . . involved with the American." Mohtashemi hastily added: "Some involvement was seen as necessary to divert suspicion."

"Continue," said Khomeini with ominous patience.

Mohtashemi swallowed hard. "Your servant Kali believed that Micheline Picard's liaison with the American had . . . that she had become blind with passion."

Khomeini's hand trembled on the blanket drawn over his frail body. "It is written, in the words of the Prophet, 'If a man and a woman are alone in one place, the third person present is Satan.' " The words were those of the Prophet Muhammad, their truth confirmed for over thirteen hundred years.

"Yes," agreed Mohtashemi. Then he continued: "Another accident was arranged—an error of judgment. Not only did it fail, but it provoked the very suspicions that your servant Kali had hoped to suppress. And now—"

"Whose error of judgment?"

"It was Kali, in his zeal for Allah."

"Not the woman?"

"No, Imam. She opposed it."

Khomeini fell back against his pillow. His skin was gray behind the white beard. "Speak plainly."

"The American is now in Paris. He is investigating IBZ, the holding company we have used to screen our investments. He will learn little from these inquiries, but . . . he has also been seen by our people in Villiers . . . and . . ."

The Ayatollah Khomeini's eyes burned as if afire with sudden fever. The eastern suburbs of Paris had been his home during both of his periods of exile in the City of Light.

". . . and in St. Genevieve-sur-Marne," Mohtashemi said.

Khomeini was visibly agitated, and Mohtashemi hurried on. "Cameron has been seeking information about Micheline Picard. He searches into her past."

"He must be stopped," the old man whispered hoarsely. "At once, Ali Akbar—eliminate the trail."

Then he collapsed onto his pillow, and his doctors hurried to his bedside. Like ants swarming upon a drop of honey.

☢ PART FOUR
PARIS MATCH

St. Genevieve-sur-Marne, France

THE TINY VILLAGE OF ST. GENEVIEVE WAS, LIKE THE CONvent that had given it its name, peaceful and picturesque. It was nestled on a side road near a small wood. Its cobbled main street and connecting dirt lanes were usually empty of traffic. Its evenings were undisturbed by modern cacophony, and the rustic, placid life that engulfed the village had changed little over the generations.

The convent of St. Genevieve had been built, stone upon stone, between the years 1631 and 1649. It had survived the Terror more than a century later. Its chapel bells had pealed to celebrate the triumph of Napoleon in the nineteenth century. It had withstood the relentless expansion of the great City of Light that kept intruding upon the surrounding marshland. The thick stone walls of the convent had shuddered to the pounding of heavy guns in both Great Wars. Its dank, ancient rooms had served as an emergency hospital ward, and in the Second World War, it had also been a haven for another group of victims—refugee Jewish children who had to be hidden not only from the Nazis but from their French toadies as well.

Only twice in those three centuries had the convent of St. Genevieve been damaged. In August 1917, a shell had struck a corner of the northeast chapel tower. The wall had stood. The shell was still visible, embedded in the gray stone about fifteen feet from the ground, nearly hidden by the climbing red bougainvillea that was in full summer bloom.

The other incident, a more recent calamity, had been a mysterious fire that had consumed most of the convent's records. Luckily, the fire had been confined largely to the office and file rooms.

Sister Eugenie remembered that night vividly—the clanging of the fire bells, the subdued excitement of the nuns and the children, as they spilled outside into the vegetable garden. They had joined a silent crowd of villagers, their faces painted an eerie orange by the dancing flames that licked the stone walls of the tower.

It was Sister Eugenie's ritual to take a short walk after evening vespers, sometimes accompanied by one of the younger nuns but more often by herself. It was just a short walk to the little wooded park at the edge of the village, and she knew every step of the way— every stone, every depression, every bush and tree and flower bed.

There was a pond in the park, framed by a grove of chestnut trees. In summer, the still surface of the pond was covered with lilies. It reminded her of Monet's pond, and over the years she had come to understand that painter's obsession with the lilies, the compositions of still water, light, and color in infinite variety.

But there was something unsettling about this evening, something that ruffled her peace of mind. She had come alone to the little grove, walking slowly, for she was crippled by osteoporosis that had left her stooped. At one time, she had been obliged to use a metal walker, a cumbersome apparatus that she had to shift forward awkwardly with both hands and lean on for support as she took each small, shuffling step. But she had slowly improved with treatment in spite of her age; now she used only a lightweight aluminum cane. She didn't mind the cane but hated the walker; she prayed forgiveness of God for the vanity that produced such feelings.

Sister Eugenie sought out a worn, gray stone bench beside the still pond. She sat motionless on the slab of granite for a long time. The peace she normally drew from the solitude, as she gazed at the play of twilight over the lily pads, eluded her.

The tall American intruded upon her thoughts; something about him was disquieting. Yet there had been kindness in his eyes that belied his rugged face, a gentleness in his voice that softened the gruff tones. Her fading faculties had not yet robbed her of such perceptions. Why, at the thought of him, did her heart flutter? It reminded her of holding a wild bird in her hands, feeling the terrified quiver in the little body, the pulsing of its tiny heartbeat against her fingers.

Do you remember a little girl named Micheline Picard?

She gave a small cry, startling a bird in a tree behind her and causing it to fly upward.

A suppressed memory surfaced like a ghost from the grave. Such

a long time ago! A quarter century at least. But in a flash she was
transported backward in time . . .

She had been a simple country girl when she entered the convent
of St. Genevieve, but having grown up on a farm she was familiar
with the raw facts of birth and death. With so many young girls in
the convent—some of them young, unwed, and pregnant, seeking
refuge from the rejection of their provincial French towns and vil-
lages—Sister Eugenie's limited knowledge had frequently been
called upon. Over the years, she had become an experienced midwife.

One cold, dank evening in the spring—April, she thought, or early
May—she had been summoned by her mother superior. A girl was
in need. Sister Eugenie must go at once to the cellar beneath the
chapel, where refugee children had been concealed during the war.

Her experience delivering babies did not lessen her concern and
anxiety and sense of inadequacy lest serious complications develop.
But the little nun hurried along damp, stone-floored corridors to the
chapel. She opened a heavy oak door behind the sacristy and descended stone steps so old that deep depressions had been worn in
each stone by countless footsteps. A string of lights—bare bulbs suspended from the ceiling—guided her.

In the narrow hall at the foot of the steps she heard voices ahead.
She hastened toward the sound. When she let herself in the small
room, she stopped, startled at the sight of two bearded men in long
black robes who stared back at her. Priests, she thought, of an Eastern order perhaps, each wearing an unusual black headdress.

The room reeked of blood and urine. A young woman lay on a
narrow cot set against the far wall. A single overhead bulb cast a
gloomy light over the center of the room, leaving the corners in
shadow. With a welling of pity, Sister Eugenie crossed quickly over
to the cot.

The girl was a child—perhaps sixteen, seventeen at most. Her face
was blanched, drenched in sweat, her homespun dress stained with
her own fluids. She was obviously in labor, having a difficult, painful
struggle to give birth to the new life she carried. The girl appeared
to be so weak that she showed no reaction at all to Sister Eugenie's
arrival. Pain created its own isolation.

One of the bearded priests moved closer to the nun. She guessed
that he was about her own age; she was in her sixties. His full beard
was white, streaked with black strands. He had heavy black eye-

brows that met at a crease in his forehead to form a fierce, perpetual scowl. His eyes were arresting; they mesmerized her.

"She is dying," the old man said in French. "Do what you can for her."

"Perhaps . . . ," she murmured, "there is still hope."

He glared as if she had uttered a blasphemy. Then he stared at the girl and turned away, as if he were turning his back on what he saw.

"I will need help . . . some towels . . . more hot water."

The old priest gestured curtly at the other man, who responded with such alacrity that Sister Eugenie became immediately aware of their relative status. The old man—she wondered whether he was a religious figure of some sect unfamiliar to her—was a man of great presence. The other scurried to do his bidding.

Soon the assistant was back, bringing blankets, towels, a kettle simmering with hot water. Over the next hour the frail girl on the cot tried to release her burden. Each time, after prolonged spasms, she fell back, exhausted and drenched in sweat. Sister Eugenie felt helpless. She was a skilled midwife, but not a doctor.

The old man asked if she could perform the necessary surgery. "No," she said, shaking her head. "I am only a nun, Father, unschooled in medicine."

"You have seen it done, perhaps? . . . You have assisted?"

"*Oui,* but . . ."

"What do you need?"

"This is something for a doctor. . . . She cannot have her child without medical help."

"There is no doctor. The village doctor is away. There is only you. You must operate."

Her protests were dismissed. He had made his decision. Without knowing who or what he was, she knew without question that his decisions were absolute. He was an authoritarian figure who overwhelmed her resistance. She was also intimidated by a terrible anger that blazed in his eyes.

She did the best she could. She was not ignorant of the procedure for a cesarean section, but the amount of bleeding astonished her. She felt clumsy, ignorant, inadequate. She knew that she was working too slowly, that the poor girl was weakening swiftly, that the authorities would not view unlicensed surgery sympathetically—particularly if the patient did not recover.

Suddenly the baby slipped free of its cage into her hands. The mother fell back, limp. Sister Eugenie passed the newborn infant quickly into the hands of the younger priest to clean and pummel it into vigorous life. She saw in a glance, before turning her attention to the mother, that the baby was a girl, black haired and perfectly formed—the tiniest, most beautiful of God's children.

But the young mother lay unnaturally still. She had collapsed in the moment of her triumph. Preparing to close her wound, willing her hands to be quick and steady, Sister Eugenie realized that there was no need for haste. She could only pray. Staring down in anguish at the lifeless girl, the nun was momentarily blinded by her tears.

"There is nothing you can do for her now," the old man said. His tone was harsh.

Without a word, Sister Eugenie took the infant girl from the younger man. She washed her gently in warm water, ignoring cries that were loud and healthy. Then she toweled the baby, caressingly, and wrapped her in a blanket.

The two men had been watching intently. Now, after an exchange of glances, they approached the nun. She held up the infant with a tired but eager smile, feeling, in spite of her sorrow over the young mother's death, that inexpressible joy at being part of the beginning of life. The old man parted the blanket and fixed his fierce gaze on the child. He confirmed that she was a girl.

Abruptly, the old priest turned away. He bent quickly over the mother, pulling down the front of her dress roughly and pressing his ear to her chest. Sister Eugenie and the younger cleric stared at him, waiting.

The old man straightened up, betraying no emotion. The light from the lamp seemed to blaze from his eyes. He spoke to his companion. In that instant, with some visceral perception, Sister Eugenie understood that the child she held in her hands, so small and helpless, was his. This old goat of a priest was her father.

In response to an abrupt command from the older man, the assistant turned quickly and, before Sister Eugenie could protest, took the infant from her. He turned toward his superior, holding the child without tenderness or love.

He asked a question in that strange tongue she did not recognize.

Hearing without understanding, she had a terrible intuition that the child's life hung upon the answer to the question. She began to tremble in fear. She reached for the baby, but the younger priest ignored her outstretched hands. His hands slid down the baby's body. Holding her by the legs, he drew her free of the blanket.

He spoke again. The question hung in the chill, damp air of the cellar room. . . .

Even now, a quarter century later, Sister Eugenie shivered at the memory. She looked about her at the shadows of the woods in the park, at the still pond with its huge lilies—and she felt not peaceful tranquility but pure terror.

For she had transported herself back to that dank little room below the chapel, and everything was starkly vivid, seen with a clarity beyond normal vision. And she knew that the young priest had been asking if this unwanted female child should be destroyed, swung by her heels to be smashed and broken against the damp stone walls. Over the years, Sister Eugenie had tried to believe otherwise, to convince herself that her intuition had been wrong. She had often prayed for forgiveness for her lack of charity—but in her heart she knew that what she had seen in the old father's eyes was a cold compassionless ferocity. After a moment, however, the old man shook his head. For another few seconds, he stared at the girl-child. At no time did he take her into his own arms. Instead he turned to Sister Eugenie and spoke in French. "She will remain here. See that she is cared for."

He stalked from the room, not looking back. His companion hesitated, handed the newborn infant to Sister Eugenie without a word, and hurried after his master up the stone steps. She listened to their footsteps until they faded away. The abandoned child began to cry, as if, even in the hour of her birth, she had a sense of loss and rejection.

"Oh, my poor dear!" Sister Eugenie murmured soothingly. "My poor child!"

Holding the infant, cuddling her against her bosom and rocking back and forth, the nun stared at the pathetic girl, so thin and young and pretty in life, so wasted in death, until she brought herself up with a start, realizing that she must fetch Father Cadieux at once. How could she have delayed so carelessly? And what was to be done with the child? There were so many questions. . . .

So many questions, Sister Eugenie thought, even after all these years. Who was the mother? Who was that frightening old priest? And was he, as she had always suspected, the baby's father?

And what ever had become of the child, little Micheline?

The tall American had been asking about such a child. It had seemed important to him. But how could he know of something that happened so long ago, in secrecy and shame?

Sister Eugenie's mind continued to clear. She remembered what a joy Micheline had been in the early years after her birth. So pretty, like her mother. So quick. So bright and saucy. Not always a happy child, for a cloud hung over her—the mystery of her origins. Yet she had not been completely abandoned; her care at the convent had been paid for, the source not known to Sister Eugenie. Only the old mother superior knew, and she had passed away long ago.

In time, when Micheline was about ten years of age, some men came for her. Not the same men Sister Eugenie remembered, but men with the same dark eyes and bearded faces, the same long robes and headdresses, the same heavily accented French. There had been long talks with the mother superior in the privacy of her office. Then Mother sent for Micheline . . .

She had returned to the convent only once. Until this moment, sitting on the stone bench as darkness enveloped her, Sister Eugenie had forgotten. Stirring up old memories brought others to the surface. On her return visit, Micheline had been a grown young woman, proud and beautiful—a stranger whom Sister Eugenie had not recognized. But Micheline had sought her out; when Sister Eugenie was summoned and arrived hesitantly, Micheline had smiled with evident pleasure. "I'm sure you don't remember me, Sister. I was here a long time ago. I am Micheline Picard."

And then, impulsively, she had reached out to embrace the old nun, who was quite embarrassed, really, not knowing what to say or do. There had been so many children, it was hard to remember them all clearly—or to identify any of them with this cool, sophisticated, smartly dressed Frenchwoman.

But of course she was the one—the child the American was asking about. Why, Sister Eugenie wondered, should such a realization cause her heart to flutter in agitation.

She rose from the bench. Though the spring evening was still mild, she felt cold. And anxious.

She wanted to return to the sanctuary of her spartan little room in the convent, home to her for more than sixty years.

As she turned away from the lily pond, she saw a reflection move across a corner of its unruffled surface. Looking up, she saw a man approaching her. He was a small, dark man in worker's clothes. Sister Eugenie relaxed. The men of the village were kind to her. Sometimes one of them would walk with her to or from the convent, protectively solicitous—as if she couldn't find her way over the terrain of a lifetime!

Only when the man was just a few steps away did she realize that he was a stranger, his face unfamiliar.

She was so intent on the man circling the pond to meet her on the path that she did not notice another figure flowing out of the shadows behind her. When she heard the scuff of a footstep she turned her head. The toe of her shoe caught a lip of one of the stepping stones set into the path, and she stumbled.

Falling, she felt strong arms lift her up. Her first reaction was gratitude. Shrunken in her old age, she was so light that the man lifted her easily, carrying her as if she were a child—but he clamped one hand over her mouth to still any outcry.

After the first moment of panic Sister Eugenie's fear began to slip from her, leaving an odd feeling of relief that this moment had come at last. Though she struggled feebly, her heart wasn't in it, and the man who had slipped out of the woods behind her—the other man now acting as a sentry—had no difficulty controlling her attempts to free herself.

He wrestled her down. She felt the cool water of the lily pond close over her as she was thrust beneath the surface. She could feel the rough hand over her face, pressing her down. Her robes became heavy with water. Her heart began to thump very rudely in her chest, like a fist pounding on a door.

She began to pray.

When the door burst open, it was not darkness that rushed in but a white, blinding light that engulfed her like music.

"I'm sorry, Luke," Frank Delaney said over coffee at Luke's hotel. "I'll be tied up all morning . . . some appointments I can't break."

"I want to talk to that nun again. Soon as possible. She *knows* something."

"Can it wait until tomorrow? Or maybe later today?"

"I'd like to see her this morning. I understand the trains are reliable. Can I get to Villiers by train? I could probably find a taxi there."

"The RER—that's the express train—should take you close. You'd have to catch the A line going east. . . . But hell, there's no need for that, *mon ami.* You can take my car."

The offer tempted Luke. A car would give him flexibility; he had no way of knowing what he was going to learn this morning or where it would lead him. "I couldn't do that."

"Why the hell not? It's my car, not InCon's, and it's yours for the day. There are good Michelin maps in the glove compartment if you get in trouble. You think you'd be comfortable driving around Paris?"

"I've driven in Mexico City."

"That should be training enough." Delaney dug his car keys out of his pocket, then scribbled a phone number onto a notebook page. "You can drop me off on your way. And Luke . . . if you need me for any reason, call this number. Any time, *comprenez-vous?*"

Following Delaney's instructions, Luke Cameron drove along the Seine to the east side of Paris near the Gare de Lyon, where he picked up the Quai de Bercy and connected with the eastbound autoroute A-4 out of the city. This proved to be a divided motorway, and the fast-moving traffic flow carried him swiftly into the valley of the Marne.

He left the A-4 near Villiers-sur-Marne, driving along side roads, until he recognized the one leading to St. Genevieve. The morning was fair and warm. Vegetable and flower gardens, bright with color, adorned the small farms, surrounded by woods of vivid green. Luke had grown up in almost treeless country; he hadn't thought of France as being so green and thickly forested. All he knew about the beautiful Marne Valley was that its woods had more than once been heavy with gunsmoke, the soil dark with blood, in battles fought over the centuries. Luke recalled reading about a fleet of six hundred taxis being rounded up to bring French volunteers out of the city to support some beleaguered British troops in one of the great World War I battles. There was something both gallant and anachronistic about the story, he thought.

At the convent of St. Genevieve, Luke was surprised to see several cars parked near the entrance. He found a group of men gathered in the entry room beyond the main heavy oak door. They interrupted their conversation to peer curiously at the stranger who had appeared among them. The elderly mother superior said something to them. Approaching Luke, she seemed agitated.

"You have come to see Sister Eugenie . . . ," she said in English. "I am so sorry, monsieur . . . you are too late."

"I don't understand."

"But she has passed away. It was so sudden."

"I just talked to her yesterday!"

"Mais oui. It is God's will, Monsieur Cameron. She is taken from us, but she was quite ready to go, you know. She had made her peace with God long ago."

"She died in her sleep?" Luke was still too stunned to think clearly.

A shadow crossed the mother superior's face. Sister Eugenie's death, unfortunately, had been an accident, she explained. The old nun had gone for her customary evening walk to the village park, something she had done almost every evening in fine weather for as long as anyone could remember. She was accustomed to sit by the lily pond in the park, her favorite place. Apparently she had slipped when she was ready to leave. She must have fallen heavily, for her shoulder was dislocated. She had drowned in the pond.

"She was not found until this morning, monsieur. We were unaware that she had not returned last night."

Dead! Before Luke had a chance to talk to her!

Tom Cameron was not found until the next day, too.

Luke stared at the Frenchmen still talking at one side of the gloomy, high-beamed room. A doctor, he supposed, and other village elders. Perhaps even a policeman. They seemed at ease in the presence of sudden death. It had been natural, after all; a very old woman falling; such things were to be expected.

What could Luke tell the local authorities? That he knew she had been murdered? He had no evidence, only conjecture. Even if he tried to explain, they would not understand.

Abruptly Luke thanked the mother superior for her help, and offered a distracted but genuine expression of regret over Sister Eugenie's unexpected passing. Then he stepped outside. The convent, protected by its thick stone walls, had been cool; the air outside was very warm.

But the walls had been no protection for the old woman. Luke began to shake with anger at the terrorist mentality that coldly justified brutal attacks on innocent victims in order to strike a blow at a perceived enemy. In the twisted corridors of terrorist thought, there were no innocents.

Then it struck him with a jolt that he was responsible for the old nun's death. He and Delaney must have been followed yesterday. Tracked all the way from Paris, from convent to convent, until they came to St. Genevieve.

How had his trail been picked up? How could anyone know . . . ?

The inner chill that had caused Luke to withdraw from the convent enveloped him like a damp, cold fog. He shivered in spite of the warmth of the day. He had visited the offices of IBZ, making inquiries about Henri Picard. And he had come to St. Genevieve to ask questions about Micheline Picard—questions, as it had turned out, that only Sister Eugenie could have answered.

He glanced up and down the dirt road that passed in front of the convent. Aside from the cars parked near the entrance there was no activity. Yet the woods on either side of the road seemed suddenly thick and dark. Had he been followed again this morning? Or were the killers satisfied with the old nun's silence?

He walked over to the black Peugeot, climbed in, and started the engine. The road was still empty in both directions. Tension tightened a clamp on the back of his neck. He drove slowly back toward the motorway.

In an unpopulated area about a half mile from the village, a gray Renault bolted out of a side lane at the edge of the woods. It tried to ram Luke's Peugeot. He had a glimpse of two men inside the gray car, and the silhouette of a gun in the hands of the man beside the driver. Not just any weapon, but an automatic assault rifle, the sickle curve of its cartridge clip clearly visible beneath the stock.

Luke spun the steering wheel as he jammed on the brakes. The Peugeot skidded sideways. The Renault shot past, missing the Peugeot's front fender by inches. The Peugeot's Michelin tires caught, stopping the skid. Luke rocked the car back onto the dirt road and stomped on the accelerator. As he did so the rear side window of the Peugeot disintegrated, a split second before he heard the hammering burst of fire from the assault rifle. It was a sound he knew from Vietnam, one that he had hoped never to hear again. To hear it now, in the peaceful French countryside, to sense the bite of minute particles of glass on his cheek, to feel his stomach muscles clench, was unreal, a nightmare.

He had gained a fifty-yard lead down the narrow dirt road before the Renault straightened itself out and set off in pursuit. The Peugeot was a more powerful car but it was also heavier; to Luke's surprise the little Renault slowly closed the gap between them. They raced through the little village of St. Genevieve-sur-Marne with its cluster of small shops, the familiar sidewalk tables beside a tiny café, a gas station with a brick planter of flowers beside the pumps.

Luke turned left at the first intersection beyond the village, thinking that he was heading back toward the motorway and that the gunmen behind him wouldn't dare try to use a military weapon on such a public thoroughfare. But after he had driven about two miles down the side road, the Renault close behind, he realized that the countryside, instead of becoming more crowded, was becoming less populated, an area of farms, open meadows, and thicker forests.

He had turned the wrong way.

At yet another intersection Luke hesitated for a second before turning right. The delay was long enough to allow the Renault to get close. He heard the crash of rapid-fire once more in his wake as he floored the Peugeot.

He began to weave and twist and double back along the roads and narrow lanes, sometimes driving straight across farm fields over tracks that were little more than worn ruts. The maneuvering gained a little distance between himself and his pursuers.

Luke slowed for a crossroads where a small country inn filled one corner. Signs and arrows painted on the stone wall pointed the way toward Champigny. Thank God for French road signs! They gave Luke some idea of where he was heading. He and Delaney had driven through Champigny, a fair-sized town. Surely he would be safe from open attack there. And it was close to the A-4, his escape route back to the heart of Paris.

Luke swung past the inn in the direction of Champigny. A forest on his right hand climbed a slope away from the road.

He didn't hear the shot, but there was a hard pop as one of his tires blew. Then he was fighting the wheel, afraid to hit the brakes hard for fear of rolling over. The Peugeot slowed perceptibly. Luke's arms ached from the strain of resisting the pull of the ruined tire.

A glance in the rearview mirror showed the Renault in the distance, racing toward him.

He plunged off the road, plowed through a strip of poppies, and came to a stop. Before the engine stopped turning over Luke burst out of the car, running in a low crouch, instinctively zigzagging as he raced toward the trees.

Bullets plucked at leaves and tree trunks as he reached the cover of the woods. Moments later he heard shouts. French? Were they yelling instructions in French or some other language? What language was it that Iranians spoke? Persian?

Luke Cameron had long legs, he was a strong runner, and he was in good enough physical condition to keep going for a long time. He could outrun his pursuers, he hoped, unless one was a marathon runner. Moreover, the forest was both dense and deep. He quickly lost sight of the men from the Renault and was fairly certain they could no longer see him. The sounds of pursuit faded away completely.

After a time he felt that he was alone in the woods. Alone and quite lost.

Through thinning patches in the foliage overhead he was able to keep track of the sun's path over the next hour. He traveled steadily north, in the general direction of the motorway and the rail line that had run parallel to the main road much of the way.

He began to think with a cooler head about the assassins. The attack had caught him not only unarmed but completely unprepared. The would-be killers were both ruthless and single minded, recklessly willing to attack in broad daylight. Their actions were typical of Europe's urban terrorists. America might be the land of crack and crime, but it had been relatively free of direct attack by terrorists. Such violence was not unknown in Paris, however, where more than one foreign diplomat had been gunned down in the street. Nor, as Luke had learned, was the pastoral French countryside a sanctuary.

He felt overwhelmed by the swift and massive response to his inquiries. Evidently the stakes were greater than anything he had imagined. So, too, were the resources of his enemies, who were able to call upon powerful forces on two continents. How could one man, alone in a strange country, fight them?

Obviously Luke's activities since his arrival in Paris had threatened someone enough to provoke a deadly reaction, but he remained frustrated by his results. What had he discovered? A vague Iranian connection to a mystery company with U.S. holdings . . . a centuries-old convent whose records had been destroyed . . . a nest of terrorists who didn't want him to dig too deeply into the background of Micheline Picard. Not much, Luke thought. Nothing that explained Tom Cameron's death. Try to throw a rope around it and you were left holding an empty loop.

Luke had crossed a ridge in the thickest part of the forest. As he worked his way down a long slope, he saw that the trees were thinning out. A smudge of chimney smoke curled upward through a gap in the trees. He had a glimpse of gray stone buildings in the distance, a town, a road, a stand of beech trees flanking a riverbank.

Pausing at the edge of the woods, he stared down at the village. Its promise of escape from his pursuers brought no elation. It mocked the failure of his mission to France.

Luke knew that, with Sister Eugenie dead, he had reached an impasse. Unlike his adversaries, he lacked the resources for an intensive probe into Micheline Picard's background or into the mysterious IBZ. Though the shadowy outlines of the plot he had stumbled upon seemed more sinister and frightening the more he perceived of them, their true dimensions remained murky and insubstantial, the common stuff of paranoia.

Luke leaned against the dark trunk of a tree, close to exhaustion, and felt the crushing weight of hopelessness. Maybe it was time to admit that he was up against something bigger than he was, that he stood no better chance against it than his father had. Maybe his best bet now was simply to go home.

Which meant, first, try to get out of France alive.

Al Trautman had been delayed that morning by the formality of presenting himself at the offices of the Direction Generale de la Securite Exterieure, the French equivalent of America's CIA. Protocol demanded such notification when an American intelligence agent entered France on an operational errand.

The DGSE was housed in La Caserne des Tourelles on boulevard Mortier in the Twentieth Arrondissement, the far northeast corner of Paris. It was an old building that had once been a women's prison. The deputy assistant director, Claude Tournier, was polite but curious. He would prefer a more frank discussion of Monsieur Trautman's purpose in Paris. Nevertheless, the DGSE was prepared to render any assistance it could. He trusted that he would be kept informed.

By the time Trautman returned to the center of the city, driving a rented Ford Escort, Luke Cameron and another man had left Cameron's hotel.

Cursing the delay, Trautman resigned himself to waiting. Whatever Luke Cameron was after in Paris, he had apparently not yet found it.

If you want to tail a man who's a stranger to Paris, there's one place you're sure to pick him up, Al Trautman knew. He'll be back for his clothes and his toothbrush and his passport. He'll return to his hotel.

It was a logical conclusion, and Al Trautman was not the only one who had reached it.

Gibson, Montana

IT WAS A CLOUDY MORNING, WITH THE WIND STIRRING UP DUST devils out on the open prairie. A tumbleweed blew up against the perimeter fence bordering the Energy Department's storage site. Emerging from the shelter of the massive, warehouselike buildings, Brad McAlister felt the wind tug at his clothes. A healthy Montana wind was not a gentle draft that merely ruffled your hair; it was a force that could disrupt even the simple act of walking across an open parking lot toward your car.

Head down into the wind and eyes tightened to mere slits, Brad discerned a figure angling closer to him. "It's a real howler," Burt Henderson muttered.

Brad nodded curtly. He didn't feel sociable at the end of an eight-hour shift. Soon he wouldn't have to put up with this grind any longer. One more payment from Kali and Brad could quit this flunky job. Not too abruptly. Anne was asking questions already. Others might become curious. He'd wait until the time was right. . . .

"You know what I mean, McAlister," Henderson said. Brad noticed that the big man was looking straight ahead, head lowered as if they weren't speaking but just happened to be walking in the same direction.

"What the hell are you talking about?"

Henderson glanced over his shoulder. "They told me not to say anything . . . but hell . . . goddamn brass," he muttered darkly.

Brad's step faltered. Panic fluttered in his chest. He told himself to keep walking. From the side of his mouth, he blurted the anguished question. "For God's sake, Burt, tell me!"

"They're asking questions about you . . . about that night you were in my control center . . . remember? . . . They caught you on film."

"What . . . what did you tell them?"

"What's to tell? You stopped by the control center . . . I was on my lunch break . . . what's so terrible about that? . . . Damn rules . . . they've got all these damn rules. . . ."

Henderson saw his car and started to veer away. "I just thought I'd tip you off. Watch your ass, McAlister. Watch your ass."

Then he was gone. Brad McAlister forced himself to continue walking into a hard breeze. His rising panic was a separate, unseen force, pressing against him like a cold wind.

The Marne Valley, France

Luke approached the town cautiously, avoiding the main road that wound through the center. The river was off to his right and a little below the town. To the west, he could see the arches of an old stone bridge over the river. Off to the left, at the western edge of town, was a small train station.

The enticing aroma of fresh-baked bread wafted across the road, drawing Luke toward an out-of-the-way boulangerie. His belly growled in anticipation. He hadn't eaten all day except for a croissant with Delaney that morning. Did everyone in France live on croissants?

The smell was irresistible. He surveyed the scene warily. No train in sight. No sign of the gray Renault that signified danger. Only a small Citroen parked near the bakery and a couple of men sipping coffee at a table out front.

Muscular, businesslike men in gray suits, one of them ill fitting. No resemblance to the assassins who had shot at Luke. They had looked like Hezbollah soldiers straight out of Beirut.

At the counter, Luke pointed at a baguette, a long, crusty loaf of bread. He also picked out a thick wedge of cheese. He could hear the men at the table out front talking, and something about the conversation caught his attention. Maybe it was his acute sensitivity to the sound, in this setting, of any language but French.

He paid for the bread and hunk of cheese. He would eat them while he waited at the train station. He intended to catch the first train to Paris.

Russian, he thought; they were talking Russian.

He started from the boulangerie, carrying his purchases. One of the Russians glanced in his direction, the one in the ill-fitting suit. Suddenly he was on his feet, pulling on his companion's arm. The second man turned and, seeing Luke, leaped to his feet so quickly his chair tipped over with a clatter.

The first man shouted. The second thrust a hand in his pocket.

Luke ran.

He ducked into a side street, down an alley, and through a narrow opening between buildings, emerging on another cobbled road. He could hear the men shouting but the words were indistinguishable, some in Russian, others in heavily accented English. This unexpected turn of events, a new threat from a totally different source, bewildered him. Consternation disrupted his thinking. Russians? Who were they? How did they figure in this wild scenario? One of them had shouted his name, for God's sake!

He tripped over an uneven paving stone and twisted his ankle. He limped on, trying to sort things out, feeling trapped. On foot, he had no chance to escape. How many were pursuing him? Were they in league with each other? Russians and Iranians? What could possibly have brought them together in some common, deadly purpose?

A side road dipped toward the river. Without taking time to reflect, Luke hobbled down the incline.

The river was a barrier. But it was also a possible escape route.

There were several small docks at the edge of the stream near the foot of the street. At one of them an old fisherman was just stepping into his small boat, reaching out to release a rope that moored him to the dock. Two fishing poles rested in the boat along with a large basket creel, some netting, a paper bag, and a folded tarpaulin stuffed under a bench seat in the stern.

The fisherman glanced up, curious, as Luke limped onto the dock. Luke dug into his wallet and withdrew a handful of franc notes, almost all he had. Without counting he thrust them toward the Frenchman. "Take me with you!" he said.

The fisherman stared at the money, surprise and suspicion and interest chasing each other across his features. *"Eh? Q'est-ce que c'est?"*

"I need your boat." Luke glanced back over his shoulder, searching for the assassins. "I must leave quickly."

"Ah, vous êtes Americain! I speak English good." A light of memory replaced the suspicion in the old man's eyes. He tapped his chest with a finger. *"La Resistance,"* he said proudly. "You are in trouble, m'sieur?"

"I will be if I'm caught."

"Ze police?" He spat into the river. "Zey are come for you?"

"Worse than that."

Luke held out the handful of bills toward the Frenchman. After a moment's hesitation, he took them and stuffed them into a pocket. "Quick . . . get down in ze bottom, I cover you." He pointed toward the tarpaulin. Luke hauled it out from under the bench seat and took its place, folding up his long legs and squirming as far under the seat as he could. The Frenchman hastily pushed the tarp around him and then, perhaps on a humorous impulse or simply to add verisimilitude, he pushed a bait pail up against the greasy tarp. Strong fish smells assaulted Like's nostrils, inescapable in his confined space.

He felt the boat tilt as the fisherman leaned over one side, then a sense of motion as the boat started to drift away from the dock. The Frenchman settled into place in the center and adjusted a pair of oars over the gunwales. Luke felt the surge as the oars dipped into the water and took hold.

The fisherman rowed out into the river, where the current carried them along. Luke listened to the rhythmic squeak and rub of the oars. The boat seemed to him to move at an agonizingly slow speed. No way it would go unobserved, he thought. Would his pursuers, seeing it, wonder? Or would they dismiss it as just the rowboat of an ordinary French fisherman, a familiar sight on the river?

"Merde!" the Frenchman muttered. For a moment the steady movement of the oars broke off and the boat drifted. It became deathly quiet. "Zey look for you, by gar . . . on ze bridge."

Through a crack in the fold of the tarp Luke peered out. He made out a portion of the bridge. The boat was heading toward one of the low arches. A man peered down, a man in a gray suit. The poorly cut suit again. Suddenly another head and shoulders appeared beside him. Both men stared at the rowboat. It would pass directly beneath them, no more than ten feet below.

The old fisherman craned his neck and waved cheerfully. *"Bonjours!"* he called out.

Then they were under the arch, slipping briefly into cool shadow. They quickly emerged from it into the warmth and brightness on the far side of the bridge.

Luke lay motionless under the tarpaulin, not even stirring to peek out. The old man lifted the oars once more, and the rhythmic dip and thrust and surge, dip and thrust and surge, began again.

"Don't look back at them," Luke whispered hoarsely. "But can you tell if they're still watching us."

There was a moment's silence. Then the old man chuckled. *"Les batards!* Why should zey watch an old man go to fish, eh? Zey are gone, m'sieur."

There was another long silence while the fisherman rowed steadily downriver. Then Luke said, "What are you called? Your name . . . ?"

"Jean Baptiste."

"Merci, Jean Baptiste. You've saved my life."

The fisherman chuckled. "I count your money, m'sieur. Is good bargain."

"Can you put me across the river somewhere? They won't be looking for me on the other side, at least for a while."

"Oui, c'est possible."

"I have to catch a train to Paris."

"No train, m'sieur. But is bus. I go near ze bus, okay? Is not far, maybe two kilometers."

Luke Cameron allowed the relief to wash over him. "Fine," he said.

The bus was even better, he thought. The men who had tried to kill him might be watching the train stations.

The slow, circuitous bus trip took him into the southeast section of Paris, the Twelfth Arrondissement, and let him off near the Gare de Lyon. From the busy train station Luke called Frank Delaney. It was late in the afternoon—the rush hour, with traffic congestion that seemed chronic in metropolises the world over, commuter stations jammed. Paris was no exception.

"Luke! Jesus Christ, where have you been? The Paris police have been questioning me. My car was found abandoned out in the country—full of bullet holes."

"Sorry about the car."

"To hell with the car! What about you?"

"No bullet holes. I ran into our Iranian friends—they owe you a new car. And listen to this, Frank. The nun I drove out to see this morning? She died unexpectedly. A sudden accident."

"You don't make it sound like an accident."

"I don't believe it was."

There was a long silence. "Jesus . . . the police didn't say anything about a murder."

"Officially, she slipped beside a pond, fell in, and drowned. Mine is the unofficial version."

"No accident."

"She knew something, Frank. Someone didn't want her to talk."

"Where are you now?"

"In Paris. I'm at the Gare de Lyon."

"I suggest you head straight out to Charles de Gaulle Airport. Go home, Luke. You're not going to learn anything else here. Go home where you belong. Maybe you'll be safe there."

"Give up? Is that what you're suggesting?"

"I'm suggesting you're in way over your head. This isn't something you can tackle yourself. Go home, go to the authorities with what you've learned, and let them handle it. The Lone Ranger's dead, Luke. I'd like to see you stay alive, and after what happened today, that means get out of France."

"I still don't know who Micheline Picard really is, or why someone would go to such lengths to keep me from finding out."

"Does it matter? You know she's involved in some conspiracy, but hell, it might not even be illegal, even if the principals are willing to commit murder to keep their secret. You don't know who or what you're dealing with, Luke."

There was a prolonged silence. Delaney was right, Luke thought wearily. Even Tom Cameron, stubborn as he was, had been scornful of men too pigheaded to admit defeat. *Tenacity is one thing, son. Trying to pull a stump with a frayed rope is another. That's just foolishness.*

He said, "My passport's at the hotel, along with my clothes."

"Okay, I'll borrow or rent a car and meet you there. I'll check you out of the hotel, get everything you need, and take care of your plane reservations. The sooner you're out of Paris, the better I'll feel. It has a violent terrorist underground, and these people are terrorists, Luke. They'll try again."

"I'll grab a taxi—"

"Listen, it's impossible to get a taxi at this hour, but you're right over the subway station. They've got maps that light up to show you how to reach your destination. You want to go to Invalides station. You can walk to your hotel from there."

"I'll find my way."

"I'll be waiting."

Canseco knew how to pick his men, Luke thought.

Gibson, Montana

BY PREARRANGEMENT, BRAD MCALISTER WAS TO CALL THE number of a pay phone on the outskirts of Gibson at ten o'clock in the morning if he had important news. The booth was next to the service bay of a gas station, whose attendant relayed his message. "I have to talk to Cal. Tell him it's urgent."

"Call back in an hour."

"Tell him to call . . ." Brad swore and banged down the phone. The attendant had already hung up.

The hour seemed longer than a car chase in a bad movie. Five minutes short of the hour, Brad picked up the phone. Kali answered, then listened in silence as Brad poured out his news.

"It's not a good idea for us to meet right now," Kali said. "I told you that. We got to cool it. You hear where I'm comin' from?"

"But they *know!*" Brad McAlister said, his voice rising.

"Take it easy, man. They don't know nothin'."

"You're not *listening* to me!"

"Where you calling from? You in that café where everyone in the place is listenin' to you but me?"

"No, no . . . I'm not stupid. I'm at home. There's nobody else in the house. Anne's at work, and the kids are out—"

"Okay, okay, no problem," Kali said quickly, thinking the opposite—that there might *be* a problem and that he, therefore, should be wary.

"What I'm telling you . . . Henderson tipped me off. That goddamn camera caught me inside the alarm control center. They asked him about it, what I was doing there. They must know. . . ."

"It don't mean that at all," Kali cut him off again. "So you were seen in the control center . . . Henderson already knew that, right? I mean, it was no secret. They're askin' him, maybe you weren't following the rules. . . . They wanted to know why, that's all. Hey, it's not as if you broke in from outside. You're a security guard! You're part of that scene."

As Kali spoke, making it all sound reasonable, Brad felt his panic begin to ebb. Maybe he was overreacting. He'd been tiptoeing along the brink since the night of the first uranium theft, jumping every time the phone rang, looking over his shoulder, thinking a car was tailing him around Gibson, when the whole idea was ridiculous. If the heavy hitters at the DOE really thought he'd done anything wrong, they'd have hauled his ass in.

"I don't know . . . Henderson made it sound as if they're serious."

"How serious can they be? They haven't even questioned you. . . . You ain't seen any SWAT team runnin' around that place. I mean, it's business as usual, right?"

"Well . . . yes."

"So no sweat, man. Hey, Brad, you got nothin' to worry about! Your part's over; you're in the clear. They call you in, ask you about being in the alarm room, hey, you stopped by to talk to your buddy Henderson. He was sick that night, right?"

"Yes . . ."

"There you are. You got to go with the flow, Brad, you know? You start to get jumpy, that's when you make trouble for yourself . . . and that could mean trouble for me. We don't want that, do we?"

There was an edge of menace in his voice, but Brad McAlister was feeling reassured enough to react. "Don't worry about me," he said stiffly. "But there's something else we should talk about. What about the rest of my money?"

"You'll get it, you'll get it. I'm supposed to take delivery maybe today."

"Maybe? Maybe I should call you tonight."

"No! You don't want to do that. No more phone calls." Kali's tone was sharp. "I'll get back to you."

"IIow are you going to do that if we're not supposed to meet?"

Kali chuckled. "Hey, you're feeling better; I like that. Don't worry, you'll get your money; you got it coming. Give me another day; I'll let you know how we'll do it. Just don't do nothin' stupid, okay? Stay cool."

"Okay."

When Brad hung up the phone Kali waited several seconds, listening for the sound of a click on the line. When he heard it, he bared his teeth in triumph, but the expression was more a grimace than a smile. Discovering that McAlister's phone was tapped wasn't good news.

Because McAlister generally left for work around 11:30 at night for the fifteen-minute drive to SMS Site Number 14, Kali was able to use the cover of darkness to set up his vigil. He knew he couldn't risk approaching McAlister's house, but he surveiled the probable route from his tree-lined street to the interstate connection.

Kali parked his Jeep in the lot of a supermarket, then walked two blocks, keeping in the shadows. He picked the lock of an empty restroom in a darkened gas station and slipped inside. The restroom had a broken window; a wedge of the mottled glass was missing from the lower left-hand corner. Through this peephole, Kali could survey the street. The lack of ventilation left a heavy odor of urine in his hideout.

When McAlister's old Mercury failed to appear at half past the hour, Kali felt a twinge of anxiety. Then he saw the headlights far

down the street, approaching slowly. McAlister wasn't in a hurry
to get to work, Kali thought.

He recognized the car when it drove slowly past the gas station,
McAlister alone in the front seat, his profile briefly silhouetted by
a streetlight as he rounded the corner.

Kali waited.

The other car appeared about thirty seconds later. It was a late
model Ford Tempo, dark blue, moving at the same leisurely pace.
At the corner it swung right, following McAlister from a safe distance.

Kali emerged thoughtfully from the restroom. He stood on the
corner, staring after the taillights of the second car.

As he had suspected, McAlister was under surveillance. If that
click on the line meant what Kali thought, McAlister's phone was
also bugged. And the poor bastard didn't even know it!

Kali's contempt for the corrupt American's ineptness had never
been greater.

At a phone booth outside the market where he had left his Jeep,
Kali dropped coins into the slot and dialed a number. This time he
knew better than to act on his own initiative. Handling McAlister
under these circumstances would be a delicate business. But failing
to act would involve even more risk to the mission. If the woman
wished to command, he thought, let her walk where the bullets flew.

Micheline Picard answered on the fourth ring, following their established procedure. "Yes?"

"It's me. We got a problem."

He had not been able to reach her earlier in the day after McAlister's initial contact. Now he reported that a few of the workers at
Wind Canyon Mine were ill. Yusef, the professor's assistant, was the
most seriously affected.

"The professor himself is not sick?" Her question was sharp.

"No, no, he is well. The work progresses."

"Good." There was no concern in her voice.

Then Kali told her in detail of Henderson's warning to McAlister,
the latter's anxiety, and Kali's decision to determine whether the
American was under surveillance. "He was followed tonight when
he left his house."

"You are quite certain of this?"

"There is no doubt."

For a moment, she was silent. "You have done well, Kali."

He felt a surge of satisfaction—and became instantly angry with himself for the feeling. Was he so easily to be manipulated by this woman? Should he wag his tail and whimper with delight when she gave him a few words of praise?

Controlling his anger, Kali said: "He is a danger to us. They will torture him, the CIA, the FBI, these tools of Satan. They will break his wrists as they broke the wrists of the martyr of Allah, Fawaz Younis. They will make him talk. He is not a man who will stand up to such interrogation."

"He is a danger to *you,* Kali. He does not know about me, is that not correct?"

"Yes."

"Nor does he know where the uranium has been taken."

Kali felt a chill. What was she trying to say?

"But you are right, Kali. He will talk. And you are too important to the cause of Allah to be betrayed in this fashion. McAlister must be dealt with."

Again he felt that leap of elation and the immediate reaction. She was manipulating him. He *knew* what she was doing, yet he wanted to hear the praise from her lips. He longed to watch her soft lips move as she spoke the words. *You have done well, Kali. . . . You are too important to the cause of Allah to be sacrificed.* He hated her, but he desired nothing more than her approval.

"Do you have a plan?" she asked.

"It will not be easy while McAlister is being watched. But he is greedy. He wants his money, his pieces of silver."

"Then you must promise him what he wants."

"Yes . . . I will use the money as a lure. For that he will do what I tell him, go where I tell him . . . where he cannot be followed easily. . . ." As he spoke Kali had a sudden inspiration, so daring that it unnerved him. But why not? Why should all of the risk be his when she claimed the glory of the late Khomeini's mandate?

"The private road to the Cameron ranch, it is long and open from the highway. McAlister could not be followed along this road without having his watchers reveal themselves."

"Yes? . . ."

"They would have to stay on the main road."

"But they would wait for his return."

"Yes, but if McAlister came at night . . ."

Eagerly Kali sketched his idea, excitement rising as he talked. He pictured the Frenchwoman listening, her red lips parted, her heart filling with admiration for his cunning.

When he had finished, there was a long silence. Then she spoke and the admiration Kali had imagined was clearly audible in her voice. *"Barakallah!* Well done, Kali! It is good."

"I will arrange it," he said, heart hammering. "It must be done quickly. If they should decide to question him . . ."

"It is your plan; you should execute it."

"I will need someone in the house . . . a backup. One of the men from the mine . . ."

"That will not be necessary."

"But we must be certain! In such matters, even with a fool and a weakling like McAlister, it would be wise to have a backup."

"You will," the woman said. "I will be there."

Paris, France

THE PARIS METRO WAS A MARVEL OF EFFICIENCY. THE TRAIN was smooth, swift, and quiet, the underground approaches remarkably free of graffiti. Even a stranger to the city, like Luke Cameron, with little knowledge of the language, could follow the clearly defined maps. He needed only to know his destination—Invalides— and at the touch of a button an illuminated map tracked his route along a string of lights. He saw that he could take the Number 1 line as far as Concorde, then change for a direct connection to Invalides.

In Paris as in all large cities, the end of the workday meant crowds on their way home. Neither aggressive nor rude, Frenchmen generally kept to themselves, avoiding eye contact with strangers.

Luke glanced quickly around him at regular intervals; he saw no small, sallow, dark-eyed men watching him.

At Invalides, Luke climbed the steps to the street. There were people hurrying through the formal gardens and along the esplanade—the length of two football fields—that extended all the way down to the Seine. Others, not in a hurry, strolled toward the river or in the direction of the Rodin Museum, a short distance away on the east flank of the huge Hotel des Invalides and, behind it, Napoleon's tomb. No one seemed to be interested in the tall American who, amidst so many tourists, did not stand out. Luke felt some of his nervous tension begin to melt away.

At avenue St. Dominique, he turned from the broad esplanade into the narrow street toward his hotel, wondering if Delaney was right in urging him to leave Paris in such a hurry. He felt uncomfortable with the advice—it seemed like running away—but there was hard-headed logic to it. What more could he do? He couldn't continue to call on Frank Delaney's goodwill indefinitely; he had already abused the man's hospitality. Hire a private investigator? Luke didn't even know where to start. Did France have P.I.s?

Perhaps more to the point, as Delaney had emphasized, limited as Luke's inquiries had been, they had proved provocative enough to make him a target for some well-armed, well-organized terrorists.

Nearing the Sofitel-Bourbon, Luke saw Frank Delaney waiting near the entrance, a few steps from the street. Luke's carryall was on the step at his feet.

Traffic along the narrow street was tuning up for the rush-hour concert, horns raising a discordant clamor, as Luke hurried forward. He saw the relief in Delaney's eyes when the natty Irish American spotted him.

"Thank God!" Delaney exclaimed, gripping Luke's hand. "I was worried."

Delaney handed Luke his passport and two envelopes, one containing his hotel receipt, the other his ticket. "InCon picked up the tab, Luke—Canseco's orders. If you want to argue about it, you'll have to take it up with him. I switched your flight to—"

Luke had reached down to pick up his carryall. Delaney broke off his statement with an odd abruptness that caused Luke to glance up. Delaney's mouth was open, but no sound came out. There was surprise in his expression, baffled astonishment in his eyes. Then Luke saw the spreading stain on the Irishman's suit jacket just above and to the right of his heart.

Delaney began to topple forward. Luke caught him awkwardly, going down to one knee. He lowered Delaney to the step. People thronged around them, forming an unwitting screen, unaware that anything had happened. No one, including Luke, had heard the shot.

He swore in helpless rage. "God damn you!" But there was no enemy visible.

He tried to hold Delaney's head up, but the Irishman was already losing consciousness, his eyes glazing over. The wound was high— high enough to have missed his heart? He might still have a chance.

Luke used his anger to lash himself out of his stunned lethargy. He had to get help fast.

A burly man in a wrinkled brown suit shoved through the crowd on the sidewalk and up the steps. Several people were now gaping at Luke kneeling beside Delaney. The sight of blood brought shocked outcries.

The heavyset man grabbed Luke Cameron and hauled him to his feet with surprising ease. "Run, you damn fool! You can't help him! You're the target!"

He gave Luke a hard shove that sent him stumbling down the steps into the crowded street. Shock jolted him like a cattle prod. The beefy man knew him! Knew the bullet that had struck Delaney had been meant for him!

Though bewildered, raw instinct told him it was not a time to reason but to run. He bolted down the street.

With long, urgent strides, he put the hotel behind him. Startled faces flashed by him, eyes widening, mouths gaping, the realization beginning to register as if in slow motion that something terrible had happened. Luke searched the stream of faces for any sign of hostility, any hint of danger. Nothing!

He plunged around the first corner, running hard now, people scattering out of his way. Still no sign of his assassins. How many were there? Stupid of him not to have anticipated that they would have known where he was staying. They hadn't needed to follow him back to Paris once he escaped their ambush at St. Genevieve. They needed only to return to the city and take up positions near his hotel.

He recognized that he was a clumsy amateur at this kind of urban guerrilla warfare. The man in the brown suit, on the other hand, had acted like a pro. Quick in spite of his age. Hard muscled. An authoritative edge to his bark, like a top sergeant. Why had he been on that particular fashionable street on Paris's Left Bank at that particular moment? Why did he intervene?

His accent identified him as an American. A friend of Delaney's? Someone from InCon? Who else on Luke's side knew he was in Paris? The man's awareness of assassins and quick intervention had probably saved Luke's life. But why wouldn't Delaney have mentioned him?

And if he wasn't from InCon, who was he?

Then Luke saw the gunmen. At least two men, possibly a third, racing down a side street, trying to cut him off. He got a clear glimpse of two assassins; both carried guns openly.

An angry protest flashed through Luke's mind. Didn't Paris have any police? How could something like this happen in the heart of the city at rush hour? But even as the question erupted, Luke knew that it was irrational. Where were the police in Los Angeles when a drive-by killer gunned down a teenager in his front yard? Where were they in Detroit or New York or Washington, D.C.? In an increasingly violent world, police everywhere had an impossible task.

Luke had veered down another narrow avenue of cobbled paving stones. He raced past small, elegant, fashionable shops. The street was not wide, the shops crowding close together, the buildings relics of another century. Above him, strangers gazed down at him from third- and fourth-floor windows, wondering at the foolishness of someone running so hard.

This time Luke heard the shot. He saw a woman duck back from her balcony, frightened by the ugly sound.

Luke dove into the nearest side street. With his long legs, he was putting space between himself and his attackers; the shot had come from some distance away.

He ducked into another short street, whirled around the first corner, pounded past a patisserie and a butcher's shop and a small brasserie. He had moved swiftly away from the public areas of the Invalides district. The crowds were thinner here, the streets not jammed with traffic. It was easier running, but the openness also made him more visible as a target. Still, he felt safer in this warren of streets twisting this way and that. His pursuers couldn't possibly anticipate his every move! He could no longer see them behind him.

What next? A taxi? Impossible at this time of day, Delaney had told him. A telephone? Call the police? The American embassy?

The questions aroused the image once more of the rumpled man who had shoved him down the steps. *Run, you damn fool! You can't help him! You're the target!*

The puzzle of the burly stranger's intervention grew. He couldn't be explained away as someone Delaney knew. No, Delaney would have confided in him. And how had the mystery man been so swiftly certain that the shot had been meant for Luke?

He had acted like . . . like a cop, Luke thought.

Luke reached a small square shaded by tall trees flanking a fountain. He huffed across the square, slowing his pace. A running man drew attention. If he had lost his pursuit, it would be better to become part of the scenery, a strolling tourist. Never mind the shirt sticking to his back, the sweat streaming down his forehead.

Beyond the square, he found himself in the midst of a street fair in front of a popular sidewalk café. He had been running generally toward the Sorbonne, the university district, and these were young people spilling over the sidewalks into the street. A juggler tossed dumbbells for onlookers; a violinist played for a dancing couple. The atmosphere was that of a spontaneous street party, noisy and colorful.

Luke plunged into the center of the happy turmoil. He pushed past dancers and drinkers, nodding and smiling. The students flashed welcoming grins at the tall American. A slim young girl with close-cropped black hair grabbed his hand and whirled around him, tempting him to dance. Luke grinned and wheeled her in a circle. Releasing her, he spun off into the crowd.

Breaking free of the carefree throng, Luke began to relax for the first time since the shot. Suddenly all the questions, suspended during his race for survival, rushed back in a flood. He also felt anew the shock and horror that had momentarily paralyzed him as he had watched the dark stain seeping from Frank Delaney's shirt onto his silk suit jacket. The absurdity of the wound seemed all the more terrible because of the amiable Irishman's fondness for elegant clothes.

Weary at last, chest still heaving and heart pumping, Luke paused to lean against the wall of a building. He tried to take his bearings. He was at the corner of a street, no wider than an alley, which ran behind a row of old buildings several stories high, sheltered at the rear by high-walled gardens.

The street was quiet. Too quiet.

Quiet enough to hear the slap of running footsteps.

As Luke swung around, a small bearded man in a white shirt appeared at the end of the street. Another man pulled alongside him. Luke could make out the angular shape of an Uzi carbine in the hands of one of the terrorists.

Luke sprang into action. He ducked around the corner and ran along the alley. He realized with a jolt of desperation that he would never reach the end of the alley in time!

A spray of bullets sent shards of stone flying from the wall beside him. Luke dove behind the cover of a high metal trash container.

Behind him, he heard the click of a latch, the squeak of an iron gate. In renewed alarm, Luke spun around.

At a glance, he recognized the Russian in the ill-fitting gray suit— the man who had been sitting at a table in front of the boulangerie where Luke had sought refuge earlier that day in the Marne River valley. As the Russian stepped back, opening the gate, Luke saw the gun in his hand.

Frank Delaney lay on the sidewalk in shock. But Al Trautman could see he was alive. Recognizing one of the concierges from the hotel, Trautman urgently beckoned him over. "He's been shot! He needs a doctor! Fast!"

"It is done, m'sieur."

"Keep people away from him. And get the police."

Trautman didn't wait for an answer. He bulled his way through the gathering crowd on the steps. His hard eyes scanned their faces.

When he broke free from the human tangle, he headed for his car. He had tipped heavily to assure it would be parked nearby, ready to leave in a hurry if necessary. Trautman moved agilely for a big man; he also had sharp instincts for where and how a fugitive might attempt to lose himself in the center of a major city. But he had no illusions about catching Cameron and his attackers on foot. With wheels, he might have an outside chance to intercept them.

As a young man, Trautman had visited Paris. Unlike many of the world's major cities, it was fairly small and concentrated at its center. It was possible, he had found, to cover much of the city on foot. Staying at pensions, living on a tight budget, the youthful Trautman had scoured Paris's Left Bank thoroughly.

The city had changed, of course, but not so much physically. The French didn't tear every building down after twenty years, Trautman thought, the way they did back home.

The narrow streets were jammed with evening traffic and people. Most of them, if the conventional wisdom applied, were not Parisians.

How many Iranians? he wondered.

How many with guns, hunting Lucas Cameron?

After encountering engine trouble with the Ford Escort he had rented, Trautman had turned it in for a white Volkswagen convertible with a stick shift. Hardly the car he would have chosen but the only one he could obtain on short notice. It took him a few minutes to get the hang of the gears after so many years of driving with automatic shifts. But the car was quick and small and nimble, well suited to the narrow streets.

Casting back and forth, Trautman worked his way east toward the university district, backing and quartering, the car windows rolled down to admit the chaos of the streets. He listened intently for the sound of gunfire.

After about ten minutes, he just about concluded that he had guessed the wrong direction of Cameron's flight.

Then he spotted the dark, bearded men in a small, battered, ugly car that vaguely resembled a vintage Citroen taxicab.

Like Trautman, the men in the Citroen were busy searching the street crowds. Their faces were Middle Eastern, he thought. Iranians, if his hunch was right. Disciples of the Ayatollah Khomeini.

The Iranians were concentrating so hotly on their own search that they didn't notice Trautman. Falling in behind them, Trautman could see the man in the passenger seat use some kind of radio mike. They were still tracking Cameron, keeping in contact with his pursuers on foot.

Trautman smiled appreciatively; the cowboy wasn't easy to corner.

He had tailed enough cars in his time to keep a full block behind the Citroen so he wouldn't be conspicuous in its rearview mirror. Suddenly the Iranians began driving so purposefully that he guessed they had received a radio message. Someone had spotted Cameron.

Trautman regretted his failure to confide more openly in the man at the DGSE, or to ask for help from the Agency man at the American embassy. But the feeling was transient. Alone, he might not be able to save Cameron, but it was too late to make other plans.

Some students spilled into the street in front of him. In rapid sequence, Trautman swore, swerved, and hit the brakes. One of the young people, laughing, slapped the hood of the VW and danced out of the way. More frustrated than angry, Trautman gunned the convertible around the next corner.

He had lost the Citroen.

It took him several minutes to find it again. The Citroen had detoured around a small square where a mini–street festival was in progress. Trautman resumed his tailing and, less than a minute later, heard the rattle of an automatic rifle.

In the distance the crackle was like fireworks, part of the street celebration. But to Al Trautman, too streetwise to be deceived, it was a gut-wrenching sound.

The little car he had been trailing braked to a stop at the mouth of a narrow alley dwarfed by rows of luxurious, nineteenth-century mansions too expensive even for the wealthy to maintain as private homes, converted now into offices and government buildings. Two men jumped out of the Citroen and darted into the alley. One carried what looked like an AK-47, the other a handgun.

Cruising past them, Trautman looked down the alley and saw two other armed men at the far end, advancing slowly.

There was no sign of Luke Cameron, but it was obvious he had been boxed in. Trapped.

Luke bolted past the open gate where the Russian waited. He raced toward the adjoining property. Another wild shot chased him. Luke heard the whine of the bullet as he threw himself at the wall.

It was a solid stone wall eight feet high. He reached the top in one jump and scrambled over. He landed on his feet in a bed of purple pansies.

Glancing over his shoulder at the wall, he wondered how many seconds before someone came over the wall after him. Then he heard the crack of a single shot nearby, and a cry of pain.

With renewed urgency, Luke trampled the bed of pansies in his hurry to reach a stone path. He found himself in a large, formal garden divided by stone walkways into neat squares and triangles of color. He headed down the central path, which led to the rear of a great, gray stone mansion.

Panting furiously, Luke reached an arched lane next to the building. From the alley behind him came a hammering burst of automatic rifle fire, followed by a high-pitched babble of cries in an unfamiliar language.

As Luke looked back, a bearded face appeared at the top of the wall. The man shouted wildly. Luke bolted toward the shelter of the covered lane that had at one time been a carriage lane. He was just a few steps from the arched opening when the Russian stepped into view.

Luke was trapped, escape cut off from the rear!

The Russian spoke in clear English. "Quick! I will cover you."

He gestured toward the front of the building. Luke sped past him, too startled to question what was happening. The Russian coolly aimed at one of the terrorists who was clambering over the wall. The shot knocked the man over like a doll in a penny arcade.

The Russian sprinted down the drive, calling to Luke. "Don't look back, Cameron! . . . Keep running!"

At first Luke thought he had shouted "Comrade!" Then he realized that the Russian had used his *name*.

Behind them, they could hear pandemonium. As they burst out of the carriage lane, a small white car turned off the street into the sweeping drive in front of the gray stone mansion. Rounding the corner of the building, the Russian waved Cameron on and swirled around to face the lane. An assailant dashed from the garden into the lane. Once more the Russian fired.

An anguished wail trembled in the air like an evening prayer. Pursuit broke off.

At that moment, Al Trautman sprang out of the Volkswagen. He took in the scene in an astonished glance. He ran toward Luke Cameron. In the same instant, the Russian whirled his head around, and his eyes locked on Trautman's.

Cop! Al Trautman thought.

American agent! thought Sergei Milov.

Luke Cameron stared at Trautman in startled recognition. Trautman threw the car keys to him. "Take the car!" he barked.

Luke caught the keys in one hand. He looked at them as if he wasn't sure what to do with them.

"We'll take care of your friends," said Trautman. "Get out of here fast, before they know you have wheels."

"I . . . I'll . . . I'll leave it at the airport."

"No!" Trautman's warning was sharp. "They'll expect you there. I don't know what you've stirred up, Cameron, but it looks like a hornet's nest of terrorists are after you. Get out of Paris. . . . Leave the car at Calais and take the Sealink ferry to England."

Luke looked from Trautman to Milov. "I can't let you—"

"You can't do anything else."

"What about Delaney? Is he dead?"

"I think he'll live. He's on his way to the hospital. If you don't want to end up there—" Trautman broke off as Milov fired at another assassin trying to reach the front of the mansion. "Go!"

Luke Cameron sprinted toward the white convertible. Whoever the blunt-spoken American was, whoever the Russian was, both men were trying to keep him alive.

Another burst of gunfire erupted as he turned the key in the VW's engine. This time the shooting sounded louder and deadlier, as the assassins brought assault weapons to bear against Trautman and the Russian. Luke could see the two men maneuvering hastily, understanding each other's silent gestures, taking cover near a corner of the house.

It was the last image he carried with him as he found first gear and screeched out of the curving drive into the street.

As Luke Cameron sped off, Al Trautman caught the Soviet agent's eyes. Cool under fire, Trautman thought. A man in control of the situation. Trautman settled down to wait for the Iranians with quiet confidence. He grinned. "When this is over," he called out to the Russian, "we have to talk."

Moscow's man nodded, not breaking his concentration. Trautman thought, *I hope he speaks English.*

He heard a strange wailing in the distance, drawing closer, and identified it as the cry of police sirens. He realized the shootout was about to come to an abrupt end.

The Soviet agent drew fire as he leaped across the opening of the lane to reach Trautman's side. "That will be the French police?" he inquired in flawless English.

"That's my guess."

He nodded toward the men at the back of the building. "They will run . . . try to escape."

"Seems likely."

"I wish to talk to one of them."

Trautman gave him a long, appraising look. "You want me to buy you some time."

Sergei Milov nodded. "I will let you know what I learn. I believe it is in the interest of both our governments."

Trautman made his decision, one he would attempt to justify later. If this is glasnost, he thought, I hope it works. "I'll entertain our French colleagues. Take care."

The Russian smiled. "I will take very good care."

Gibson, Montana

"**W**HERE ARE YOU GOING?" ANNE MCALISTER ASKED.

"I have to meet somebody," Brad replied evasively.

Was he having an affair? That was her first thought. He was nervous, obviously, but it appeared a different kind of nervousness. His anticipation, she was quite certain, was not for a sexual liaison. There was an apprehension in his demeanor.

"I wish you'd tell me . . ."

But even as she spoke the words, she was not sure they were true. Did she really want to know?

"I told you already . . . it's done. After tonight. I'm seeing this guy. He owes me some money . . . it's a development deal. Okay, maybe it's not something you want to invite the Internal Revenue Service to witness, but it's nothing terrible. Not like I'm an ax murderer." He essayed the old Brad McAlister grin.

"Won't you be late for work?"

"Yeah . . . you're right, I better get going." He hesitated, then said, "Honey, I can't tell you what this is all about. But believe me, it's over. After tonight I'm out of it. I'm seeing Cal—this guy. And I'm telling him this is the last time, I don't want to see his face again. That's the truth. You've got to believe me."

"I want to."

"You'll see," Brad insisted. "Things will be different. Without all those bills hanging over us . . . That's been our problem, honey, worrying all the time, not knowing how we're ever gonna get out of the hole. It'll be different now . . . you'll see."

As he left the house, stepping outside onto the porch into the cool darkness, the image that lingered in his mind was the doubt in Anne's eyes. It must be like that for a couple when one of them has been unfaithful, he thought. The woman would look at the man that way as he was going out, wondering if she could ever trust him again. He felt a pang of lost innocence, the realization that the rapture of their first years, when they believed in each other so completely, could never be recaptured.

Then he thought of Cal. With a feeling of pure hatred.

This was followed by a sudden concern. Never should have used Cal's name in front of Anne. That had been stupid. But what the hell. After tonight, he could tell the bastard where to go.

When he turned the ignition key, the battery groaned wearily, and something twisted in Brad's stomach. God in heaven, not now! Not tonight! Then the engine caught, stuttered, and coughed into life as he pumped the accelerator. He felt a dampness of sweat on his upper lip.

Backing out of the drive and heading down the street, beneath its nave of old oak trees, he reviewed in his mind the latest and, he hoped, last phone call from Cal.

Brad had always thought Cal's system of telephone cutouts and secretive meetings had been a little melodramatic, something Cal must have seen in a spy movie. This morning it had become clear he was wrong. Cal's precautions had not only been necessary but were probably the only reason Brad was not up to his neck in hot water.

Brad had left his message at the gas station number. Cal had called back an hour later. But he had sidestepped Brad's questions, refusing to talk. Instead, he had told Brad to meet him for lunch at the 4-B's restaurant attached to the motel. Brad had waited by the counter. But no sign of Cal. Instead, Brad received another phone call. The restaurant owner, who knew him, handed him the phone from behind the cash register.

"What's going on?" Brad had demanded when he heard Cal's voice on the line. "Have you got my money?"

"Don't talk," Cal said, "just listen. I'm being tailed."

"What?"

"I could be wrong, but I don't think so. I've seen this same car too many times wherever I go."

"Oh my God . . . ," Brad whispered hoarsely. "What are we going to do?"

"Take it easy. It's not a problem. They're probably tailin' everybody around here who looks foreign to them."

"Who's them? For Christ's sake, Cal, don't you see what this means?"

Cal's voice was hard. "I told you to shut up and listen. It could be the DOE. Or the FBI. Who knows? It doesn't matter. They don't know anything, you got that? Anyway, you got nothin' to worry about. You're in the clear."

"I told you they were asking questions about me."

"If they really knew anything, do you think you'd still be walkin' around loose?"

"But it means they know that . . ." Brad looked about him apprehensively. Ted Dickerson, the owner, nodded at him pleasantly enough, but there was the beginning of a little frown creasing his forehead. "What . . . how are we going to meet?"

"That's why I set this up. If they really *are* tailing me, you don't want to be seen meeting me. That means we can't meet in town. I can lose the tail, that's no problem, but they might pick me up again in town."

"Where can we meet?" Brad was beginning to have a very bad feeling. He was suddenly very sorry that he had ever met Cal.

"You know the old Cameron place? Outside of town, maybe fifteen miles or so?"

"Yes, sure," Brad said, surprised.

"Meet me there tonight. Eleven o'clock. That'll leave time for you to get to work on time."

"But . . . isn't someone living there?"

"You mean the Frenchwoman? Yeah, she was living there. I did some work on the place for her. That's how I know it's safe. She moved back into town. She couldn't stand it out there; too lonely, I guess. . . . She must've missed the bright lights of Gibson," Kali added with a chuckle.

"What . . . what if you're followed?"

"Hey, man, don't sweat. I'll lose them, no problem. That way, you can just drive out there on your own, meet me there, pick up your filthy greenbacks and drive off. It's perfect. A place like that, out in the country, there's no way they could tail me without my knowing it, you dig?"

Brad McAlister wished once more Cal didn't feel the necessity to affect his clumsy slang. "I suppose so . . ."

"It's perfect!" Cal repeated. "The money's in cash," he added. "Used twenties and some fifties, just the way you wanted it."

Ted Dickerson was looking impatient. Brad said, "Listen, I've got to get off this phone."

"Meet me at the ranch tonight, eleven o'clock. Then you're out of it. After that we don't meet again, is that clear?"

"I'll see you then," Brad said, Cal's last words bringing a rush of relief.

Now, leaving the bright lights of Gibson behind, he wondered if his euphoria hadn't been premature. He was even a bit nervous about meeting Cal in such a remote place at night. Not that he thought Cal would try to pull anything, but . . .

If he did, the little bastard would get a surprise.

Brad flipped down the lid of the glove compartment and removed a black leather holster. Inside the smooth leather sheath was a Colt Cobra, a modern and powerful handgun. There was nothing unique in Montana about owning and transporting a gun, though the rifle in a pickup was more popular. He liked guns; he enjoyed hunting and shooting. And he was a crack shot. If little Cal tried something funny, Brad might shoot his balls off.

He remembered that moment of bitter hatred he had felt when he stood on the porch. . . .

Leaving Gibson, Brad McAlister self-consciously studied the highway behind him to check whether a car might be tailing *him*. For a while, he felt tension in his gut when a dark-colored Ford hung behind him for several miles. Then it turned down a side road, its headlights disappearing in the distance as Brad continued on.

He laughed nervously. Cal was overdramatic. Maybe he was

jumping to wrong conclusions, Brad told himself. Guilt did funny things to you. He checked the rearview mirror again. The night was overcast. But he could still see for some distance back along the road. There was nothing moving.

He convinced himself that he had merely imagined being followed. But as a precaution, about a quarter mile before reaching the dirt lane leading into the Cameron ranch property, Brad pulled off the highway, doused his lights, and switched off the engine. With the window rolled down, he sat for several minutes, watching, listening. The wind was restless, stirring the brush along the side of the road into scratchy motion.

In the distance, he saw a car's lights approaching from the east at high speed. He watched it bear down on him. It whooshed past without slowing. He waited until the bright red taillights disappeared. The car's headlights would have illuminated any car parked behind Brad off the highway.

There was nothing.

Satisfied, Brad revived the Mercury, rolled ahead a short distance, and turned down the long private road that led to the Cameron ranch house.

He felt a tingle of tension as he neared the house. A downstairs light was on, and a porch light illuminated the yard behind the house.

He pulled the Colt Cobra from its holster, checked the safety, and shoved the gun into the side pocket of his short jacket. He kept a wary hand on the gun as he stepped from the car and quietly shut the door.

No sign of Cal.

The soft laughter came from behind him. "Hey, man, what's your problem?"

Brad spun around. His right hand pulled free of his jacket pocket, clenching the Colt.

The bearded man he knew as Cal jumped back a step. He threw up both hands in mock surrender. "Hey, don't shoot, don't shoot! What is this, man, you come here to rob me? Didn't I tell you the money's yours?"

"Where is it?"

Cal nodded toward the house. "In the kitchen on the table, waiting for you. What's with the gun, man?"

"Let's just get this over with. After you, Cal. No funny stuff. This is a .45 Magnum, and I know how to use it. It makes a hell of a hole."

"I bet it does."

Cal seemed surprisingly unruffled by the gun or Brad's warning—which could mean that he had no tricks up his sleeve. Still, it would be better to take no chances, Brad thought. He had the situation under control, why not finish it that way?

"You lead the way."

"Suit yourself, man. But you don't need that gun. Just don't trip or anything."

"Don't worry about me."

"I'm not worried about nothin'. You wanted your money? You got it, okay?" Cal pushed open the screen door and stepped into the kitchen.

Still cautious, Brad McAlister followed the bearded man inside, keeping two steps behind. His gaze was drawn instantly to the round maple table and the shoebox resting on the table, stuffed with money in neat, rubber-banded stacks. He felt an easing of his jitters.

As Cal turned to grin at him and Brad stepped toward the table, he saw motion out of the corner of his eye. Something slammed down on his right hand with enough force to break it. Pain shot up his arm and the Cobra flew from nerveless fingers, clattering onto the linoleum floor, skittering toward Cal.

Looking around in pain and astonishment, Brad saw the French-woman watching him with cool dark eyes. He looked at her hands, wondering what she could have hit him with. It didn't occur to him that a slight woman like this one could have struck him with the edge of her hand with such force.

A sudden rush of anger overwhelmed the shock and pain. She wasn't supposed to be here! Cal had lied to him! Yet the money was there on the table; what the hell was going on? What could a beauti-ful, sophisticated woman like this have to do with Cal?

Then he saw Cal make a move toward the Colt on the floor. With grim satisfaction, Brad sprang into action. He felt a need to take out his anger and confusion on the most available target. Brad weighed two hundred twenty pounds, well distributed on his large frame, and he hadn't lost all his athletic skills. Cal wasn't much more than half his size; he couldn't have weighed more than a hundred fifty. It was a mismatch, but Brad didn't care.

As Cal bent to retrieve the gun, Brad lunged for him. But the bearded man wasn't reaching for the gun at all. He seemed to change direction in midmotion. He spun toward Brad. His leg flicked out. He drop-kicked Brad in the groin. When Brad doubled over, locked into position by the unbelievable pain, Cal's knee shot up and caught him on the chin. He went down as if he had been clotheslined.

He lay on the floor, writhing, his hands clutching his loins in a reflex protective action. Cal hacked, clearing his throat, and Brad felt a spray of spittle. The humiliation didn't seem important. Nothing was important but the pain spreading through his gut.

That and the realization, screening through the pain into his brain, that he had made a terrible miscalculation.

The Frenchwoman looked down at him, with open contempt. Even as his terrible pain turned into nausea, he couldn't help staring up her legs under her skirts. She ignored his lecherous gaze. "You are a stupid man, Mr. McAlister, as well as a greedy one."

"Why . . . why are you . . . doing this?" His voice was high and strained, the words coming out in gasps. "What . . . kind of . . . people are you?"

"You dare ask that, a man who would sell his soul for a cardboard box filled with money?"

"It's not my fault. . . . It wasn't my . . ." Brad's words failed him. There were none that would answer her question.

He saw the contempt in her eyes. And the cold dismissal.

"It is Allah who puts the gun in our hand," she said.

He did not know that the words were those of Ayatollah Ruhollah Khomeini.

The woman turned to the bearded man beside her. "Kill him," she said.

Joe Springer sat in the parked Ford and glowered at the Washington agent, who was lighting up another cigarette. The goddamn car reeked of tobacco smoke. Hell, the so-called experts said it was just as bad for you as lighting up yourself.

He wound down the side window, letting in more of the pure night air. Fred Hawthorne, one of the field agents dispatched by FBI headquarters in Washington, said, "He's coming out."

Springer stared down the dark lane toward the Cameron ranch, with a twinge of surprise. McAlister hadn't been there long. Fifteen, twenty minutes maybe. In another five minutes, Springer would have been tempted to cross the prairie to check what was going on at the house. Good thing he hadn't.

Until tonight, he had tended to dismiss Brad McAlister as a minor figure in the investigation.

Tonight had changed the picture. Tonight put McAlister back into the plot—along with Luke Cameron.

Springer didn't know what the connection was between Cameron and McAlister and the stolen uranium. But there was a connection.

McAlister's Mercury zoomed past them. The FBI surveillance vehicle was hidden behind a screen of brush, but Springer caught a glimpse of the lone figure behind the wheel, the collar of his jacket turned up as he had seen it earlier.

"Let him get up the road a ways and don't use your lights," Springer said. "And douse that cigarette."

With a shrug, the agent smashed the cigarette in the ashtray. He had already received a tongue-lashing from Springer for tossing one out the window. "We gonna pick the son of a bitch up?" he asked.

"I don't know; you tell me. Washington seems to be running this show."

"I say we should pick him up and sweat him."

"Our orders are to maintain surveillance."

"Yeah."

They followed McAlister's car back toward Gibson, carefully keeping about a quarter mile behind. As they neared the edge of town, a pickup pulled out of a side road in front of the FBI car. Hawthorne turned on his headlights and maneuvered the pickup as a screen between the surveillance car and McAlister's Mercury.

The suspect stopped at a diner off the highway southeast of Gibson. He hurried inside. Approaching from the east, the two agents were still a hundred yards away when they saw the man emerge from the Mercury and enter the diner. They cruised slowly into a parking place. Something about that brief glimpse bothered Joe Springer, but he wasn't sure what it was until later.

A row of parked cars lined the front of the diner, with the Mercury in the middle of them. There was an empty space next to it, but the G-men parked down at the end.

"Want a cup of coffee?" the Washington agent asked.

"One of us better stay put. You go ahead if you want."

Hawthorne shrugged. "Yeah, I guess you're right. He might come out in a hurry."

He lit up another cigarette. With a weary sigh, Joe Springer slid out of the car into the fresh air.

Twenty minutes later, Springer was becoming concerned. "I think one of us better go in there."

"He's probably having dinner."

"It's beginning to feel wrong. I'm going in. Wait here just in case."

Five minutes later Springer burst out of the diner and sprinted past the row of cars to the FBI vehicle. "Get on the phone!" he said. "He's gone!"

"What do you mean, gone?"

"I mean he's given us the slip! He's not there. And that means he burned us. He knew he was being tailed, so he dumped the car here where we'd wait for him to come out. He's gone, Hawthorne! Will you get on the goddamn phone? I don't care what your team leader says, I want the bastard picked up! Tonight!"

Joe Springer drove to the Cameron ranch the following morning. The Frenchwoman turned out to be as beautiful as he had been told she was. He felt a tightness in his chest as he studied her. For the first time in his life, he discovered that the cliché about a beautiful woman was literally true: *She takes your breath away.*

She was also more charming and cooperative than he had expected. Yes, she knew Mr. McAlister; his wife worked for the Gibson Bank. And he *had* stopped by the house the previous night, quite late—so late in fact, that the car's approach had made her a bit nervous, since she was living there alone. McAlister had appeared agitated, she said. He was looking for Luke Cameron. He seemed disturbed that she was unable to tell him where Cameron was. Her account was simple and straightforward—and convincing.

She smiled warmly when Springer thanked her for her help.

Driving back toward Gibson, Joe Springer could find no reason to doubt the Frenchwoman's story. The key to the uranium theft, he told himself, was still the missing Luke Cameron.

But Springer was also beginning to wonder how Brad McAlister could disappear so easily. And why.

Paris, France

F ROM A SMALL, WINDOWLESS ROOM ON THE TOP FLOOR OF THE
Soviet embassy, Sergei Milov used a secure line to call his superior, Colonel Vitaly Novikoff, at Moscow Central. In spite of the late
hour in Moscow—it was after ten—Novikoff was not only in his office but he sounded alert. "Milov! How is Paris?"

"It is quite beautiful."

"The churches? You have found time to visit Notre Dame?"

"Yes, Colonel . . . very impressive."

"Impressive, is it? Ha! Yes, Sergei Andreyevich, it is most impressive. And the women of Paris . . . you have enjoyed them, my ardent
young friend? Are they not also impressive?"

"There has been no time, Colonel."

"No time? Make time, Sergei, make time! Who knows when you
will see Paris again?" After a sobering pause Novikoff's tone turned
from playful to brisk. "You have news for me?"

"It is as we suspected."

Milov gave a well-prepared capsule summary of his investigations
since his arrival in France. At the end, Novikoff interrupted him
sharply.

"This American agent—is he CIA?"

"No, Comrade Colonel, he works for the United States Department of Energy."

"Ha! Then he was in Paris for the same reason as you, Milov. The
Americans have also been a target for nuclear theft. Their Energy
Department is in charge of producing and storing nuclear weapons
materials."

"Yes, it would appear that the American was on a similar mission."

"And he was drawn to the same potential source for these attacks—the Frenchwoman. What have you learned of her?"

"The Iranians have attempted to cover her background, but some
things are known. I questioned one of the Iranians who participated
in the attack on the American civilian. The agent Trautman was
agreeable to my questioning the man before the French authorities

could intervene, on the understanding that I would inform him of what I learned. I trust that was satisfactory, Colonel."

"Mmmm . . ."

"It was . . . an agreement, Colonel."

"Which you were not authorized to make. But it's done. Go on."

"The woman is only half French. Her father was Iranian, and she is loyal to revolutionary Islam. Obviously she cannot be acting on her own behalf as a . . . a . . ."

"A loose cannon on the deck?" Novikoff suggested.

"Precisely, Colonel. There can be little doubt of the ultimate responsibility for the concerted attempts to steal nuclear materials, both in the United States and the U.S.S.R."

"And that is?" Novikoff prompted, though he knew the answer.

"Khomeini."

By the time Luke Cameron reached Calais the next evening—after a pleasant drive through the green French countryside, cruising with the top down on the VW convertible and wishing that he were here under different circumstances—the swift and ruthless roundup of Iranian nationals and Islamic adherents had begun in the southern Soviet republics of Azerbaijan, Armenia, and Georgia. Glasnost might prevail throughout the U.S.S.R.; protests might be tolerated; provincial nationalistic fervor might be allowed to find its voice; elections might be held and party officials defeated. But an attempt to steal or sabotage the Soviet Union's closely guarded nuclear arsenal provoked a response of brutal efficiency that Stalin himself might have envied, savage interrogation of its victims followed by pitiless death.

While the roundup was under way, Sergei Milov received the joyful news he had been waiting for. The directive came from Vitaly Novikoff:

Milov—
You are relieved of your investigation relating to recent criminal actions against the Soviet Union. You will proceed directly to Moscow and report to me for reassignment. In the interest of carrying out any unfinished inquiries you may have in Paris, your departure has been delayed for seventy-two hours. Don't waste the time.

Novikoff

Tehran, Iran

S HORTLY BEFORE DAWN THAT SATURDAY MORNING, MAY 27, Ali Akbar Mohtashemi slowly climbed the winding staircase to the mosque tower. It was too early for the morning prayer, which waited for dawn. For Muslims the world over it was the same.

Scholarly debate had never successfully eliminated all question of the precise moment when dawn arrived and the first prayer of the day might be heard. One tradition held that the moment came when the first rays of light were sufficient for a man to distinguish between a black thread and a white thread held out at arm's length. Eager believers sometimes vied with each other to be the first to praise Allah for the birth of a new day.

That moment had not yet come when Mohtashemi dismissed the attendant from the tower and stood alone, gazing out over the city, peaceful and quiet at this hour. Always at such moments he felt close to the desert. Standing in the tower he could feel its presence just beyond the city walls, he could smell it in the hot dry breeze.

He had been awakened by an aide when the first news began to arrive from the U.S.S.R. Hundreds of soldiers of Allah had been seized in the southernmost Soviet republics. Reports coming in hourly from informants detailed a sweeping roundup of the Islamic faithful. Nearly one-fifth of the population of the U.S.S.R. was Muslim, but of these a much smaller percentage were militant fundamentalists. These had been targeted. Anyone who had demonstrated for Islam or shown openly fundamentalist views was suspect. Anyone with relatives in Iran, or who had traveled across the border to Iran, was automatically arrested.

The loyal followers who had been in charge of the Russian option had been caught in the comprehensive sweep. Few had escaped, and those were in hiding.

Their mission was aborted.

Ali Akbar Mohtashemi knew that his personal fate rested upon the outcome of the nuclear missions he had authorized. Already his chief rival, Hashemi Rafsanjani, was maneuvering behind the scenes in anticipation of Khomeini's death, lining up the voices of weakness and modernism, the enemies of the true Islamic Revolution. Only a stunning success could now stop the appeasers, Mohtashemi thought bitterly. The Russian failure would only strengthen Rafsanjani's hand, make doubters waver. . . .

Mohtashemi was hesitant to approach Khomeini with such terrible news, even at this moment of the Imam's weakness while he recovered from drastic surgery—or perhaps because of it. His wrath could be terrible, and no one could be certain where and against whom the blow would fall.

Just before dawn Mohtashemi descended from the tower and went to his own room, which had been set aside for him in the hospital so that he might remain close to the Imam during the crisis. There, in privacy, he knelt facing Mecca, the birthplace of the Prophet of Islam, as the tremulous call to morning prayer was heard. He prostrated himself and whispered, *Al-hamdo-lellah!* Praise to God!" He asked nothing for himself, but only that the will of Allah be fulfilled.

Shortly after morning prayers the devoted Ahmad bin Razi came to inform him that the Imam was awake. The two mullahs hurried along the silent corridor to the hospital room, passing the nurses busy at their stations, ignoring the furtive glances of attendants and doctors and armed Revolutionary Guards outside the ayatollah's room. The latter recognized Mohtashemi as he approached and quickly stepped aside.

Heart beating heavily, Mohtashemi entered the room.

The usual throng of doctors swung toward him, their eyes and mouths disapproving as they recognized him. They disapproved of anything that might disturb the Imam in his weakened postoperative state, but they also feared and resented Mohtashemi's closeness to their spiritual leader.

Khomeini's eyes were closed and he breathed in a shallow wheeze that disturbed the mullah listening to him. But after a moment the eyelids fluttered over the sunken eyes.

Khomeini stared at him for a long moment. Then he said, *"Che khabar-e?* What is the news?"

Mohtashemi swallowed, but it did not even occur to him to fail in his duty to tell the Imam what had happened.

Khomeini's reaction astounded him.

The old man dismissed Mohtashemi's expressions of concern and disappointment. Khomeini's mood was surprisingly calm. Coals of anger and hatred burned in his breast against the hated Soviet infidels, he said, but all was not lost. Where one hand was cut off, the other might still strike.

For the present the Soviet option had failed.

The Satan option was still alive.

In the hands of the daughter he had never acknowledged . . .

In the late 1960s, after his departure from France for Najaf in Iraq, where with Soviet help over the next ten years he sent his revolutionary message across the border to his followers in Iran, rarely had Khomeini given any thought to the bastard child he had left in the care of the nuns of the convent of St. Genevieve. If the child had been a boy, he might have acted differently. A girl child, after all, was unimportant.

Khomeini's legitimate children were loyal and devoted, if undistinguished except for his eldest son Mostafa, whom he still mourned. He had no need to acknowledge another offspring, born out of wedlock to a pretty little French waif.

It was Ahmad bin Razi, who had been with him during his exile in France, who had suggested that the girl might be brought to Iran to be properly educated in the teachings of the Prophet. Khomeini had considered the suggestion. The girl was not of pure blood—in the veins flowed the blood of infidels—but she was also his daughter. He decided that, although she should remain in France, one of his loyal mullahs should undertake her education and religious training. She could not be left among the Christian nuns.

Involved in his passionate goal of bringing down the hated Pahlavi regime and replacing it with the true order of government obedient to Allah's wishes, the ayatollah had dismissed the girl from his thoughts. When he returned to Paris after more than a decade's absence, after being exiled from Iraq at the shah's insistence, he found himself a major world figure, the leader of militant Islam. Paris became his stage.

One day a slim young girl was brought to him. She was but thirteen years of age, shy, beautiful, intelligent, and spirited. She was everything the plain, unexceptional children of his household were not. Heretofore aloof and indifferent toward her, he began to take an interest, though he did not reveal it to the girl herself.

During the next year in France, preoccupied with the increasing unrest in Iran and his role in exploiting the dissatisfaction many Iranians felt for the shah's secular reforms, Khomeini nevertheless saw the girl many times. He found her enchanting. He ordered that she be educated well in the truth of the Koran—and trained as a servant of militant Islam.

After the revolution exploded in the streets of Tehran, the Grand Ayatollah returned in triumph to his country early in 1979 as its rightful ruler and spiritual guide. He lost no time in restoring Iran to the traditional ways of Islam. The girl remained in Paris until she was of sufficient age to choose to be given terrorist training in Iran. Though the camp to which she was sent was a thousand miles from Tehran, the revolutionary fervor she displayed brought her to the attention of Ali Akbar Mohtashemi, who at that time was in charge of the terrorist training camps. He had duly reported her progress to the Imam, to whom it brought an inordinate satisfaction. He had not been wrong, he thought, in choosing that she might live.

Back in Paris, now a trained and active terrorist as well as a woman whose striking beauty affected all who saw her, she had served the revolution with such passion that she had become a leader of the Party of Allah in the French capital . . . and it was she who had first communicated to Mohtashemi the idea for a blow against the forces of evil that would reverberate down through the centuries.

It was right that the sword of Islam should be placed in her hands. . . .

"The message to my daughter," Khomeini said at last. "It is ready to be sent?"

"Yes, Imam. All preparations have been made."

"The time has come," the Grand Ayatollah whispered, so low that only Mohtashemi could hear him. "Send it, Ali Akbar. Let the truth be heard!"

Gibson, Montana

T HEY HAD RIGGED UP A CART FOR YUSEF, WHO WAS TOO WEAK to stand up. He had been wracked by stomach pains, vomiting, and violent headaches. He could no longer keep anything in his stomach.

From the cart Yusef looked up at Hassan Kamateh with a weak smile. His black eyes seemed huge in the drawn face. "It is completed, Professor?"

They both stared through the thick glass window at the table on which the gleaming ball rested, suspended in its metal cage. It was about the size of a soccer ball, and it had been machined absolutely smooth except for a single opening that penetrated to its heart. The opening, like a miniature tunnel, was now filled with paraffin.

The gleaming steel ball was the outer casing for the nuclear heart of the bomb.

"Yes," Dr. Kamateh said. "It is ready."

There remained only the casting, using the wax process, of the nuclear bullet that would be smashed into the bomb to trigger a chain reaction, and the completion of a suitable firing mechanism for the bullet. Kamateh's work, as he had explained to Kali, now centered upon the adaptation of a high-powered rifle to his needs.

"I did well, Professor? Is it not so?"

"You did well, Yusef."

Kamateh felt both affection and pity for his young assistant. Yusef would not survive this week. His system was ravaged by severe radiation poisoning. The use of remote handling devices for manipulating the nuclear materials during the casting process had not saved him.

Two others had vomited during the night. The zeal of the youthful terrorist contingent at Wind Canyon Mine was subdued this morning.

Kamateh pitied all of them—victims of a fanatical despotism masquerading as religion.

He stared at the gleaming bomb behind its protective wall. He told himself that he had to do it. He had never really had a choice.

Kamateh felt no professional pride in his achievement. There was only horror.

Tehran, Iran

T HE SMALL CLINIC, WHICH CONTAINED EVERYTHING FOR CARE
and treatment to be found in the most modern medical facility,
including a complete trauma center, was near the Grand Ayatollah's
home in north Tehran. It had been taken over by the Imam's physicians nine years ago, in the aftermath of the successful revolution,
after he had suffered a heart attack. Since Khomeini was also the
potential target of his many enemies, including the survivors of the
shah's SAVAK, or secret police, it was felt that a fully equipped and
staffed private hospital near his home was essential. A similar clinic
had been established near his Qom residence.

On that Saturday the Imam's family had gathered around him,
subdued but optimistic. The unblinking eyes of the concealed video
cameras recorded their greetings, their anxiety, their expressions of
devotion. Ahmad bin Razi, whose closeness to the Imam was resented by some members of his family, had withdrawn in respect for
their privacy. A dozen of the two score physicians on the medical
team were either in the room or watching the television monitors.

At 4:06 P.M. the panel displaying in vertical strokes the dancing
rhythm of the sick man's heartbeat, and recording the beat with
steady blips, suddenly changed.

The line flattened.

The blips became an uninterrupted single note that, in the hushed
silence of the room, was like a scream.

Ruhollah Khomeini had suffered a massive heart attack.

PART FIVE
ZERO TIME

MONTANA'S THREE-YEAR DROUGHT ENDED IN A GULLY-washer. The day began sunny and warm, with distant thunderheads building up over the mountains and mushrooming a mile high. By midmorning, the black clouds were tumbling overhead in a stiff breeze, and the rumble of distant thunder had become resounding explosions close enough to make you jump. The gray curtain of rain that began to obscure the mountains appeared from a distance to be a welcome wetting. But it arrived in the Gibson vicinity as a torrential downpour, wind and rain so violent that stout tree branches broke like twigs. Anyone caught outside was pummeled by driving raindrops that stung like pellets, and had to struggle to keep his feet.

Out on the plains the rain gushed into washes and gullies, quickly overflowing them, then drained into canyons and ravines. A ravine fifteen feet deep filled to the brim as fast as an agile man could climb.

One of the many dry washes in the foothills south of the Cameron and Halston ranches was transformed into a raging rapids, five feet deep, within minutes after the storm arrived. Its sandy bottom was swiftly scoured deeper by the rocks and branches and other debris that became part of the flash flood. The water picked up everything in its way and swept it along. A body that had been buried about three feet under the soft sand was torn loose and tossed into the violent stream. Battered by rocks and trees, the body was finally heaved up on the bank where the wash encountered the north-south state highway. The floodwaters boiled across the road and raced on.

A semi, southbound out of Gibson, speeding too fast in the rain, started to aquaplane when it hit the spill of water, which was a foot deep where it flooded the highway. About a quarter mile down the road the skidding truck jackknifed out of control. The rear end of the trailer hit the soft wet shoulder and tipped over into the water-filled dip beside the highway.

The truck driver, Lester Bigman, cursing and slamming the heel of his palm against the steering wheel, calmed down after a few minutes. The cab was leaning but still upright; Lester figured he would remain drier inside the cab than he would be the instant he opened the door.

The trucker used his CB to call for help. The wind and rain slammed against the side of the beached truck with so much force that the huge rig rocked and groaned. The water seemed to pour out of the sky in solid sheets. Lester began to worry that the cab might keel over, him along with it. "Jesus . . . wish I could trade in this damned semi for an ark," he muttered.

After about twenty minutes, the full fury of the storm passed on, settling down to a steady, drenching downpour. Not long afterward, Lester Bigman saw the revolving roof light of a Montana state highway cruiser approaching. One of the patrolmen, wearing a yellow rain slicker, barged out of the car, splashed over to Lester, and shouted up at him. He called for Lester to climb down and get in the patrol car. Reluctant to leave his shelter, Lester grudgingly complied. He got soaking wet as he had anticipated before reaching the back seat of the car.

"You got anything flammable or explosive or toxic in there?" the patrolman demanded after they had settled inside the car and shut the doors. Steam clouded the windows.

"Nope," said Lester. "It's canned goods . . . mostly apple juice."

"You independent?"

"Yep." No company to pay his insurance premiums, he thought sourly.

"Heavy load, huh?"

"Yep, heavy enough."

"Guess you were goin' too fast."

"Nosiree!" Lester said indignantly. "Ran into a flash flood across the road back there. You must've crossed it yourself."

"Guess it's quieted down," the patrolman said.

His name was Dave Lancaster. He took down more details about the accident, Lester's route and destination, his insurance and registration. While they were still talking, a second patrol car arrived. After a conference one of the newly arrived patrolmen began posting warning lights. Most of the truck was clear of the road, with only the engine and cab jutting out onto the macadam. A call was placed to Gibson for an emergency truck and a tractor. Uprighting the trailer might even require a crane. The cargo would have to be off-loaded.

After all this was settled, Lester Bigman accepted a ride back into town with Dave Lancaster and his partner. They set off slowly in thinning rain, the two patrolmen talking.

It was Lester who saw the body.

A strangled sound rose from his throat; he was too startled to get the words out. Lancaster glanced back at him, puzzled. "Mother of God!" Lester Bigman gasped. "Stop! There's a body there! Beside the road!"

The patrol car backed, the officer at the wheel peering through the rain. He stopped abruptly.

Beside the road lay the body of a big man, battered beyond recognition. Lancaster guessed every bone must be broken. Apparently the man had been caught in a flash flood and sucked into the wash.

Lester stared along the shallow gully. With the rain thinning out, the violence of the water had already abated. The gully, dry only an hour or so ago, was now overrun by a respectable stream. Yet it lacked the force to bowl a big man off his feet and drag him to his death. Must have been a stranger to these parts, Dave Lancaster thought, someone ignorant of how quickly these gullies and washes could fill with an avalanche of water.

There was no identification on the body.

That was the first oddity that bothered the patrolman. While his partner called for an ambulance and the trucker, Lester Bigman, was throwing up beside the road, Lancaster gingerly examined the body. The many bruises and cuts, he guessed, would obliterate any evidence of foul play. But the appearance of no wallet or I.D. of any kind, bothered Lancaster. At least it caused him to make a more critical examination. The coroner would have found the wound anyway when he examined the body. But Dave Lancaster didn't need a doctor to tell him what an exit wound from a bullet looked like, especially a hole made by a soft-nosed bullet that had emerged from the back of the skull.

A piece of luck, he thought, that the back of the head hadn't been crushed, obliterating the evidence.

Lancaster guessed that the man had been shot, then buried in the gully. The flooding after a long drought had washed the recently buried body into the open. *Evil will out,* thought Dave Lancaster, a member of the defunct Gibson Theatrical Company.

Doc Hastings, who served as coroner for Gibson County, unzipped the body bag and stared at the battered face. A flicker of recognition crossed his face. "God in heaven!" he exclaimed aloud. "It's Brad McAlister! He's a sack of bones!"

In spite of his intimacy with death, the doctor was shaken. He had known Brad McAlister since he was a boy, had treated him for minor mishaps, had cared for Anne during three pregnancies, had called at the house when one of the boys came down with whooping cough, had mended the other boy's broken collarbone. (He was dismayed that he couldn't remember the boys' names . . . there had been so many patients, so many children . . . Brad, Junior, that was one of them.)

"Know him, Doc?" Dave Lancaster asked.

"Yes, I know him. He was a patient of mine. Where did you find him?"

"South a ways, just off the state highway. You better give me the name. His kin'll have to be notified. . . . Married?"

"Yes. His name is Brad McAlister. I'll tell his wife. I know her. . . ."

"It might be best," said the patrolman, relieved. After seven years on the force, he still hated to walk up to a stranger's door, with ill tidings that would shatter the lives behind it.

"I'll take care of that, officer," the doctor repeated. "But you'd better inform Sheriff Thayer."

"I reckon so. . . . It was a bullet that did that to the back of his head, wasn't it?"

"Yes, it was. And it was no accident, no random hunter's shot. It was an execution. From the angle of the wound I'd say someone had him kneel down, put a gun to his eye, and blew his brains out."

Ed Thayer received the news of Brad McAlister's murder shortly before three o'clock that afternoon. He reached Joe Springer within the hour. Springer informed the A.D., Ted Chandler, who had been sent from Washington to take charge of the SMS Site 14 field investigation. Chandler promptly relayed the news by telex to FBI Headquarters. Third in line, Springer informed Lee Hamilton, the head of the NEST team.

At five o'clock Rocky Mountain time, it was seven o'clock on a muggy evening in Washington, D.C. George Bush was sipping a predinner scotch on the rocks when the FBI director requested an urgent meeting. A half hour later, the director handed Bush a copy of the telex from Montana.

"What does it mean?" asked the president.

"They're showing their hand, Mr. President. They must know McAlister's murder would alert us, and they don't care. It means, Mr. President . . . whatever is going to happen is coming down soon . . . and they don't think we can stop them."

Micheline Picard—how she despised the name!—arrived at the mine in the late afternoon. It was the first time she had been present for evening prayers. A satellite dish had been installed so the men, isolated at the mine, would be able to watch television. A video tape recorder had also been provided, and at sunset, when all true believers faced Mecca, scenes of the holy city were shown in this remote mountain hideout by video tape.

The chant of the muezzin filled her heart with longing for the most vivid years of her life, which were spent in the vast Iranian desert at the Behjeshtieh revolutionary training camp for women. It had been the closest she had come to feeling part of her father's life.

Until now.

A tremor ran through her body as she waited, a shiver of desire and fear.

A subdued Kali, humbled by the message he carried, had brought her the news. She was to come to the mine this evening. The Imam himself would speak to her.

Short-wave radio communication, using a powerful transmitter and transceiver, had already been established between Wind Canyon and Iran. It was at the mercy of the elements, she had been told; interference could interrupt the signal. The Americans, should they choose, could also jam it, making clear reception impossible. "I do not think they will do this," Kali had said. "They will be more interested in recording the message for analysis. And they will monitor the airwaves in search of our response. It is for this reason that we can only listen in silence."

Micheline nodded, impatient with the explanation. Only one thing mattered: to hear *his* voice, so long withheld from her. Abandoned as an infant, ignored by her father for the first ten years of her life, she had dreamed of such a moment since childhood, as an orphan dreams of a prince who will one day come to claim her.

She had dreamed not of a mere prince but of the Imam who was in a direct line stretching over a thousand years to the Prophet Muhammad—her father, Ayatollah Ruhollah Khomeini.

Within the mine, the young *fedayeen* watched her covertly, their voices hushed with new respect. Dr. Kamateh had greeted her politely, confirming in response to her terse questions that the bomb was nearly complete.

"I must know for certain before I respond to the Imam."

"You will have what you wish within twenty-four hours. There can be no absolute certainty, you understand, that we can produce nuclear fission. It may be only a fizzle."

A light flicked in her eyes like a snake's tongue. "Which means?"

"A great cloud of dangerous, dirty radiation but no chain reaction. No explosion."

"Is this possible?"

Kamateh met her challenging gaze with sad eyes. "No. If my calculations have been correct, the outcome is almost certain. I will test the firing mechanism in the morning. After that . . . you will have your weapon."

"Good! And you, Dr. Kamateh, shall have your reward."

"I wish only the safe return of my family."

Micheline learned that the professor's young assistant had died that morning. She heard the news with indifference. Yusef had served Allah well, she said. He was blessed in hastening his journey to heaven. Because he had died in the service of Allah, he had achieved *shahadah,* the martyrdom that was every Muslim's most cherished wish.

The transceiver in the main cave crackled to life. The transmission capability would remain silent, but the receiver, linked by cable to an antenna at the top of the mountain, could pick up and enhance any signal on the chosen frequency. One of the young soldiers, who had a facility for electronics, fiddled with the dials, trying to tune in the signal precisely. The sound was garbled, fading in and out.

Then suddenly, clear as if the speaker were inside the cave:

" . . . the destruction of American imperialism, the scourge of the earth. Until the cry, 'There is no God but God,' is heard all over the world, there will be turmoil and struggle. You, my children, have taken the Islamic Revolution into the City of War. The true soldier of Allah does not sit at home, waiting for his enemy to attack. He carries the battle into the enemy's camp, where the evil one rises up trembling from his sleep.

"You are true believers. You are our children, our brothers. For all who believe in Allah are our brothers, and those who do not believe are our enemies. Satan is everywhere, even beside those who kneel in prayer facing Mecca. But you have chosen to battle against the evil one. Because of you, who keep the words of the Prophet alive in your hearts, the forces of good will triumph. Islam and the teachings of the Koran will prevail!"

Within the great cavern, there was absolute silence, filled only with the voice of the Ayatollah Khomeini, the sound frayed at times by static, fading in and out, yet holding his listeners in a hypnotic trance. The mood of fright and uncertainty and gloom that had overtaken them after the death of Yusef and the appearance of similar symptoms in several others changed to a rapt euphoria.

Micheline Picard waited, her heart beating anxiously in her breast.

"And now I speak to you, my daughter. In the history of man, it is sometimes given to one to serve God more than others. It is you into whose hands the sword has been delivered. I have sworn that, as long as I am alive, I will never stop using the sword to smite the evil agents of the United States and the Soviet Union. You are my daughter. Your hand is my hand that grips the sword, your arm is my arm, your blood is my blood."

For a moment, the voice faded out. Micheline sat motionless, trembling, a thickness in her throat, tears of joy streaming down her face. Everyone in the cave was staring at her in awe. Even Kali was dumbfounded. He took the words of the ayatollah as rhetorical, not even considering the possibility of their literal truth. *But who was she, that the Imam himself would address her in such terms?*

"Beware, my daughter, of the man Cameron. He is an agent of

Satan. He travels in the devil's name to Paris to seek out your past, that he might acquire knowledge to use against us.

"You, my daughter, will lead my soldiers against the enemy. You will show the corrupt no mercy, for they must be destroyed. Evil can only be cured by fire. You now have in your hands the mightiest of all weapons to show the world the strength of Islam!

"Do not recite the *suras* of mercy, my daughter and my children. Recite *suras* of *qital*. . . . For to kill your enemy is also a form of mercy." The voice seemed to gather strength and power, echoing through the stone chamber inside the mountain. "How I wish I could be with you! For there is no joy sweeter than to die beside your friends on the road to Paradise. Islam, my children, is an eternal tree. It is watered by the blood of martyrs shed in holy war. Without this nourishment it will not grow; it will wither and pass away. But every time the blood of martyrs is shed for our cause, the tree grows stronger.

"My children! My daughter! This world is but a passage, the Narrow Path toward the true life which is only in the hereafter. We have been placed here in this low, earthly life only to serve Allah, and it is your privilege to render Him the highest service.

"Remember not the beauty of the blossoms, but He who made them so!

"Remember not the weakness of your enemies, but the strength of your arms!

"Remember not the fear of death but the joy of heaven!

"Death to Satan! Satan's armies are but shadows, and shadows cannot fight; shadows are afraid of the light.

"I have said that my son Mostafa was the light of my eyes. He now lives in the true joy of the hereafter. But a new light has been given to me that I might see my enemy. You, my daughter, are now the light! Let it shine in the eyes of the Great Satan, that it might blind him! Unleash the power! The moment has come. The evil one trembles! Death to Satan!"

As the ringing charge echoed through the cave, the transmission abruptly ended. And after a tick of stunned silence the chamber exploded in screams and cries.

"Khomeini, Khomeini, the beloved one!"

"I shall kill him who has killed my brother!"

And, over and over again, "Death to Satan! Death to Satan!"

For an unwanted girl child, a passionate dream of winning the love and praise of the fierce old man who was her father had led her into terrorism. This was her moment of fulfillment. Her eyes overflowed, and gooseflesh prickled her arms. She had dreamed of such a moment in a thousand fantasies. But no mere fantasy could approach the reality. No ecstasy would ever equal it.

She was the true heir to the legacy of Khomeini. Only she had the power to give him his final triumph!

Washington, D.C.
The White House

THE PRESIDENT HAD ASSEMBLED HIS CRISIS MANAGEMENT team in the situation room beneath the White House. He glared at the DOE's Eric Sanderson, who had just reported on an incident involving a NEST agent and an American fugitive in Paris. "One of *our* people engaged in a shootout in the heart of Paris?" the President repeated with cold fury. "How in the world did *that* happen? Who *is* he? What's he *doing* there? What the hell is going on?! I have Mitterand sending me a protest and leaking it to *Le Monde*. . . . Now our media are demanding answers."

"No one expected a shootout, Mr. President," Sanderson said.

"No one expected! Who've we got running around over there, a bunch of Lone Rangers?"

"No, sir. Our man was following a suspect who had flown from Montana to Paris."

"Someone involved in this uranium theft?"

"We don't believe he's the thief, but . . . he's somehow involved. He was attacked by what we believe were Iranian terrorists. One American was shot. Our agent intervened to save the intended victim . . . a man named Cameron . . . Lucas Cameron."

George Bush exchanged glances with Mel Durbin. Iranians again, the glance read. Low on the totem pole in a meeting at this level, the NSC staff specialist was savvy enough to know when to keep his mouth shut and listen. The president turned to William Webster. "All right, that brings us back to this short-wave broadcast by Khomeini. You're sure it *was* Khomeini?"

"There's no doubt of it, Mr. President."

"And you think his message was directed to someone here in the United States?"

"That is our conclusion."

"And the substance of his speech . . . ," said the President. Though Khomeini had spoken in Farsi, a language expert at the National Security Agency had provided a complete translation within an hour after the broadcast. "Another diatribe against the Great Satan . . . What's that phrase in Farsi?"

"Shaytan Bozorg."

"That's it; the Great Satan . . . Every devoted son of Allah is obliged to spill his blood . . . if that's what it takes to spill some of ours. That's the substance, isn't it? Hardly a new message from our nemesis, the ayatollah."

"It's new if he's talking directly to someone inside our borders," said Bob Shirek of State. "It all ties in, Mr. President . . . the theft of uranium, this Iranian-born physicist who has apparently been kidnapped, the attempt by Iranian assassins in France to gun down an involved American . . . and now Khomeini's fire-and-brimstone speech on the glories of martyrdom while carrying out *qital.* It's a blueprint for a blow against the Great Satan . . . a strike at our vitals . . . a nuclear strike, I would guess . . . something so dramatic that it would fire up his followers and make them forget about losing the war in Iraq."

Bush nodded in appreciation for the succinct summary. "What is *qital?*" he asked.

"Killing," said Shirek grimly. "Killing to carry out the will of Allah. Killing and being killed. It's the sure way for a Shiite to get to heaven."

The president rose and ambled over to the long mahogany cabinet against the wall where trays had been set up with a morning snack— coffee, milk and sugar, doughnuts, and Danish. He poured himself a cup of coffee, waving off the eager offers to do it for him. Hesitating, he poised two lumps of sugar over the target, then defiantly dropped them into the cup and stirred to dissolve them. Watching him, Mel

Durbin thought he understood the president's deliberate break in the discussion. It not only gave him time to think without distraction; it also offered to others the same opportunity. Bush had assembled these men not only because of their official status but because of their keen intellect.

After the interlude, he settled back in his place at the center of the long oval table—a more dominating position than the end locations. George Bush said, "Where is this man . . . uh . . . Cameron . . . now?"

Mel Durbin would describe the next moment as a pregnant pause. Then Eric Sanderson said, "We don't know, Mr. President."

The president looked at him in silent rebuke. "Why am I not surprised?"

Sanderson flushed. "Our agent helped him escape. . . . We know he went to England. We assumed he'd book a commercial flight out of Heathrow. We contacted the Agency"—a nod toward William Webster—"they had a man at the airport to meet him. But he never showed up."

"How do you know he went to England?"

"We know he caught the ferry from Calais."

Bush turned toward the CIA's director. "Anything to add, Bill?"

"Lucas Cameron works for a large international construction firm called InCon. An InCon Lear jet left England for the United States the same day Cameron arrived. The flight plan gave its destination as Houston, Texas. It flew the polar route, which brought it over Canada. The plane stopped to refuel at Minneapolis–St. Paul before continuing on to Houston."

"Cameron was on the plane when it landed in Houston?"

"No, Mr. President. We think he got off in Minneapolis. He probably headed for Montana."

The President stared at him. "InCon . . . I know that company. Hell, I know the chairman of the board. What's their role in all this?"

"We think they're just helping one of their own. The American who was shot in Paris—we believe the bullet was meant for Lucas Cameron—also works for InCon. . . . Their people are outwardly cooperative," Webster added, "but the man who might shed the most light on InCon's role is Cameron's boss, a man named Canseco, and he's conveniently out of the country right now. They say they're trying to reach him. . . . So are we," the CIA chief finished dryly.

"Cameron is no backwater cowboy, judging by the way he's kept a jump ahead of the world's best intelligence agency." Now it was Bush who spoke dryly. "What's his game? Why's he going to Montana?"

"He moves like a man on a mission," Webster said. "I think he may be after the same thing we are. Find Cameron, and we might find our uranium."

"This is all very interesting," General Vuono growled. The Army Chief of Staff was not known for diplomacy. "But if that crazy old man in Iran has his way, that uranium is going to be used to flatten American homes and offices and churches. I respectfully suggest, Mr. President, that you send a meaningful message to the ayatollah warning him of the consequences if he takes his Holy War to American soil."

"A message has already been sent," the State's man, Bob Shirek, said smoothly. "We are evaluating various sanctions."

"He doesn't give a damn about our sanctions," the general snorted. "He'd be more impressed if we bombed his oil fields . . . a raid on Kharg Island maybe . . ."

"That option hasn't been closed," the president said quietly.

"Warn him, Mr. President! Warn him he'll be held responsible!"

George Bush shrugged. "The ayatollah is in seclusion. His health is failing. His subordinates are maneuvering for power. We're not sure who's in charge. Who should we address this message to?"

"We could send a message they'd all understand."

"The answer isn't in Iran, General." Bush's gaze probed the faces of the representatives of the Defense Department, the FBI, the Energy Department. "It's in Montana."

Helena, Montana

"**J**ESUS H. CHRIST!" LEE HAMILTON WAS INCREDULOUS. "You helped the guy get away?"

"That's right."

"You let him escape in *your car?*"

"The alternative was to let him be killed."

"And you gave this fucking *Russian* carte blanche to interrogate one of those fucking A-rabs while you played tag with the fucking French police?"

"Why do I get the idea you don't approve of my methods," said Al Trautman mildly. And Iranians aren't Arabs, he added to himself.

The operational head of the NEST field team had met Trautman at the airport, with Trautman's telex message fresh on his mind. It had presented the bare bones of the rescue of Lucas Cameron from Iranian assassins in Paris. Hamilton had seethed in silence during the short ride from the airport to the motel. Now, in the privacy of his motel suite—he had booked three connecting rooms for members of the team to use in Helena, with a fourth set aside as a conference room—his anger had found, at least in Al Trautman's view, a new eloquence.

"Did it occur to you," replied Trautman serenely, "that the terrorists might be the bad guys? If they were so eager to kill Cameron, maybe it was to our advantage to keep him alive. That's the way I saw it . . . and I was the man on the spot."

Hamilton glared at him. "And the Russian? Weren't you carrying glasnost a bit far?"

"Ivan and me, we made a deal. He'd interrogate the Iranians while I bought him a few minutes before the French police got there. We'd share what he found out."

"And you *believed* him?"

"I had two choices. I could take a chance or come up empty. He seemed okay. . . . We had a deal."

"Seemed okay? He was a Soviet fucking spy!" Hamilton sneered.

Trautman gave him a benign look. "Aren't you even a little bit interested in what I learned?" he asked sweetly.

Hamilton's anger, already sputtering, gave up like an engine running out of gas. "Don't be cute. . . . All right, out with it."

"The Soviets have had similar problems . . . break-ins, attempts to steal nuclear materials. This Russkie—Milov's his name—he was sent to France to investigate the Iranian connection. He stumbled on Cameron in this suburb where the Iranians hang out. . . . Seems there's quite a group of them in France, militant Muslims loyal to the Ayatollah Khomeini's revolution."

Now that he had Hamilton's complete attention, Trautman felt a strong urge to light up a cigarette. He resisted the impulse but enjoyed the thought. Sometimes temptation produces its own satisfaction, he thought. "Don't ask me how Cameron uncovered the same trail the Russians were following, but he did. Adding what Milov told me with what we already knew, I came up with this scenario: These terrorists—or the Iranians who back them—plan to hit the two great powers at the same time. They're trying to steal nuclear weapons or the materials to make them. That suggests they aren't planning any ordinary, everyday terrorist action. They're thinking big. They're planning a nuclear surprise.

"Anyway, here's what we know: Cameron went to Paris to investigate a French holding company, IBZ International S.A. It's not really French, Milov says, that's just a front. The money behind it is Iranian." Trautman paused for effect. "IBZ has bought up a lot of property around Gibson—including the Gibson Bank. Cameron's old man might have been on to them. He was killed in a freak accident. Convenient. Too convenient. Cameron began asking questions. He became curious about a woman who works for the company . . . here in Gibson . . . a Frenchwoman."

The commander of the FBI's antiterrorist task force assembled in Montana, Ted Chandler, had been leaning casually over the back of a chair he was straddling. At Trautman's last words, he sat up alertly. "Micheline Picard?"

Trautman smiled. "A beauty, from what they tell me. In Paris and Villiers, I'm told, she's group leader of a bunch of Iranian hotheads. Now she's in Gibson when some uranium turns up missing. As they say, the plot thickens."

Chandler excused himself abruptly and left for an adjoining room. Trautman heard him bark orders to a field agent, then speak on the phone. He talked for about fifteen minutes. In the bedroom designated as the conference room a sober silence descended on the group as they separately absorbed and analyzed Trautman's report.

Trautman grinned at young Rob Gillespie. The kid did himself proud, Trautman thought, coming up with a winner from all those miles of videotape taken at the DOE site.

After Chandler returned, Hamilton said: "The question is, do we pick her up?"

"That won't find us the uranium," said Chandler. "The director says we should learn more about IBZ and the woman. The Bureau will be digging in Washington and Paris and through Interpol. But we can't move on the woman until we have more than we do right now. Right now, we don't have a legal reason to arrest her or even prevent her leaving the country—not unless we find a bomb in her suitcase."

"We don't want to violate the civil rights of terrorists," said Trautman sarcastically.

Hamilton eyed him as if Trautman's rumpled suit, even more disreputable after his long overseas flight, offended him. "Let's take a look at IBZ's properties here. Maybe we'll find a place where they could hide some uranium." Hamilton's gaze suddenly sharpened. "Didn't that company take over Lucas Cameron's ranch property?"

"Uh huh," Trautman said.

"Where's Cameron now?"

"Helluva good question. I contacted the CIA in Paris and London so the Agency could pick him up and give him protective custody."

"And?"

"He's disappeared." Trautman glanced across the room at Chandler. "That still true? Your people haven't traced him?"

"All we know is that he's in this country. As I said, we believe he deplaned in Minneapolis. He's probably on his way here . . . if he's not here already."

"Well, we don't have to wait for a reason to pick *him* up," Hamilton said. "He could unlock this whole thing for us."

"If he had the answers, he wouldn't have been running off to Paris to seek them," Trautman said. "Maybe we should just leave him loose. He seems to have a way of stirring up the mud from the bottom."

Hamilton rolled his eyes to the top of his head like Fernando Valenzuela about to throw a screwball. "Spare us the homespun rhetoric."

Trautman grinned amiably. "It's the Montana in me. Maybe I've been in Montana too long. . . . But then Luke Cameron's a Montanan."

"What's that supposed to mean?"

Trautman's fingers patted his shirt pocket, as if searching for a phantom pack of cigarettes. "Let me tell you a little story I heard. It's about this town in Montana called Wolf Point. It's somewhere up in the northeast part of the state on the Missouri River. Seems back in the nineteenth century some early Montanans, fur trappers, were having trouble with wolf packs. So what they did is, they poisoned a few hundred wolves one winter. They gathered up the frozen carcasses and stacked them like cordwood near the point in the river. They were sending the wolves a message. There's a plaque up there by Wolf Point today that tells the story. The plaque says, 'It taught those varmints a lesson. No wolf has darkened the door of a house in this town since.' "

Several FBI and NEST agents, including Rob Gillespie, grinned appreciatively. Lee Hamilton scowled. "Are you going to explain what this has to do with Lucas Cameron?" he asked irritably.

"Like I said, he's a Montanan. That story about Wolf Point and its plaque is still true about the people who live here now. What I'm suggesting is, Cameron thinks his daddy was murdered . . . murdered by wolves in human clothes . . . maybe led by a beautiful she-wolf. I'm thinking that Cameron is going after the varmints."

Trautman slumped back in his chair, suddenly feeling as rumpled and tired as he looked. Jet lag, he told himself. The frequent flyers claimed jet lag wasn't as bad traveling west as it was going east. Those who made that claim, Trautman thought, weren't on the down side of fifty.

"You seem to have a glorified opinion of this man," muttered Hamilton.

"He's done all right. One man, on his own . . . he's done about as well as the DOE, the FBI, the CIA and the KGB all rolled together. Leave him out there . . . maybe *he'll* find what *we're* looking for."

"I agree," Ted Chandler said crisply, before Hamilton could respond. The NEST man, disconcerted by this unexpected support for Trautman's strategy, bit his tongue and kept silent.

The FBI official continued: "First we have to find Cameron. I've assigned half a dozen agents to track him down and put him under surveillance. That will leave a dozen agents to investigate the Frenchwoman and this French-Iranian holding company. Our antiterrorist assault team is on standby. You'd better get some sleep, Trautman;

we may need you. I suggest you alert your NEST team to be ready
to move on a minute's notice, Mr. Hamilton. We're getting down
to the crunch. We've got a catastrophe to prevent from happening."

Trautman regarded him gloomily. All the power that the mighty
U.S. government could mount to stop this catastrophe probably depended on one man who just wanted to avenge his daddy.

The InCon executive jet landed at a private strip on property
owned by a Houston-based oil company doing exploratory drilling
in Montana. A friendly but taciturn oilman, driving a Jeep Cherokee,
hauled Luke south, then west, across the prairie over back-country
roads. There was no sign of human habitation in any direction.

Luke was surprised to see signs of recent moisture. Some desert
flowers were in blossom, and the creeks seemed to be running higher.

"Yep," the oilman said in response to Luke's question. "Had a
little rain day before yesterday." That was all he said; it seemed to
cover the subject.

Just before sunset they reached civilization. In Bozeman Luke's
driver dropped him off at the Frontier Pies Restaurant & Bakery.
The oilman said he couldn't stay for supper; then without another
word, he drove out of Luke's life.

Inside the restaurant Luke found Justin Cranmer waiting for him.
They found a booth in the dining room, which offered rustic western
decor without the discomforts. The waitress appeared immediately,
and they ordered two beers, steaks, and French fries.

"Good to see you, Luke," Cranmer said, appraising his friend
across the table and noting the unfamiliar lines of fatigue and dis-
couragement about his eyes and mouth. "Want to tell me what happened?"

"Has anyone in Gibson been asking about me?"

"An FBI man named Springer. He's the agent in charge over in
Butte, which doesn't explain why he's in Gibson."

"I know him."

"I'm your lawyer, in case I hadn't told you. That allows me more
discretion how to answer questions about you." Cranmer's gaze was
frankly curious. "What's going on, Luke? Springer isn't the only government agent in town. I get the impression something heavy is going
on."

"More than I can handle," Luke said. The weary tone matched

the bleak resignation in his eyes. "Would you believe terrorists chasing me through the French countryside and shooting at me in the streets of Paris?"

The arrival of the waitress with their beers gave Cranmer time to recover. Then Luke Cameron recounted his experiences in France, beginning with the murder of an old nun he was trying to question and culminating in the wild attempts on his own life. With interruptions, the narrative lasted through salad into the steak.

When Luke finished, the lawyer silently attacked his steak as he digested the news and the food together. Then he spoke up. "There's something you should know. There's been a sequel here in Gibson. Brad McAlister is dead. Murdered."

Luke's fork stopped halfway to his mouth. He put it down slowly. His first thought was of Anne and the kids. "How?" he asked. "What happened?"

"He was shot through the head and dumped in a gully. A heavy storm washed his body out, or he might never have been found."

Luke sat back, appetite gone. He tried to absorb the shocking news. Thinking back to the evening he spent with the McAlisters, he remembered Brad's nervous irritability and Anne's transparent unhappiness. Brad had been involved in something—something that had made him nervous. Apparently he'd had good reason to be nervous. Whatever it was, it had cost him his life.

And then it hit him. Brad worked at the nuclear facility; he was killed. Luke's father was prying around the nuclear facility; he died mysteriously. An Iranian-connected holding company headquartered in France purchased an obscure ranch next to the nuclear facility; Luke's prying questions about it flushed out Iranian terrorists in France.

"It's that nuclear storage site," Justin Cranmer said, echoing Luke's thoughts. "Has to be. I know this sounds crazy, but I think there're nuclear terrorists right here in Montana."

Luke nodded slowly. The pieces were beginning to fit. Brad McAlister was the piece that had been missing. As he traced the ruthless pattern of violence that was emerging more clearly, Luke felt a resurgence of the anger that had driven him to France. The words of his father's letter came back to him as clearly as if Tom Cameron spoke them: *All I can tell you, son, is there's something happening here I*

can't handle alone. And it troubles me. You're the only one I know
of who could maybe solve the mystery, the only one I can trust. . . .

They were the words of a frightened man, Luke thought. That was
the thing that had jarred him the most about Tom's letter. The old
man had been scared, as Luke had nearly been scared off by the terrorist attacks and the sheer hopelessness of fighting something so big
and impenetrable.

"What is it, Luke?" Cranmer asked softly. "What are you getting
into your head?"

"The bastards!" Luke said. "They had me ready to quit. By God,
the one time my dad asked me for something, and I was ready to
turn my back and walk away."

"Tom never asked you to get yourself killed."

"Maybe there are worse things. Like giving up. This thing has to
be stopped, Justin. Tom saw that. It's just taken me a little longer."

"I think it's time for you to go to the authorities, tell them what
you know."

Luke shook his head. "They've been keeping up with me . . . may
even be ahead of me. But they haven't yet solved the case, or they
would have arrested Micheline Picard."

"You're convinced she's part of it?"

"A gentle old woman died so I wouldn't find out."

"I just don't think you should go it alone. Too dangerous."

"The government doesn't need my help. That was a U.S. agent
who saved my hide in Paris. If he's at all typical, the government
is on top of this case. What I'm doing is for myself . . . and Dad."

Luke sat silently for awhile, his mind at work, oblivious to Cranmer. "I may have one little edge," he mused. "Provided that Micheline Picard hasn't heard what happened in Paris. She might not
know."

"Might is an unreliable word, Luke. You'd be taking a hell of a
gamble."

"Maybe . . . but it's worth taking. I'm calling her tonight."

"Sleep on it, Luke."

"No, tomorrow may be too late."

Cranmer frowned, registering his silent objection. He thought
about what to say, how to put it. Then he realized that no carefully
reasoned lawyer's brief matched up against Luke Cameron's deep
anger and the terrible conspiracy he had stumbled upon.

The lawyer shrugged and said, "At least eat some pie. Why do you think I picked this place to meet?"

Luke managed a grin, and Cranmer waved the waitress over. They both ordered the night's special: fresh peach pie. After savoring the last bite and washing it down with coffee, Luke had one more thing to say. "If you don't hear from me tomorrow night by this time, you can call Ed Thayer. He'll know where to take it from there."

He borrowed some change and headed for the alcove next to the Bucks and Does restrooms. He had noticed a pay phone there.

Micheline Picard sounded delighted. "Luke! Where have you been? I have been so very much worry about you!"

"No need to worry. I just had some business to take care of."

"I think you have left without saying good-bye."

"I wouldn't do that."

Her voice softened. "I am ver' glad you are back. I will see you, yes?"

"I was hoping we could get together."

"But of course! You will come to your ranch—you see, I still think of it so. I have buy some horses to ride. I am not so good. Maybe you will teach me to ride better, yes?"

"You've taken up riding?" He pictured her astride a horse, elegant in jodhpurs, white silk blouse, and riding boots. It was, undeniably, an appealing image.

"You will come in the morning," she insisted, making it sound like a command. "It is the best time, I think, to ride."

"Tomorrow morning? About nine? Would that suit you?"

"It is ver' good for me." The soft purr in her voice became a yearning. "I am hope you will not be in so much hurry to go away, Lucas. Is possible?"

"Anything's possible."

Hanging up, he felt unsure and a little guilty. But he asked himself, wasn't she playing the same kind of charade? He realized there was only one answer.

Justin Cranmer was waiting by the cash register. "My treat," he said firmly. He fished two packets of matches with the Frontier Pies logo from a glass bowl and gave one to Luke, who shoved it absently into his pocket. The lawyer appraised Luke's expression. "I guess you got what you wanted."

"Yes."

"God help you if they're waiting for you."

In the kitchen of the Cameron ranch house, as she hung up the phone, Micheline Picard felt Kali's hostile stare.

"That was Lucas Cameron," she said.

"He is not dead, then."

"So it would seem."

The discovery that Cameron had gone to France had been a shock, but no more than the revelation that the Party of Allah in France had been ordered to eliminate him. The voice on the phone from Paris, as clear as if the speaker had been in the room with her, had been respectful. "It is for your protection. The orders came from the Imam himself."

The thrill had shot through her like an electric charge. *He protects me!* But there had also been confusion, dismay, a moment of frantic grief, until she learned the assassins had failed.

After a moment's silence, she said, "Cameron wishes to see me. I have ask him to come here."

"Good. I will succeed where your friends in Paris failed. I will kill him."

"You will do as you are told. I must know what he has learn. Our people in Paris say he was investigating IBZ, but he found nothing."

"Was it IBZ, or was it you he was searching for?"

She dismissed the question with a toss of her fingers. "It is no matter, there are no records, nothing for him to find."

"Then why are they still worried?"

"They believe he has fail, but they are not certain. We must know—we are too close to all that we have work for."

"Why should he tell you anything? If he suspects you—"

"Suspicion—what is that? He does not *know*. Why else would he wish to see me?"

Kali made no attempt to conceal his sneer. "You are too eager to be with him again. To go horseback riding!"

She gave a Gallic shrug. *"Eh bien,* perhaps it is so. But it is also necessary."

She turned away. Her cool demeanor concealed the trickle she had felt along her spine when she picked up the phone and heard Lucas

Cameron's easy drawl. She hated the idea that Kali could see through her, perceiving motives of which she was herself uncertain.

"Tomorrow," she said quietly, "we will have our answers."

Tomorrow, she thought. And she shivered.

Earlier in the afternoon, while Luke Cameron was flying westward, a sleek, black aircraft soared steeply over the Pacific Ocean from the runway at Beale Air Force Base in northern California. Quicker than the naked eye could follow, it reached a cruising altitude of 80,000 feet, its arrowlike silhouette no longer visible from the ground to the naked eye.

Nicknamed the Blackbird because of its black epoxy coating, the SR-71 measured 107 feet in length and could streak through the stratosphere at speeds well in excess of 2,100 miles per hour. In less than thirty minutes, it was sweeping across Montana at 90,000 feet above the earth. With swift efficiency, America's oldest stealth aircraft began its mission—aerial surveillance.

For a panoramic view of the terrain on both sides of its flight path, the plane carried optical bar cameras that could produce images of superb quality in color or black and white. Other cameras mounted in its underbelly, shooting straight down, took black-and-white photos so clear that it was possible in enlargement to see objects on the ground as small as a book. In some photographs, it was possible to read the book's title. Once the SR-71 had returned from a mission over the Soviet Union with pictures so sharp that photo analysts could determine which Soviet soldiers had neglected to shave that morning.

Ninety minutes after the automatic sequence cameras began clicking away above Montana, they had recorded overlapping images covering the entire state.

The Blackbird returned to base less than four hours after takeoff. Luke Cameron and Justin Cranmer were gulping down their ice-cold beer in the Frontier Pies Restaurant & Bakery in Bozeman, unaware that their movements had been filmed by the SR-71's cameras passing over them earlier in the afternoon.

At Beale Air Force Base the plane's cameras were detached as soon as the SR-71 coasted to a stop. The undeveloped film was deposited in a courier pouch, which was rushed aboard a companion SR-71 already fueled. The sleek aircraft soared into a glowing Pacific sunset, swung in a wide circle, and raced eastward into the gathering darkness.

At Andrews Air Force Base outside Washington, D.C., an unmarked car waited to speed the pouch to CIA headquarters at Langley, Virginia. A team of expert photo-interpreters had been called in for night duty. They sipped coffee and listened to the Yankees-Orioles game while they waited. One of the men wondered aloud what could be important enough to receive the highest priority on their agenda. His companion said he had his own priority; he just hoped the Orioles would win the game before the film arrived.

Joe Springer said, "We've obtained a flight log from an InCon private jet out of MSP—that's Minneapolis–St. Paul—to a private airstrip north of Livingston, Montana. Sure as cats have whiskers, Lucas Cameron was on that plane, and somebody met him." The FBI man from Butte surveyed the glazed doughnuts in the glass display case behind the counter of the cafe. "You can bet he's here in Gibson right now."

"Who met him?" asked Ted Chandler.

"I'd guess his lawyer . . . coy character name of Cranmer. He disappeared from town yesterday and got back this morning."

"Coy?"

"Yes, coy . . . He tells us that Cameron isn't a fugitive under any warrant, that he hasn't been accused of breaking any U.S. laws, that his activities are his own business, that any further discussion would violate lawyer-client privilege."

"Coy," agreed Chandler who, like many FBI men, had a law degree himself. "How do you read the situation?"

"My guess is that Cranmer met Cameron and drove him back to Gibson. That means Cameron got here sometime early this morning. Cranmer probably lent him his truck—I think he bought it from Cameron—to get around. We'll find it."

"Keep on it."

Joe Springer nodded and signaled the waitress. One more doughnut couldn't hurt.

Driving up the long gravel road to the ranch house, past the sentinel line of cedar trees his grandfather had planted, Luke Cameron was stirred by nostalgic feelings, as if he had been away a long while, not just for a few days. The rustle of the trees was as familiar to him as the smell of sage or the silhouette of the hills far to the south or the homely structures of house and barn and sheds casting long shadows in the morning sun.

Luke's eyes swept the yard as he reached the old homestead. He told himself that he was looking for hired hands. If Micheline Picard had taken up riding, she should have hired someone to care for the horses and the stables. But there was no one in sight.

Luke stepped warily out of the pickup into the empty yard, staring at the silent house. He wasn't watching for ranch hands, he knew; he really expected to see terrorists with beards and assault rifles. Here in Montana, in the place that had been his home, he could almost persuade himself that the events of the past few days had been a dream.

But it was no dream. His father had died not far from here.

So had Brad McAlister.

The door banged open and the Frenchwoman skipped down the steps, her face alight with pleasure, her arms opening out to embrace him. While he stood awkwardly, she gave him a quick, impetuous hug and reached up to pull his mouth toward hers.

She drew back and cocked her head, dark eyes speculative. They twinkled, Luke thought; by God, they actually twinkled. It was unsettling to realize she could make her eyes light up that way at will. "You are very naughty, Lucas, running off like that without saying a word about where you go."

"I went to Paris," he said, without having planned it, watching her intently.

Her surprise seemed genuine. "Paris! *Main non*—it is not possible! Oh, Lucas, you should have tell me! I could have gone with you. Oh, I would love to show you my Paris!"

"There wasn't really any time for sightseeing. I had a meeting with one of the people who works for InCon—my company." That much was true enough, he thought. "But Paris is beautiful."

"It is not the same," she said, almost pouting, "to visit Paris alone. You must see it with someone else."

Luke wondered how far she was going to take this display of affection. What she had felt on the night she surprised him in the nude had been real. It had had little to do with affection. "We . . . we have to talk about some things," he said slowly.

"Oh, there will be much time for talk. *Ce matin* . . . this morning you will ride with me, yes? I wish to see more of your ranch, where you ride when you were a boy, is it not so?"

It was not a suggestion. She had obviously made plans. He decided to play her game, waiting for the next move, convinced now that she had no intention of causing him immediate harm. A sniper in the house or barn would have saved the trouble of a gallop across the countryside.

Besides, he was curious about where so apparently innocent an invitation would lead.

He had also not entirely banished the image he had conjured up of the Frenchwoman racing along on a horse. She was not wearing the jodhpurs he had imagined, but tight-fitting jeans and a cotton blouse. No matter. He knew before they turned toward the barn that she would look splendid on horseback.

Though Micheline tried to ignore her excitement, she realized that it was making her slightly giddy. She must be careful, she warned herself. Because of Kali's heavy-handed blundering, Cameron was obviously suspicious of the reason for her presence in Gibson; he was not sufficiently schooled in deception to hide it.

The lone stable hand, a dark-haired, silent youth in jeans, T-shirt, and wide-brimmed straw hat, kept his head down and merely nodded when Micheline Picard told him to bring the horses. She had given him his orders earlier, and in a moment he emerged from the barn leading two horses already saddled. One was a sleek, black Arabian mare, as stunning as her mistress. The other was a big, rawboned buckskin Luke Cameron clearly liked at first glance, as Micheline had hoped.

Kali, also following orders, was nowhere in sight.

Micheline swung easily into the saddle astride the elegant mare, which pranced and snorted eagerly. The Arabian was a spirited handful even for an expert rider. But Micheline waved at Luke, flashed a smile, flicked the reins, and cantered off, leaving him to climb aboard the long-legged buckskin and follow.

Despite her coy suggestion on the phone, she didn't need riding lessons from him. The mullahs had taught her to ride in the country-side near Paris when she was still in her teens, and the *moujahedeen* had added to her skills in the Iranian desert during her terrorist training. She was as supple and united with her horse as the desert nomads who had ridden such animals for centuries.

After a short distance Luke caught up with her. They rode in silence for a while. Micheline liked riding, liked the familiar feel of the horse beneath her, the muscular roll when she let the well-rested mare stretch out a bit. She savored the clean, pungent smells of sage and grass and earth still damp from the recent rain. Cameron, she saw, was also enjoying the ride in spite of himself. As they rode he appeared to relax, pointing out landmarks—a cottonwood he had climbed as a boy to approach an eagle's nest, a dry sinkhole where once two hundred head of cattle had been able to drink their fill, a clump of brush in a draw where he had surprised a small black bear. "We both ran off in opposite directions as fast as we could run."

He moved ahead of her a little as he became more animated, and she was able to study him covertly. Whatever he had learned in Paris, he was not yet certain about her. He didn't know who she was or why she was in Gibson. For the moment, at least, they could almost believe they were just a man and a woman together, as they had been that one night. . . .

The reminder brought warmth to her cheeks. She tried to banish the memory, replacing it with another. She saw him on the buckskin as the quintessential American, tall and lazy and soft spoken, the cowboy hero on his horse she had watched as a child on those rare occasions when the nuns took the children to the village cinema. But it was the muscular naked body stepping from the shower into a pool of reddish light that kept dominating her thoughts.

She hated the feeling of weakness the vivid image quickened. *He is the enemy of Islam*, she reminded herself. The temptations of the flesh and spirit that were so much a part of Western culture were evils against which her father had preached and fought, which she herself was committed to destroy. And yet . . . without her volition her thighs tightened against the muscular rhythm of the mare's movement. She felt the dizziness she had first experienced standing in the darkness of Luke Cameron's bedroom, watching him, discovering passionate desire for the first time in her life. Because of it, she had wanted this last day alone with him, in spite of the risk. She had maneuvered it like an experienced temptress, justifying it to herself as she had to Kali by insisting that she had to know what Cameron had learned about her and IBZ. Only then could she act, she told herself. Until then, she would play the French coquette to his American cowboy. . . .

They had been riding at an easy pace for nearly an hour when Micheline Picard pointed ahead to a strip of cottonwoods and willow brush in the distance at the foot of a slope now painted with the deceptively pretty blooms of prickly pear. A narrow creek bed accounted for the brush and trees. Just beyond it was an old wagon road, little more than a dirt track that wound southwest through low hills to the edge of the Bar-C range, where it intersected with a minor state highway.

"I will race you to those trees!" Micheline called out.

"Hey, it's too warm to run these horses—"

But with an excited laugh she kicked the black Arabian into a run, and Luke Cameron could only reluctantly join the chase. The willing buckskin ran strongly in response to Luke's urging, but in a brief race it was no contest. The sleeker, lighter Arabian mare had been born to race. She not only held her lead but pulled away. Micheline Picard's laughter pealed back to Cameron like a mocking challenge.

By the time he reached the creek, which had a shallow trickle left from the rain, Micheline had already dismounted. She produced a blanket and a small picnic basket from the saddlebags the Arabian carried. Spreading the blanket on the bank of the creek, she opened the picnic basket. Both horses were turned loose to graze on the tender young grass along the creek bed.

The basket contained fruit and cheese, sweet rolls, and a bottle of French wine.

"Wasn't the wine jostled?" Luke asked, amused.

"I'm glad you are in good humor, Lucas. I am also ver' glad you could come this morning."

"Are you?" She could see the puzzlement in his eyes, and she turned away quickly to hide a secret smile. She wanted him off balance, disconcerted, uncertain of himself or her.

The cheese and fruit and a sticky bun with walnuts on top were delicious—the first picnic fare, Cameron assured her, that he had ever washed down with white French table wine beneath a tall cottonwood on the Montana plains. He recounted a story his father had once told him about European nobility who had come west in the nineteenth century to slaughter buffalo in sporting hunts (Tom Cameron had had something vitriolic to say about such sport); stopping for evening camp, the hunters would set out gourmet condiments on white tablecloths laid with fine china and silverware—and pour French wine into crystal glasses to wash down their buffalo steaks and pemmican.

At last, pleased with his responsiveness, Micheline lay back on the blanket, locking her hands behind her head and staring up through the leafy branches of the cottonwood at the immense blue sky. The position drew her blouse taut, outlining her small, firm, unfettered breasts. Her heart was pounding.

Luke Cameron sat close beside her in a deepening silence, making no move. She felt his steady gaze upon her but did not yet meet his eyes. Would she find desire there—or something else?

"I visited the offices of your company in Paris," he said.

"Yes?"

"You said your father worked for them."

"It is true."

"I couldn't locate him . . . or any record of him."

"They tell you . . . ?"

"They told me nothing."

"Yes, I am not surprise. IBZ is ver' . . . *confidentiel.*"

"Very," Luke said dryly.

"You ask about me, too, yes?" she murmured, as if the idea pleased her. She stirred on the blanket, and the movement brought her hip into contact with his. She felt an electric shock, then a glowing spot of heat. Neither of them made any attempt to withdraw the contact.

"Yes. You're like your father . . . very elusive."

She laughed lightly. "It is the privilege of a woman."

"What's your real connection with them? Why did they send you here?"

"But I have tell you," she protested. "I am a scientist. Do we need to talk of these things?" The moist circle of heat where their hips touched glued them together. She found it difficult to concentrate on his words, or on the feelings of alarm they should have awakened. She had warned herself to be careful, but the warning seemed very remote now. She had been right; he had learned little in Paris, nothing that threatened her or her mission. There was no risk in these moments together, no tempting of fate, only the tempting of a man. . . .

As if of its own volition her hand strayed toward the front of her blouse. The top button was already loosened. As her trembling fingers found the next button, her need seemed to spread outward from the core of her body like liquid fire. Her voice quivered as she spoke. "You could help, Lucas," she teased him.

"Is that why we're here?"

"Is that such a bad reason? Or have you forgotton so soon?"

"No . . . I haven't forgotten."

"Then why . . . ?"

"I think you know."

She lay still. The pounding of her heart was loud in her ears. "Do you not wish to enjoy these moments together?"

"Are they to be the last?"

"Do not be so quick to wish beautiful moments to end."

But his words were chilling. And when at last she turned her head to meet his gaze, she saw no ardor there, nor warmth. His stare was flat, and if there was any readable expression at all it might have been . . . contempt.

She sat up abruptly. Even the air was suddenly cooler, the brilliance gone from the day as a cloud covered the sun. She understood that nothing was possible between them. Too much had happened. It had been foolish to imagine otherwise . . . foolish and dangerous. For a schoolgirl's fantasy she had been willing to jeopardize everything, even her father's dream. *Forgive me, my Imam, oh beloved one!*

After another moment she said, her tone cool now, all animation gone, "You are right, Lucas, we have little more time together. You will not understand, but . . . that is why I was happy to see you."

"I figured you had a reason."

She cocked her head piquantly, but the dark eyes were shrewd. "If you think so badly of me, why did you come? Did you not think it dangerous?"

"I wanted to find out what you were up to. I decided the best way was to ask."

"Yes . . . that is so like you, I think." She gave a hard little laugh, as if dismissing a pointless feeling. "Also, I think, you do not take me seriously. You think, she is only a silly woman."

"I've never thought that."

"No? So be it. Nevertheless, I will show you what I am up to, as you Americans say. You can do us no harm now. It is too late to stop us."

"Will you also explain why you had my father killed?"

The harsh question ended all pretense of goodwill between them. If he had expected her to flinch, he was disappointed. Instead, she rejoiced in the moment. Like hot metal plunged into cold water, her resolve hardened. She was herself again.

"That was a mistake," she answered coolly. "I would not order such a thing. It was . . . a stupid mistake."

She saw the quick flare of anger in his eyes. That his father's death could be dismissed as a stupid error shook him so deeply that he was close to losing control. He looked as if he wanted to hit her.

"I do not think you will strike a woman," she said. "Besides, there is someone nearby with a gun. I have only to summon him."

"I heard him coming in the brush. Brush makes too much noise, he should have stayed on the road."

Micheline Picard flushed. So Kali had crept close to spy on them, disobeying her command!

Looking past Cameron she said, "You see, Kali, you are not so clever as you think."

"Let me kill him now."

As Cameron turned his head, Kali stepped into view, climbing out of the gully beside the road, a rifle in his hands. He eyed the American with a malevolent stare.

"I think not," Micheline said. "We will take him to the mine."

"He is too clever. It is dangerous to keep him alive."

"Would you have us leave another body to be washed out onto the road? That has warn the police and the FBI."

Kali seemed to shrink from the rebuke. His expression became surly. His eyes sought Cameron again and flared with hate.

"How far is the vehicle?" Micheline Picard asked.

"A short distance, less than two kilometers."

"Bring it."

"You will be safe with him?" Kali asked. "Now he knows."

"Don't be foolish, Kali," she said. "He knows all the time."

"Then take my gun. He might—"

"That will not be necessary." She withdrew a .32 automatic from the picnic basket, where it had been hidden beneath a towel. "Now leave us. Bring the van."

After Kali had disappeared, trotting along the dirt road to the south, they waited in silence. They both heard the growl of a car laboring along the dirt track. Moments later, a large, enclosed Ford van appeared in the distance, painted blue with flame stripes on the side panels.

As they watched the vehicle's approach, Micheline spoke with a new edge of steely pride. "It is not a small thing I do, Lucas Cameron. I am glad that you will know. It is something the whole world will soon take notice of."

"So another murder or two are of no consequence."

"You talk like a child," she said scornfully. "You fought in a war; you know that men die in battle, that women and children also die."

"Then it's war we're talking about."

"Yes. A war that . . . that will not end until all the world knows the truth of Islam."

She saw at once that he was not surprised, and she knew then that he had learned too much while in France. The realization brought her an odd relief. If ever there had been any doubt about his fate, it was now removed.

A full set of the reconnaissance pictures taken during the SR-71's overflight of Montana, along with the photo analysts' report, was delivered to the White House at 9:48 that morning. The president, who had an appointment with the Chinese ambassador at 10:00, did not see the photos until nearly 11:30. After studying them, he convened a meeting of the Crisis Management Committee for 1:30 P.M. This gave the FBI's analysts time to complete their own evaluation of the photographs. They made blowups of key areas of the Wind Canyon mountain range in the southwest part of the state.

George Bush met with Mel Durbin in his study an hour before the emergency meeting. He laid the key photos out on the glass-topped coffee table for the national security specialist to study.

"Thank you for including me in on this, Mr. President."

"Nonsense, Mel. If you hadn't brought this to my attention, we would have been slower to respond. What do you think?" The president nodded toward the blowups. "Even enlarged, it's hard for me to see anything sinister or revealing."

Durbin studied the photos. Each had a number corresponding to a numbered square superimposed over a map of Montana. At first,

Durbin saw only small areas of shadow and light. But after examin-
ing some of the enlargements, he was able to identify the shapes of
trucks and people in an area overlooking a deep canyon. A dirt road
corkscrewed up the mountain to a shelf where the vehicles were
parked near some sheds. An area of shadow defined what he decided
must be the main entrance to a mine. Along the face of the cliff, there
were several other openings.

"It has been identified as an old gold mine, abandoned near the
beginning of this century when the gold played out," the president
said. "A French-based holding company, IBZ International, whose
principals appear to be Iranian, bought the mine nine months ago.
They're actively engaged in mining gold that I'm told doesn't exist."

"How come this is the first we're hearing about it?"

"It's not exactly headline news, Mel. I mean, the part about a
French company buying a gold mine. That's what they're all after,
one way or another, isn't it? The French, the Japanese, the Germans,
the British, they've all been scooping up whatever pieces of this country they could get their hands on." George Bush, who had pursued
his dream down in Texas and found liquid gold, paused reflectively.
"Things are changing out there in America's heartland, Mel. The
drought, lakes drying into sinkholes, outsiders snapping up land that
stayed in the same families for generations . . . it's all changing."

"Yes, sir. Not all for the better."

"Nosirree! What's happening to us, Mel?" Like most politicians,
even in casual conversation Bush fell naturally into the clichés of
speechmaking. "What happened to Americans investing in America?
Investing in our future? Why is it that it sometimes seems as if the
only people who believe in America's future are people who are seeing us from afar? What happened to our faith in ourselves?"

"We haven't lost it, Mr. President," Durbin said. "Maybe it gets
misplaced once in a while."

George Bush grinned. "Make a note of this whole investing in
America thing, Mel. I've got a feeling we can use it, maybe work
it into a speech." He glanced once more at the reconnaissance photos
of an important piece of the heartland of America, and his grin faded.
"Maybe sooner than I'd like."

Bush glanced at his watch, and began to gather up the photographs. It was time for the meeting to begin, and it would take them
five minutes to reach the situation room. He spoke in a low voice

as they left the study and started down the corridor to the president's private elevator.

"The FBI has been running a parallel investigation of IBZ International and its holdings. The Wind Canyon Mine showed up on its list, but the Bureau didn't obtain that information until late yesterday." They stepped into the elevator. "If we'd obtained the list last week, the name of the mine might have had no meaning. But we can now associate the activity at the mine with the information from Paris. . . ."

"They add up to one helluva story," Durbin said. "A scary story."

The elevator was tiny, offering little elbow room for two men. It hummed down through the White House to the layered floors beneath it, deep underground. George Bush said, "I want the FBI to move on this today."

"Today?" Mel Durbin felt like he was at the top of a rollercoaster about to plunge down the first incline.

"It's still morning in the Rockies . . . a little after eleven. In two hours, we'll know whether we're right . . . or too late."

The CIA's analyst provided a needlessly long, detailed explanation of the photographs and the specific objects that could be identified in them. One of these was a sentry posted near the top of a ridge. It was even possible to see the rifle in his hands. "It's an AK-47," the analyst said.

"There's little doubt, Mr. President," William Webster said after the presentation was complete. "We've located the terrorists' hideout."

"Do we know the stolen uranium is there?"

"I believe I can answer that, Mr. President," said Eric Sanderson. The Energy Department's task force chief had arrived late at the meeting, obviously agitated. He had waited impatiently through the photo analysis. "I'm sorry to be late, Mr. President, but I was delayed by a call from the NEST team leader in Helena. He'd just received word from our flyby of the Wind Canyon Mine. As we suspected, there are high levels of radiation in the area of the mine."

"You can detect that from the air?"

"When we know where to look, yes. From the readings, it's almost certain the material is—or has been—inside the mine. Otherwise we would have detected the radioactivity during previous flights."

"All those overflights aren't giving the game away, I hope," the President said with a frown.

"Overflights are common in Montana . . . I think they call it . . . Big Sky, Mr. President. Our man just got his reading and flew on. He didn't linger over the area."

"Your readings show that radioactive material is—or *has been*—in the area. Does that mean the material might not be there now?"

Sanderson hesitated. Then he nodded unhappily. "We can't be certain the nuclear material is still in the mine. But I'd give odds that it is."

A sober hush fell over the room while the president digested the information. The evidence, he knew, was conclusive enough to act on. But action in these circumstances involved risks. What if the uranium—or a bomb that likely had been fashioned from it—had already been moved from the mine? Then the terrorists would be forewarned; they would be more difficult to locate. They might even be panicked into a premature, suicidal nuclear attack.

Everyone waited in breathless silence for the president to speak. He caught Mel Durbin's glance and nodded solemnly. Then Bush turned to the FBI director. "It's your show now. Send in the attack force. I know what I'm asking of them. If there's radiation around the mine, anyone who enters will be at risk. The NEST scientists will accompany your people?"

"Yes, Mr. President."

"Do it," George Bush said decisively. "Shut that mine down; seal it; do whatever you have to do. That's an order."

The FBI director didn't hesitate. "The men know what they face, Mr. President. They're all volunteers. With your permission . . ."

He glanced toward the array of phones on a long table at the side of the room.

The president of the United States nodded.

The FBI director picked up a blue phone, tapped out a number, and gave the order. "Red attack," he said tersely.

Luke Cameron was forced to lie face down on the flat metal floor in the back of the speeding van. The fact that his captors were confident enough not to tie his hands gave him no comfort.

Micheline Picard rode up front with Kali. Neither of them spoke. Luke sensed tension between them, perhaps even animosity. How could he make use of that? He focused on this thought without finding an answer. He noted that *she* seemed to be in charge, not Kali. This man was probably an Iranian terrorist, imbued with Ayatollah Khomeini's sixth-century views of women's rights. Yet the man took orders from her. Was that what rankled? Or was it something more personal?

After more than an hour of jostling on the floor of the van, Luke sensed from the whine of the engine that they were climbing. Then they turned off the smooth highway onto a twisting, bumpy road. The wheels churned up clouds of dust. Luke didn't have to be able to see to know where they were going. From the crest of a ridge near the top of the mountain, he had peered down at this switchback road that led directly to the Wind Canyon Mine.

The van crawled in low gear up the last steep grade, swung through a tight loop, and suddenly bumped to a stop. Kali turned off the engine. The sudden silence beat against Luke's ears.

For a moment no one moved. Micheline Picard looked back at Luke. "Do you know where you are?"

"Yes."

"But you do *not* know what is inside."

"I have a feeling I'm about to be educated."

"Yes. Now you will understand."

As he climbed out of the van and squinted against the brightness, he beheld a band of silent youths surrounding the brightly painted vehicle. They were all younger versions of Kali. Most carried automatic weapons.

Just teenagers, he thought. Yet every one a trained terrorist.

Luke felt Kali's eyes upon him. When he met his baleful gaze, Luke was jolted by what he saw. Though Kali carried a rifle, his hand moved toward the handle of a knife in a leather sheath at his hip. Then the Frenchwoman strode in short, feminine steps past them toward the entrance of the mine, and Luke saw the sea change in Kali's eyes. The lust for her was as naked as the hatred he had for Luke.

He means to kill you, Luke thought. *And she won't be able to control him.*

The advance units of the FBI's antiterrorist task force converged on Wind Canyon by car. Others were lifted by helicopter from the staging area in a far corner of the Helena airport. They landed both west and south of the canyon. They looked like commandos of any of the world's elite assault forces, with their camouflage clothing blending into the background, blacking under their eyes to reduce sun glare. Most bore Colt Commando rifles, a variant of the army's M-16A1 automatic rifle, but a few carried M-21 sniper rifles. They moved with swift, silent precision, reacting instantly to the slightest signal or word from their squad leaders.

Two units were already in position when the blue van was spotted climbing the mountain road toward the mine. They were not close enough, even with field glasses, to identify who was in the vehicle.

Ted Chandler, the FBI agent in charge of the attack force, approached the Wind Canyon range from the northwest, flying in one of three Hughes 500 MD helicopters. The white-coated NEST scientists and technicians, who would evaluate the immediate nuclear hazard in the target area, rode in the other two helicopters. Lee Hamilton had remained at the Helena base to direct communications and logistical support for the mission. Al Trautman, who sat beside Chandler in the chopper, had tried not to smile when he heard about Hamilton's assignment.

The radio in the lead helicopter crackled into life. The pilot handed the speaker to Ted Chandler, who pressed a button. Trautman recognized FBI agent Joe Springer's voice. "—not here," he said.

"I missed part of that," Chandler said. "Repeat."

"I'm at the Cameron place. The house is empty. The place is deserted except for a kid in the stables who doesn't seem to speak English."

"Any sign of Lucas Cameron?"

"His pickup truck is here. Negative on him or the woman. I've got men out looking for them now."

"Can you get anything out of the stable hand?"

"I doubt it unless we get a translator out here. But there is one thing . . . There's been horses in the stables within the past few hours. They're not there now."

Chandler scowled. His glance met Trautman's; the burly NEST agent shrugged. "Maybe they went for a ride."

"Wait a sec," Springer called over some static, "I'm getting more input from one of our people." After a brief pause, he came back on the line with an edge of satisfaction in his voice. "We got the horses. And there are fresh tracks of a heavy vehicle on a back road near where the horses were found. . . . Also the footprints of a second man."

"Anything else?"

"Yeah," Springer said. "A picnic basket."

Chandler and Trautman exchanged glances. "She suckered him," Trautman said, raising his voice over the throbbing of the rotors. "They've got him."

Chandler nodded slowly. He wondered whether Cameron had walked into the trap openly, and if so what he had hoped to accomplish. "See what else you can find," he barked into the speaker. "What about the Halston place?"

"Two squads moved in thirty minutes ago. They rounded up about a half dozen field hands who look like they were recruited from the streets of Beirut. A couple of them tried to get away in a truck, but they didn't make it to the main road."

"No resistance?"

"Not so's you would notice," Springer said dryly. "Hey! . . . maybe we could trade them for our hostages. . . ."

"All right, Springer, good work. Let me know if you find anything else."

"You going in?"

"We're going in."

There was a brief pause before Springer said, "Yeah . . . Good hunting."

Rough hands propelled Luke Cameron into the mine. Hostile shouts and spittle rained over him, awakening nearly forgotten television images of American hostages in Iran.

Inside the mine, Luke's eyes made the adjustment from the sunlit glare of the mountainside to the artificial glow of overhead strip lighting—parallel fluorescent tubes linked like long, thin sausages along the full length of a gallery that had been carved out of the mountain.

Not sure exactly what he had expected to find, Luke gazed in amazement at a series of concrete-reinforced workrooms along the back wall of the cavernous room. Snakes of heavy-duty electrical wiring wriggled across the floor and spilled outside. They climbed the mountain, Luke guessed, to hook into the Montana power company's lines. A bewildering array of equipment filled the workrooms and the crowded spaces around them—a large lathe, a drill press, a milling machine, welding equipment, even a compact furnace in a separate room with an outside vent. Several rooms, dominated by large tables cluttered with tubes and equipment, resembled miniature laboratories. One with an observation window contained what appeared to be remote-handling equipment.

At the center of it all was a small man in his forties, with curly gray hair and a trimmed mustache. His neatness was in sharp contrast to the ragtag young terrorists all around him. His large, slightly protuberant dark eyes reflected dismay at first sight of the tall newcomer being hassled and spat upon by the untidy young Iranians. The older man had been supervising several terrorists, who were moving an apparently heavy apparatus from one of the workrooms toward the mine entrance, sliding it across the floor on plank runners.

When Cameron was hustled into the mine, the work stopped, and the workers stared. His eyes quickly surveyed the contraption encased in a heavy wooden frame; it was just about large enough to hold a standard-sized oil drum. His heart flopped like a fish in the bottom of a boat. In that instant, Luke understood what the gray-haired man was. Luke also knew what Micheline Picard and her ragtag band had achieved in the bowels of this mountain.

Luke stared at the gleaming, machined steel ball, about the size of a soccer ball, suspended at the center of a web of steel rods and cables. Locked into place at an angle above the steel ball was the sawed-off barrel and firing mechanism of a high-powered rifle. Its muzzle was directly over the opening of a hole bored into the heart of the steel ball.

Luke Cameron knew the steel was the outer casing for a uranium core. He was looking at the nightmare that had haunted the second half of the twentieth century—a homemade nuclear weapon.

Luke only half heard Micheline Picard questioning the scientist.

" . . . there is a digital timer," the small man said. "You simply set the timer for the exact second you wish the initial firing sequence to begin."

A van, Luke thought. Anonymous in spite of its vivid flame stripes, or perhaps even because of them. It could be driven anywhere, parked anywhere, the bomb sitting undetected on the floor of the vehicle, hidden from curious eyes.

"The device can also be triggered by a radio signal, which will release a powerful electrical impulse into a high-explosive charge. This fires the nuclear bullet into the core, initiating a chain reaction which is contained by the steel casing and thus magnified enormously. This all takes place, you understand, in nanoseconds."

"There is no danger during transit? This is true?" Micheline Picard pressed him.

"There can be no chain reaction without the initial detonation, which must be triggered manually or by remote control. Until that is done, you will simply be transporting a lump of enriched uranium inside a steel ball."

"*Bien,* that is good."

Hassan Kamateh said nothing.

"You have serve Allah well, Dr. Kamateh. You will be rewarded."

The scientist did not reply. His glance fled from hers, touching Luke's in passing. The triumph the woman so obviously felt was not reflected in the physicist's eyes. Luke saw only despair.

He followed Kamateh's glance toward two cots at the far end of the gallery, separated from the center of activity. On each of the cots lay a thin youth with a sickly pallor and haunted dark eyes. *Something has gone wrong here,* Luke thought.

He also took note of two tunnels near the cots leading away from the gallery. One, larger than any of the other visible shafts, had lights strung along one wall. The other tunnel was completely black. Presumably of no use to the terrorists, it had not been wired.

The Frenchwoman turned to Kali. "We leave as soon as it is dark, you understand? You will bring the van as close as possible to the mine."

The entire bomb apparatus, including the metal cage and its wooden frame, would slide easily through the double rear doors of the van. Once the vehicle left the area of the mine undetected, it would become a mobile weapon of monstrous destructive power. In any large city, Luke Cameron thought, such a van would be, for all practical purposes, invisible.

Kali had set his rifle down and was directing several of the younger men. One went outside, proudly carrying the keys to the van.

Micheline Picard watched Luke. "You think we are of small con-

sequence," she said, demanding his attention. "You do not fear us
because we are so far away. Here in your own country, you feel safe.
But you are safe no longer. We have come into your City of War
to take from you the weapon of terror."

"To kill more innocent people?"

She shrugged. "You talk to me of killing? These are the word of
the imperialists who would enslave half the world to make more
profit and to feed your crave for drugs? It was *you* who gave the
world this weapon, Lucas. Now it is your turn to discover what you
have create. The master will feel the bite of the whip across his own
back."

She was far too cool, Luke thought, too much in command. At-
tempting to bait her seemed futile. Still, he had to try. . . .

"You talk as if killing thousands of people is a holy mission. Where
are you planning to set this thing off? Do you have any idea what
it will do? Not just now, but for generations to come?"

"We have give this much thought," Micheline answered quietly.
"We have even consider setting it off, as you say, in your own Mon-
tana. It would be easy to drive tonight to Billings or Great Falls.
There would be no risk. But that would not be enough."

"My God, you mean there wouldn't be enough people killed." The
revulsion in Luke's tone left her unmoved, and he tried to shake her
composure. "I'm not the only one who's suspected you. The FBI is
already investigating. You won't get far in that van. Where . . . ?"

He was stopped by the expression of satisfaction in her eyes.

"It is not so far to Denver," she said, as calmly and reasonably
as if they were discussing a vacation itinerary. "And we have travel
these road. No one notice us."

"How can you do this?" Luke whispered.

"We do not kill for the sake of killing, Lucas. I have tell you, it
is an act of war we do. We strike where Satan will feel most pain.
And the Denver airport, it is, how do you say, a hub? To destroy
it will do much damage. So your people will know fear. So they will
not soon forget."

Appalled by the revelation of the target, Luke looked about as if
he sought to escape the punishment of her words. Once more his
gaze was arrested by the two cots pushed against the rock wall at
the far end of the gallery. The pity Luke felt became the focus of
his rising anger—and a last, reckless gamble.

The idea that had come to him seemed an act of desperation, but he began to walk rapidly along the gallery. "What about these children?" He gestured toward the two sick youths on the cots. "Are they just martyrs to the cause? How many more will there be? How many others are sick? What is it, doctor?" he called out to the scientist. "Radiation poisoning? Isn't that a pencil radiation counter sticking out of your pocket? What kind of dosage have they all been exposed to?"

As Luke raised his voice, Kali started toward him. Blood darkened his face like a mask. Luke was only a few steps from the cots. The youths lying there were too weak to raise themselves up. They could only stare helplessly at the drama bursting upon them. The pity Luke felt ignited rage.

"Stop!" Micheline Picard commanded.

"He must die!" Kali cried. The knife seemed to leap from its sheath into his hand. Its six-inch, double-edged blade glittered under the fluorescent ribbons of light overhead.

"No, Kali—I forbid it!"

But the bearded man's fury was out of control—perhaps even lacerated to a greater frenzy by the command from a woman, especially this woman. His knife, once drawn, would not return to its sheath.

Catlike, Kali rushed toward Luke, who was still several steps away from the dark mine shaft that was his objective. Kali was too quick. He came between Luke and his goal.

Luke realized that the Iranian was chanting the kind of litany Khomeini's Revolutionary Guards had shouted in the streets of Tehran—and outside the American embassy. "There is no God but God! Death to the unbeliever!"

Kali leaped forward. His knife blade dipped deceptively and then slashed upward. Twisting clear, Luke felt the tip of the blade caress his stomach with a touch as cold as an icicle. There was a sudden stickiness about his waist.

Inside the mine the crack of a gunshot was magnified a hundredfold. It echoed within the gallery and along the satellite tunnels. The reverberations beat painfully against Luke's eardrums.

Kali stopped as if, like a mime, he had run into an invisible wall. Lifting the knife higher, he tried to lunge at Luke. A second shot struck him high on the chest and jerked him around as if a powerful hand had seized him. He pivoted toward Micheline Picard, stared at the pistol in her hand. Disbelief gave his expression a look of shocked innocence.

He sank to his knees. His hands dug into his chest, fingers splayed out, as if they might stem the flow of blood seeping over his shirt front.

"Why did you not listen?" Micheline cried. "You know I am the ayatollah's daughter—my commands are *his* commands. Who dares defy Khomeini defies all Islam!"

The magnitude of his error was in Kali's eyes in the moment before he pitched forward onto his face.

In spite of his astonishment, Luke did not hesitate. He broke for the unlit mine shaft six feet away.

He wasn't sure later if Micheline hesitated for a split second before she fired, or was simply caught by surprise. He heard the shot as he plunged into darkness. Something plucked at his sleeve and ricocheted down the tunnel.

An automatic rifle chattered.

Careening into the echoing blackness of the shaft, Luke tried to sort out the swift tattoo of sounds. It took a moment before he realized the automatic gunfire hadn't come from inside the mine, where its roar would have been deafening, but from outside.

Incredulity over Micheline's words added to his confusion. My God, was it possible? Khomeini's daughter? It explained so much. . . .

Luke heard Micheline calling out orders in a strange tongue—he recognized only his name. Footsteps pounded toward him. He turned and plunged blindly into the tunnel.

From the FBI command helicopter, Al Trautman stared down at Wind Canyon and the fractured rock face of the mountain. The camouflaged figures of the FBI's assault force swarmed over the ridges. Above the whirring of the chopper's rotors he couldn't hear gunfire below, but he saw a terrorist sentry on the ridge catapult down the mountainside in a cocoon of dust and rocks.

Others in the attack force approached the mine from below along the switchback road. Trautman watched a truck crawl up the grade and stop across from the mine entrance, separated from it by a deep chasm. A squad of men carrying assault weapons spilled out of the truck and sprinted for cover. There was a burst of gunfire from one of the tin mine shacks, and one of the attackers went down. Instantly a hail of gunfire etched a polka-dot pattern across the entire face of the shack. The firing from inside the shack ceased.

At Trautman's elbow, Ted Chandler also peered down at the action. One of the terrorists on a rise shook his fist at the chopper, swung his weapon toward them, and fired a wild burst. The helicopter veered sharply away. At the same moment, an FBI sniper from the attack force picked the Iranian defender off his perch with a single rifle shot.

Then the terrorists were in full retreat, scurrying for cover or fleeing toward the main entrance to Wind Canyon Mine.

Trautman heard the relief as well as satisfaction in Chandler's voice. "We've got it under control. I've seen only one of our boys go down." He tapped the pilot on the shoulder and shouted, "Take us down!"

Glancing at Trautman, his expression tight, Chandler said, "I just pray the damn thing's still inside the mine."

Trautman stared downward as the mountain rushed toward them. If Chandler's prayer came true, their descent was akin to dropping into the mouth of a live volcano.

In the situation room beneath the White House the atmosphere was tense and the conversation cryptic. An ominous question hung like a specter over the room: Would some unsuspecting American city feel the fury of a nuclear explosion before the day ended? George Bush was in control, outwardly calm and assured. But the worry lines in his face seemed deeper.

He rose to stretch his legs. The others, following suit, gravitated into small clusters, the rivalries and affinities asserting themselves. People from the Pentagon and Foggy Bottom filtered to opposite sides of the room. The FBI and DOE contingents huddled together; it had become their joint operation. The CIA people were shut out and appeared unhappy. The White House advisers formed their own clique.

At the center of this solemn assemblage, the president of the United States was isolated and aloof as always, with the ultimate responsibility weighing heavy on his shoulders. The others could speak freely. They wouldn't have to follow their own advice or accept the consequences personally. George Bush had held many posts near the seat of power; until this moment he had not really understood how crushing the weight of responsibility could be.

Mel Durbin drifted over to the president's side next to the long mahogany sideboard. "Can I get you something stronger, Mr. President?" Durbin nodded at the cup of coffee Bush held.

"Not right now, Mel. I could use a drink, but I don't dare."

One of the phones rang. They were of different colors; this one was blue—a direct line to FBI headquarters. Bush didn't stir. The FBI chief picked up the blue phone. The DOE's Eric Sanderson stood beside him apprehensively. A somber hush fell upon the room. All eyes were upon the FBI director, watching, waiting.

The director hung up. He glanced at Sanderson, gave him a knowing nod, then crossed the room to the president. "The attack has started," he said.

George Bush felt a tightening in his chest. "The bomb?" he demanded. "Is there any sign of the bomb?"

"Their readings indicate the presence of uranium. If the terrorists have built a bomb, it's probably still inside the mine."

"How long before we can get confirmation?"

"A matter of minutes, Mr. President. Our people have landed, and the terrorists have been driven back inside the mine. There have been casualties."

"Any escapes?"

"The attack force has its orders. The entire area has been isolated and sealed. No one can get out."

"Good! That's the way I want it."

"Yes, Mr. President."

Bush turned aside and the FBI director sidled off to repeat to the others what he had just told the president. Mel Durbin found himself alone with Bush again. He studied the dark hollows under the president's eyes.

"What made you decide to attack at once?"

"The situation demanded action; the mine was the only known target. The alternative would have been to wait and wonder, to guess and gamble. It's still a gamble, Mel—a terrible gamble. But it's better than doing nothing. I felt the odds favored action."

"How will Khomeini react? Have you made any contact?"

"We've sent messages to him, but he hasn't responded. He's probably waiting for events to determine what his response will be. Whatever happens, I'm sure his response will be disagreeable."

The NSC specialist thought of Jimmy Carter agonizing over what to do after Khomeini's screaming Revolutionary Guards stormed the American embassy and took fifty-two hostages. One president's crisis inevitably influenced the next president's actions. Neither Jimmy Carter nor Ronald Reagan had been able to handle Khomeini. Now it was George Bush's turn.

Durbin met the president's eyes. Bush smiled grimly. "Nail-biting time, Mel," he said softly. "Men dying on that mountain right now. The only question is . . . will it end there?"

The chain reaction of events inside Wind Canyon Mine produced incipient panic.

Some of the teenage terrorists stood stupefied, staring in disbelief at Kali's body. It lay sprawled face down on the floor of the gallery between two rusty rails that had once been used for cable cars hauling raw ore to the surface from the mine shafts. The rails, framing the body of the dead man, formed a grotesque tableau.

Other youths gaped at the woman who had dared to kill him. Her proud declaration echoed in their minds: *"I am the ayatollah's daughter."*

One of the terrorists, as if emerging from a trance, started to drag Kali's body away from the center of the gallery. Speaking in Farsi, Micheline Picard stopped him with a firm command: "Never mind him now; he betrayed Allah and our cause." Then she addressed an older youth, armed with a Russian Kalashnikov. "Hassim, take others with you, as many as you need. Find the American and bring him back."

The youth, having witnessed what happened to Kali, asked querulously, "If he resists . . . we are to fire . . . ?"

She hesitated, but only for an instant. Her cool self-assurance had begun to ease the air of panic inside the mine, though she was far more disturbed than her tone and demeanor suggested. "If he resists, you will shoot. He must not escape."

Proud of having been singled out, Hassim quickly rounded up a dozen others. "Come with me! Those who stay behind, be ready to die. No one must enter the mine." He glanced toward the woman for approval of his initiative.

"Bien," she said. "Now go!"

As they rushed off, Micheline felt a quivering that she resisted by an effort of will. She could not lose control, or reveal weakness to her followers. Kali's death, and Luke Cameron's escape into the mine, had shaken her. Even more alarming was the gunfire outside. Like the rumble of an avalanche, it was the sound of disaster.

Out of the corner of her eye she saw Hassan Kamateh take a step toward the mine entrance. "Do not think of trying to leave, Dr. Kamateh," she said sharply. "You are one of us, yes? The Americans will not ask before they shoot." As if to punctuate her comment, a burst of automatic fire erupted outside, almost drowning out a man's scream.

Micheline stared at the entrance, listening to the rattle of gunfire echoing through the canyon. Then she looked at the bomb sitting on the floor in its cage, ready to be loaded into the van. She had to fight back a feeling of sick despair. She had come so close! It was as if Allah was punishing her for the weakness that had permitted her to betray her father's cause, succumbing to her yearning for the American. No words now could hide the truth. She had risked everything for a few moments with Cameron—and earned only his rejection. She had heard only the song of desire whispering in her blood, drowning out the voice of the man she worshiped above all others, her father. In her grief she shuddered. Tears glistened in her dark eyes.

"You are not well, *mademoiselle?*" Hassan Kamateh's question was solicitous. It stung her.

"Quite well, *m'sieur.*"

When she turned toward him, she was outwardly composed. The sorrow within her would never die, but a proud determination settled over her features. She would not yet admit defeat. She had not advanced so far only to see her mission aborted. The Great Satan would yet feel her father's wrath.

"The Americans must guess we have a bomb," she said to the physicist. "They will not dare to attack us here in the mine." Her thoughts were racing now, sifting her options. "Is the bomb ready?"

Hassan Kamateh was silent, his eyes haunted. He looked ill, she thought irritably. Like Yusef and . . .

"Tell me! The bomb, she is prepare to fire? Show me the . . . the *mécanisme,* Doctor, the works. You will have the honor to be a martyr to Allah's will."

Kamateh made no move. After a moment he shook his head.

Deliberately, she holstered her small pistol and grabbed an AK-47 from one of the child terrorists, who gave it up with reluctance. She thrust the rifle at Kamateh's chest. The little physicist staggered back, trembling violently.

Then a terrible premonition began to form in Micheline's mind. She turned quickly toward the bomb, seeking its digital timer. Yes, there! It could be triggered manually, Kamateh had said earlier. She had feared the loss of Kali's expertise with mechanisms. But she could do it herself.

Remote detonation from a safe distance was no longer an option. All that mattered was that the sword must fall. Now!

"Hurry! Show me what to do. There is no time!"

Kamateh blinked at her, his eyes moist. "It is no use."

"What . . . what do you mean?"

"I cannot do it," he said softly. "I can't!"

In the blackness of the mine shaft, Luke Cameron blundered into a low ceiling beam. It cracked him with such force across the forehead that he staggered. Momentarily dizzy, he stumbled against a side wall, cracking an elbow, and tripped over some unseen object on the floor of the shaft. He fell headlong, scraping patches of skin from hands and knees.

Behind him came the shrill voices of pursuers. He saw the stabbing arcs of flashlights. One sent a powerful beam far down the shaft where Luke had fallen. By good luck the light passed over his head.

Scrambling into a side tunnel, he made out the faint definition of shapes from some unidentified source of light. He was in a narrow shaft, a short connecting artery.

Feeling his way along, he penetrated an opening with his left hand.

The narrow artery led back toward the main gallery, which was the source of the faint glimmer of light. The empty space Luke had found in the dark was the opening, buttressed by a wood frame, into a small storeroom.

Luke fumbled in his pockets for something he suddenly remembered: a souvenir packet of matches Justin Cranmer had picked up at the cash register of the Frontier Pies Restaurant. He had pocketed one and tossed another at Luke, who had absently slipped the matches into his pocket.

The voices of pursuit were dimmer, fading along another corridor. He opened the packet, closed one eye an instant before striking so that he wouldn't be completely blinded when the light flickered out, and scraped the match into flame.

The tiny flare seemed brilliant in the small, dark room. He saw boxes of equipment, some open, others stacked along one wall. In a separate stack in one corner, an open wooden box contained packets of plastic that resembled putty or artist's clay.

Luke's heart skipped as he recognized the brick-sized packets in their plastic yellow wrappers. During heavy construction work, he had used similar packets of plastic explosive. The C-4 plastique in these boxes had been manufactured in Czechoslovakia.

The match burned his fingers and he dropped it. The proximity to the explosive caused a pang of anxiety, but the reaction was reflexive. He could hold a match directly to the plastic explosive without risk.

He heard footsteps not far away, shouts. Darts of light danced along the shafts nearby. Luke risked a second match to search frantically for what he was certain had to be in the storeroom. He found what he was looking for in a separate cardboard container: detonators.

Luke blew out the match. Working in darkness, he stuffed four packets of plastique under his shirt, first jamming detonators into two of the packets, like birthday candles.

He crouched in the entry to the storeroom, listening to the sounds made by the searchers. Then he slipped out of the room into the narrow tunnel and moved back the way he had come.

Just before reaching one of the main shafts, he felt air stirring against his cheek. Then the beam from a flashlight struck his eyes like a fist, blinding him.

Luke threw himself to the side. In the same motion he kicked out with his left leg—not at the man who had surprised him or the rifle he carried, but at the flashlight. His kick missed its immediate target but connected solidly with the man's arm. The flashlight flew from his fingers and struck the rock wall. Glass splintered.

The light went out.

Luke wasted no effort trying to run. The man he had blundered into must have heard him coming. He had waited alone in the darkness for Luke to reach him, too cunning, or too eager to be a hero, to call for help. Now he let loose a full-throated holler. The yell guided the hard edge of Luke's right hand swiftly, powerfully to the man's throat. His cry broke off like a stick of wood snapping.

The man slumped against the wall behind him and began to slide to the floor. Luke heard the clatter of his weapon as it fell from his fingers. Frantically scrabbling across the floor of the shaft on his hands and knees, Luke tried to find the automatic rifle. The man's shout must have been heard. Others would be arriving at any moment.

Luke's hand closed over the stubby barrel of the AK-47.

As he scooped up the weapon, shouts rang in the shaft off to his left. Spears of light fenced along the tunnel, like the weapons in the *Star Wars* movies. Luke fired a single short burst in the direction of the light beams to delay pursuit. Then he plunged deeper into the mine.

As Luke fled, the search behind him became more organized. There were at least a dozen terrorists, working back and forth along the network of tunnels. Luke ransacked his memory for a pattern of the shafts he had followed. But their number and the disorienting darkness defeated him.

Not all of the shafts were totally dark. Some borrowed light from others with access to the surface. As his eyes became more accustomed to this strange new world, he began to distinguish shapes in the dimmest light, like a fish in the near total darkness at the bottom of the sea.

Luke recognized the main shaft when he crossed it again, not only from its larger size but from the rails trailing along the floor, half buried under dirt. The lesser shafts were becoming more and more hazardous as he was driven away from the main gallery. They were shorter, more easily penetrated by the quick thrust of a flashlight beam. And most dead-ended. If he were trapped in one of these, the deadly game of hide-and-seek would end abruptly.

He ducked just in time to evade a low overhead beam. All of his senses were adapting. He began to think, in snatches, about his plight. What in the world was he doing here? His meeting with Micheline Picard, his rejection of her attempt at seduction, had accomplished what he hoped, leading her to reveal the full scope of her operation and more—the startling truth of her identity.

But Luke realized that he had played his maverick role recklessly, unwilling to wait for the government agents who were following the same paths. He had made it personal, he thought; he had let his anger against the terrorists rule his reason. It had been a quixotic gesture. But damn them, he would do it again!

He turned away from a shaft, warned by the sound of running footsteps. A sudden burst from an automatic weapon filled the mine with its hellacious hammering. A scream echoed through the corridor. The firing stopped. Frozen in place, Luke was momentarily deafened. He thought, *They've shot one of their own by mistake.*

As his ears began to clear, he heard the creaking of the framework of wooden posts and beams that supported the shafts. The mountain seemed to tremble, and dust sifted down into the tunnels. Luke felt it on his neck.

A shout rang out, shrill with alarm. From the bowels of the mountain came a deep rumbling. Not fifteen feet from where Luke Cameron stood, the roof of one of the main arteries collapsed. The rumbling became a mind-numbing, demoralizing roar that blotted out every other sensation. Luke was hurled off his feet into the darkness.

Ted Chandler had set up his command post on a ridge above the Wind Canyon Mine—the same lookout Luke Cameron had discovered when he first came to scout out the abandoned gold mine. Al Trautman, who had landed with the FBI officials, was on the helicopter's radio, talking to his boss at the motel in Helena. He could see white-coated NEST agents fanning out from one of the other choppers that had just landed. Unlike the first White Jackets who had arrived, these men were not taking readings with their radiation counters. They deployed over the face of the mountain, moving quickly and purposefully. Trautman saw a small packet one of the men was carrying.

"What the hell's going on?" he demanded of Lee Hamilton over the radio. "People in white jackets are running all over this goddamned mountain."

"They're checking every exit shown in the plan that's on file."

"What do they intend to do?" Trautman asked the question, though he had already guessed the answer.

"Seal the mine," Hamilton said calmly.

"Jesus Christ," Trautman whispered.

"I'm acting on the orders of the president. No one gets out of that mine."

"What about Luke Cameron? Does the president know about him? He's a prisoner inside that hole."

"The FBI will try to rescue him."

They could never get Cameron out now, Trautman thought. God damn it, Hamilton knew that!

Trautman threw down his headset and stalked away from the command helicopter. The chattering of automatic weapons fire on the mountain had begun to subside. Trautman realized that the fire-fight was almost over.

Some of the NEST agents who had been swarming over the face of the mountainside were now returning, scrambling up the few animal trails or climbing wherever they could find footholds on the cliff face. They were empty handed.

Al Trautman felt a chill.

No one knew how far the terrorists had progressed with their bomb. The whole mountain could go. Here he was standing on top of the ridge, and the whole damned thing could blow.

He thought of Luke Cameron, trapped in the mine with the survivors of Khomeini's band of holy warriors. No way out, Trautman thought. He doesn't have a prayer.

During his days as a prisoner of the Iranian terrorists, Hassan Kamateh had seen in their single-minded obsessiveness all that he had feared and rejected in the recent history of his homeland—the perversion of religious fervor into a violent elitism, the warping of a message of love and faith into vengeful killing. Through threats and intimidation they had sought to make him a reluctant soldier in their holy war.

He had never really had a choice.

"What have you done?" the beautiful Frenchwoman whispered. She had said she was the Imam's daughter. What an incredible thing to meet such a woman. His wife would be—.

He shut off the thought of wife, children, hope.

"Tell me, Doctor. You *must* tell me."

"There is no bomb."

Shock, skepticism, disbelief succeeded themselves in her dark eyes. "What is this, then?" she cried, gesturing toward the polished steel cylinder in its crate. *"Non, non,* what you say, is not possible."

"It will not explode. It will only produce what I described to you once before . . . what is called a fizzle."

Again she shook her head, unable to accept what he was saying. "I must have the bomb. I must have it. Satan must know we have enter his camp in the night, that he is weak, that his ocean protect him no more."

"There will be a massive release of very dirty radiation," Kamateh said quietly. "It will destroy all of us who are near it." He paused. "But we are already the walking dead. There has already been intolerable exposure. Why do you think Yusef died? Why do you suppose others are dying?"

"Ne jamais . . . you could not . . . you would not do such a thing. You would not sacrifice your wife, your children, yourself. . . ."

But the doubt was in her eyes now, the dawning realization that what she was hearing, dreading, was the truth.

"I had no choice. I had no choice." For Hassan Kamateh the repeated words were numbing, a soporific designed to keep the unbearable at a distance before it destroyed his sanity. "Your father—if he is indeed your father—does not speak for Allah. He is the voice of unreason. I could not deliver into your hands—into his hands—the most terrible of all weapons."

In a last gesture of defiance Hassan Kamateh started toward the exit from the gallery, ignoring the automatic rifle in the woman's hands. Whether she pulled the trigger or not was a matter of indifference. He was already doomed, along with his loved ones. Only his adopted country, America, had escaped the terror—this time.

She shot him when he was ten feet from the exit. The chatter of the AK-47 was followed, as if triggered by it, by a deeper, louder series of explosions. A mass of earth and rock thundered onto the ledge outside the mine, blocking the opening. Kamateh felt the mountain heave and shudder in the same instant the bullets slammed into his chest. Pain and blackness enveloped him.

He fell into the bullet stream, which exploded his skull like a melon.

●

The massive explosions blanketed all openings into the mine and cut off power lines. For a few seconds the auxiliary generator in a nearby shaft continued to throb. Then it too sputtered into silence.

Wind Canyon Mine was as black as a tomb.

Micheline Picard stumbled blindly. Her nose and throat were clogged with dust, and her chest ached from the struggle to breathe. From far off, it seemed, came feeble cries of anguish. Then these were also stilled.

She was isolated in the darkness, alone with her despair.

Sinking to her knees, she wept, not for herself but for her father. Allah had punished her for her weakness. She had no wish to live with her failure.

And how could she have misjudged Kamateh so badly? What was the hold this country of infidels had had upon him, that he could betray his own people, his own children?

She wondered if Lucas Cameron, like herself, crouched in the blackness, waiting for life, like the light, to be snuffed out, his thoughts tumbling helter-skelter, as hers were, a kaleidoscope of memories, regrets, shattered dreams.

A part of the gallery collapsed, hurling her off her feet, sending another choking cloud of dirt and debris over her. She crawled on hands and knees, trying to escape the dust, and her hand brushed over a human face.

She froze, trembling. The tumble of her thoughts came to rest.

He is with Allah now, she thought, kneeling beside the unknown youth who had come so far to fight in her father's name. He has no regrets. He goes with joy into heaven.

She had failed, but it was only one failure. A war was not a single battle. The dream to which her beloved Imam had given such a powerful voice, the dream of a united, triumphant Islam, would not die with this one soldier of God, or with her.

She rose slowly to her feet, lifting her face, lifting her thoughts toward Khomeini, remembering, oblivious of a deep rumbling of the cavern that shook the dirt floor beneath her feet. Rocks and debris fell all about her.

He chose *you*, she thought. In the end it was you he sent into Satan's camp to fight in his name. To die in his name. Even in failure there was victory. The world would know—.

With a great, shuddering roar the roof of the gallery collapsed upon her.

Gasping from the dust that choked the mine shafts, Luke Cameron crouched against the wall, waiting for the mountain to stop shaking. The collapse of the adjoining shaft, the crunching and roaring, the sensation that the whole weight of the mountain was about to crush him overwhelmed his senses.

Gradually the rumbling diminished. Coherent thought began to return. Luke heard moans of pain and cries of panic. And, farther away, excited voices that drew closer as he listened. He reached a quick conclusion: some terrorists had been buried in the cave-in; others had survived.

Suddenly the mountain shuddered once more, this time in response to a series of explosions evidently timed to go off at once. The beams directly above Luke stirred and groaned ominously. The voices from a nearby tunnel acquired an edge of panic.

To Luke Cameron, the timed sequence of explosions conveyed a clear message: the mine was under attack and all exits were being sealed off.

The attacking force was shutting off escape. And bottling up the bomb. An underground nuclear explosion would cause far less radiation danger, if any at all.

He thought of Micheline trapped with her juvenile terrorists inside the mine at the center of a nuclear firestorm. In spite of everything he was moved to pity. No one should die that way.

But then he was in the same predicament.

From another shaft, closer to where Luke crouched, came a fresh babble of voices. The Iranians were beginning to move about once more, assessing their situation. It could be unpleasant if they found him; they would surely take their vengeance out on the infidel.

Luke retreated on cats' feet along the shaft in which he was trapped. The cave-in left him only one direction that was open. Almost immediately, he heard cries of discovery. The survivors had found his hiding place.

He ducked back and forth from one shaft to another. As he retreated, his options diminished. There was now only one main core. The satellite tunnels were short, the connections few. Luke heard the Iranians calling out to each other. As they closed in on their quarry, excitement raised their voices a pitch; they sounded even more like the voices of children in a game of hide-and-seek.

Flattening almost to the floor to evade a stabbing beam of light, Luke dove into a side shaft. It was a tunnel so narrow that his elbows brushed both sides, so low he had to scuttle along in a crouch over the rugged floor.

A cooler current of air caressed him.

Peering along the shaft, Luke thought he saw a lessening of the total blackness. Heart thumping, he scurried forward faster. As he penetrated deeper into the narrow tunnel, he felt the floor rising under his feet.

At first, he guessed it was an illusion, born of desperation. Then the climb became steeper.

He had found it—the long-forgotten shaft bored from the western face of the mountain.

Behind him the shouts of the eager children of Khomeini's *jihad* drew closer in a rising frenzy.

Crouching low, Luke scrambled up the shaft, feeling its walls tight on either side. As he climbed, the drag pulling on his thighs, light began to seep through the darkness, turning the tunnel ahead of him to predawn gray.

He scurried faster, rabbitlike, in a half crouch. The walls and roof of the shaft took shape around him, the spaces widening. Then, as he made out a thin horizontal strip of light ahead, his heart leaped. The barrier!

Luke raced toward it. After the darkness of the mine's interior, the dim light that beckoned him seemed bright as the flashlight beams dancing in the tunnel behind him.

He ripped down the top board, then another. Both gave way easily, the wood long ago rotted, the rusty nails unresisting. With two boards gone, there was room enough for him to squeeze through.

He was sliding through the opening, dragging his last leg over the top, when footsteps rushed toward him from below. With a shriek, one of the Iranians threw himself at Luke's trailing leg, clawing at his boot. Hands seized it, pulled. Luke pushed out with all his strength.

The boot slipped off. Luke tumbled over the barrier.

Behind him the attacker's wild bearded face appeared. Luke

clubbed at it with the stubby barrel of the AK-47 he still carried. He felt a shuddering impact. The face vanished.

Voices filled the shaft below him, approaching fast.

Working swiftly, Luke packed the plastic explosives stuffed with detonators at the base of the wooden barrier. A staccato burst of gunfire engulfed the shaft. Bullets smacked into the wooden planks. Luke heard one of them flick through the wood and sing past his ear.

On the western side of the barrier, the mine shaft was both higher and wider. Luke ran headlong, covering as much ground as he could with his long, loping strides, until he heard screams at the barricade.

He swung around. Not far enough, he thought; not nearly far enough.

But one of the terrorists was climbing through the opening Luke had forced at the top of the wooden barrier.

Luke raised the AK-47. For a moment he hesitated. He thought of the ayatollah's daughter, of the children who followed her, of the mountain mass above them all.

Then Luke squeezed the trigger. Bullets stitched a path across the floor of the shaft near the barrier, caught the lead terrorist as he dropped through the opening, and finally found the explosives Luke had packed along the base.

The force of the blast blew Luke Cameron off his feet. He catapulted into chaos.

It had begun and ended in less than thirty minutes. From the command post, Al Trautman had watched the younger men of the FBI assault force mount their brief, furious attack. After all the shooting and explosions, the FBI commandos and NEST White Jackets had retreated as rapidly as they could scramble from the immediate vicinity of Wind Canyon Mine. Two of the helicopters had already lifted off. Ted Chandler's command chopper would be the last to leave.

If the bomb exploded, Trautman knew, he would never be able to outrun it. He waited with a calm fatalism.

The dust settled slowly. The explosions had blocked every known access to the mine. The rumbling of cave-ins deep within the massive cliffs could no longer be felt.

The radio in the command chopper crackled. Trautman heard Lee

Hamilton's voice. "Trautman? Chandler? Are you there? What the hell's happening?"

Trautman ignored him. He watched Ted Chandler, who was communicating over a walkie-talkie with the FBI squads. Trautman heard him say, "Pull back fast as you can. Keep your eyes and ears open." Trautman was surprised to see two White Jackets still out on the mountain, using their radiation detectors.

Some Iranians had been taken prisoner. They had been on sentry duty and, Trautman reflected cynically, had not elected martyrdom, with all its glories. They could fill in the missing pieces, he thought.

Still ignoring Lee Hamilton's impatient questions over the chopper's radio, Trautman turned away from the mine. It was now a tomb.

He glanced down the steep western slope of the ridge on which he stood. He blinked in disbelief, then stared again.

A tall man, white with dust, stumbled out of a hole in the western face of the mountain and collapsed on a narrow path. Someone shouted. Two commandos sprinted toward the fallen man, their Colt automatic weapons held in both hands, ready to fire.

"No!" Trautman bellowed. "For God's sake, don't shoot!"

He broke into a run, slipping and sliding down the slope to a steep trail. *By God, he'd made it!* Trautman exulted.

He scrambled around an outcropping of rock and saw Luke Cameron below him. The dazed, dust-coated figure was trying to sit up. One of the FBI agents had him covered with his Colt assault rifle.

Trautman reared up above them, chest heaving, legs quivering. Goddamned thin air; he gasped; he couldn't run at this altitude.

But he could manage a single shout: "Luke Cameron, you son of a bitch!"

Cameron swiveled his head to peer up at him. For a moment, his expression was blank. Then a tired grin cracked the white mask of dust.

Trautman, his heart still banging against his ribs, grinned back at him.

The FBI director laid down the blue phone and stared across the situation room at the president. His cheeks sagged with relief. "It's over," the FBI chief said.

"And?"

"No big bang. We're one hundred percent sure the bomb is inside the mine. Most of the terrorists were trapped with it. There have been massive cave-ins but no nuclear explosion."

George Bush sighed audibly. "Did anyone get out alive?"

"A few Iranians were captured, three of them wounded. . . . Oh yeah, that cowboy, Lucas Cameron, somehow found a tunnel through to the other side of the mountain before the mine collapsed."

"Then those who were trapped inside were all part of the terrorist group?"

"There was one exception, Mr. President. According to Cameron, a scientist named Kamateh was caught in the mine. That's the UCLA physicist who disappeared. Cameron had the impression he was there under duress."

The President digested the report silently. All eyes in the situation room were on him. A silent euphoria had lifted the tension that had gripped the room all day. Bush did not change expression; yet his face somehow reflected the euphoria.

"Maybe he didn't complete the bomb," Bush said quietly. "Or . . . maybe he sabotaged his own creation."

"We'll never know," said the FBI director.

Bush glanced at him. "Did you have any casualties?"

"One man wounded, that's all. A clean operation."

"What about that tunnel . . . the one the cowboy used to escape."

"It caved in behind him. He may have helped to cause it with some explosives he found in the mine."

Bush allowed a fleeting, wry smile. "I want that opening sealed off anyway," he said. "I want that mountain to be tight as a drum." He looked slowly around the room, his gaze pausing deliberately on each man. Then he spoke with quiet emphasis on each word. "I want this clearly understood. This incident never happened. I want it buried deep. Deep! Presumably, Khomeini wanted a propaganda coup, a morale boost. I don't want him to succeed! We know he's dying. His apparent successor, Hashemi Rafsanjani, appears to be eager to stabilize Iran and normalize its relations. His radical rivals might want to use this incident to disrupt the healing process. I don't want them to succeed! Nothing happened. Nothing! Do I make myself clear?"

It was a moment before the others fully comprehended what George Bush had decided. Then, one by one as the president's gaze probed, they began to nod agreement. A few appreciative smiles appeared.

"What about the woman?" Mel Durbin asked. "Do you think the Russians are right? Do you think it's true? That she was really Khomeini's daughter?"

Bush assessed the question carefully before he spoke. His words were emphatic. "As far as I'm concerned—and this entire administration—we know nothing of any such woman. She never existed." He leaned forward and, without undue force, slapped his hand against the table. "There was no woman. There was no bomb thing. There was no threat. It never happened."

Leaning back, for the first time in recent days, the president felt a great weight lift from his shoulders.

We dodged the nuclear bullet this time, he thought.

Moscow

CAPTAIN SERGEI MILOV HAD JOINED HIS KGB SUPERIOR, COLONEL Vitaly Novikoff, for dinner at the Novoarbatsky Restaurant. The waiter, an opinionated man, convinced both of them that the Kiev-style cutlets were excellent that day. The taste of the tender veal confirmed the man's credibility. During the meal, Novikoff drenched his tonsils in vodka with his customary imperviousness. He said not a word about Milov's accomplishments in Paris or their effect on his future.

At last, over double-strength black coffee and cognac, Novikoff leaned back, patted his solid belly, and said with satisfaction, "George Bush has dealt with our problem."

"With the Iranian terrorists?"

"Yes, of course."

"How do you know?"

Novikoff regarded his protege with an expression of pity. "What a question, Milov! From a KGB man!"

There was amusement in the colonel's eyes, but as it faded to a more sober stare, Milov grew uneasy. Were his hopes to be crushed again? Is that why Novikoff, earlier while they were enjoying their beef bouillon with *Pirozhki,* had casually mentioned the nationalist uprisings in Georgia?

"There is something I must tell you, Sergei Andreyevich."

"Yes, Comrade Colonel?" Milov's heart was beating heavily.

"It affects the KGB . . . all of us."

Milov's apprehension increased, but now it was blended with confusion. He waited anxiously while Novikoff studied his cognac, surveying the last drops at the bottom of the glass.

"General Sidorin, that great hero of the revolution, died of a heart attack while you were en route to Paris. He was not an old man, Milov, only seventy-six at his last birthday, but his health had not been good. His widow, as you know, is much younger."

Natalia! Now completely bewildered, Milov stared at his superior. He didn't know how to respond.

"She grieves, I am told. Perhaps, as an old friend, you would find it possible to call upon the poor bereaved woman to offer your consolation. . . ."

"Yes . . . yes, of course, Colonel," Milov stammered.

Novikoff smiled. "I am sure the opportunity will present itself. Especially since you have been posted to Moscow Central as my assistant."

At the expression on Sergei Milov's face, Novikoff roared with laughter.

Tehran, Iran

R UMORS OF A GREAT STRIKE AGAINST THE ENEMIES OF ISLAM flew about the city of Iran, but there was no word from the Grand Ayatollah himself or those close to him. No one knew how the rumors started.

He has cut off the hand of Satan, the whispers said.

America cowers before the wrath of Khomeini.

Crowds gathered in the streets. Anti-American signs appeared, and youths ran in packs shouting, "Death to Satan! Death to America!" But when there was no word of any kind, the fervor of the demonstrations began to ebb. Stones were thrown at the old American embassy compound, but even this symbolic gesture could not feed the passion of the mobs.

In the Iranian parliament, the prime minister gave a speech that lasted over an hour, denouncing the imperialist partners of the devil, comparing the American president Bush to the hated Iranian shah Pahlavi.

The Ayatollah Ruhollah Khomeini remained in seclusion at the clinic near his residential compound. Word of his cancer surgery and subsequent heart attack had been withheld from the public. One of the surgeons who had spoken too freely, boasting of operating upon the Imam himself, had been arrested at his home and taken away. No one knew what had become of him. No one else talked.

A few loyal mullahs closest to the Imam, including another ayatollah, came to the clinic to pay their respects. Even they found Khomeini inaccessible. He was said to be weak, brooding, and unresponsive. He seemed to have become frail overnight, one of the visitors commented on leaving. He was little more than a husk in which the spirit still lived. There was death in his eyes, another said.

Clinging to a slim thread of life after his second heart seizure in four days, Khomeini waited for word to speed across the ocean from America, the news of his final triumphant blow against the enemies of Islam.

There was only a deepening silence.

During those periods when his mind was lucid, he thought frequently of the enchanting child who had first come to him in Paris, filled with curiosity and pride and fear, a creature of fire and beauty. Why did she not speak to him now? What could have happened?

Silence answered him.